EXTERMINATION ON PIKE PRIME

SERVICE TERM
BOOK 1

NICHOLAS TAYLOR

CONTENTS

This book is dedicated to my wonderful wife, Stacia. Without her, none of this would have been possible. Thank you so much for always being there to listen to my random ideas and for all the evenings I've kept you awake, talking to you about drones, and aliens, and ships, and planets, and this idea I had for a space elevator that...

You get the idea.

Stacia, thank you, and I love you.

PROLOGUE

PROLOGUE

ECTO-3967814HB, affectionately known as Molly by her human crew, was observing a star—a red dwarf, to be exact. The star was as ordinary and unremarkable as any other red dwarf, but Molly didn't care. After all, she was a science station, and while her crew imparted personality traits onto her, she, of course, had none, as she didn't have a personality... because she was a science station.

Two crew members were actively discussing a book they had both been reading while they waited for Molly to complete her analysis of some data on the red dwarf.

Molly was analyzing a variety of data from her extensive suite of equipment. Some of it noted a flash of light, indicating a ship jumping into the area—something that was not on the schedule for today. Other equipment detected the presence of a new gravity source in the same area. Molly scanned the vicinity, confirming the presence of a ship.

Molly checked for a transponder. There was none. She checked for low-data AltComms pings from the ship. There were none. The ship was not from humans. Molly scanned the vessel in an attempt to identify if it belonged to a friendly race, a hostile race, or perhaps an altogether new race.

The search returned, informing Molly that the ship was from a known race—the Erie, to be precise. They were hostile. Molly did all of this work in milliseconds, of course, with the humans completely unaware.

Molly notified the human crew that a hostile ship was in the vicinity. The humans were surprised and began to grow worried. Molly noted that the ship had changed directions and was headed their way. Simultaneously, Molly's sensors detected a group of missiles the Erie ship had launched.

This triggered two things to happen. One was that Molly sounded an alarm for the crew to get to their ships and make an emergency jump out of the area. The other was to ping the Human Federation Defense Forces to notify them that she was being fired upon.

The humans panicked, scrambling to their ships. As they did, Molly tracked the incoming missiles. She showed two minutes to impact. The humans were in their ships, and Molly began the undocking procedure.

The missiles were now one minute out. At this time, Molly was pinged that a Human Federation Defense Force ship would be jumping into the area.

The crew members undocked their ships, pulling away.

Thirty seconds from impact, the human ships made an emergency jump out of the system to safety. Moments later, Molly was struck by three Erie missiles that were way too overpowered for the task. Molly exploded into bits and pieces, chunks of her flying in all directions to forever litter the red dwarf system.

Molly went offline.

ONE

I woke to my alarm, a gentle ringing in my head that no one else could hear. It was coming from my Cerebral Central Processing Unit, or CCPU. As I opened my eyes, the alarm stopped. I felt slightly tired, but soon that feeling evaporated as my CCPU encouraged hormone production, making me feel rested and awake. I rose from the bed, telling my CCPU to open the window blinds.

The blinds opened, sending shafts of warm light into my room. I padded across the soft carpet to the window, which looked out over the Sound. A few birds were in the air over the stony blue waves, weaving around each other and occasionally diving into the water. I pulled on a pair of shorts and shoes. I left the front of my house, jogging along the street, passing by lines of little homes.

As I ran into the woods, the trees rose from the ground, cutting off most of the light, save for the few mottled spots on the forest floor. The air was thick with humidity. I could feel it trying to cling to me as the heavy scent of dirt and life filled my nose and lungs. My CCPU played music in my head, setting a tempo for my jog.

I didn't need the exercise; no one did. My CCPU and biotech

ensured that I, along with the rest of society, was in perfect shape without us having to do anything.

I started up a modest incline, pushing myself to the beat of the music, and my heart picked up. The path became rough, with rocks and tree roots curling around. I stepped around them, trying to see them as an obstacle course, making my morning run a game. I tried not to think about the day's events, but they came to mind anyway.

Today I would leave for my compulsory term of government service. Every twenty-year-old did so. I would serve my five years like everyone else. I knew that during that time, I would learn valuable lessons while helping to keep society running and all the other shit they told us growing up. But I was still a little apprehensive. Starting one's term of service was one of those big stepping-off points in life. It would change people's lives in ways they couldn't foresee, doubly so for the position I'd signed up for, and that sense of the unknown put me on edge.

I'd signed up for the Human Federation Defense Force Spaceborne Division. My fellow recruits and I would be responsible for protecting the Hunter system and all of its planets, along with the rest of the Human Federation if needed, from both alien and human threats. I could practically hear the recruiter in my head talking about what an honor it was to serve. I didn't know about the whole it being an honor bit, but the HFDF had sounded like the best service option for me.

I should have felt excited about joining the HFDF. I would have the opportunity to see other worlds on the government's dime. I would also have one of the more exciting Service Term jobs. And who doesn't want to blow stuff up? It wasn't so much that I was worried about dying. War had changed since the days of my parents' youth. Now drones did the dying, not people. There was danger, to be sure, but it was minimal and manageable.

I came to the top of the hill, to a spot where the trees gave way, showing the Sound in the distance; beyond it, the skyline of Orion City sparkled. I paused as I looked out at the city. It was the first city built on the planet Orion and therefore carried the planet's name. If you were on Earth, we were located in the Orion constellation, hence our name. I'd been to Earth several times; it was where my parents were born over three hundred fifty years ago, in a time when humans still aged. They'd been in their seventies when humans developed ageless-ness, being some of the first to be treated with the technology. They were part of the first generation. They'd seen a lot in their time and had been part of the first wave to colonize Orion.

My half-brother and sister, who were also considered first-genera-tion, had a similar history. If I was being honest, that's probably what had me feeling trepidation about leaving for the HFDF. I'd grown up in the shadow of people who were the generation that had founded the Human Federation. My parents had done many great things in their lives, and thus far, I'd managed to graduate from high school. *Good job, me!*

I started running again.

My parents had seen combat shortly after becoming ageless during the last human war. They'd told me it was a dark, bloody time in human history, stopped only by the ability to travel faster than light, allowing us to colonize other worlds. Barring them, no one in my family had been in the armed forces since the founding of the Federation.

My friend Liz said she thought I'd joined the HFDF in an effort to prove myself. I'd told her that I had joined because when my time in the HFDF was done, it would be a big plus on any resume and would teach me leadership and work ethic. All true statements, but I knew she was right.

I was coming back down the hill, heading towards the house. It was empty when I'd gotten up. My parents had commitments that had taken them off-world two days earlier. They were upset not to see me off, but I had told them not to worry about it, that I'd see them when I was done with basic in a few months.

I jumped in the shower, washed off the sweat from the run, and walked into my room. In the corner was an HFDF-issued suitcase that had been delivered the week prior. Inside, it contained a few brochures about the Spaceborne Division and a new recruit uniform. The uniform was a baggy gray jumpsuit that looked to be of the one-size-fits-all variety. The case was for personal items only, and I was not to bring any clothing items or toiletries, as the HFDF would be providing those for me. The case was carry-on sized, and something that you would have thought would make packing for five years difficult, but it wasn't. If anything, it was hard to find items I wanted to take with me.

I could access all of the photos and videos I'd taken or received over the years via my CCPU, along with any form of audio, video, or written entertainment. The guy I'd talked to at the recruiting department said that when he'd left, he'd only taken a couple of things but found that he filled his case up quickly as his ship stopped at various planets. He'd sent most items back home. Apparently, his was a pretty typical story. So I packed a deck of cards, a baseball, and a glove. Before I closed my case, I decided to toss in my sunglasses. None of the items seemed necessary, but what if I was the only person who showed up empty-handed? I didn't care that much about appearances, but I didn't want to get labeled as the sad loner guy before my first day even started.

My CCPU pinged me, telling me a taxi would soon arrive to take me to the train station. I took one last look around my home before leaving. As I did, I felt a slight pang of sadness at the thought of leaving my childhood home. I found the cat and scratched behind his ears.

"You're not going to have me around to wake up in the middle of the night anymore, buddy. You'll have to stick with Mom and Dad," I said.

The cat purred deeply.

My CCPU pinged me again; the taxi was out front. I carried my case outside to the cab. It was a large glass dome, with the main body being a bright mustard yellow. It was driverless, and the door opened as I approached. I tossed my case in and plopped down on one of the cushy seats, feeling it mold to my body. My CCPU pinged a message from the taxi asking if I was ready to go and if my destination was still the train station.

As the taxi started to pull away, I looked back at the house. I smirked at how cliché the act was, but it still felt odd leaving the place, knowing it was no longer my home as soon as I'd walked out. I knew it had little to do with the structure itself. I'd stay here again on leave, but it was the knowledge that I was no longer under my parents' roof and care. I was entering a new stage in life, one without the ever-present safety net of my parents. Sink or swim, it was up to me now. I was on my own.

The train station was busy with mid-morning traffic, lots of people and drones moving around. I saw a familiar group of people in similar jumpsuits milling about. I came up behind one with a baggy blue uniform, her black hair in a ponytail. I slapped her ass, receiving a satisfying yelp of surprise and then anger as she spun around. Flint shone in Monica's dark eyes for a moment until she registered who'd slapped her. Her expression turned into a playful glare. Next to her, a man with short black hair and dark skin started to laugh. Monica turned her gaze to Charles for a moment before returning it to me.

"Alex, I could have, and should have, decked you," Monica said, then she leaned in, giving me a hug, "nice outfit by the way, black and dark gray, mmmm," she joked.

"Yeah, you're looking pretty good too," I said, nodding at her blue suit.

She glanced down at her own suit and tugged on its baggy legs. "Yeah, that's fair."

Monica, like everyone else in my circle of friends, was also entering her government service today. Monica was going into law enforcement. Most of her training would take place in Orion City. Next to her was Charles; he was going into exploration, something that would keep him off-world for most of his time in the service. Across from him was Liz, in a baggy white suit with red lines along the seams. She had long bronze hair and blue eyes framed by a soft face. Liz was going into medicine.

Lastly, there was Jon, whose suit was bright day-glow orange. Jon had an average build, and he wore a broad smile that never seemed to fade. He was going into logistics. He chuckled at Monica's and my exchange, running his hand through his shaggy sandy hair.

"How long have you guys been here?" I asked.

Liz answered, "Not too long; I got here about five minutes ago. Everyone else just showed up," she said, tucking a lock of bronze hair behind her ear.

We began to walk as the PA announced that the train to Orion City was about to depart. Jon and Charles clapped me on the shoulder as a greeting.

We shuffled with the rest of the crowd to a platform where a train hovered slightly above the ground. It was all smooth lines and glass. There was the slightest of hums as I approached it and climbed up the stairs inside.

I found a seat with my friends next to a large window. I shoved my case under my seat and settled in. The train began moving, and the trees outside passed by in a blur. As the train moved, it lifted in the air, allowing wildlife to pass beneath it without harm.

"I got us on the 15:40 lift up to the station," Jon said to Liz and me, "that should give us plenty of time in the city and still make it to your ships just fine."

Liz and I would be going off-planet for training. Liz was headed to a station that functioned as a school, while I was bound for the planet Arrow for basic training. Jon's training would be mostly done on Orion Station. As for Charles, he'd be planetside for the first part of his training, as would Monica.

The train moved quickly, the scenery outside changing from trees to houses to buildings. As we approached the city, I could see a line reaching from the ground up into the sky, seemingly forever. The space elevator, or Lift as it was known, was set a small distance away from the city. Around it was a massive terminal that moved both people and goods onto the elevator and up to Orion Station.

I looked away from the elevator, gazing at the gleaming city. Glass and polished metal dominated the landscape. The air was filled with all manner of drones of various sizes, moving about like rivers in the sky. Some of the drones were commuter buses carrying people around the city, while others were small delivery models. Lower to the ground, I could see other trains moving along unseen tracks. Our train started to slow as it came to its destination. As we disembarked, I tried not to run into people with my case. I was mostly successful, but I still managed to nail some poor guy in the shin. All of my friends had a case of their own, though Monica's was by far the smallest. She'd only be staying at the academy for a week before she could commute into training every day.

We all moved like a herd of cattle into the station and downstairs to street level, where more people crowded about trying to make their way up the stairs to the train. Once we were away from the station, things calmed down, and we could all walk together without running into people. The day was turning warm, and I wished I could go out onto the Sound instead of reporting for duty.

As we walked, we joked around and talked about where to go for lunch. We settled on a place near downtown where we could sit for a while. I requested that we sit outside if possible, and Liz agreed with me. Neither of us would be enjoying the outdoors any time soon, and it seemed neither of us was going to pass up one of the few chances for fresh air we could get.

For Liz, the station she'd be on was massive, but a station nonetheless. For me, I had Arrow to look forward to. It was a small red-brown planet further away from our sun, Hunter, than Orion was. Every system seemed to have one or two planets like Arrow. It didn't have as much gravity as Orion, and its atmosphere was significantly thinner. The planet suffered from massive sandstorms that blew with enough force to shred flesh off you. The people there lived in giant cities that were really just incredibly large buildings that could withstand the storms, provide air, and increased the gravity. The cities were nice, and they had gardens and all that, but it wasn't like the real outdoors.

The restaurant seated us on their second-story terrace. I looked over the menu, joining in small talk. I wasn't sure what the food would be like in the service. The recruiter had told me it was good when you were on base or on a ship. But he was a recruiter. It wasn't like he was going to say to me that it sucked. I wasn't being sent away to some distant planet far removed from society. I was going to be spending a lot of time on other populated worlds and would have free time. Today's lunch wasn't my last meal.

"So, what are you guys looking forward to the most about your service?" Jon asked, as if it hadn't been all we'd been talking about for a month.

Monica spoke first, "Making the world a safer place," she said with a cheesy grin. "I'll get to take down bad guys here on Orion and other parts of the system. I'll be making a difference while the rest of you are playing around."

Liz rolled her eyes. "Yes, because healing people is a waste of time," she retorted. "I'm looking forward to being able to help people and to learn more about medicine. Besides, after my service, it will be easy to find a health job on any planet... not that I'm planning on moving to another system."

"I can't wait to get off-world," Charles said. "I'm going to go to planets no one else has ever been on. Help with terraforming and explore the cosmos. I honestly don't see myself living on Orion again. But don't worry, I'll visit when I can," he said with a grin.

I wasn't surprised to hear that. Charles had been itching to get off-world his whole life. It wasn't that he didn't like people; he was plenty social, and from my understanding, he'd be living in close quarters with people while exploring other worlds. But Charles found true wonder in the universe. He wasn't meant to stay on just one world.

"You guys know me; I can't help but get into how things move around," Jon said. "I can't tell you how excited I am to work on the Lift. And after my service, I'll be able to work on a cargo vessel, someday even captain one," he said.

"Um, Captain Jon, where is my new shirt?" Monica snickered.

Jon pointed at her with a smile. "Delayed due to customs. Some grunt officer got all high and mighty and held up the shipment."

Everyone laughed.

"How about you, Alex?" Liz asked. "What are you excited about?"

I shrugged. "I get to blow stuff up. I think it will be good for me, and I get to help protect the Federation from hostiles. Also, how cool will it be jumping from a spaceship onto a planet?"

Monica nodded her head at that, and everyone else told me I was crazy. They were probably right. I was sure the desire to jump from a vessel hundreds of kilometers above a planet, to go through that planet's atmosphere just to fight a bunch of aliens, was a little crazy. But hey, we all need hobbies.

The mood turned as we started talking about the negatives of service. So many people we had graduated with weren't going to be leaving our hometown or county. Many would be serving locally, and their schedule wouldn't change much, if at all. They'd still be seeing the same people in the same places. Not for us. Monica wouldn't be allowed to serve in her hometown, so she didn't show preference. She'd bounce around Orion and Arrow for a while, along with one of the many Satcities that orbited the system.

Liz would spend a good deal of her time serving on one of the medical corps' many hospital ships. The ships were sent wherever needed, be it a natural disaster or helping the HFDF. That said, it was possible that Liz would spend all of her time helping people with routine medical treatments and scans.

Charles would be in some far-off section of the galaxy before we knew it, and Jon would spend a lot of time on Orion. He'd be assigned to some freighters that did government work and would also spend a little time assisting the HFDF on one of those freighters if needed. Like Liz, he wouldn't be seeing action but would be staying high in orbit.

We wouldn't see each other again for a few months. It felt like a slight hit to the gut. I'd grown up with each of the people sitting with me. We would be able to talk via our CCPUs, but it wouldn't be the same. Five years from now, we'd each be on a different path in life. We all felt slightly depressed when we left the restaurant a few hours later.

We slowly made our way to the Lift's Terminal, where Monica and Charles would catch ferries to their respective training, and Jon, Liz, and I would catch the Lift up to the station. At least the three of us would have a few more hours together. I liked Charles, and Monica was fine, if not slightly annoying sometimes, but I was going to miss Jon and Liz the most.

At the terminal, we said our farewells; even Monica looked a little misty. Then we parted ways. Liz, Jon, and I turned to a large doorway labeled "Space Lift."

As we walked into the terminal, we were greeted by a large cavernous room that stood several stories above us. Skylights made up almost all of the ceiling, bathing the smooth grey walls and polished floors in light.

Our CCPUs guided us as we joined the throngs of people moving down corridors that lead to gates. We joined others on a giant conveyor belt that carried us deeper into the terminal. Jon confirmed that our car to the station left in an hour as we moved along on the belt.

A hall and another conveyor belt later, and we were walking down a concourse to our gate. The concourses were separated by large gaps with tracks where the Lift cars traveled from gate to gate and then to the Lift itself.

I glanced up, seeing small drones flowing like little streams above us as they carried items around. Jon was all smiles as he watched the drones above us and the Lift cars moving around outside as they made their way to or from the elevator. It was all very orderly; each car would detach from the elevator and move to a different part of the terminal for loading and unloading.

Jon looked around wide-eyed, and for a moment, I shared his awe. The cars were large, each one being several stories tall. The elevator had sixteen tracks, eight dedicated to up traffic and eight for down. The elevator could move thousands of people and thousands of tons of goods each day.

The concourse we were traveling down was lined with loading gates where people entered their cars. I could see out windows across to the neighboring concourse where a car was docked.

At the gate, a woman told us we could board, and we walked directly onto the car. There was a set of stairs that would take you to the upper or lower levels of the car, and in front of us were rows of seats looking out of floor-to-ceiling windows. We managed to get seats in the front, looking out between concourses as cars moved past.

After a while, a monotone female voice came over the PA, "Thank you for riding the Lift today from Orion City to Orion Station. We will be undocking momentarily and starting our taxi to the Lift. Our trip up to Orion Station will take one and a half hours. On the car's upper level, you will find the cafeteria and lounge where drinks and food can be purchased." The car gave a slight shudder, and we began to move. "In the event of an emergency, this car is designed to disengage from the Lift and return to the surface of Orion. Should the artificial gravity fail, please try to make your way back to your seat and fasten your seat belt." There was nothing about what would happen if there was a loss of pressure once in space. I knew if that happened, we would just plain die. Thankfully, there hadn't been a Space Elevator accident resulting in a fatality on any world in over one hundred and fifty years.

The car was turning onto a track that would take us to the Lift. In front of us was the back of another car. Two grooves ran from top to bottom; inside the grooves were gears that clamped onto the elevator's tracks, lifting it into space. We moved slowly down the track until we came to a T-intersection. The car before us turned at the T, and we waited as several cars with space freight containers went by. Jon bounced in his seat.

"Did you know each of those cars can carry over four hundred tons of cargo?" Jon asked.

"No," Liz said, "I didn't know that. That's a lot of crap."

"And each track on the Lift has its cars separated by ten-minute intervals. Our car will attach and start moving up while another car comes in to attach, and so on. At the station, we will detach, and then ten minutes later, another car will come and detach. It's crazy efficient." Jon gushed, "The Lift is made of nano-material and has hundreds of cars running on it at all times. The Lift even self-repairs..."

I started to tune Jon out as he started talking about the Lift's gravitational controls. It wasn't that it wasn't interesting, but I'd heard about the space elevator about a thousand times and wasn't going to pretend like I hadn't, as Liz was doing. Instead, I watched as we turned on the track that would take us to the Lift. It was impressive. A massive black cylinder rose from the ground, going all the way up into space. The cars, which moments before had seemed big, now looked small in comparison. I could see cars moving up and down the various tracks on the Lift. They looked like kids' toys compared to the large structure. Our car was next in line.

It spun around, its back facing the Lift, giving me a view of the waiting cars. There was a little whine from the gears moving to grip the track, and then the ground started to fall below us. The car's gravity controls made it feel like we weren't moving at all as the car began to move.

We rose above the terminal, giving us a fantastic view of the city. The car picked up speed as it went, and soon the city was below us, with all I could see being the countryside. The view from the Lift was second to none. Even when I'd been in space, the view from the Lift had been better. Space was almost too far away. Clouds whipped by the window as we moved, and I settled back in my seat, listening to Liz and Jon talk. With each kilometer the car moved away from the planet, the more nervous I became. I wasn't sure I was ready for my whole world to turn upside down.

As the car moved up, the horizon transitioned from the greens of the area around Orion City to the black of space, with Orion now a bright, vibrant expanse below us. As we got closer to the station, even Jon's enthusiasm started to wane. This was really happening.

My siblings had told me that beginning your service was tough, but once you got through the start, it would become the best five years of your life. I hoped they were right. The higher we got from Orion, the more we could see in space. Ships in all shapes and sizes were moving around. We whizzed by a stationary freighter.

The female PA voice came on again and said, "We are now arriving at Orion Station. The station is perpendicular to Orion. As a result, once detached from the Lift, the car will rotate to align with the Station. While the gravity inside the car will make you feel as if nothing has changed, if you are looking outside one of the windows, the change in perspective can cause motion sickness. It is advised that you set your CCPU to inhibit nausea. Thank you."

I did as the voice instructed. I couldn't feel the car slow down, but it must have as metal passed before the window, and suddenly we were at the Station. Like the voice had suggested, the station looked like it was on its side. The world moved as the car detached and aligned itself with the station. Orion was no longer below us but to our right. The car moved down tracks until it came to a stop at a gate.

"Thank you for taking the Lift today. Please ensure that you have all of your belongings with you. Have a nice day," the monotone voice said.

I grabbed my case's handle and followed the procession of people out of the car and into the station's concourse. It seemed smaller than the terminal that I'd been in an hour and a half ago, but I knew that was wrong. As I looked out the windows, I could see massive cargo ships, as well as black-hulled military vessels, along with all other manner of ships. Drones were flying cargo containers to ships off in the distance.

"Whoa, look at that one," Jon said, pointing to a ship in the distance. "That's got to be a galaxy-class cargo ship. They have a cargo capacity of over five hundred thousand tons!"

"Wow dude," I said, trying not to curb his enthusiasm. Logistics sounded like hell to me, but if Jon wanted to deal with cargo and all that stuff, good for him.

We walked through the main terminal silently until we got to an intersection that would take us to different places. Jon was going to be staying on the station while Liz and I had ships to catch on opposite sides. Jon didn't have too long until he had to report in.

"So this is it then," Liz said with a tear in her eye, "we'll keep in touch?"

"Yeah," I said.

Jon brightened, "Let's promise to do dinner or lunch back home one year from now. A year isn't that long, right?"

I thought about it. A year wasn't that long, and I'd be home on leave a few times before then.

"Yeah, dinner or lunch in a year," I said, "we'll celebrate one year in the service." As I said this, my nerves started to fade a bit. What could happen in a year?

We all shook on it and then went our separate ways, a bounce in our steps. By this time tomorrow, I'd be on Arrow in training. Part of me was nervous about that, but that was now becoming a small part of me. The other part was starting to think about what I said at lunch.

Hmm, I wonder when I get to jump out of a ship? I thought, smiling.

TWO

The counter at my gate had an enormous window that offered a view outside the station. Before me was a small, sleek, black, windowless ship. I wondered why military ships were black. My CCPU, sensing my curiosity, pulled up a search, showing me what it assumed was the best answer.

Text flowed over my vision.

THOUGH MOST ENEMIES HAVE THE ABILITY TO DETECT SHIPS AND OTHER OBJECTS WITHOUT THE USE OF OPTICAL SENSORS, MILITARY VESSELS ARE BLACK AS A SAFE MEASURE FROM OPTICAL VIEWING. WHEN IN BATTLE, AN ENEMY MAY BE FORCED TO USE LINE-OF-SIGHT TACTICS, WHICH COULD BE HINDERED BY THE DARK COLOR OF THE SHIP.

I figured the lack of windows was pretty obvious for a military vessel, and something I was sure I'd be grateful for someday. For today though, I wasn't overly excited about being in a tin can without any view of the world around me. I'd never been to Arrow, and it would have been nice to see it when we got there. *Arrow's station does have windows, you know,* I told myself.

I walked down a gangway that led to a door inside the ship. The interior of the ship was a light gray with rows and rows of large, comfortable-looking seats. I was happy to see that the walls were vid screens showing the view from outside the ship. I had my CCPU check my seat number and made my way to it.

My parents had told me about the military from when humans had first become ageless. They'd said that conditions were far more comfortable than when they were my age, but still not as nice as civilian life. I had hoped that things had changed in the hundreds of years since they'd been in the military, and so far, so good.

There was a thud next to me. I turned to see a man my age with dark skin and short hair settling himself in the chair beside me. He shifted in his chair and turned to me, extending a hand.

"Miron Sweeting," he said, taking my hand.

"Alex Taylor," I replied.

Sweeting looked at the screen. "Man, I am sure glad to see those," he said. "When I saw the ship, I was sure it wouldn't have windows... well, it doesn't I guess, but with the vid screens, it doesn't feel that way."

"Same here. I hear we'll spend a lot of time on ship during our service. Do you think the troop ships will have vid walls?" I asked.

Sweeting looked thoughtful. "Not sure." His eyes went out of focus for a moment; I assumed he was checking his CCPU. "Looks like they do. Well, in squad rooms at least."

I sighed. "Good, I would have gone crazy if they didn't. My parents said the old troop carriers didn't have them."

"No kidding? How old are your parents?"

"First-gen."

Sweeting looked impressed. "No way! Man, that's cool, you must have all kinds of older siblings. But I bet it was hard to get away with anything growing up. I hear after how many kids they've had over the years, you can't get anything past a first-gen."

I laughed. "You have no idea. And I do have a bunch of siblings and all that," I said.

"So how first-gen are they?" he asked.

Questions like this were pretty common. You would have thought that with how many people were on Earth when humans stopped aging, there would be first-gens everywhere, but there weren't. Humans had spread across the cosmos, and in the early days, there had been many conflicts before humans even left Earth. And that wasn't counting the billions that hadn't left at all. Many of the people who left Earth to start colonies had been younger, looking to get away from the masses on Earth in hopes of finding a better life, or, like in the case of my parents, a chance to explore the universe. I frequently had to remind myself that when my parents were my age, the thought of going to Earth's moon in their lifetimes was a fantasy, let alone living on other planets.

"They were in their seventies when the tech came along," I said.

"Dang!" Sweeting exclaimed, "so they're like super first-gens. That's cool. I'm my parents' first kid, but my great-grandparents are first-gen too; they live on Hydra... So what's it like?"

I shrugged, "nothing special. You have a lot to live up to, I suppose."

Our conversation was interrupted as a voice came over the PA, letting us know that the ship was about to leave dock. Sweeting and I looked at the vid screens as the station started to creep by us. As we pulled away from the station, I received a CCPU message from the ship, letting me know that I could access any of the exterior camera feeds. I did so, selecting the view from one of the bow cameras.

My vision was taken over by the feed from the ship, and I was only slightly aware of things around me. Orion Station was massively large, and way bigger than I could have ever imagined. As a kid, I'd never actually taken the time to look at it the few times I'd left Orion, but at the moment, I could start to see Jon's fascination with it.

I couldn't see all of it yet, but what I could see seemed unreal. The outside was a light gray, with the ships in dock looking like little spikes on a cactus. There had to be tens of thousands of people on the station at any given moment. My mind boggled as I thought about the number of people that must pass through daily, not to mention the cargo and raw materials that flowed through it.

As the ship backed away and turned, I switched views. I could see little dots moving all around the station. I zoomed in on some, seeing that they were cargo drones carrying containers to and from the station; there were thousands of them. I zoomed out and could see other ships coming into view. Some were black like the one I was in, but most came in a myriad of colors and sizes.

Soon, the ship turned towards the planet Arrow, our destination, and I pulled up the aft camera. I saw Orion as a giant blue and green sphere. It was beautiful. I watched my home start to shrink as the ship accelerated forward. The view of Orion got smaller and smaller more rapidly as the ship sped up; soon, Orion's moon whizzed past us in a blur. I turned off the feed and looked back to Sweeting.

"Aft feed?" I asked.

He smiled, "it was a sight to behold, wasn't it?"

"Yeah, it was."

Watching Orion fade made me wonder what it would be like to see other worlds. I'd been to Earth before but hadn't been anywhere else. A list of worlds started running in my head, and the types I'd like to visit. I'd only ever been to Earth and Orion, the latter being chosen for colonization because of how similar it was to Earth. I'd always wanted to see one of the Human Federation's water worlds or one of the frozen moons with thick atmospheres and lakes of liquid nitrogen. My desires aside, I knew planets like Arrow were the norm among the rocky worlds, and on a societal level, I saw their appeal.

"So what made you want to join the HFDF?" I asked Sweeting.

He didn't have to think long, "it sounded like fun. Some of my friends think I'm nuts. But I mean, come on, we get to blow shit up and jump out of ships!" he said.

"Nice, me too. You're Spaceborne, I take it?" I asked.

"Sure am. Don't you think it will be a good time?" he asked.

I couldn't help but smile, "my friend Liz thinks I'm crazy for looking forward to it. She even talked to my parents about it."

"It is crazy; she was right." He chuckled, "but that doesn't mean it won't be fun. From what I hear, you spend a lot of time in drills with other groups in the HFDF. The recruiter said that you go to a bunch of worlds. Well, unless there's a conflict. Do you think we'll see any action?"

I thought about it. "I don't know, but my gut says we will. My recruiter said that most people see at least one combat deployment in their Service Term, if not more."

"Mine said the same thing," he said thoughtfully.

I considered this for a moment. The thought of killing aliens on other planets should have seemed somewhat worrisome for me, but it wasn't. If anything, I was a little excited. I was sure that excitement would disappear or fade once aliens were actually shooting at me.

"But he also said that the vast majority of combat we'd see would be pretty one-sided. There aren't that many races up to par with us. And of those that are, we're friendly with them," I said.

He nodded, "yeah, mine said things along the same lines. I won't lie, I'm cool with that. I don't think I would be as excited if I thought I was gonna die," he said with a chuckle.

I laughed, "I hear you there."

I spent most of the trip talking with Sweeting. We discussed what we thought the service would be like and our hometowns. Sweeting was easy to talk to, and I hoped we'd at least be in training together, but I wasn't overly optimistic about it. It helped pass the time, though.

When Arrow Station came into view, I was amazed at how similar it looked to Orion Station. My CCPU found that virtually every planetary station looked similar, as they shared many of the same design specifications. We docked at the station and disembarked. Sweeting and I retrieved our cases at the gate and made our way to the elevator. As the car went down, I looked up anything interesting I could find about Arrow and the city we were going to, even if we'd only be passing through.

Sweeting snorted a laugh.

"What?" I asked.

"Look at the history of the Arrow Space Elevator," he said.

I did, seeing what was so funny. Supposedly when the elevator was installed, the residents wanted to name it, like the people of Orion had done with the Lift. The people of Arrow, however, claimed they wanted a name that fit with the planet's name. After a fair amount of debate, the name of the elevator was coined *The Shaft*, after the shaft of an arrow. City planners accepted the name but hadn't understood why some people always giggled about The Shaft until years later when a local celebrity said on a talk show that her favorite pastime was going up and down The Shaft all night long. This spawned open mockery of the elevator, something that had always been a quiet joke.

When city planners got the punchline, they officially changed the name of the elevator. However, the citizens refused to let the name go, and The Shaft was still the term every media outlet and person used for the elevator on Arrow. I chuckled to myself as a curious search found no less than one hundred adult films centered around The Shaft. I decided that maybe the people of Arrow were my kind of folks.

As we got to the bottom of the elevator, I started to get a grasp of Arrow. It was much smaller than Orion, had a thin atmosphere, and I knew that cities used artificial gravity to keep everything in town at 1g. The ground was a muted reddish-brown, and below us was a city that sprawled for kilometers. The city was one large structure with glass on the top that could be covered in bad weather. I could see towers rising all over the city. While it inspired respect, Arrow City was far from attractive. It looked industrial and cold, wrapped in metal and glass.

One thing that did stick out to me was that the airspace was rela-tively void of drones and aircraft. Over Orion City, the sky seemed to have nearly the same, if not more, traffic than the ground. Again, I turned to my CCPU with the question. It said that the weather was such an issue on the planet that it too regularly interrupted air traffic. As a result, all of the city's supply routes were in the megastructure.

It made me wonder how horrific the storms could be.

The inside of the terminal looked much the same as the one on Orion, with the difference that it was part of the city. The city extended out from the elevator, making it the center of town. We got on a tram that ran through the city, and it felt odd never to be outside as the tram moved. Instead, we passed by shops, businesses, and residential areas.

We were in a lower level that couldn't see through one of the city's skylights. Despite that, the city felt surprisingly open. The ceilings we could see showed the view from outside, with some even showing what must have been the views of other worlds and space. It felt surprisingly open. It was nothing like the buildings on Orion. Orion City gave you the feeling of being in, well... a big city. Arrow City, on the other hand, didn't. It somehow felt smaller and open, though it was anything but. Finally, we reached a small military port and got on a shuttle.

The port was as no-nonsense as the ship we'd taken to Arrow had been. Sweeting and I joined other people in baggy gray jumpsuits as they walked into the shuttle. I managed to find a seat next to a window, and Sweeting plopped down beside me. I was starting to feel the trip, and all I wanted to do was sleep. *Soon, you can sleep soon,* I told myself.

We passed the edge of the city and found that it was at least fifty stories tall above ground. Workers and drones were on the city limits, building more of the city as it grew across the landscape. Machines dug into the ground, showing that Arrow City had just as many subterranean levels as above ground. I wondered if at some point, the planet would become one giant city.

The shuttle flew over the ruddy landscape that had no trees, grass, or any plant life at all. It was a barren wasteland. The only thing you had to look at was the contour of the land itself. It wasn't that it was ugly per se, rather just simple, unadorned, and almost naked. There was a kind of beauty to it, but not one I found myself attracted to. The sun had long set when the shuttle stopped at a large base. Like Arrow City, the base was all metal and utilitarian. It wasn't as tall as the city had been, but from the shuttle window, I could see that it spanned a great distance.

As the sky had darkened, it came alive with stars. Without much of an atmosphere to diffuse far-off city lights, the sky was clear. It was around 21:00 when we arrived at the training base. I wasn't sure how long I'd been awake. We got off the shuttle; even Sweeting moved sluggishly. I followed the directions that my CCPU gave me to my quarters. Most of the people who had been on the transport with me had been on the shuttle, and now we all shuffled through the base together as a tired mass.

The halls of the training base were a bland gray, with closed doors lining them that people would sporadically come in and out of. I noticed all of the people wore the same clothing I did. I was happy to find out that Sweeting and I were going to be rooming together; we came to a door that was ours. The door slid open, revealing a gray room with five bunks built into the walls. On the right and left sides were two, and on the far wall, one was close to the ground. Above it, a vid display showed the names of the people in the room and the bunks that we were to stay in. Mine was below Sweeting's on the left side.

Next to the bunk was a compartment that fit my case perfectly. Seeing where my and Sweeting's bunks were, and considering seating on the ship, I would have been willing to bet that almost everyone from the ship going into the Spaceborne would be in my training platoon. Further, I was sure most of them were likewise standing in their rooms with new friends they'd made on the trip.

I thought about waiting to see who else would be coming to my room but decided to go to bed instead. Sweeting was doing likewise. I read some instructions on the vid display saying that we were to dress and undress inside our bunks as this room was co-ed, unless we didn't mind being seen nude, and it didn't bother our roommates. I wasn't sure that I wanted any first impressions to be with me or someone else in the buff, so I decided I'd undress in my bunk. It said that we would be getting a new uniform tomorrow that would remove itself when in the bunks. I perked up at that; that sounded kind of cool.

I got in my bunk more tired than I had been in a while and, using my CCPU, closed a screen to the room. The screen snapped down, and I was instantly in pitch black; there was no light or sound from the room outside. I shifted, noting that the mattress and pillow were actually pretty soft. I accessed the bunk with my CCPU and turned on some lights so I could undress. There was a place where I could put my clothes at the base of the bed. It wasn't easy; the bunk wasn't tall, but I managed. Next, I looked through the bunk's options, seeing that I could change it to any scenery I liked. I tried setting it to outdoors near Orion City. Instantly, my surroundings transformed as if I were in the forest. I couldn't see the top or sides of the bunk at all. I could hear crickets chirping and wind blowing in the tall trees around me. I grinned; this was pretty nice. I'd seen tech like it before but didn't know I'd get to use it in training.

I switched everything back to black. I pulled up my itinerary for the morning and saw that I was to be up by 06:00. I set an alarm in my CCPU, then told it to help me sleep. I closed my eyes, drifting off.

THREE

I struggled to fully wake up in the dark, silent bunk and had to use my CCPU to help me along. There was a message waiting for me, telling me to log in and integrate with the base's computers. I followed the instructions, which caused a flood of information to stream through my head.

Another message from the base appeared:

ARROW TRAINING BASE: WELCOME TO ARROW
TRAINING BASE. PLEASE GET DRESSED AND PROCEED
TO THE 'HEAD' LOCATED AT THE END OF THE HALL. IT
IS HIGHLY RECOMMENDED THAT YOU DIRECT YOUR
CCPU TO HAVE YOUR BODY DISCARD ALL BODY HAIR,
AS YOUR COMBAT SUIT WILL BE ABLE TO BETTER
CONNECT WITH YOUR SKIN. YOU MAY LEAVE THE
HAIR ON YOUR HEAD AND A SHORT BEARD IF YOU
WOULD LIKE. QUEUE UP AND AWAIT FURTHER
INSTRUCTION.

Odd though the request was, the recruiter had told me to expect it.

I told my CCPU to lose the hair, which would come off in the shower. I set the hair on my head to stay in place, but told it not to let my beard grow.

I synced up my wishes with base functions in my CCPU, so I wouldn't have to send conscious commands to use anything in the base. The bunk wasn't all that big on the inside, and it was a bit of a pain in the ass to turn around and reach into the bin that held my uniform. After I got it though, I found that it was even more of a pain to put on. Eventually, with many grunts and a few choice words, I got it done and was relieved that the screen to the bunk was opaque. The screen slid open as I rolled, and I swung my legs out and stood. The screens of the other bunks across from me and the one on the wall opposite the door were all closed.

"Morning, man," Sweeting said, jumping down from the bunk above me.

"Hey, how'd you sleep?" I asked.

"I could get used to the bunks for sure, but fuck, I hope we don't always have to get dressed and undressed in them, you know? I really thought I might get stuck there for a moment."

"You could always walk around in your birthday suit," I pointed out.

He laughed. "You're gonna have to do a little bit more romancing before that's gonna happen."

Across from us, another bunk started to open. It was the lower one, and a girl with long brown hair and blue eyes awkwardly slid out. She stood, her recruit suit baggy on her. She looked at Sweeting and me.

"Alex Taylor," I said, extending my hand.

"Krista McLeod," she said, taking mine and then repeating the process with Sweeting.

She took a moment to run her fingers through her hair in an attempt to smooth it out.

The bunk on the far wall opened up, and a guy with short brown hair, dark eyes, and a lean build slid out. We repeated the handshaking; his name was Betts.

Lastly, the bunk above McLeod's opened, and a guy with wavy blond hair and green eyes got out.

"The name's Miron Sweeting," Sweeting said, extending his hand with a warm smile on his face.

"Good for you," the guy said with a chuckle and an eye roll as he walked out of the room.

I watched him go, sighing on the inside. There was always a prick wherever you went, my father had told me. He'd never been wrong about that. He'd also warned that if there wasn't a prick that I noticed, then that meant I was the prick, and to shape up. Bright side? I'd identified this group's prick, so I was in the clear.

McLeod scowled slightly. "That's Meyers; we got in at the same time last night. I was hoping that his attitude was just because it was late."

"Maybe we won't be with him," I offered.

"Nah," Betts said. "My brother is in the infantry. He said that whoever you room with is your Fireteam, and that doesn't change your entire time in the service unless you're in a replacement company, which we aren't. I checked this morning before I got out of bed."

I thought about that for a moment. The people with me now would be my teammates for the next five years. My life and theirs might be in each other's hands. It was an odd sort of feeling, to be sure.

"We're stuck with him?" McLeod said morosely.

"That sucks," I said. "Well…want to go to the head?"

We left the room and joined a line in the hall leading to a door marked "HEAD." I waited my turn until I got to the door, which thankfully didn't take long. It opened, and I stepped inside to stand in a new line that ended in a large gray circular room with several doors. When I was third in line, I got a message.

ARROW TRAINING BASE: WHEN IT IS YOUR TURN,

PROCEED TO THE NEAREST OPEN DOOR AND AWAIT INSTRUCTION.

When it was my turn, a door to my left opened, and I walked into a much smaller room. The door closed behind me. Inside the closet-sized room was a bin marked "Dopp Kit" and another marked "Suit." Across from me was yet another door. The whole affair felt odd.

ARROW TRAINING BASE: DISROBE, PLACE CLOTHING INSIDE OF THE PROPER BIN, AND WAIT FOR THE NEXT DOOR TO OPEN.

I did as ordered, placing my clothing inside the bin. The other door opened into a brightly lit cylindrical room. I stepped inside onto a squishy grate. The door behind me closed. The room was tall and narrow. The walls shone with bright white light.

ARROW TRAINING BASE: RAISE YOUR HANDS AND CLOSE YOUR EYES. YOUR SHOWER WILL COMMENCE AT ONCE.

I closed my eyes and raised my hands hesitantly. Jets of pleasantly hot water pelted my body from above, and then the jets moved down my body until they sprayed my feet. Next, soap was squirted on me, and I was told to scrub my head and body. Following that, more water rinsed me, and then hot air blew on me, drying me off.

I opened my eyes as the wall in front of me opened to yet another room. There, I found a new suit to put on and a case labeled "Dopp Kit," which contained a toothbrush, comb, and other minor toiletries. There was a little sink to brush my teeth with and a mirror to comb my hair. The base reminded me to be quick about my preparations.

ARROW TRAINING BASE: TAKE YOUR DOPP KIT WITH

YOU. THERE IS A STORAGE AREA IN YOUR BUNK FOR IT. EACH DAY THE CONTENTS WILL BE STERILIZED. THE NANO-MATERIAL ON THE BRUSH WILL ENSURE IT NEVER WEARS OUT, AND THE TOOTHPASTE RESERVOIR WILL BE REFILLED.

I took the Dopp Kit as the wall, also a door, opened into a narrow hallway. There were other recruits in the hallway; we all walked to a door that let us back out into the hall where our rooms were and the line of other recruits. I went back to the room where McLeod was waiting.

"What'd you think of that?" I asked, not entirely sure about my opinion on the shower.

"I'm not too sure how I feel about standing in a car wash every day. Don't get me wrong, the water was nice and warm, and I'm clean..." she said.

"But not like your normal shower, yeah, I know what you mean. I couldn't decide if I was being treated like a car or a cow," I commented.

She nodded and said, "Both seem pretty accurate."

The door opened, and Betts and Sweeting came in.

"Did you guys order the deluxe wash? I did, and man, the wax and spotless rinse were amazing, let me tell you," Sweeting joked.

After that, we left the room and went to the mess hall, following maps from our CCPUs. The mess hall was huge, with hundreds of people in it. Most of them were not in the new recruit suits like us, but formfitting charcoal gray ones that looked like they were made out of some sort of rubber or nano-material. They were padded enough that you couldn't see exactly what the person looked like without the suit on, but like bathing suits, there wasn't much left to the imagination. I'd seen plenty of cops before, and they wore those suits, but in blue. Each of the people in the mess hall had a sidearm in a thigh holster. I didn't expect to see my fellow trainees packing at the breakfast table, but I also hadn't expected to be herded into a car wash for humans either. *Life's full of new experiences,* I thought.

We walked up to the food line, and one of the people in the suits was right in front of me. I'd never really paid close attention to the ones cops wore, but I inspected the person in front of us now. The sidearm was rectangular in shape, with the holster connected to the thigh, its form blending seamlessly with the suit. The suit went down the woman's legs, transitioning into boots, and up to the base of her head. The arms were long, ending at her hands. The back of the suit looked bulkier than the rest of it, but it still mirrored the contours of her body.

I was up next to get food and ordered an omelet. We sat down, still with no sight of Meyers, and dug into our food. It was good, which was a pleasant surprise. In my parents' days, the HFDF had limited food supplies, so they'd eaten a lot of nutrient packets. Again, I was thankful things had changed. I made a mental note to tell my dad. He'd given me no end of grief about the lack of food once I'd enlisted. In retrospect, he probably knew things were different from his time and just wanted to get a rise out of me. *Dick.*

After breakfast, we followed CCPU maps to a classroom filled with fifty other recruits, Meyers among them. Standing at the head of the room was a rather severe-looking man with a bald head. We sat down together, watching the man up front who finally spoke—well, yelled.

"Good morning, recruits! My name is Major Cortez! You will call me Sir or Major. Welcome to your orientation. Let's get started!"

Cortez started to pace. "I will be responsible for your training. My team and I will monitor and customize training routines for you for the duration of your Service Term. We will not be on the ship with you when you leave here, but rest assured that I will be watching you.

"You might be wondering what makes me qualified to do this. Well, let me tell you. I am first-generation and have been in the military since a time when drones were little more than remote-controlled airplanes. Before you ask what that is, I suggest you use the computer in your head to find out! I was seventy-five when agelessness came around. I'm as first-generation as you can get. I spent my mortal career training pukes like you and have been doing so since becoming ageless. I have fought in more wars than you can imagine and witnessed the evolution of war."

He stopped pacing, turning to look at us. He was loud, yes, but didn't seem like the movie drill sergeants that I'd come to expect.

"Now, it used to be that basic training was not like what you will have here. There was a time when people were the weapons and not drones; those people, unlike yourselves, did not have advanced biotechnology controlling their bodies. Your body, as you know, will not age past twenty-five. Your CCPU also controls how much fat and muscle you have, along with just about everything else about you. Better still, you have pounds of synthetic muscle material to augment your natural body. You cannot get sick, and you can heal from almost anything. What you may not know is that you are pound for pound stronger and faster than your non-ageless ancestors by a long shot.

"In my non-ageless physical prime, the least of you would be at least twice as strong and fast as me. You could take more damage than I would have been able to; your bones are stronger, and you have a computer inside your head augmenting everything about you! Though untrained you are, my highly trained non-ageless self would have been hard-pressed to beat any of you in hand-to-hand combat. So much so that it would be laughable. For that matter, you would have been able to outstrip me in every other category. You have finer motor skills than I had, better sight, smell, and hearing. That computer in your head does more for you than you know. How many of you sat around in school memorizing multiplication tables?"

No one raised their hands. He laughed. "That seems stupid to you, doesn't it? After all these years of relying on your CCPU, many of you have undoubtedly memorized a good deal more than I did at your age. But you have never taken the time to learn how to do it. Your CCPU helps your brain to do it in a way you don't have to think about. That has been your entire life.

"Thus, we get to the first difference in training. In my time, we had to train our bodies and make them stronger and better. There are literally no exercises that you can do that will make you better than what your CCPU can tell your body to do. Nor will your CCPU let you push your body to a point where you would achieve meaningful emotional and psychological growth. Here, you will not have PT like I had. Also, unlike wars of the past, while you will know how to fight and kill with the best of us, your primary job is to direct drones and not get killed! It is possible and likely that none of you will die in the service if you do your job correctly and the drones take the risks. If you stay in the service past your Service Term and enter the ranks of the career troops, you may go years without firing your weapon in combat, instead using solely drones.

"We also have much better medicine than in my time. If you do not have brain damage, you can be fixed. I once saw a man lose his head, literally! A medical drone was close enough to recover his head and put it in stasis before his brain could start to die. He made a full recovery and fought again in the same campaign.

"I'm not telling you this to make you think it's okay to get hurt. Don't be dumb, but don't be overly fearful either. While the tech in your body might be able to keep you alive, that doesn't mean that you'll be effective. If you lose a leg, you won't be able to magically walk out of whatever the situation is. Get hit in the heart, and your biotech will have to work overtime keeping your brain alive; as a result, it will knock you out. You aren't very useful when you're asleep. Understand what I'm getting at here?"

We all shouted, "Sir, yes sir," indicating that we did get what he was saying. Lesson number one from the HFDF: don't be stupid and try not to get blown up.

He stood before us and waved his hands over his body, which was covered in the same suit I'd seen others in.

"This is your combat suit," he said. "It is made up of nano-material and other small equipment, the minutiae of which you can read about in your spare time if you so choose. Most of you have heard of nano-material and interact with it on a daily basis, but don't give it any thought, not seeing the true miracle that it is. First off, nano-material is not nanobots, though you have plenty of them running in your blood-stream. Nano-material forms into whatever it is told to. It can also be made out of seemingly endless types of material. Your suit is made of several different materials. Some will camouflage you; others will help your strength and speed. You will be forty percent faster in these suits and three times stronger! They harden to stop shrapnel and projectiles fired at you. They allow you to be in space without harm or under hundreds of feet of water. They will convert your body heat into energy. On that topic, they will keep your body at a constant tempera-ture in almost any environment!

"They are designed in a way that, regardless of the environment you find yourself in, you will be in perfect comfort. Why? Is it because the HFDF really likes to make you feel good? Not really. If you aren't distracted by how cold, hot, or whatever you are, then you can focus on your job. It also means your body won't be wasting energy trying to heat you up or cool you off. Plain and simple.

"These suits are your life! You will wear them from this day forth until the end of your service. They will remove themselves from you when you command, which will be when you are in your bunks or shower. They will recycle your body's fluids, and when you have them on, they catheterize you to take care of your body's waste. You will literally never feel like you have to go to the bathroom when in combat. On a ship or in training when not in exercises, you will still need to go to the restroom the old-fashioned way."

He raised a finger. "Before one of you nitwits asks this question: No, you cannot get a hard-on when the suit has you cath'd! You won't even feel it happen." He patted his sidearm. "Today, you will be issued a sidearm and holster that will meld with the nano-material of your suit.

You will carry your sidearm at all times, even on leave. Your sidearm works with your CCPU. You will not be able to shoot one another with them, so don't bother trying. We will teach you how to shoot tomorrow, but you will get your sidearm today. For those of you with firearm training and carry licenses, which is about twenty percent of you, your sidearm will be functional."

I listened as Cortez talked about vambraces that we would put on, which held grenades and breaching charges. He talked about the nanomaterial in the vambraces that could extend out into whatever we needed. He warned that they were mainly used for throwing arms for the grenades and climbing appendages that would allow us to cling onto and thus scale almost any surface, but they could also be used as weapons in close-quarter fights. Our boots had the same type of material, allowing them to make tread for each environment we were in, and the toe had extra material again for climbing. I was floored by the amount of tech I'd have attached to my body for the next five years.

After lunch, we went into a separate room with little fabric partitions where our suits were. I walked into a partition and saw a black block on the floor with two handles. We'd been told to strip, grab the handles, and integrate with the block. I bent down, grabbing the handles; my CCPU integrated with the block. It flowed almost like a liquid, covering my body. As the suit slid over my skin, it felt almost cold but warmed up immediately. I lifted each foot as the boots molded around them.

My CCPU showed a myriad of options related to the suit. As Cortez suggested, I set it to intuitive with the physical augmentations off for the time being. The suit was the most comfortable thing I had ever worn in my life, and I understood the need for no hair on my body. The suit used my body heat to recharge its power cells, but it also stopped any itching or discomfort I might have. Body hair would have had a higher chance of itching, thus wasting energy.

I walked around, feeling out the boots. They too, were comfortable, contouring to my feet and giving me more support than I honestly thought was possible. Outside of the partitions, everyone was walking around. The boots hugged my ankles but not in an uncomfortable way; just in a supportive grip. When I tried to bend my ankles, they moved with ease, the boots responding fluidly.

I could change the level of input I received from the outside world as well. I could feel pressure, heat, and texture as if the floor, air, or whatever I touched was being felt by my own skin. I could also dull the sensations, isolating myself from the world, or even just allowing certain senses to come through, limiting different sections of my body to feeling different things. It was an odd sensation to have full control over how I perceived the world around me.

Cortez started to talk again. "You will all be getting messages about fat and muscle mass. You will need some fat on your body for energy and nutrients in a fight. You do not want too much fat, however, and conversely, you don't want too much muscle. Your CCPU can access what the HFDF deems to be the best for your body. What it won't tell you is where fat deposits should be. I suggest keeping yourself balanced."

My CCPU pinged me with a message about what the HFDF thought I needed. I wasn't overly surprised when it said that my body was within the tolerances the HFDF would have recommended.

I turned to Betts. "Do you have to change anything?" I asked.

He shook his head. "Nope, you?"

"Nah. Sweeting, how about you?"

"You can't change perfection," he said, looking at McLeod expectantly, then smiled. "I'm not that dumb."

She laughed. "No changes for me."

"I bet that's something that's a holdover from when people didn't just keep their bodies in optimal condition," Betts said.

"I could see that. My parents said that when they first had the ability to change their fat and muscle mass, they went a little crazy with it. They said people got a little extreme with their bodies," I supplied.

I'd seen plenty of pictures from my parents' lives pre- and post-ageless technology. They'd gone from normal to old to ungodly fit and attractive and back to a sane version of themselves.

Next, we got our sidearms, the MIP, though everyone just called it their pistol or sidearm, and a holster. The gun was blocky and bulky. It felt solid in my hand, and despite how utilitarian it was, it felt well-balanced and comfortable. I got the impression that it was a lot tougher than I was. The front had nano-material that could be shaped into whatever I needed. I held the holster to my leg, and it melded with the suit. I placed the gun inside the holster and integrated with it.

ARROW TRAINING BASE: ALEXANDER MICHAEL TAYLOR, YOU HAVE A VALID LICENSE AND TRAINING. YOUR SIDEARM IS ACTIVE. YOU MAY FIRE IT AT ANY TIME. PLEASE NOTE THAT YOUR GUN'S SAFETY WILL ENGAGE WHEN YOUR FIREARM IS POINTED AT OTHER PEOPLE UNLESS YOU FEEL THREATENED. THANK YOU.

We went back to the classroom and were told to stack up the chairs and move the tables to the side of the room. We did so, sitting on the floor. The suit supported my body, making me comfortable despite the hard surface. Cortez stood before us. His suit changed, flowing over his hands, covering them with gloves. His head and face were covered in a helmet that flowed over his head in several solid, obviously non-nano-material pieces. The helmet was opaque with a curved ridge down the center.

"The front of your helmet can sense nearly every spectrum of light and gathers light across its entire surface. You will be able to see in any light situation, and if you look up at the sky, you will be able to view space as if you had a telescope! You can switch light spectrums at will or overlay them in whatever way you like. Your helmet can also pick up heat and electric signatures, along with being able to measure the density of objects around you. You can see through most objects, which will come in very handy. It gathers sound that you cannot hear with your normal ears; it will use this to help you not only hear but build visual maps of your environment like sonar. It has light sensors in a band around the sides of your head and over the top of your head. You can see feeds from any direction. Your helmet will detect movement and just about everything else. Thankfully, you don't have to process all of that information. Your CCPU puts the supercomputers of my youth to shame. Also, your CCPU will link up with your troop ship via altcomms, giving you access to your own computer aboard the ship, increasing that power. Give the helmet a try."

I activated the helmet, which flowed over my head. I closed my eyes, and when I opened them, I was confused. The room looked the same. I reached up but couldn't touch my face; the helmet was on! A HUD pulled up in my field of view, giving me information. I could customize it to whatever I wanted. I grinned; this was too cool. I looked at Sweeting, his helmet on. He nodded at me. I overlaid heat in my vision, then remembered Cortez had said we could see through walls. I turned that on and could see through the walls but not the suits.

Like physical sensations, the helmet gave me full control over what I sensed in the world around me. Even more so in many ways. New sounds and sights were opened to me. I could hear things that before I couldn't. The helmet analyzed the air around me, giving me information, though I had no sense of smell. That felt a little odd, but I could see where, on alien worlds, my sense of smell could be a hindrance, not knowing what things should or shouldn't smell like. My CCPU showed me a range of presets for the HUD and the ability to make my own or to put it on intuitive.

I was having fun playing with what I could see. I was able to narrow down the colors that were displayed, excluding everything but the color I wanted. When I wasn't telling the helmet to do something, it went back to a "normal" mode. As I paid more attention to the normal mode, I saw that it was anything but normal. I could see perfect detail in my peripheral vision. Everything was in focus. I asked my CCPU why this was and found that while I felt like my eyes were open, they really weren't. Everything I was seeing now was information fed to my CCPU, which in turn processed it and sent it to my brain. Everything was in focus because my eyes weren't actually doing anything. My CCPU had no reason not to keep everything crystal clear. It was cool but discomforting at the same time. My CCPU said that my view and the feeds from my helmet were considered "hyper-real" and that while I would get used to it, many users reported a sense of satisfaction when the helmet was removed after long periods.

Cortez informed us that they recycled the air we breathed when attached to our packs that we'd get tomorrow. He also told us that on other worlds during conflicts, we would leave our helmets and gloves on at all times. That was fine with me; I could see where being so connected to everything around you could be addictive.

After a few more hours of training with the suit, we were dismissed for dinner and then bed. When we got back to the room, Meyers was already in bed, his screen shut.

I slipped into my bunk, shutting the screen. The suit slid off me and into a compartment at the base of my mattress. I relaxed on the bed and pulled up my messages. I found one from Jon chatting about what he'd learned on his first day, and others from Monica, Charles, and Liz. They had a group chat open that I joined, reading all of the comments for the day.

They'd apparently had more free time than I did because the list of comments was long. I sent a quick message to them about my day and told my CCPU to put me to sleep. My brain felt like it was going to explode with information about the suits and how to use them. I was already overwhelmed, and in the morning, we'd start learning about the drones we'd command and how to use them. I smiled. We'd also start using our suit's physical abilities too and get to shoot our sidearm, and we'd also get our rifles. I was excited to go to the range.

FOUR

The following day, I woke up and joined the others in my room lining up for the shower. The shower was the same as the day before, with the change that I had my Dopp Kit. While I was in the shower, my suit, with all its computers, components, and nano-material, was washed separately. After breakfast, we reported to the same classroom we had the day before, with instructions to sit with our Fireteams.

I sat at a desk next to Sweeting and McLeod. An irritated-looking Meyers sat next to Betts and a girl from another Fireteam with long dark hair and brown-green eyes. She tried to greet Meyers, but he didn't respond. She looked at me, giving me a "what's his problem?" look. I shrugged. I turned my CCPU's visual ID on and saw her name was Veronica Royle. I sent her a message.

> ME: I don't know what his problem is. He's been a prick since we landed.

> ROYLE: Lucky you.

Major Cortez entered the room, followed by a cart stacked high with boxes. Cortez swept his hands at the cart. "These are your packs. They will cling to your suits wherever you place them and will mold to your body. They aren't like the backpacks you used when you went camping or to school," he explained.

We learned that the packs contained purification equipment that integrated with our suits, allowing us to breathe and drink our own water and air indefinitely. They held medical gel that the nanobots in our bodies could use to heal us, nutrient packs to feed us, extra storage for ammo blocks, etc. About half of the pack was filled with a nano-material block that we could use to make shelter, bedding, rope, or even a compact wall to deflect low-caliber rounds. Cortez told us we would use it mostly for rope and shelter with a flat surface to sleep on.

"If you are fighting on a planet like Arrow with sandstorms, you can use this block to create a shelter for you to lay in while the storm passes; it will not be able to provide you with a thick wall, but a wall that most rocks and debris will bounce off of. Now, you might have noticed that I haven't talked about the bit at the bottom of the pack," he said, pointing to a rectangular block at the pack's bottom. "This is your entry unit. It can detach from the main pack. When you are on a ship, you are required to have it on."

I took a closer look at the entry unit, feeling uneasy. Next to me, McLeod looked a little pale.

"Yes, Miss Royle," Cortez said.

I followed his gaze to Royle, her hand in the air. "You mean that's what we use to enter a planet's atmosphere?" Her voice sounded a little unsure, as though she thought she was asking a dumb question.

Cortez grinned wickedly. "What, you don't think it will work?" Before she could answer, he laughed. "There are two parts to entering a planet's atmosphere: this," he detached an entry unit from a pack and held it up, "and a space anchor built into your suit. It is at the base of your neck on your back. It is small and very useful!"

Unconsciously, I touched the base of my neck. Cortez reached around his waist with the entry unit, which stuck to him. He crouched down on the floor, curling up into a ball. The entry unit flowed along the base of his back and under his feet and rear, spreading into a large dish on the floor. Cortez looked up with a smile. "The unit is a heat shield, but with an amazing ability!" He stood, and the heat shield stayed on the ground as he walked around it. "When I was your age, we weren't very good at converting heat into energy, but that's not the case now! Your Space Anchor will try to hold its place in space, wherever that might be. You can do other things with it too, but that will come later. What this means in this instance is that it can slow you down if you are falling, say from a spaceship.

"But it takes a lot of power to slow you down enough not to burn up in a planet's atmosphere, not to mention still keeping you from splatting on the ground! Enter the heat shield," he waved his hand at the shield on the floor, "it will slow you down, *and* as heat is generated from the friction with a planet's atmosphere, it will convert that heat into energy for your space anchor. In effect, the more heat your entry generates, the stronger your Anchor becomes, and the more it slows you down. That means that you will never be moving fast enough to exceed your suit's heat limits." He smiled at us in a way that told me he was immensely enjoying our discomfort.

No one asked any other questions. We were ordered to grab a pack and line up to go into another room where we'd learn about some of the drones we'd be commanding. When it was my turn, I grabbed a pack, which was surprisingly light. I wasn't sure what I'd been expecting. The pack wasn't as light as a regular backpack, but I thought it would have been heavier for some reason. After all, it was what would keep me alive on alien worlds. Shit that keeps you alive is usually heavy, right? It didn't have straps; instead, a small nano-material handle allowed me to sling the pack across my back.

As I put it on, I felt my suit cling to it and move it into place. As this happened, I was flooded with information as it integrated with me. I rolled my shoulders and couldn't feel the pack at all. I saw other people putting them on and noticed that the handles melded back into the pack once in place, and the pack reshaped itself to contour the person's body more. Not a regular backpack indeed.

In the next room, we were introduced to a host of drones. The first one we learned about was a Basic Infantry model, called BIs for short. It looked exactly like we did, with a pack and all. The BI, while it had the same appearance as the people around me, clearly wasn't human. It was subtle, and I couldn't pinpoint what was wrong with how it held itself, but it just felt off to me.

Cortez explained that the BIs were the most common drones we'd use, with each of us usually being responsible for five to ten of them. They all looked a bit different, with some being a little taller, some shorter, and some narrower of shoulder. Many even appeared to have breasts.

"You and I will always know these are drones, as would any human; while you have all undoubtedly interacted with drones that are indistinguishable from humans, these do not need that level of intricacy. The enemy does not have the lifetime of interaction and human observation you do. The BIs look like you so that the enemy doesn't know who is a drone and who is a person. Your job is to command them, and their job is to do as you say and to keep you alive. They will be your camouflage.

"That's not to say that you won't be fighting. You will be. If you were to keep out of every engagement, you would stick out to the enemy. Much of your job will be to look the part of a non-consequential unit.

"The BIs hold a lot more ammo than you do, and their central computer is about twice as powerful as your CCPU. This means you can get more ammo from them and network with them, along with every other computer in your suit, guns, and pack. This will give you a lot more computing power than you have with just a CCPU."

Cortez showed us his back and pointed at his pack. "Do you see those three rings? They are about seven centimeters across. Those are called Whiskers, and you and each BI in your command have three of them. Play with the Whiskers," he ordered.

I watched the Whiskers launch from Cortez and hover above him. I fully connected with my pack, and as promised, I could see my computing power increase drastically as each of the computers networked. My HUD also shifted to a new view. On the left side of the HUD, I saw a menu with an option for robotic equipment. I focused on it, and the menu twirled open. I saw a section that said "Whiskers." I saw the three Whiskers on my pack. I integrated with them and executed the launch command. The little rings launched, and I saw options to see data from them. There were also options for having my CCPU process data for me. A quick check showed a wide array of choices for what data I would be served and what would be ignored. I closed the section and connected to a visual feed from one of the Whiskers.

A view from the Whisker took over my vision. I smiled as I looked down at the top of my head. These things could be handy. I had the Whisker move around and focus on different people in the room. Like my helmet, I could zoom in the view, though not to the same extent.

"These are your eyes and ears in the field. They are for your drones as well; that's why drones come with their own. Whiskers can fit in tight places, they can change color and make no sound, and they will help you find targets and figure out how to kill those targets. You can access the feeds of every Whisker under your command or the command of your drones. Further, anyone can access the information from anyone else's drones and Whiskers, though you cannot command them."

I could see that you could get overwhelmed in a hurry with all the information you had at your disposal. Between the suit and Whiskers alone, I found it hard to focus on just one thing. We broke for lunch after that, with Cortez telling us to keep our packs with us. Royle and her Fireteam joined us for lunch; so far, we all got along well, barring Meyers, who sat slightly on his own, trying not to talk to anyone.

"So what's your problem, man?" Sweeting finally asked Meyers.

"I'm not here to be chummy," Meyers said as he looked at his food.

"So you're here to be a dick?" Royle asked.

Meyers chuckled and gave Royle a disdainful look. "God, you're one of those people who have to be liked, aren't you? Shit, the next five years are going to be long."

Royle snorted and pointed at me and the rest of my Fireteam. "No, it will be for them with you on their team."

Meyers didn't seem inclined to retort.

We all laughed awkwardly.

"Hey, thanks," I said.

But Royle had a point. I sighed on the inside. How were the next five years going to be? I liked Sweeting, Betts, and McLeod, but Meyers? I glanced at him. He was sitting, looking ahead with a haughty expression on his face. I'd met plenty of assholes in my life, but not one like Meyers. I wondered why he was like this. He was in the HFDF and Spaceborne, so he wasn't dumb. It was surprisingly hard to get into the military. The testing I had taken was pretty extensive. He knew he'd be spending the next five years with all of us. Why would you want to alienate those people? Further, why would you want to do that to people you'd be in combat with?

That's what bothered me the most. The chances of us going into combat during our Service Term were high. Did I want Meyers to have my back? He left a short time later, and Betts turned to me.

"I really don't want to deal with that guy for five years," he said.

"I was just thinking the same thing," I said.

McLeod nodded, and Sweeting said, "He's a prick, but he seems to keep to himself. Maybe he won't be that bad." He said, trying to sound optimistic.

Betts shook his head. "I kind of doubt he'll be able to avoid us too much; we're in the same Fireteam. You know we will have to work together a lot over our term."

Sweeting shrugged. "Yeah, fair enough."

"I don't like the idea of being in combat with someone like that," I said, then sighed. "I know I've just met the guy, but come on."

Royle piped in. "I hadn't thought about that. That's a good point. Again, sucks to be you guys." She winked.

Sweeting chuckled.

After lunch, we went to the shooting range. I knew the base had several ranges, some of which were outside. This one wasn't. I'd never seen a shooting range so big in my life. There were hundreds of lanes. I looked down one, seeing that it extended far into the distance. We were led to a cart with racks of guns.

I was introduced to the Standard Issue Rifle, lovingly known as the SIR. The SIR we were assigned was to be our service weapon for the remainder of the time we were in the service unless it was damaged, lost, or a better unit developed. Cortez informed us that the SIR hadn't been updated in a decade and was designed to be tougher than we were.

I lay down at the firing line, looking down the range. I inserted what appeared to be a solid block of heavy metal, called an ammo block, into my SIR's ammo slot. The SIR itself was unremarkable-looking. It was rectangular with a pistol grip and an adjustable stock that automatically adjusted itself to best fit whatever position I was in. Its top sight integrated with my CCPU and suit, giving me a targeting reticle that showed where the round would go. I didn't have to sight the gun the proper way with this setup, which was something I would have to get used to. As I connected with the SIR, I could see its power level and the amount of power the current round took to fire. I made a mental note of that. Though the SIR didn't use chemical propellants for regular bullets, I could see the need to watch the power cell. I continued my inspection of the rifle.

There was a grenade magazine near the front and a block of nano-material that could transform into a T-pod or any other type of mount I could ever want. That was very cool. The material could grip onto walls to steady the gun, turn into a bayonet, or whatever I needed.

Several small chemical reservoirs for propellants or explosives were built into the weapon's stock.

My CCPU showed that the SIR was designed to be relatively easy to modify, allowing for more chemicals, grenades, or non-lethal configurations. While I found it unlikely that I'd be using a lot of non-lethal options during my time in the service, the explosive stuff sounded fun.

I looked at the targets at the end of the range. They were over a kilometer away from me, but my suit zoomed most of my field of view into the targets, so they appeared to be only a meter away. I could see my immediate surroundings in my peripherals, and my HUD showed a map of my surroundings, indicating friendlies or unknowns. There was no sneaking up on an HFDF troop; I could see. My targeting reticle waved frantically before me as the SIR's muzzle moved a bit this way or that.

"Turn on your stabilizers!" Cortez ordered.

I thought about the stabilizer, and my CCPU prompted me that there was an option. I rolled my eyes, wishing I had thought to look through the SIR's and my suit's manuals. I turned on the stabilizer. My suit went tight and rigid around my upper body, and the targeting reticle slowed in my field of view. As I tried to move, my CCPU compensated, making it so I could only move a fraction of a centimeter without effort.

My mind went back to when Cortez talked about ageless humans having higher fine motor control. I wondered if my CCPU was doing anything to my body to help with the stabilization. A quick search showed that my assumption was correct. My CCPU was working in conjunction with my suit to limit and smooth my range of motion.

Badass.

Cortez's voice boomed over the range, "Constrict your movement to your field of view. You will find a setting in your CCPU called Steady Fire Platform. Turn it on and leave it on. Your body's range of movement will be limited depending on how far zoomed in you are. Turn on your SIR's advanced targeting, which will adjust your reticle for bullet arc, atmospheric conditions, and the type of round you are firing. In this mode, it will also ascertain your target's range and density and adjust the power when the gun shoots," he laughed once, "it even looks for friendlies and will adjust range or round type to avoid hurting them while still killing the bad guy!

"On the topic of projectiles, you have over three hundred different types of rounds you can use; your gun makes the round from the block as you shoot. In the field, should your ammo start to run low, you will have little drones called Reloaders that can be placed on almost any surface, and they will make you more ammo. You can fire in semi-automatic mode, burst mode, or full auto. In burst mode, you can not only decide how many rounds it will fire per burst but also what each round is. Full auto has similar options. It's very handy, let me tell you, but you can get pretty damn consumed messing with it in combat. SO, when you drop into a combat situation, command will give you recommended rounds to use. Load those rounds into your SIR's favorites and tell *it* to decide what type of round to use, and you will rarely want anything other than semi-auto.

"We try to conserve ammo while in combat. One of the key take-aways from training here will be resource management. Yes, you can make more ammo, provided you find a suitable surface to pull materials from. But making ammo takes time, meaning you need to know when to deploy Reloaders. Also, your drones do not have long-term thinking abilities, so if you don't manage your ammo and run out, you will be good and rightly fucked. Likewise, if you are stingy with your ammo, you will also be fucked. Your HUD can show you burn rates and use data from your suit and drones to find the best spots to make more ammo.

"But we aren't in combat today, so have some fun!" he said. I couldn't see him looking down the range, but I suspected he was smiling.

I sighted in on a target about the size of the end of my thumb. With my advanced targeting, I could tell my CCPU what targets I wanted and in what order I wanted them. It would also try to let me know if something seemed to be more of a threat than something else. I centered the target, my body going still. I breathed out and slowly squeezed the trigger. There was a small pop that was hardly audible and a slight push on my shoulder from the gun firing. The round I had set was large enough that I should have felt a kick, but with the SIR's recoil system, the force of the kick was like someone flicking you. The target, a black spot of nano-material, now had a hole in the center of it.

I grinned. I heard people firing around me, with many shooting a lot faster than I would have. *I wonder.* I targeted the next piece of material quickly this time and didn't breathe like I was supposed to, and pulled the trigger. Again there was a little pop and a flick on my shoulder, and the target had a hole in it. I started to laugh.

"TAYLOR!" Cortez bellowed. *Damn it, I didn't mute my suit's speaker.* "What is so funny?"

I sat up, everyone on the range looking at me. Well, their heads were facing me, but we all had our full suits on, including helmets and gloves, so I couldn't see their expressions.

"Just learning that I don't have to control my breath and shoot right...Sir," I said.

Cortez barked a laugh after a moment. "Your records here show you placing in a few shooting contests back on Orion," he laughed harder, "how does it feel to find out that years of practice don't mean squat anymore and that you can hit targets with ease that you wouldn't have even dreamed of hitting before?"

I thought for a moment, then said, "Kind of pissed right now, Sir. I won't lie to you."

He laughed again. "I bet! Don't worry yourself too much. If you try to hit anything past two clicks, you'll need that training. I should say two clicks on a 1g world." He said, changing his tone to that of an instructor, "While this range might be 1g, Arrow is not. That means your rounds would go further, hence why we stabilize you and expect you to be able to hit anything a click and a half away. And for those of you wondering why we don't just teach you how to shoot without stabilization, let me explain. As I said, Arrow is not 1g. Every planet you go to will have different gravity and a unique atmosphere.

"In short, if you had to do this the old-fashioned way, you'd have a learning curve on each deployment for anything other than close-quarters combat. That's not how we work. We in the HFDF don't believe in fair fights. Thus, we give you every advantage we can. You will have more speed and accuracy in close and long-range fights than your enemy. You will learn how to control your drones and prioritize targets in such a way that you can drop a group of hostiles before they even know what's happening. Now get back to it!"

After we were done at the range, it was time for us to interact with the drones. My Fireteam joined a group of people in a giant airlock. The inner door closed with a clang. My helmet engaged, and my hands were covered by the suit's gloves. My HUD showed the pressure in the room drop rapidly as the air was purged out. As the air left, most sound went with it. The outer door opened, and I stepped onto the surface of Arrow. My suit showed the temperature outside drop, but I didn't feel it. What I did feel after a few steps was an odd falling sensation as the base's gravity fell off, being replaced with Arrow's. I had a moment of slight vertigo as I adjusted to the change.

I looked around. Behind me, the base stood as a gray monolith. It rose high above us, its towering form casting a long, sharp shadow across Arrow's reddish-brown landscape. In front of us, I could see a group of BIs standing in neat rows. As they stood in this formation, I could see how it would be easy for aliens not to be able to tell humans from drones. They didn't stand perfectly still. I could make out the slight rise and fall of their chests as they simulated breathing, and occasionally, one would appear to shift its weight slightly.

"Each of you will work with two BIs today. You will be doing nothing more than going for a walk with them. You can tell them where to go and what to do. You will receive a waypoint of where to walk to and the path to take. Your CCPU will slowly add information and features for you to look at, along with any updates you might need. Have a nice walk," he said sweetly.

My CCPU pinged me, letting me know that I had a waypoint. My HUD overlaid it in my field of view. I could see the waypoint as a blue vertical line on the horizon. As I focused on the point, information flooded my CCPU. The waypoint was three kilometers away. In my path, there was what looked like a large ridge. The waypoint pulsed, letting me know there was more information or options for it. I accessed them, seeing that the waypoint came with a set of sub-points giving me my path to take.

At the same time, my CCPU notified me that I could control two of the BIs. My HUD also showed where they were. I looked at the formation of drones. Mine had blue highlights over them. My CCPU prompted me with a message saying I could change any of the colors I wanted. The formation of drones started to move, my two walking toward me. As I integrated with them, I started grasping just how much they could do, and conversely, how much I had to pay attention to.

I could order the drones around with verbal commands, intuitive commands, or a mix. My CCPU recommended using the mix. I set the BIs to that. As I integrated with them on the side of my HUD, a list pulled up. Currently, that list showed the BIs, named 1 and 2, along with my waypoint. I started to walk to the waypoint, telling my BIs to stay with me. They did so, walking along at the same pace I did. As I walked, my list updated with all the other people and drones. There were icons representing humans and drones; all of the names were in gray.

My HUD blinked, showing me a little map. I pulled it up. Everything on the list was on the map. I could see what my CCPU thought were others' predicted trajectories, speed, distance from me and others, and…

I tripped on a rock, almost toppling over. As my brain registered, "oh shit," my BIs moved on either side of me, catching my elbows and helping me up. I stopped walking and looked at the BIs that now stood placidly at my side. My CCPU told me that if not for my suit, I would have broken the big toe on my right foot. I concentrated on one of the BIs, seeing that there was a section where I could see a decision tree. I pulled up the tree, seeing a long list of decisions that they had made.

When I tripped, my CCPU sensed I didn't want to fall and, using the intuitive command, told the BIs to help me. That was kind of cool. I wondered how I was supposed to walk around and not eat shit all the time. My CCPU answered my question by letting me know that my suit sensed what was around me, and obstacle avoidance could be added to my HUD. In the case of small objects, my suit could help me avoid obstacles without me having to think about it. I turned that on and started walking again. Occasionally, I felt my suit push my feet one way or another as it dodged smallish rocks.

As I walked, I could tell that none of the people in my platoon had the same path. We each appeared to be wandering in random directions. I picked up my pace a bit and tried to pay more attention to my surroundings. My CCPU continued to add more features and information, and I soon had to start organizing it. Thankfully, there were recommendations for how to do that. Thirty minutes into the walk, my CCPU let me know that the Whiskers on my pack and those of the two BIs were going to deploy.

I had already been messing around with looking at the world from the BIs' perspectives, but god damn, the Whiskers increased that by an order of magnitude. As they observed the world around me, that information became available to me. I could also direct them where to go. I told the BIs to manage their own Whiskers and instructed mine to orbit the area—an area that was getting smaller with each step. What had looked like a hill turned out to be a rock face that went up about twenty meters. As we got closer, I zoomed in on the face, not seeing many places to go up. The waypoint showed me going over the rock face.

I sighed. Just a walk, huh?

———

LATER THAT NIGHT, MY HEAD WAS BUZZING WHEN I LAY IN BED. HOW WAS I supposed to handle a group of drones? Just the two BIs I'd had already overwhelmed me. On the flip side, going up the rock face was fun, and jumping down the other side was as well. But the information was insane! On the way back home, Cortez shut off our ability to use intuitive commands for a while, making us verbalize what we wanted the drones to do. It wasn't hard, but counting the Whiskers meant ordering around eleven drones while trying to walk and talk simultaneously. I'd been so busy with that I hadn't even noticed everyone else and their drones.

Dinner had been pretty quiet. Sweeting didn't even say anything. We'd all looked like zombies. After we ate, I just wanted to go lie down. I shuffled into my room and flopped down in my bunk. As the screen closed, I felt myself wake up a bit. Of course, now that I could rest, my brain decided it was time to be awake.

I didn't want to go to sleep yet, but I didn't feel like getting out of bed either. So I pulled up my friend's messages from the day. I started to read them and stopped. *No more text for the day.*

Liz was the only one in an overlapping time zone. I pinged her to see if she was awake. She was. I opened a line to her.

"Hey, how's it going?" I asked.

Her voice sounded in my head. "Hey! I'm doing alright. How about you? How's training been?" she asked.

"Why just alright? And training is crazy."

"I shouldn't say just alright; I'm just fried. I haven't had to think this hard in a long time. So what's been crazy about your training?"

I launched into my story of the day and was happy to learn that while she hadn't been dealing with drones all day, her brain was just as full as mine. It was nice being able to talk to her. It had only been a few days, but talking to her added some normality to the day. She told me how our friends were doing in their training, so I didn't have to read through the message thread. As we talked about the others, it was easy for my mind to calm down, and soon enough, we were both yawning.

"Alright, Liz, I think I'm gonna go to sleep. This was good though. It helped me clear my mind," I said.

"Me too," she yawned. "Talk to you later."

I closed the connection, set my bunk to be in the woods of Orion at night, and went to sleep.

FIVE

I stood in a preparation room, going over my inventory. We had spent weeks learning about all of our equipment, along with intense combat training. We'd worked in teams, spent countless hours on individual simulations, and trained heavily with drones. I'd never been pushed so hard in my life, and I'd also never failed so much. It wasn't that each training exercise got progressively more challenging like a game; instead, Cortez and his team seemed to be able to keep you far enough out of your comfort zone to learn, but not so far out that you quit.

We were now entering the drill portion of our training. Cortez reminded us in the morning that we'd be scored and ranked within our Fireteams, and that Fireteams would be ranked against each other. Over the coming weeks, the many types of drills we would run would determine who became Fireteam leaders and help command establish which teams to pair to make squads. Like our Fireteams, we'd be in the same squad for the rest of our time in our Service Term. Likewise, the Fireteam leader would maintain that position for the rest of the term as well.

In the prep room with me were nine BIs and two spherical hovering drones nicknamed Basketballs, or BBALLs for short. They flew and had a small, short-range gun along with small charges. They weren't as powerful or as armed as the BIs or myself, but they were incredible when it came to clearing buildings. Quick and small, they were hard to hit, allowing them to rush up or sneak up on an enemy. I named them BBALL 1 and 2 in my CCPU, and the BIs 1 through 9.

The prep room wasn't large, with only a tiny table at the end for ammo blocks. The walls and ceiling I saw were just projections from my helmet. However, if I touched the walls, my suit would make them feel real. The floor was mostly nano-material, and while I waited in the training room, that nano-material, along with structures—robotic and otherwise, were forming parts of the environment where the drill would take place. The ability to project different environments had obvious advantages. The only real pain in the ass was if a recruit tried to interact with an object that was purely a projection. So far, I hadn't run into this, but if it happened, my CCPU would make the object shimmer, so I knew not to interact with it.

The rounds we used wouldn't be fake. They were frag rounds that broke apart on contact with a hard surface. I'd been hit by plenty of them; they stung like a hard flick for just a moment.

I ran over the drill with my CCPU. The living participants would be my Fireteam, each with the same POD makeup of drones I had. We were all against each other. There were also five Heavy Infantry Drones, one for each of us in the area that we needed to deal with before we could do anything else. The Heavies were honestly the biggest concern I had. As for the others in my Fireteam, I tried to think of who would be the largest threat—not Sweeting. He was a great person but a little too carefree when it came to the drills. McLeod struggled with everything, so that shouldn't be a problem. Meyers could be good but also had a temper that got the best of him. Betts would be my primary threat. He was calm and intelligent.

Before joining the HFDF, I wouldn't have thought the humans controlling the drones mattered. After all, the drones were highly effec-

tive killers, but as I'd learned, they were only as effective as their operators. There were a few reasons for this. The first was that they didn't
do well with strategy in combat; their computers needed to be rugged
with lots of redundancy, not advanced. Second, if an operator was
sucking it up, their BIs had to dial back a bit to keep the operator from
being noticed. We all had the same drones, so no one had an advantage. It was how we used them that counted.

The prep room dissolved away. Behind me was the table and what
looked like a stone ledge. All around me were ruined, burned buildings, most of them homes. In the distance was a concrete structure that
rose above the other buildings. *There*, I thought. Our job was simple:
take out our Heavy and then take out every other member of our
Fireteam; whoever did that won. If people were still alive after thirty
minutes, whoever had the highest score won.

I crouched down and moved quickly to a chunk of concrete on the
ground, my drones following suit. Our training ran through my head,
particularly the OODA loop. It stood for observe, orient, decide, and
act. When we'd learned it, I was reminded of some of my father's
favorite acronyms and sayings growing up. I could almost always hear
him saying them in the back of my head. But the OODA loop was a
pretty handy way of working, I had to admit.

I crouched down and observed what was around me. Most of the
burnt-out buildings looked to be a mix of wood and brick construction.
Orient, I was on the outskirts of the arena. I looked over the chunk I
was behind and ducked back down. *This is why you have drones*, I told
myself. I activated my Whiskers. I nicknamed them W with a number.
The Whiskers fanned out, gathering data, making a map of the area,
and finding potential hiding places.

Explosions sounded in the distance. *Is someone already taking on their
Heavy?* I tried not to get anxious or worried about not moving quickly
enough. Just because someone was moving fast didn't mean they were
moving smart. I focused on the map in my HUD and set waypoints.

"Move forward with caution," I ordered my POD.

The BIs started to move. As they did, their suits changed colors and added a pattern to help them blend into the area. My suit did likewise. I moved forward, keeping low and taking cover wherever I could. As the Whiskers searched the area, my map took on more detail. I tasked a BBALL with covering our backs. I wasn't overly worried about another person sneaking up on me this early in the drill, nor this close to the arena wall. But everything we did was scored.

I heard more explosions in the distance and heavy weapons being fired. Someone was definitely engaging their Heavy. As I moved, I swiveled my head back and forth, allowing all of my helmet's sensor suite to get a full picture of the area around me. I hugged the corner of a pale green house. Its roof was missing, and I could see angry scorch marks along the walls. Just ahead of me was a small building that also looked to be in bad shape.

"Hold," I told my POD.

A few Whiskers zipped over to the building. W23 pinged a contact alert. It hugged the lip of the building, and I pulled the feed from the Whisker. The Heavy was in a parking lot, moving around in a lazy circle. I'd thought the Heavies were cool from the first moment Cortez showed them to us—a feeling I still had... whenever I didn't have to fight one.

They were large drones that didn't resemble humans in the least bit. Three meters tall and bipedal, they had two arms with massive guns that could fire just about any size round you could think of. They had two smaller front and rear guns, a grenade launcher, several rockets, and a missile defense system on top of them. Oh, and the SIR's rounds had difficulty penetrating the Heavies armor from long range. Yay for me.

For the most part, the Heavies were handy for getting the enemy's attention and dealing damage. They weren't overly fast, nor were they even remotely stealthy. But I had to be careful dealing with it. Unlike the BIs, you couldn't tell where the Heavy was putting the bulk of its attention. Each weapon had a dedicated targeting system that could act independently of the drone's primary system. So it wasn't like you were fighting one drone; it was like you were fighting five or six.

We were lucky that the Heavies usual complement of five Whiskers was missing for the drill. When the HFDF had come up with this monstrosity, it hadn't been enough that they could kill just about anything. They also had to make it so hiding from one was nearly impossible at close range. I might have been able to sneak up on it more than normal, but its onboard sensors weren't anything to sneeze at.

I told the Whiskers to search the area and make a detailed map. I made sure I was out of sight and thought of what to do. As more Whiskers got eyes on the Heavy and its surroundings, the map updated with lines of fire each weapon had. *Think, Alex,* I told myself. The parking lot of the building was lined by other small structures. This could work to my advantage. At close range, the SIRs could punch through the Heavies armor, and the buildings might give my drones cover. But on the flip side, I'd lose drones that I would need later.

We had small rockets that we could use. I looked at the map, seeing it updated with the internal structures of the building. There wasn't much that the Heavy or we couldn't shoot through. I could have a BI fire a rocket, but the Heavies defense system was fast as hell. I could have multiple BIs fire rockets, but as soon as they fired, the Heavies guns would target them, and again, about that fast-as-hell missile defense system. Before the Heavy went down, it would take out drones. I sighed, deciding what to do.

While it might have been fun to go toe-to-toe with the Heavy, I wanted to win. That meant keeping my head down and out of the fight. I started setting waypoints on the buildings and one behind me in a covering position.

"Move to waypoints," I ordered my POD.

I moved to a new position that gave me plenty of cover for when the shit hit the fan. As I hunkered down, my HUD toggled to a view that took up almost all of my field of view. I watched as the BIs moved, the Heavy seemingly none the wiser.

"B2 through B5, load rockets. B6 through B8, switch to heavy armor-piercing rounds," I ordered.

I waited as the drones moved into position. Each of them was fully in control of its Whiskers, using them to avoid the Heavy and to begin coming up with firing solutions. The explosions in the distance stopped, and a message popped up in my HUD, letting me know that McLeod was KIA along with all of her drones. I felt a pang in my gut for her; she tried so hard but wasn't progressing. *You can help her later,* I told myself.

As the drones neared their positions, I watched the Heavy, trying to time my attack. I sent a BBALL arcing over the parking lot, firing down from above. The Heavy wheeled around, its guns coming up buzzing as they fired. The BBALL dipped below a building as the next one started its run. There were dings of bullets on metal as it passed over the larger drone. The Heavy turned to the new threat.

"Get in position," I ordered my BIs.

They moved up to the edges of buildings or into windows.

"B4 and B5, fire," I said.

The two BIs popped out of their cover, firing rockets at the Heavy. Its defense system targeted a rocket, taking it out. B7 and B8 shot at the defense system. The Heavy took out the other rocket. The BIs took cover. The shit had truly hit the fan. The Heavy started targeting multiple BIs who dove out of the way as concrete and stone crumbled under a barrage of fire. The BIs popped up again, firing rockets; again, the defense system took them out as B7 and B8 tried to hit it. As large rounds went through the building, I heard them hiss in the air above me.

B3 registered a minor hit to its left arm. It pulled back as it tried to find cover. As the Heavy turned more of its attention toward B3, I looked at the map. B6 had moved down to the ground and was nearest the Heavy; thus far, it hadn't been spotted. I plotted a quick escape path for it.

"B6, target the defense system; rocket BIs, time firing with B6."

B3's pack got tagged, sending the drone rolling off the edge of the building it was on. Its anchor brought it to a jerking stop before it hit the ground. I sent the command to fire. B6 left cover and opened up on the defense system with heavy rounds. At the same time, three rockets were launched. There was a ping as the system was hit by B6 and taken out. The back guns on the Heavy rotated to target B6. Before it could fire, the rockets hit. There was a series of booms, and the Heavy went down.

"B7 and B8, secure the target."

The BIs moved to the Heavy, confirming that it was indeed out of commission.

I rolled onto my knees, got up, and moved in on the smoldering remains of the Heavy. I didn't get too close, though. Even though it looked destroyed and real to me, I tried to remember that this was only a simulation; the Heavy was still there in perfect condition, and while it wouldn't shoot at me, I didn't really care to trip over an arm or leg that I couldn't see. Videos of people doing shit like that seemed to end up in all of the platoon members' inboxes. I looked at my POD's ammo reserve, seeing that we were down fifty percent on our rockets. That was fine. I might have been a little worried if I knew I'd have armor to deal with or vehicles. I could have gotten dinged in my score for wasting the rockets, but my rationale would probably keep me from getting docked.

There was more gunfire in the distance as my POD moved towards the central building. We took cover wherever we could, searching for enemies. My helmet's display changed, giving me the best view I could get, which was pretty awesome. I saw through smoke, and my vision overlaid with some heat signatures. I gave a cover command as BI6 detected something. I sat tense and viewed its feed as it looked around a corner. There was another Heavy walking around. I relaxed. It was probably the one assigned to McLeod.

We got up and started moving carefully. Because we took ours out, this Heavy wouldn't pay us any attention unless I was dumb enough to fire at it, in which case it would pay us the type of attention we didn't want. We were moving along the rubble of a building when a Whisker pinged me. I lay flat on the ground. My POD was not in a good position, half of us on one side of the street and the other half on the other. I looked down the road and cringed as figures appeared. My CCPU told me it was Sweeting's POD. The drones were programmed to match their commander's behavior; our ID systems did not let us know who was human or not. Sweeting and his POD were moving around, not appearing to seek cover. *What are you doing, Sweeting?*

In the center of the street, a figure stooped and looked at the Heavy, which didn't fire. My CCPU wouldn't tell me if the figure was Sweeting or not, but I assumed it was him based on the way he moved. The BIs' body language and movement might be enough to fool alien races, but they couldn't fool other humans. I also doubted a BI would take the time to look at a drone that wasn't a threat. Sweeting knelt in the street, looking at the Heavy, which was paying no attention to him. I knew it wouldn't run into him or do anything to give away his position. Instead, it lazily turned away from Sweeting and his team.

I ran through different fields of view, trying to spot all of Sweeting's drones, and, more importantly, his Whiskers. I couldn't find them all. Sweeting lifted his SIR, pointing it in my direction. *Shit, he found you!* Sweeting shot. There was a ding of metal being hit, but not next to me. The Heavy rounded on Sweeting, and his POD opened fire. *That idiot shot the Heavy?* He knew better. I could picture Sweeting thinking it would be funny to shoot at the thing, just to see if it really would pay attention to him. Well, it was.

The area around Sweeting's POD exploded as bullets tore apart cement and wood. His BIs started to fire at the Heavy, and Sweeting dove behind some debris. As he did, an idea came to me. The Heavy would not assist me or my POD; we would be ignored. But there was nothing in the rulebook stating that I couldn't help the Heavy.

I separated my BIs into subteams. Three BIs on each team.

"Subteams two and three, fan out, find Sweeting's drones and take them out. BBALLS, wrap around back. Subteam one, sniping positions, take out assisting drones," I ordered my POD, joining subteam one.

My POD moved out, doing as commanded. Soon Sweeting's POD was being pelted by grenades from my subteams, and I zoomed my view into where Sweeting was hiding, waiting for him to pop up. He tried to run for cover, and I shot a three-round burst at his chest, dropping him. My HUD had a list of names on it and statuses; now Sweeting's read OOA for Out of Action. I'd get more points for a headshot, but I wasn't looking for a kill. Sweeting's drones, like mine, had a primary mission which was to keep their operator alive. If this were a real battle, Sweeting's suit would be keeping him from bleeding out and keeping his brain alive. So long as his brain was alive, his drones would try to get him to safety and a place where a medical drone could get him.

BI2 fired on one of Sweeting's BIs that darted out to retrieve its wounded commander. Sweeting's BI dropped. His drones hadn't figured out where we were yet, and honestly, the Heavy was a bit more important, so I wasn't worried about being found. Also, with Sweeting out of the game, his BIs were entirely on their own when it came to making decisions. In short, between the Heavy and me, Sweeting was fucked. Another of his drones went down as another came for him. As the third BI ran out, there was covering fire in my direction, but the Heavy took out the drone going to Sweeting and then turned on the BIs providing cover.

My subteams reported that they had taken out Sweeting's BBALLs, and he was down to two drones. I gave the order to come back to me. In the street, the two remaining drones fired rockets at the Heavy. They exploded in the air as its defense system took them out. Just to make sure I got full credit for Sweeting, I aimed and shot him in the head before moving out. Next to his name, it changed from OOA to KIA.

In my HUD, I also noticed that Meyers was marked WIA, meaning that he was badly hurt but still able to fight. *He might be missing a limb or something; was it the Heavy?* Meyers' status updated to KIA. I sighed. Meyers would have been easier. It was just Betts and me. I moved to the central building quickly, the arena silent. Betts and I had trained together a lot over the last couple of weeks; I knew how he thought, and he knew me. It would be a race to the central building. Taking and holding it would be the top priority.

I wasn't entirely sure how the scoring worked, but I knew that taking and holding tactically sound positions counted for a lot. We got to the base of the building, which looked to be some old office building, most of the windows blown out, with smoke coming from a few of them. I entered through one of the ones with smoke coming out of it, and my display changed so that I could see. In the smoke, the display was an overlay of thermal vision and a type of sonar. I moved quickly with my POD, clearing the doors along a hallway as we worked to a stairwell.

Once in, I used my Space Anchor, telling it to go up. The name for the device was deceiving. While its original intent was just to enter an atmosphere and stop troops from falling to their deaths, troops soon found new uses for the device. It drained the power cell heavily to make it do something other than stay in one spot in space, but it was possible.

I shot up with my POD, moving between the gap of the staircases. I watched my Anchor's power meter fade quickly, but the building was only a few stories tall. When I reached the top, my power cells were down to twenty percent, just enough to break a fall, though the building wasn't so tall that my suit couldn't absorb the impact.

BI3 opened the door, and the rest of subteam one filed into the hall. We split up, looking for sniping positions; my BBALLs hung by the stairwell entrance to make a trap, or so I thought. As we spread out, gunshots tore through the walls, and the BI next to me dropped. I knelt, firing from the direction the bullets had come from.

One of Betts's drones came out into the hall, and I shot at it. I moved into a room and took out another waiting for me. There was a sting in the back of my left leg, which gave out, dropping me to the ground. I rolled and fired at a BBALL, hitting it. An alert came up on my HUD: YOU ARE HIT. YOUR LEFT LEG IS UNUSABLE. Next to my name on the Fireteam list, my status went to WIA. *Awesome.* I moved up to the wall, telling my BIs to avoid my area. I wasn't going to go down as Sweeting had as bait.

I dragged myself to another room and waited, using my map to command my remaining drones. There weren't many left. My heart pounded; everything felt so real. I tried to think. I needed to get out. If I could get picked up by a medical drone, I'd be marked as surviving the simulation. The door to the room I was in burst open, and I fired at it. A hand reached around the door frame and tossed in a grenade. There was a flash, and my display went black except for big red letters that read "YOU ARE KIA." I couldn't move; my suit went rigid.

A few moments later, my body could move, and my display cleared. I was in a white room atop a platform. All the drones were retreating back to prep rooms, leaving the humans. Betts wasn't far from me. He walked over and extended a hand to help me up. I placed my SIR behind me on my pack and let my helmet remove itself.

Betts did likewise. "That was fun," he said.

I couldn't disagree. "Yeah, how long were you waiting for me?"

"Not long," he shook his head. "Almost didn't have time to trap you. Sweeting?"

"Took on a Heavy, and I helped the Heavy," I said with a smirk.

Sweeting yelled from below, "Yeah man, that was messed up using me as bait and then shooting me in the head!"

He laughed and gave me the finger. We walked to the ground level and found Sweeting and McLeod, who'd apparently been killed due to three 20mm rounds to the chest.

"Ouch, that will do it," Sweeting said.

She shook her head, looking disappointed. We found Meyers walking back to the entrance of the arena. He didn't say anything to us, but he stared daggers at Betts. Outside of the simulation room, we went back to our main classroom. Ours was the last Fireteam to go for the day, so when we returned to the classroom, rankings were posted on the board. Only the top ten people in the platoon were listed, and they were in alphabetical order. Betts and I were on the list along with Royle.

She came up behind us and slapped Betts and me on the back. "Looks like we did okay." She looked over at Meyers. "Sorry, Happy." She'd taken to calling him that. He glared at her.

"At least I wasn't killed by my Heavy," Meyers said, looking at McLeod.

McLeod looked down, ashamed. Next to the list of top fighters was the list of the top three Fireteams in the platoon, and any joy I felt from being in the top ten individuals vanished as I saw that my Fireteam wasn't on the list.

"It's my fault. I'm horrible," McLeod said dejectedly as she looked at the list of Fireteams.

"You're right. You are horrible, and it is your fault," Meyers spat.

"Shut it, Meyers. We're supposed to work as a team; it's everyone's fault," I said. "I'll help you, McLeod."

She brightened a bit.

"I'll join," Betts said.

McLeod's face flushed. I felt guilty for not helping her sooner. Cortez had drilled into us that while we needed to be the best we could be, we'd be nothing if our Fireteam was weak. Today drove that point home for me.

Meyers looked at Betts and me as if he wanted to say something else but decided better of it. He was odd like that. He'd make comments but rarely follow up on them. I had assumed that we'd be constantly arguing, but that hadn't been the case barring a few occasions.

SIX

My CCPU sounded a gentle alarm in my head, and I began to wake up. As I stirred, I remembered what today was. Today was a day off. Usually, we only got an evening off here and there, but today was different—it was a whole day. As soon as my suit was on, I rolled out of my bunk. I was soon joined by the rest of my Fireteam. We all made our way to the mess hall; even Meyers seemed to be in a good mood.

We only got a full day off every few weeks, but it wasn't just the day off that made the day special. It was what you could do. Later in the evening, Betts, McLeod, and I had simulator time booked, but during the day, we had other plans.

On full days off, leaving the base without permission was not allowed, and even if you got permission, you'd waste half the day traveling back and forth to Arrow City on a shuttle. However, there were things to do on base. On our first and only day off, Cortez offered to show us around a canyon on Arrow. He'd gotten permission for shuttles, and we'd had to get up ungodly early. But the canyon had been like nothing I'd ever imagined. We climbed rocks and explored caves, with the culminating part of the day ending with Cortez showing us how to stargaze with our suit's helmet. It had been amazing.

Today we were going to a pool that was only for troops in training. Each company had access on full days off. The HFDF had a lot going for it, but like all large organizations, it had some downsides. One was that if we weren't in our bunks or in the shower, we were to be in our suits. That meant all the time. Sure, you could play any sport you wanted, but it was all in the suits. The pool was different. While there, we could wear military-issued swimsuits. Silly as it seemed, I was pretty excited not to be in my suit for most of the day.

Our suits, while comfortable and awesome in every way, had the significant downside of being mandatory, making me just itch to get it off. They could have said we had to walk around naked in the base, and I'd have been down for it.

We made quick work of breakfast and then made our way to the pool's locker rooms. As we walked, my CCPU pinged me, letting me know that in the locker room, I would find a block of nano-material that would be my swimwear for my time in the pool. My CCPU then asked what style of bathing suit I wanted. My level of caring about style was nonexistent by this point, so I picked whatever the first option on the list was.

The locker room consisted of walls of lockers, each the size of a suit in its block form. I walked to the one my CCPU told me to, and the door opened. Inside was a much smaller block of nano-material. My suit flowed off my body. I grabbed the smaller block and held it to my waist. It flowed into basic trunks. The trunks seemed a smidge form-fitting, but whatever. I placed my combat suit in the locker. Betts, Sweeting, and I made our way out of the locker room. The pool was indoors, of course, as being outside on Arrow without a suit would mean certain death. The room was large with high ceilings where an artificial sun shone down on us. The pool itself was also big, with several hot tubs around it. A map on a vid wall showed where a place to get snacks and drinks was. I grinned. I'd landed in paradise.

Betts, Sweeting, and I started to walk in when McLeod came out of the women's locker room. We all stopped. When I'd first entered the pool, I'd only kind of noticed all the people in black nano-material swimsuits. I'd been more occupied by the pool itself and looking forward to relaxing. Not now. We'd spent weeks on end in our combat suits. The most skin I'd seen on another human was their face and hands. All of our suits went up most of our necks, and the women had kept their hair up in tight buns lest their helmets give them a haircut when they engaged.

McLeod stopped and looked at us, her eyes going up and down, her face flushed, and her mouth fell open for a moment before she snapped it shut, composing herself. Not that I could judge. I'd always thought of her as cute but nothing exceptional. In all fairness, no one looks "exceptional" in a combat suit. After not seeing a woman in anything other than a full-body suit for so long, McLeod was a goddess. She was in a black bikini that contrasted amazingly with her creamy skin. And how had I not noticed before how her body curved in all the right places? Her perfect belly and her chest... oh my god. Her face was framed with long brown hair, and... what was I doing? I felt my own face flush, and my heart did a little flip as it picked up.

I shook my head, "Hey, McLeod..." I said awkwardly.

Next to me, Sweeting and Betts started looking anywhere but at McLeod. If she noticed my blatant check-out, she didn't let on. Instead, she still looked a little flustered.

"Hey guys," she said, her voice a little off.

Eyes, Alex, look at her eyes! Or her mouth, that was fine, look at her mouth. Fuck, don't look at her mouth. God damn it, what was wrong with me?

"Let's go sit next to the pool," Sweeting said, breaking the awkward silence. We turned to the pool, and I found myself looking at the rest of my company. Every other woman looked just as amazing to me as McLeod.

I turned, whispering to Sweeting, "Is it just me, or is everyone in our company insanely hot?"

He looked at me conspiratorially, "Dude, I'm in heaven right now, but it's kind of messed up, ya know? Those suits are awesome and all, but they ain't, well..." He glanced at Veronica Royle.

I stopped listening to him. Royle was walking up to us. She was also in a two-piece suit and, like McLeod, looked terrific. Her hair was long and dark, her blue-green eyes bright. It took sheer force of will to keep my eyes from shooting down her body. I failed.

She smiled as she walked up to us, "You boys checking me out?" she asked.

Betts turned red, but Sweeting just laughed, "Yeah, I'm not gonna even try to get out of that one."

She smiled and gave us all an obvious once-over. I tried not to let my face turn as red as Betts. "No judgment here." She stood next to me, "I think I know what our company will be doing this afternoon."

We all barked a laugh. As we did, I caught McLeod's eye, and we both looked away quickly. We walked to the pool and tried to relax. After a bit, I didn't feel like I was thirteen anymore, and I could hang around by the pool with my Fireteam and Royle's without feeling like the universe's biggest perv. That said, what Royle had said when we arrived seemed accurate. People were leaving the pool in twos, each heading for their respective locker rooms.

People in training hooked up. This wasn't new. In your downtime, you could do whatever, and there were no regulations against it. There weren't many options for places to go, which limited you to someone's bunk. That meant your Fireteam knowing you were fooling around with someone in your bunk. It kept most people from doing too much. But that didn't look to be the case now.

We'd been working hard for weeks, and the stress levels were starting to turn up. I'd have been lying if I said I didn't want to blow off some steam. After a while, Sweeting and Kwasny from Royle's team left hand in hand.

"There goes two more," I said with a laugh.

Betts left an hour later with a girl from another platoon, leaving Royle, McLeod, and me. Thankfully, Meyers hadn't joined us once we left the mess.

After a while, Royle took off with a black-haired guy from another platoon, leaving McLeod and me alone. It was kind of awkward again. The pool was turning into a meat market.

"Do you want to go get lunch?" I asked.

She shot up from her chair, "Yes, please," she said hurriedly.

We changed, and I met her in the hall going to the mess. As I saw her back in her combat suit, I felt more normal, but I couldn't get the sight of her or anyone in the company out of my head.

"That place..." was all she said.

"Right?"

"I mean, I get it, but..."

I shook my head, "Yeah, I know what you mean."

We ate lunch, discussing the simulation we were going to run that night. It wouldn't be until after dinner, but it gave us something to talk about. We walked back to our room. There wasn't anything else I wanted to do for the day. I thought I'd check up on what my friends were up to, and as exciting as it was, maybe do some studying.

We were the only ones in the room, though Betts and Sweeting's bunk screens were closed. I chuckled, "I guess we know what their plans are."

"Yeah," she said with a laugh.

"I guess I can't blame them; it has been a while," I admitted.

"That it has," she said with a nod.

I noticed her eyes flick to my open bunk for just a moment. All I could think of was her in that bikini. She was just looking at me, chewing her lip. Fuck, did she know how insanely sexy that was? Okay, time to get the hell out of dodge.

"I get wanting to blow off steam," I said. *What the fuck! Alex, how is that getting out of dodge?*

She turned red, and I could almost see the wheels turning in her head. I'd just made an incredible ass of myself. She nodded, her eyes darting again.

"Your bunk or mine?" she blurted. "I'm sorry. I can't believe I just..." I cut her off. "Mine."

She nodded, "Okay," she smiled tightly, "just blowing off steam, though." She confirmed.

"Totally!"

What are you doing? She's in your Fireteam, moron! I told myself, but the thing was, my brain was no longer calling the shots. We fidgeted for a moment. God, was I bad at this; thankfully, she was too.

"Sorry, I normally don't do the hook-up thing..." I said uncomfortably, "not that there's anything wrong with it!" I added hastily.

"Yeah, me either," she said nervously, "but yeah, nothing wrong with it. Um... okay... here we go."

She took my hand awkwardly and led me to my bunk. McLeod slid into the bunk, her back to the wall. I got in after her, lying on my side. I felt my heartbeat quicken as the screen closed. It was dark for a moment, and then we were bathed in soft light. The space felt incredibly tight. I tried to scooch closer to her. If I were to create a top ten list of un-smooth things I'd done in my life, this would take the first eight spots, hands down. Hesitantly, I placed my hand on her waist.

She looked as nervous as I felt. I tried to smile. I felt her hand on the arm of my suit.

"I'm being awkward. I'm so sorry," she said.

"No, no, it's me," I countered.

She sighed, "Alright, so we both suck at this."

I chuckled, "Yeah, I don't have much experience with the whole hooking up with a teammate in a bunk thing."

She laughed, and it broke the tension a bit. As she laughed, I looked at her face, my gaze settling on her soft blue eyes. She was pretty. I'd just never taken the time to look. My eyes traced along her face, and without thinking about it, my hand went up and swept some of her long brown hair away from her cheek.

"I think I could get used to it," I said.

Her expression softened, "Yeah?"

"Yeah."

I leaned in and gently pressed my lips to hers. After a moment, I felt her lips move as she leaned into the kiss. My hand slid down to her hip, and I kissed her again, feeling how soft and warm her lips were. I gently sucked her lower lip and felt her body pressing against me in the most wonderful way. I kissed her again, deeper this time; her lips parted, allowing my tongue to slide inside and up the roof of her mouth.

All of the awkwardness was gone now. All I could think of was McLeod, her lips on mine, and her body against me. Her suit began to remove itself, and with a thought, mine followed. I felt my hand on the soft, warm flesh of her hip, and I slid it to the small of her back, pulling her into me. She moaned softly, and I felt what little self-control I had left cracking. I kissed her more passionately, my hand moving up and down her back.

Her skin was so soft, and I couldn't get enough of it. We broke the kiss, and the smoldering look in her eyes broke me.

"I have wanted to do this since the moment I saw you come out of that locker room," I admitted.

She bit her lip. Fuck, with the look in her eyes and her biting her lip, I was done for.

"When I came out, I wasn't sure I'd ever wanted to sleep with someone so bad before in my life," she admitted.

"Yeah?" I asked, smiling.

She kissed me, "Yeah. Sweeting and Betts were nice too, but," she bit her lip, smirking, "I'm happy how this worked out. I have weeks' worth of stress and tension I need to take care of."

"Fuck, Krista," I said and kissed her again, pulling her close.

My hand moved to her waist, and I tried to roll her onto her back.

As it was, the only way for her to be on her back was if I was on top of her. Something I fully planned on happening, but not yet. She half-rolled onto her back, and I kissed down her jaw and neck, loving the effect it had on her breathing. My hand moved up her thigh as my lips found her breasts. God, I'd been thinking about her chest all day.

Her moans deepened as my lips found her nipple and my tongue swirled. A moment later, when my hand made it up the inside of her thigh, she groaned. I'd never felt anything so silky before in my life as my fingers found that delightful little bundle of nerves between her legs and began to move.

"Fuuuck, Alex," she moaned, her hips rocking against my hand.

I kissed her lips and neck and continued to work, extracting every ounce of pleasure I could from her. Fleetingly, I wondered how good the bunk's soundproofing was. As I took her over the edge, I felt my own need rising.

She tried to roll onto her back, and I hit my head on the ceiling twice as I got on top of her. This was now taking nine of my life's top ten un-smooth moments. But as I felt the inside of her thighs against my legs and looked down at her, it was all worth it. I took in her body, feeling myself aching to be inside her. I kissed her, enjoying the moment. Her hand touched my cheek, and I broke the kiss to see excitement in her eyes.

Her head tilted slightly, and she smiled in the most seductive way, "Have fun blowing off steam."

How did she know everything to say? I kissed her and then groaned as I pushed inside. Her back arched, and I felt pure ecstasy as I sank in.

"Hmmmm," she breathed.

I groaned, "Christ... you feel amazing!"

My hips began to move, slowly at first, but as the energy in me built, I pumped faster and harder. Her moans egged me on, and she placed her hands against the bunk wall, pushing herself down. I lost myself to the feel of her legs and body writhing. Her head went back in a moan, and I tensed and shuddered, feeling weeks' worth of tension and stress explode into Krista McLeod.

I looked down at her, our breathing heavy, and kissed her. I tasted the salt of her sweat. "That was fun," I said.

She smiled, nodding. "Yes, it was." She kissed me.

"I could do this all day," I commented between kisses.

Her chuckle was breathy. "Yes, please."

A while later, I woke up from a nice nap, McLeod half-laid on me, her head against my chest. I ran my fingers through her hair and down her back. She'd occasionally kiss my chest or neck. It was so relaxing.

She looked up at me, smiled, and kissed me.

"Today's been a good day," she said.

"Yes, it has," I agreed.

She got serious. "But this isn't anything. It's just sex, right?"

I nodded. "Yeah, totally."

She sighed in relief. "Good. Sorry, I just don't want to make working together difficult."

I smiled. "I hear ya." I thought for a moment. "But if we ever need to blow off some steam again..."

She grinned. "Oh, we'll blow off steam again." She winked.

Her saying that turned me on. She glanced down.

"Looks like steam isn't the only thing getting blown today. It's my turn to be on top," she said as her lips began trailing kisses down my chest and abdomen.

Again, we lay in my bunk, with McLeod on top of me this time. My arms wrapped around her waist. My CCPU let me know that dinner would be starting soon. Hunger aside, for my part, I was fine lying like this the rest of the day.

I sighed. "Dinner is soon."

"I am kind of hungry," she said.

I couldn't argue, but I didn't want to leave the bunk. It wasn't just the sex; we'd had a good afternoon. I hadn't really talked to McLeod on a deep level before. I had today, and she was so different than she usually was. She'd always seemed a little shy and unconfident in train-ing, but in the bunk?

"I'm hungry too. And then training." I smiled.

She scowled. "Yay, I get to continue to suck at combat."

I squeezed her. "You're getting better. Don't be hard on yourself. Your scores are improving."

She looked down at me and smiled. "You're sweet." She leaned down and kissed me softly. I kissed back, holding her.

She lifted off me, her pale blue eyes looking at me in slight panic.

"Fuck!" she said. "This isn't just blowing off steam, is it?"

I thought for a moment, then deflated and said, "Sorry."

She smiled tightly. "Me too." She huffed, looking concerned, chewing her lip this time in a very non-sexy way. "Can we do this? What if you become Fireteam leader?"

I was happy to hear her say that she felt the same way. And I was surprised I felt that way about her.

Her eyes went out of focus. "Well, there's a provision in the HFDF if one of us becomes a Fireteam leader. So long as our squad leader is fine with it and monitors that no one is being treated differently... we'd have to grant a bit more access to our CCPUs while together," she said.

"If I even get the job," I said. "Do you want to do this?" I asked.

As I spoke, my hand absently ran up and down her back, and I realized just how badly I wanted to do it. There was something comfortable about Krista. Once the awkwardness was over, everything just clicked. Spending an afternoon in a tight bunk, fooling around and talking seemed like the most natural thing in the world.

She looked at me for a moment, then nodded. "I do, like kind of a lot. You?"

I smiled. "Yeah."

She leaned down and kissed me again. "Good."

Our suits slid back over our bodies, and we rolled out of my bunk. At dinner, we sat next to each other, with Betts across from us.

"Sorry you have to go into training with me," McLeod said to Betts.

"I know there are other things you could be doing." She shot an unconscious glance at a red-headed woman at another table—the one Betts had spent his day with.

Surprisingly, Betts didn't turn red. "Today was fun and amazing, and all that, but neither of us are relationship types. We had our fill and worked out a little arrangement." He looked at McLeod and me, inspecting us. "Did you two? No, you didn't!"

McLeod turned red, and I looked at my food. Betts laughed. "Well, good for you guys. When I saw your screen closed, I figured you had someone in there with you, but not McLeod!" He laughed again. "Just blowing off steam?" he asked.

"Not entirely," I admitted.

He looked thoughtful. "My brother hooked up with one of his teammates."

"How'd that work out?" I asked.

Betts shrugged. "Good, they've been married twenty-five years."

"Was one of them in command of the other?" McLeod asked.

He snorted. "Yeah, she was. If you're going to ask if it was an issue, the answer is no. Service Term troops have different regs; our squad leader will watch our every move and decision. Shit, the HFDF wants us to be in this for life. Teams of career troops are almost all composed of couples. Do you really think they didn't know what would happen when they made that little flesh fest today?" he asked.

That felt better and somehow creepy at the same time.

"Come on, you don't think...." McLeod started.

Betts chuckled dryly. "They wanted us to do exactly what we did." He put down his fork. "It did two things. One, it made it so no one will feel awkward about fucking in their bunks. That's good for morale. And if they manage to get some people into a relationship, then good for them. Either way, the Service got a lot more interesting for us."

"Yeah, unless said relationships mess with teams," I said.

Betts shook his head. "No, they wouldn't. Trust me. The HFDF knows what they're doing. Just accept it." He dug back into his food.

———

BETTS, MCLEOD, AND I MADE OUR WAY TO ONE OF THE BASE'S VR simulation rooms. The room was long, with five VR pods on each side. The pods looked like elongated clamshells, their tops opening to allow someone to lie inside.

We each walked up to a pod and got in. The lid closed on top of me, plunging me into darkness. I closed my eyes, then opened them. Well, I felt like I opened them, but I knew I was looking at a projection from my CCPU.

We were all in a generic landscape—a depiction of terrain that could be found everywhere on Arrow. Betts and McLeod were next to me. Right now, there were no drones or enemy units.

"So what are you thinking tonight?" Betts asked me.

I thought for a moment, trying to figure out what would be good.

"Why don't we work on zoning?" I suggested.

Betts nodded. "Am I the bad guy?"

"You know it," I said.

He chuckled and ran off into the distance, leaving McLeod and me. I assigned her a standard POD of BIs. They materialized behind us.

"Betts, she's going to hold this spot; just come at us from one direction," I instructed.

"Roger that."

I looked at McLeod. "Okay, so zoning—you've got this," I told her.

She sighed. "Okay."

She took control of her BIs and allowed me access to her CCPU, which would show me her decisions and why she made them. For me, it would be like I was a ghost. Nothing would interact with me, and I could walk through whatever I wanted. It was kind of fun. I could also stand in the shoes of any unit, seeing what they were seeing.

I pulled up McLeod's feed. She was getting her drones in place to defend her current position. In the distance, Betts' drones approached. When they were in range, I called pause. All of the drones froze.

McLeod and Betts came up next to me.

"So tell me what you're thinking on this," I asked McLeod.

While I could see her decisions, it seemed to help if she had to vocalize them.

She looked at her drones. "I'm in a bad spot; I'm dead center in my POD. I could be targeted."

She rearranged her POD, making her seem less important. That was good; she'd had issues with that. This seemed to be something common with her. When she had to stop and look at something critically, she could see where she was going wrong, but she didn't seem to be able to do it in the moment. I had Betts start his attack. His goal was to force McLeod to focus on her zones.

Zoning was a simple concept that could be more or less easy to implement. It was easy if the enemy was coming right at you and you were in a good spot, or if the enemy were pushovers. It was much more challenging if your position was shit or the enemy was competent.

The beauty of everything being networked together was that you knew what everyone was shooting at. McLeod's display was overlaid with tinted squares. Each square was a zone. All you had to do was shoot stuff in your zone, and you didn't have to pay full attention to the other zones. If something was about to cross into your zone, your CCPU would let you know, and if a drone went down, you could re-zone. Coupled with target sequencing and our firing system, a small team could hold off a large number of hostiles.

McLeod started to fire at enemy BIs. I could see where her attention was being pulled and started to notice something. She wasn't trusting the other zones. As an operator, you had to pay attention to everything to a certain degree. This was why you tried to put yourself in a place where you'd fight the least. That said, the drones were very good at killing stuff, so you didn't have to give them all of your attention. She was also looking at everything at once, trying to take in the whole picture all the time.

Betts' units were closing the gap. As he did so, she was starting to get stressed out. Her ability to hold her own zone went down as her stress levels increased. She also started messing with her drones, which then suffered, making them less effective. The other danger she would run into is if she started to suck enough, her BIs would take their abilities down a notch. After all, their primary mission was to keep their operator alive—something they couldn't do if said operator stuck out like a sore thumb.

"McLeod, constrict your view to your zone; let the BIs do their job," I said.

She did so, and I saw her view shrink to just her zone and a small area around it. As it did, her suit also constricted her movement. I could see in my CCPU that her stress levels went up a bit.

"Pause," I said.

The drones stopped moving.

"What did I do?" she asked, dejected.

I talked just to her, muting our conversation from Betts.

"Hey, what's got you so stressed?" I asked.

"I don't know. I'm worried I'll mess up like I always do," she admitted. "I guess I can't keep everything straight. I start to do badly, and then instead of fixing the issue, I make it worse."

It was odd. That afternoon, she'd been so confident when it was just the two of us. I just needed her to channel that now.

"You can do this. You do great at the firing range, and your BIs don't have any issues hitting anything. Just focus on your zone, and let your CCPU reassign zones as needed," I told her.

"Okay."

"Unpause," I said.

The attack continued. She focused on her zone, treating it like the firing range. Her rate of fire increased, and as it did, the enemy was slowly being pushed back. She began to relax more as well. Her CCPU showed that she was starting to feel confident. I had Betts push her harder but didn't tell her that he was going to do it. She did fine, staying in the zone and holding her position.

I opened a line with Betts. "I think she's just overcomplicating it. She's trying to take the whole fight into account the whole time. It's overwhelming her. Once she calms down, she does fine."

"I can see that. So what now?" he asked.

I thought for a moment. "We let her win tonight. Let's slowly build on zoning, forcing her to focus on one part at a time. Once she's confident with a piece, we add another."

"Can do," he said.

I continued to watch her work. She was doing much better now.

———

LATER, I LAY IN BED THINKING ABOUT THE DAY. BETTS AND I HAD A GOOD idea of where to take McLeod's training now, and I was convinced that she could improve. I had to remind myself that while McLeod was having a hard time in our Fireteam, she wasn't the lowest-ranked person in the platoon or company by a decent margin. While being with higher-ranked people pushed Betts, Meyers, and even Sweeting, it seemed to make McLeod struggle. *I just need to get her confidence up*, I told myself.

I tried not to think about the HFDF for a bit. I'd have tomorrow to deal with it. Instead, I looked at messages from my friends, sending them a few of my own. It was late when my CCPU pinged me. It was McLeod.

"Hey, what's up?" I asked.

"I didn't wake you, did I?" she asked.

"Nah, I was up," I said.

"Mind if I join you?" she asked.

"Sure," I replied.

I sent the command to my suit to put itself back on. After it was done, I opened the screen, and McLeod slid in. I shut the screen.

"Hey," I said.

She situated herself on me as comfortably as she could. I wrapped my arm around her waist.

"Hey there. So tonight wasn't weird at all," she said.

"No, it wasn't," I agreed.

"So we're really doing this?" she said, looking happy.

"We are," I said. "It doesn't sound like the HFDF cares."

"The opposite, if anything," she said.

I yawned.

"Sorry I came over here for this. I could have used my CCPU; I can let you sleep," she said.

She tried to shift, but I held her. "I'm fine."

She smiled. "I guess I could set an alarm for before we're supposed to wake up and go back to my bunk," she suggested.

"I like that idea," I said.

I gave the command to remove my suit, as did she. She lay in my arms as we dozed. We couldn't make a habit of this, but it was nice for tonight. Her skin was just as smooth and soft as I'd remembered from earlier. As I ran my hand down her back, I felt myself relax. We rolled onto our sides; there was thankfully enough room to spoon. Her body molded to mine, and I held her close. Her hair tickled my nose. I told my CCPU to make it so I didn't feel my face get tickled. As I did, I chuckled softly.

"What?" she asked.

"Just thinking about my dad, that's all," I said.

She turned to look at me. "You have a naked girl pressed against you, and you think of your father? You might want to explain that one."

I laughed. "It's just... it's just when I had my first girlfriend, he gave me some advice." I smirked, thinking about it. "He told me that before he was ageless, he loved to cuddle, but hair always tickled his nose. He told me when he got a CCPU, he always made his face not feel my mom's hair. He always reminded me to do that when I'd start seeing someone. Your hair tickled my face, and I told my CCPU to make it stop. I just thought it was funny because he would be proud."

She rolled over to face me. "That's good advice, I guess. But I'm still not sure how I feel about you thinking about a parent when I'm in bed with you. Hmm," she kissed me, pressing her body against mine. "Are you thinking about anybody else now?"

"No, I'm not," I said. It wasn't a lie either.

She grinned and wrapped one leg around me. "Good," she said as she kissed me again. Man, I was going to be tired tomorrow, and I was totally okay with that. Everything else in the world vanished, replaced with only Krista McLeod.

SEVEN

I pressed myself against the exterior wall of a warehouse. My BIs positioned themselves on either side of me as my Whiskers scanned the area, trying to figure out who was shooting at us. The warehouse I was cowering behind was located amidst a cluster of other industrial buildings, all cast in the same red-brown light. The buildings may have been brightly colored once, but the glaring light from the surface of Arrow had washed those colors out.

We had moved from one simulation or drill to another. We had virtual reality simulations that allowed us to learn quickly, even simulating the feel of movement and gravity—or, in some cases, the lack thereof. But in those, you knew you were in a VR pod, so your mind didn't take things as seriously as it should. Next, we moved to the training arena; it added the reality that we were actually moving around. Still, when you stepped on something in the arena, even if it looked like it might collapse, you knew it was some structure that your CCPU was imposing an image on. You were inside the base, and your mind knew that.

Not here. We were on the surface of Arrow, with its thin atmosphere and weak gravity. Our surroundings were manufactured and built for the purpose of training. If a rooftop gave way, we would really fall to the ground. Our Space Anchors and suits would keep us from getting hurt, but for our minds, things were as real as they could be before actual combat.

I pulled up a feed from a Whisker with a view of a training drone. They were built in modules and covered in nano-material so our trainers could come up with any size or shape enemy they saw fit. These enemies looked a little like grasshoppers standing on their hind legs with the head of a wasp and several long arms. In those arms was a gun. That was really the only thing that didn't change much. While the HFDF wanted our training to throw as much at us as possible, they weren't about to design a bunch of unique weapons that mainly did the same task. So the enemy was holding a SIR.

I took a moment to focus on the map on my HUD. The map was constructed using data from every HFDF unit in the area, providing a clear picture of what we were about to face. The building we were against didn't have any windows along the wall we were on. That was a good thing, as thermal and sonar showed that the building was full of enemy units.

Whiskers had themselves planted to the building walls, using the sounds from inside to build an ever more detailed map. On the other side of the building was a wide street lined with one- and two-story buildings. My map lit up with little red dots indicating enemies. We were outnumbered, and the enemy had really good positions. If Meyers Fireteam was a democracy, I'd vote for avoiding the street.

I took a moment to run down all of the stats I had on my drone POD and my situation. Per Meyers' orders, neither I nor any of my drones had taken the time to place Reloaders on anything around us. As a result, I saw that my ammo reserves were down to ten percent. Most of my drones were faring the same. My Space Anchor was also nearly drained, save for a small burst that would keep me from falling to my death and a little extra. I couldn't access all of that power unless I started to fall. I had enough energy to boost a jump, maybe. I looked up to the roof of the warehouse. I could probably make it up there by jumping and using the anchor. It looked far up, but Arrow's gravity sucked, so I should make it if I needed to. That said, I really didn't want to go on the roof.

My CCPU notified me that there was gunfire in the distance. It was Betts making his way to a waypoint at another spot along the warehouse. I sighed. I knew where this attack was going; we all did. Meyers would have us jump on top of the roof and run at the enemy, guns blazing. It would be fast and violent, but if it worked, Meyers would have the quickest completion time for this simulation in the company. Which was his goal; hence, not taking time to reload or, you know, do anything the right way.

I tried not to get frustrated. For training purposes, my CCPU's privacy settings allowed command not to hear my every thought but to read my intentions and feelings about other team members. That was also the reason I couldn't ignore Meyers. While he was being graded on how we all felt about him and his intent behind commands, we were all being graded on how well we followed those commands, regardless of their stupidity.

"Fireteam, ascend to the rooftop on my mark," Meyers said.

"Fireteam leader advise, I am low on ammo and Space Anchor charge," Betts said, concern evident in his voice.

"Fireteam, do not waste my time with information I already have," Meyers responded curtly.

I clenched my jaw; *what a prick.*

I got ready to jump, and when the command came, I leaped into the air, using up the last of the power in my anchor that I could control. I ascended, my fingers clasping the edge of the roof. I heaved myself up. The lack of gravity and my suit's help made it easy. I came up on the roof and stayed low for a moment as my drones and the rest of the team arrived. Meyers motioned us forward, and we kept low as we approached the roof's edge.

Below, I saw numerous enemies. They had obviously set a trap for anyone who made a break down the road. I looked at the end of the road to the objective. It was a squat building that, for the purpose of today's simulation, represented a communications building.

On that note, why was it always a communications building? I could count on one hand how many objectives had not been communications buildings. Okay, I could count on one hand around this type of op; we weren't always taking or holding buildings. Why couldn't it be something different every now and then? Someone had voiced this during a lecture once. Cortez apologized for the monotony of it in a tone of sarcasm that could only come from an instructor. He explained to us that the HFDF training team had better things to do than come up with different labels for buildings and then asked us not to be asses. We hadn't brought it up again.

I opened a line to Betts.

"Betts, how's your ammo? I have a little if you need it."

"At ten percent, how much do you have?" he said, annoyed.

"Also ten percent; this is not good."

"That it isn't," Betts replied.

My CCPU told me Meyers had taken command of all my drones save for two. On the bright side, I had fewer drones that were about to be sans ammo to worry about. As he was the Fireteam leader, he could take anyone's drones except the two BIs that always stayed with their original humans. Meyers had everyone else's drones too, except Krista's.

"Fireteam. McLeod, you go down the center, take the objective if you can, distract if you can't. The rest give her covering fire," Meyers ordered.

What? This was insane. Before anyone could say anything, Meyers gave the order to move out. Krista and her POD jumped from the roof, landing hard on the ground. She sprinted forward, her drones forming up to protect her. From the buildings along the street, the enemy came out shooting at her, taking out drones left, right, and center. It was happening so fast that none of us had time to react. I raised my rifle, trying to give her cover, but not to much effect. With the limited number of drones, our ability to zone was almost impossible. Meyers had deployed the drones in his command to flank around the buildings on the street. Krista wasn't a distraction; she was bait. Hostiles were popping out of windows and around buildings to fire at Krista and her POD.

Krista got tagged in the leg, went down, then got hit several more times. My list of team members showed her as OOA. Two of her BIs rushed to her, pulling her away from danger. This was a function that Meyers could not override, but he could tell them where to take her body to await EVAC. He instructed them to take her to the middle of the street inside of a crater in the ground. The enemy was ditching cover as they moved on to what was left of Krista's POD. I moved up to the lip of the building and propped my SIR on the edge. The nanomaterial inside gripped the concrete lip, stabilizing the gun. I was fully exposed to enemy units, but I needed the best position possible. I began dropping hostiles as they moved forward.

Bits of concrete filled the air as some of the enemies turned their attention to me. BI1 was grazed by a round and took cover as it loaded its last ammo block into its SIR. My SIR ran out shortly after, and I ducked below the lip of the building to avoid fire.

I slammed an ammo block into my SIR. I knew it was a drill, and Krista wasn't hurt, but my heart pounded in my chest, and I zoomed in on the enemy, firing as quickly and effectively as possible. The enemy fired back at us. On a map in the corner of my vision, two medical drones were inbound, but Meyers directed the drones to the worst place possible. The enemy was moving to surround her.

I felt a cold that my suit could not fix, and I stopped firing for a moment. Meyers had used Krista as bait when she ran and now while she was hurt. The enemy swarmed around her location, her last drones getting taken out.

Next to her name in my HUD, Krista went to KIA.

There was a simulated explosion that filled my field of view as mortars took out the enemies around Krista's body. Meyers had zeroed the mortars on the EVAC location for Krista. In this drill, Meyers had three mortar drones that were pounding the area as they cycled through targets. Two Heavies were also entering the street, buzzing enemy units who were scrambling for cover. A small part of my brain registered that if this had been real, not only would I have just watched my girlfriend die and been powerless to stop it, but her body would have just been blown to bits with the mortars. I tried not to feel sick; this was just a drill, nothing more.

"Fireteam, advance on the objective!" Meyers ordered.

I launched myself from the roof as fire erupted everywhere. The drones Meyers sent to flank were here, and the Heavies hammered the enemy with gunfire. I sprinted down the street; around me, the ground exploded with grenades. Normally, at the bottom of our packs was an entry unit, but for today's training, it had been replaced with a power-cell that our anchor used to simulate when we'd been flung in the air by something. I jerked to my left, lifting into the air as a grenade went off beside me. I landed rolling, my suit's damage report showing that my right arm was hurt and numbed, but my suit would compensate for the injury. My CCPU told me my arm would be functional on its own in less than twenty minutes, as it sent nanobots to the area.

It was all fake. I knew this. There was no explosion, and my arm was fine; my CCPU was just numbing it so I learned what it would be like in real action. But I couldn't help but feel a slight panic. Betts' status changed to KIA.

I kept running towards the objective, noting that I only had one drone left. It went down. Two more drones from my old POD detached to come to my aid, but a siren sounded, and the drill was over. I stopped running and looked at the objective building atop which stood Meyers, jumping and waving his arms.

He got over the comms, "That's right! I have the best time in the company! I'm going to be your Fireteam leader, suckers! Hahaha!"

I muted him.

"They aren't going to give him command of anything," Betts said over an audio comm line that Meyers wasn't a part of.

"I hope not," Krista said.

Our squad leader and trainer for the day, Sergeant John Monroe, got over the comm, "Fireteam Alpha, get back to base for debrief." He didn't sound happy, but from Meyers' body language, he didn't seem to notice that.

———

We all sat in a bright room with two rows of chairs facing a large screen. Each row had five chairs; we all sat in the front row, waiting for Monroe to come in. Meyers sat on the far left, smugly, next to him Sweeting, then Betts, me, and on the right, Krista. She hadn't said anything since we got back to base. I wanted to put my hand on hers or something to try and make her feel better, but barring Betts, no one knew we were together yet.

Meyers leaned forward with a grin, pointing at Betts and Krista, "You two are dead. What are you doing here?" He laughed.

Betts' face darkened, but he didn't say anything. Krista just looked forward. Behind us, a door opened, and a tall, lean man with dark skin and a bald head entered the room. Sergeant John Monroe. He was one of several squad leaders our team had worked with, and he was my favorite. After the Fireteams had leaders, the teams would be paired up with other Fireteams to form squads. Monroe and all of the other squad leaders in our training would be taking one of those squads for the duration of our term.

Monroe was fair and level-headed. He also seemed to know just how to help you and deliver news. All of the squad leaders seemed to be like that. Like most of the squad leaders, Monroe was usually calm and controlled, but he didn't look that way now.

As he stalked in front of the screen, our stats for the day popped up. At the top was the time it took our team to complete the drill. It was in green text; all of the other text was red. That wasn't what you wanted to see. Monroe looked at Meyers, who was grinning with pride. Monroe smiled at him, but the smile didn't feel kind to me.

He pointed at the simulation time, "Wow, Meyers," he said, pacing. "I've never seen a score like this before, you know that? After your training here, I'll have my third squad. Do you guys know what that means?" he asked.

"Nah," Meyers said.

Monroe stopped walking and said animatedly, "It means that once I was like you guys, here on my first term. Like you, I worked with every Fireteam in my platoon and company, so that's what, like...two Fireteams per squad...five squads per platoon, and twenty squads per company, so that comes to what, like...forty Fireteams per company? So I worked with forty Fireteams when I was in my first term, and *now* I'm on my fourth term. See, so that means that I've now worked with one hundred and sixty Fireteams, and I've never seen anything like I did today!"

Meyers' grin widened, and he gave a slight shrug as if to say *I know I'm amazing.*

Monroe looked at Meyers, his hands clasped under his chin. "And you did it all at the small, small cost of sixty percent of your drones and two human lives." His smile vanished, his expression turning to rage. "TWO! Two human lives, Meyers!" he roared.

Meyers didn't look so smug anymore. Monroe came close to him, tapping his forehead with two fingers. "If this wasn't a drill, two of your teammates would be dead, Meyers! Two!" He shouted, waving his fingers in front of Meyers' face. "Do you even comprehend how bad that number is? Or are you too stupid to get the point of the training here? What is the job of the Fireteam leader?"

"To get the mission accomplished," Meyers said, his face red with anger.

Monroe stepped back a few paces, "To get the mission accomplished? NO! Your job as a Fireteam leader is to accomplish your mission with the least loss of human life possible! Not in the shortest amount of time, and not with the highest losses possible." Monroe was back to pacing. "What part of that do you not understand?"

Meyers looked up at Monroe. "I thought my team coul—"

"Don't you dare say handle it!" Monroe cut him off, shaking his head. "Meyers, this is training, not combat. Your ability to lie to me today is much harder than in actual combat. Let me remind you all that according to the law, the Human Federation cannot access your personal thoughts from your CCPU unless you grant them permission in accordance with the Thought Protection Act. That means your CCPU can't rat you out unless you tell it to.

"In actual combat, you will find yourself giving data to command on a regular basis so that they can come up with training for you or help you in some way. In a real situation, it will also let you exonerate yourself from accusations should they arise. But we are not in combat; we are in training, and each and every one of you has granted the HFDF partial access to your CCPU. That means I know your intentions behind your actions, I know your thought process behind them, and your emotions." He looked at Meyers. "So do not try to lie to me! Because I know that you did not use McLeod as a distraction but as bait. I know that you hoped she'd be injured and that her drones would go to her aid when she was. I know you wanted this so that you could focus the enemy on her so that you could attack them. I know that you did not allow your team members to use their surroundings to make more ammo with their Reloaders because you wanted the best time and thought reloading would waste time. I know that you do not care about them." He chuckled without humor. "I even know that you thought it was funny how scared McLeod must have been and that you were disappointed that in this simulation, unlike real combat, your team members wouldn't feel anything when they got shot."

I felt a disgusted expression cross my face as I watched Meyers. Monroe continued, not looking at the rest of us.

"You were disappointed that it wasn't like in the real world, where it takes someone's CCPU a split second to stop the pain, and in that split second, the person feels themselves getting shot." Monroe was up close to Meyers now, his voice low and cold. "I know that you thought it was funny when one of your teammates was marked KIA. I know you put Sweeting where he was so that he got pinned down and that you knew that Betts and Taylor would do their job and try to support their teammates despite their lack of drones so that you could sprint to the finish line and claim your reward. You, James Meyers, are a piece of shit." He finished, his voice soft, dripping with disgust and malice.

Next to me, Krista sniffed. I placed my hand on her forearm and squeezed gently.

Meyers looked like he was about to talk but didn't get the chance.

"If this had been real, Meyers, and you were dumb enough to give command access to your CCPU, you would have just landed yourself in jail for several decades at best, but more likely, you would have been executed."

The color drained from Meyers' face.

"As is, you will not go to jail. After all, everything today was a simulation. However, Private Meyers, it is my opinion and the opinion of every trainer in the company, including Major Cortez, that you never receive a command during this service. Not even your Fireteam or squad leaders will be able to put you over other people." Monroe said evenly. Meyers looked down as Monroe went on. "Further, you can consider yourself under probation. If you don't follow the commands of your acting Fireteam leaders, then you will be transferred to a post where you can't do any harm. Should you fail at that post, you will be dishonorably discharged. That also means no causing any problems inside of your Fireteam. I'd recommend keeping your assholishness to a minimum."

Monroe's expression changed as he looked at me. "Private Taylor, tomorrow you will be the Fireteam leader; at the end of the day tomorrow, we will announce who will be permanent Fireteam leaders. That is all. You are dismissed."

We all stood and left the room, walking in silence to the mess hall with Meyers in front of us. I pulled up a CCPU message thread with the rest of the team.

> ME: WOW.

> BETTS: Served the little bastard right. Who uses a teammate as bait?

> SWEETING: Dude is crazy. I'm glad command sees that. There's no way I'd go into combat with him if he was in charge.

> ME: Ditto. Mcleod, you ok?

She was next to me, looking ahead at Meyers' back with a mixture of hurt and hate on her face. We all got food, and Meyers found a table on his own to sit at. I was halfway through a burger when Krista finally broke her silence.

"He chose me because I'm the weakest," she said.

I put down my food. "He chose you because he's a dick and has it out for you. Plus, if he used Sweeting, Betts, or me as bait, we'd punch him after the simulation."

Sweeting lifted his cup. "Hear, hear to that! Taylor is right, McLeod. He picked you because he knows you wouldn't do anything about it afterward. Taylor is right, Betts; he or I would probably try to beat his ass."

"So I'm a coward then?" Krista asked.

Betts shook his head. "No, you're controlled enough not to lose your cool. What we're saying is don't try to figure out Meyers' thinking. You've come a long way."

"But I'm still the weakest," she protested.

It was true; I really couldn't argue that. Betts and I had been spending our evenings in simulation rooms and on the range trying to help her out. And it had worked; Krista did great with her drones, but she freaked out if she had to make decisions in battle.

"You are ranked third on defensive maneuvers," I told her.

"Yeah!" Sweeting said. "And compared to these two," he pointed at Betts and me, "that's like saying you are first! These pricks have some of the highest scores in the company, let alone our platoon."

Betts frowned at that, and I tried not to smile. Krista smiled a bit.

"Well, I guess I can do one thing right then. Sorry, I'm being a downer," she said.

"I think after someone did what they did to you today, you have the right to not be all that happy," I said. "The bright side is now we know he won't have the chance to do that in real combat."

"Thank God for that," she said.

I picked my burger back up and started eating again. Sweeting cracked a joke, and she laughed.

———

LATER, I DECIDED TO GO TO THE RANGE AND FOUND ROYLE PRACTICING. I walked up to the stall next to hers. She had her suit's helmet on per the range safety rules, as did I. She opened a comm line.

"How fun was your day?" Her voice was sarcastic.

"It was a total blast, never better," I said as I raised my sidearm and squeezed off a few rounds at a target. "Saw your Fireteam did good, number one for the platoon. Good work."

"Thanks. I've got a good team; Retz is a bit of a jerk, but every village has its ass, right?"

"You're telling me. Man, you should have seen Monroe rip into him, told him if he had done that in real combat, he could have been executed."

"Yikes," she fired at a target that moved back and forth, up and down. "Well, I hope that puts him in line."

"Yeah, like the end of it. Monroe told him that he'll never be in command of anyone. Well, at least not on this term of service. I don't know what would happen if he signed up for another. So do you think you'll be Fireteam leader for your team?"

Royle holstered her sidearm and came into my stall, leaning against the wall. We couldn't see each other's faces, but I still turned to look at her. It just seemed rude not to.

"Maybe, I don't know; Kwasny is pretty spot on, ya know? But what about you?"

I shrugged and turned back down the range. "I bet you get it. As for me, I don't know. Betts is better than I am. Don't tell him I told you that."

"Yeah, but he doesn't want the job, and I hear that counts for a lot when they figure out who to pick. And I'll blackmail you with that statement later, don't worry," she said.

I chuckled. "He may not, but if he's the best choice for the job, he should get it. From what little time we've been here, it doesn't seem like the HFDF screws around," I said.

"That they don't."

In my bunk that night, I thought about the drill for the day. After a bit of prodding, Krista joined me. I opened the screen, and she slid in. It closed, and our suits removed themselves. She lay in my arms for a few moments.

"How are you doing?" I asked.

She sighed. "I'm still bothered," she said, looking at me. "Thank you for not beating up Meyers."

"It took effort," I said.

She kissed me, a small smile touching her face. I squeezed her gently.

"So tomorrow," I said.

"Tomorrow," she echoed.

We'd decided not to be open about our relationship until the Fireteam leader was picked. If it was me, and command said we couldn't be together, we didn't want Meyers' shit about it for the next five years.

"What if they say no?" I asked.

"That would suck," she said.

"I'll turn down the position," I decided on the spot.

"No, you won't," she replied. "You'd be good at it. You can't throw away a huge opportunity for a relationship that just started."

I looked into her eyes. The last few weeks had been wonderful. I knew we were in the honeymoon phase, but I was worried about losing what we had. But she was right; I couldn't throw away a big opportunity for a new relationship.

"But for now, we need sleep," she sighed. "We have a big day tomorrow, and I don't want to think that tonight is our last night." I kissed her goodnight, and she turned over. I spooned her, which was really the only way to sleep two in the bunk. God, I hoped the ships had bigger beds.

I lay there thinking. I'd been Fireteam leader several times now, and tomorrow was weighted the same as any other time. Command would look at who the best person for the job was and give them the command. I knew that, and I knew that I should just want what was best for the team, but I wanted the job. I wouldn't get paid more or anything like that. If anything, I'd get a whole lot more work, but I wanted it anyway.

I started running through the members of the Fireteam in my head and what they were good and not so good at. Sweeting scored middle average for the Fireteam in whatever we did; he seemed to be just as good defensively as he was offensively. Sweeting's problem was he didn't take anything too seriously. He would never let anyone get hurt, but he didn't push himself. Middle of the pack was where he liked to be. Meyers was anything but a team player. He scored well enough, but I wouldn't want him to have my back, nor did I think the rest of the team did. Betts was easy. He and I went back and forth for having the highest scores in the group, with him taking the top spot more often than I did. Krista was right earlier. She was the weakest link... unless I put her in defensive roles.

I thought about what Krista was good at. She was great with her drones, and she could hold positions and even do a good job if you gave her a clear objective. It was not until she had to think on her feet working offensively that she ran into problems. If I told Krista to hold a building, she'd do it just fine; if I told her to give someone cover, she'd do great.

I had no idea what the simulation would be in the morning, but I started to form a basic plan in my head. Krista would work on holding and giving cover. She would be in a support role. It didn't sound glamorous, but support generally acted as an anchor for the team. If they go, then things go sideways in a hurry. Betts and I would make up an assault force. Meyers could be used in more solo-type objectives that didn't require him to play with others. And Sweeting could be a switch hitter, going from offense to support as needed. As everything clicked into place, it felt right in my head. I squeezed Krista's unconscious form just a bit and closed my eyes. I wanted to be rested for tomorrow.

EIGHT

I crouched down, waiting for the drill to begin, with my drone POD of eight BIs and two BBALLs. My teammates were scattered in the nearby area to simulate what it would be like if we dropped onto an enemy world. I couldn't see anything yet, as the drill hadn't started, but I had a rough idea of my surroundings based on the intel provided to me before we began. We were positioned on the outskirts of a small city, and as soon as the drill started, all hell would break loose.

We would face a simulated humanoid enemy, which was training jargon for standard HFDF drones. They were considered mid-level as far as technology went, indicating it wouldn't be a walk in the park. It also meant that, unlike insect races that tended to send in droves of fighters, today's enemy probably wouldn't do that, so no high body count. We were to take and hold a factory. Pretty straightforward as far as orders went. And it was nice that we were taking a factory and not a communications building for a change.

My helmet's feed into my CCPU started, and I was surrounded by Arrow's bleak red-brown landscape. My suit changed colors, blending into my surroundings, and I deployed my Whiskers.

I moved quickly to a large rock. I pressed my back to it and directed a Whisker to check the area. It spotted an enemy walking in the near distance. I kept low and got ready to pop out from behind the rock. I watched the Whisker feed, waiting for the right time. I poked out from behind my cover and fired a three-round burst. The enemy unit jerked as the rounds hit and fell to the ground. I ducked back behind the rock, waiting to see if there was return fire. As I waited, I set a waypoint on the map nearby to gather at.

The Fireteam met in a ditch near a clump of industrial buildings. I told the mortar drones and Heavies to take cover nearby. I ran through the list of strengths and weaknesses of each team member I had compiled the night before. I tried to match those skills with the situation at hand. While time wasn't my primary concern, I didn't want to take too long to accomplish the objective. I pulled up a map of the area. Buildings weren't arranged in any seeming order, with streets sometimes only going for a few blocks. It would make navigating our way around difficult, something I'm sure Cortez had in mind. My CCPU found our objective building smack in the middle of town.

I told Krista and Sweeting to set up defensive positions along the ditch, giving us time to plan. I also ordered the mortar drones to lob a couple of shells into the west part of town, away from our current position. The decoy wouldn't work for long, as I had already taken down an enemy troop that would soon be missed if it wasn't already. I formulated a quick plan and sent it to the team.

"McLeod and Sweeting, you two give us cover when we move. Betts, Meyers, and I will make up the primary assault force. Betts, you take the center. Meyers and I will take your flanks," I said.

I sent a series of waypoints for each team member, including myself. Along with them was a set of guidelines for when to move from one waypoint to another. Krista and Sweeting would be spending their time leapfrogging behind the rest of us. Our intel showed that the enemy was concentrated in the northwest part of town. My path for Meyers brought him around the back of the objective building, with

Betts and me focused on the side facing the enemy. I then pre-targeted mortar volleys and ordered them to fire.

As the first shells hit, I gave the order to move out. I came out of the ditch, my SIR pressed against my shoulder. As the mortar shells exploded, there was a loud concussion that my helmet masked out. With the explosions, dust, and smoke, my helmet overlaid thermal into my vision, showing hostiles scrambling for whatever cover they could find. I set my SIR to auto-round selection, giving it a handful of choices. I then aimed at an enemy behind a wall as I moved and fired. The round punched through concrete but was deflected by something in the wall, probably rebar. Rebar that wasn't there the last time we'd trained on this course. I reset my display to overlay metallic and density views, confirming my assumption about the wall. I chided myself for taking the building for granted.

"Fireteam, be advised the course has changed," I said.

"Confirmed structures have been reinforced, and the streets no longer have piping," Krista replied. I was impressed she'd thought to check the streets.

I kept the change in mind as I approached my first building. My POD's Whiskers flew about, giving us a view inside. Five hostiles were in the building on the floor above us. I pinged Sweeting the info, and his POD sniped all but one of them, who escaped out a door. My CCPU calculated which building he—it was heading to, and I zeroed a Mortar on it, taking the building out.

We moved ahead, pausing at each building, allowing Krista and Sweeting to approach and set up defense. As I waited, I pulled up a map of the battle. Betts was pressing forward at a consistent speed, not rushing ahead but being smart. Meyers had the most distance to cover, and I gave him control of the Heavies. He was using them effectively, making excellent time. I watched as Krista's POD covered him with amazing skill as she removed flanking groups of enemies with seeming ease. I smiled, happy I had put her in the right position.

I started moving again, taking ground and buildings in small spurts. We weren't far from the objective building. Though I wasn't sure if we'd be asked to hold it or not, that was one of the mission's to-be-determined factors. As we got to the objective, I told Meyers to wrap around the building and clear out anything trying to get out.

"Command, we are about to take the objective. What are our orders?" I asked.

Monroe got on the comms, "Fireteam Alpha, you are to hold the building until assistance arrives. If you cannot hold the building, you are to destroy it. Acknowledge."

"Acknowledged command, we will hold the building or destroy it," I responded.

We pressed forward; Betts was entering the objective building, sweeping through it. The rest of us joined Krista and Sweeting, taking up defensive positions. I checked ammo and resources across the Fireteam.

"Use your Reloaders," I ordered.

I took out my own, placing them on a metal patch next to me. My drones did the same. They started working quickly to produce new ammo blocks. Each unit had three Reloaders; they were handy little things. Each was a small disk that held various nano-bots and who knew what else. I couldn't imagine the technology that went into something as seemingly simple as the Reloaders. All I knew was that they kept us in the fight. I also took a moment to ensure the BBALLs had full ammo storages. If the orders were to take, hold, or destroy the building, I figured we'd be in for a bit of a ride.

The team complied, soon restoring their ammo. Then we hunkered down and waited. I'd moved the Mortar drones to a covered spot on the roof, having them pick off groups of enemies that the Whiskers found. Help did not arrive. I sighed. There were simulations where you had a simple, straightforward objective. In those, you were either destined to win or lose. They were usually pretty obvious. Then there were ones you weren't sure what was supposed to happen. This was one of those. It felt like it could go either way to me, either a win or a loss.

"Advise one of my Whiskers just got taken out after sending me this," Meyers said.

Meyers included an image showing heavy armor. Damn, this one looked like it might be a loss. The core of our score would be how effectively we got out of dodge if we were supposed to lose. I would also be graded on how well I'd done deciding when it was time to leave.

"Command, be advised we have armor heading our way, requesting air support," I said.

I doubted it would come.

"Roger Fireteam Alpha, air support inbound," Monroe said.

"Air is on the way," I told the team.

Command was certainly trying to keep me on my toes about how this would go down. Above us, a drone screamed overhead, firing missiles at the enemy armor. Plumes of smoke and fire rose into the air along with gunfire. A rocket streaked up, striking the drone and blowing it apart.

I pulled up feeds from Whiskers, seeing that the armor was destroyed but that the enemy was coming in force with a large group and its own heavy infantry. We braced for the attack. As we did, I told drones to place charges in the building in case we had to blow it. I also ordered the human team members to find the safest places they could. I laid on the floor on the other side of a wall from Krista. I was not planning on getting into the soon-to-be fight. Early in our training, we went through simulations like this where we had the choice of fighting in the front lines with our drones or taking cover and commanding them. We learned in each of those simulations that you don't take the line. The drones were faster and better at some things than we were. It was better to blend in out in the open or in more dynamic situations. But, on pure defense, we could do a better job leading our PODs from safety. Also, since the drones didn't have to dial down their capabilities to keep us from being noticed, they could work faster and more effectively.

I began checking my POD's zones, looking for holes in them. While it was safer for all of us to be out of the line of fire, I recognized that it left us five rifles short. If our zones started going to hell, we would have to fill those slots or retreat.

The simulations where we went to the front were fun; I won't lie, there's something about going all out and going down in a blaze of glory, but that's not what I wanted today. The enemy made it to our building, and the ground shook as a mortar hit us. Concrete and debris fell on us in small chunks. I terminated my normal vision, leaving only the thermal, metallic, and density views. Another mortar shell hit us. It felt real... too real.

"Boss, you feeling this?" Betts asked.

There was another thud. The shells used in training were fake. What we felt and saw were mostly BS. It had to be. After all, you can't count on what debris will fly around when you legitimately blow something up. Yes, each shell had a small charge, but it was just to give the feel of the real thing. That's not what this felt like at all.

"Shit, there must be something wrong with the drones; those are real mortar shells," I said, realization taking hold of me.

I looked through the view of one of my drones, seeing it tag an enemy that got back up, confirming what I thought. During simulations, despite what our CCPUs said, we fired frag ammo that broke apart on contact, thus not doing any actual harm. The enemy shot the same, and we all pretended it was real, except an enemy got back up this time. I sent a clip of this to the team.

"Advise there is something wrong in the simulation; our rounds won't work. I'm contacting command," I said to the Fireteam.

"Fucking pain in the ass," Meyers grumbled on the comm.

For once, no one was going to argue with him.

"Fireteam leader, what do you want us to do in the meantime?" Betts asked.

I sighed, "Keep working as if everything is still working correctly until command gets back to us."

"Command, there is a problem with the drones. They are firing real rounds, requesting simulation end," I said.

"Roger Alpha, we are investigating," Monroe said, his tone slightly strained.

"Command is checking," I said to the team.

There was another thud.

"I don't like this," Betts said.

"I'm with you; prep for EVAC. I'm not sure how much actual abuse this structure is supposed to be able to handle," I said.

"Fireteam Alpha, advise drone error found. Help is on the way. We cannot end the simulation. This is a real fight now. Your ammo and weapon safeties are removed," Monroe said, his usual calm marred slightly.

As he spoke, I felt a jolt of oh shit, and then an odd calm fell over me, and I was still for only a moment before springing into action. With Monroe's words, my CCPU notified me that my SIR was now fully functional and no longer in training mode, along with the rest of my team and drones.

"We're getting out of here. There's a problem with the drones; we are using real ammo. McLeod, Sweeting, pin them down long enough for Betts and Meyers to move back," I instructed, "this doesn't change our retreat plan; it just means we can't fuck it up."

I took command of the Heavies, moving them toward the enemy. Next to me, the wall was torn to bits as bullets ripped through the concrete. BI4 was shredded, pieces of it flying. That was disquieting. I felt that jolt of fear again. The Heavies began to unload on the malfunctioning drones. Betts and Meyers moved out, high-tailing it to another building. Sweeting went next, leaving Krista and me. She'd only lost a handful of drones.

"McLeod, retreat past Betts's position and cover his retreat," I ordered.

As she started to move, one of the Heavies blew. I looked out a hole in the wall, and my blood ran cold. The enemy armor from before was also part of the malfunctioning drones. It was back up. It felt like my heart stopped beating for a moment before a calm clarity came over me. I pulled up a map of the area. We couldn't hold back the armor; there was no way. We were never meant to. In the simulation, air support took out the armor. This was now outside of the scope our trainers had planned.

On my map, it was obvious that moving quickly wasn't going to be an option. The city was like a fucking maze, and if my team jumped from roof to roof, they'd be easy targets for snipers. I could tell the drones to hold the area, sending each team member with their two mandatory BIs. That would pull fifteen guns from holding the malfunctioning drones back. The other issue was that while the drones were great killers, they needed an operator to truly unlock their potential. I made what seemed like the only decision I could.

"Do you want me to help you hold them back?" Krista asked.

It's like she knows what you're about to do. I took command of every drone I could, bringing them to my location.

"Fireteam, run like hell, get out of here. There are no enemies at our backs. I will hold them and get out before I blow the building," I ordered.

Betts, Sweeting, and Meyers bought my lie and continued booking it; they weren't still in the objective building getting hammered like Krista and I were. She knew I was lying. She hesitated for a moment.

"Krista, go," I said over a line to her.

"Thanks," she said, her voice thick. She touched my shoulder.

She sprinted from the building. I breathed a sigh of relief; at least she was getting out. I felt like my CCPU should be pouring stress-reducing chemicals into my blood, but it wasn't. For some reason, I was calm in a way I had never been before. I picked up my SIR, moving back into the building, sending drones before me, drawing all of the enemy's attention. They started to enter the building as drone after drone went down. I had an idea. I set the timing on the charges with my CCPU; even if I died, at least my teammates would make it out. The wall to the room I was in burst, and an enemy came in. I shot it, bits of metal flying off. The wall next to me crumbled, and another one of the enemy troops came in, but too late for it. I detonated the charges.

My display went blank, and I was immersed in darkness for a moment, feeling nothing. Then my display came back online, reading "simulation end." I blinked. What?

"Now that's what I'm talking about!" Monroe yelled over the comms, "Good work, Taylor, report back to the staging area!"

My display reactivated, and I saw an enemy drone standing in front of me. It held out a hand. I took it as it helped me up. My CCPU pinged, letting me know that I was in control of all the drones in the area and to take them with me to staging for repair. The malfunction was fake. Instantly, I got angry, and then I laughed.

"That was all BS?" Meyers asked on the comms.

"It was a simulation, and I can still see what you're thinking, soldier, and that's not a nice thing to think of your Commanders," Monroe said.

"You guys earned it!" Meyers spat.

For some reason, that made me laugh more. I felt tension leave in a shaky, steady flow.

———

I SAT IN THE MIDDLE OF MY TEAM IN THE DEBRIEFING ROOM, A BEAMING Monroe standing before us.

"I knew that you guys could do it," he said. He pointed at the vid screen behind him, which pulled up our scores and our Fireteam's score against that of other Fireteams. My jaw nearly hit the floor.

"That was the highest score?" I asked.

"Of this training group, yes, it was," Monroe said. His expression became serious, "By this point, you all know how to command your PODs, but commanding each other is different." He looked at me, "Today, you showed that you know your team's weaknesses and strengths. You used them, and when everything went bad, you saved your team first and sacrificed yourself. Add to that, you completed the mission. As a team, you have come together to help other members out where they needed it." He said, "Taylor, you started that, didn't you?"

"Sweeting and Betts played a big role..." I started to say.

"I know they did, but when McLeod was having a hard time, it was you who started to pitch in, and you who took the most time. And did you see her today?" Monroe asked, pointing at Krista, "Did you see her tear it up out there?" He looked her in the eye, "McLeod, when you started, you were the worst recruit we had bar none, and now you're ranked fairly well overall, but in support... well, let me just be the first to say there aren't many people here that I'd rather have covering my back than you."

I watched Krista as she smiled, obviously trying not to show emotion, "Sweeting, Betts, and Alex—uh, Taylor did it; they helped me." She tripped over my name a bit.

Monroe nodded, "They helped you, that's right. That is what a Fireteam does. They help one another. Meyers, you need to get on board." He said, but then quickly moved on, directing his comments to me, "But you were the one who figured out how to help her. You figured out how to best use each member of your team to ensure that they did their best. You picked the best person for the job, even if that meant you didn't get credit for it. And you were willing to sacrifice yourself for your team, and that is just one of the reasons why you're the Fireteam leader. Welcome to command. Congratulations, you are promoted to Corporal."

Monroe grinned at me, extending his hand. I took it in a firm shake, not really believing that I got the Fireteam leader spot. Sweeting and Betts clapped my shoulder. Betts looked happier than I felt and a little bit relieved. Krista gave me a hug, and Meyers sat, waiting to be dismissed.

"Now!" Monroe said, "From here on out, you will be working in squads. We basically have your squads figured out, but over the next few weeks, we might make some changes. As of right now, you are Fireteam Echo. We have you paired for the time being with Fireteam Delta, which is under the command of Veronica Royle. You have the rest of the day off. Enjoy it. Tomorrow, we will hit the ground running. Congratulations, Fireteam Echo, you did well."

Monroe spoke as we started to leave, "Taylor, McLeod, please join me in my office."

She looked over at me, nervous. I felt a pit start to form in my gut. We followed Monroe down the hall to his office.

The office was modest in size, containing only a desk and a few chairs. The wall to the left featured a floor-to-ceiling vid screen that currently displayed the HFDF logo spinning slowly. Cortez stood by the screen, turning to look at us impassively as we entered.

"Take a seat," Monroe instructed.

We complied, while Cortez remained standing.

"I'm sure the two of you know why we are all here together," Monroe said.

Krista and I nodded.

"It's about our relationship and my promotion," I said.

"Yes, it is," Monroe confirmed. "What do you think I am going to say?" he asked.

I thought for a moment before responding, "That we need to end it."

"I could also say that you can stay together and assign McLeod to another team," he suggested.

Krista tensed.

"I don't want to damage the team," I said in a hurry. "We will get over it, sir."

Cortez laughed, "The hell you will!"

He eyed us as the vid screen changed to display charts and graphs, with a large green 87 at the center.

"So long as you two are around each other, you will have feelings for one another, feelings that will deepen over time. This will lead to dissatisfaction and distraction in the field. You are both great recruits, and the HFDF would like to keep you if possible. No, you two being apart and in the same unit won't work," he explained.

Krista looked down, and I felt like shit.

"What unit will I be with?" Krista asked.

"The one you're in now," Cortez replied, as if stating the obvious. "Christ, the two of you have each read the regulations about this about a hundred times."

"But the regs say it's up to command," I said.

Cortez nodded, "Thank you for stating the obvious, Corporal. It might not have occurred to you that both Sergeant Monroe and I are commanding officers. Yes, it is up to us." He pointed at the 87 again, "This is the chance we are giving your relationship over the next ten years. An eighty-seven percent chance of success. That's a likely second term for each of you." More graphs appeared, and he looked at Krista, "Did you know that once you two got together, both of your scores started to trend up? McLeod, your tactical scores skyrocketed, and Taylor, your command and empathy scores went up. Hell, your relationship with McLeod all but gave you what you needed for us to make you a Fireteam leader.

"For you, McLeod, you've always struggled with a lack of confidence, but that's much less of an issue now. You are now scoring higher than we had anticipated. We estimate a ninety percent chance that this relationship will help anchor your Fireteam together. Fireteams are our families when we are deployed. This will help yours feel that way."

"Even Meyers?" Krista blurted.

Cortez scowled, "Don't interrupt me, Private. To answer your question, no. But that's another issue."

"So we can stay together?" I confirmed.

"Yes, you can," Monroe said. "Today, we tested to make sure there weren't going to be any issues. You had to notice no one else had a simulation like yours."

"That crossed my mind," I admitted. "How did that test me?"

"It didn't," Cortez said. "We knew what you'd do in the end. Once we saw how you used McLeod, we confirmed that she won't negatively impact your ability to command. The real test was for you." He pointed at Krista, "You could have disobeyed orders and stayed, but you trusted your commander and did what you were told regardless of how badly you wanted to disobey. There will come a time when you won't obey that kind of order, but that time will come for your whole team."

Monroe looked pleased, and Cortez's expression showed warmth, something that was rare. "Aside from how this helps the HFDF, I truly hope you two do well. You have been good for one another. The HFDF wants you to succeed, as do we."

Monroe went over some of the finer details regarding Krista and me being together, but as Cortez had said, we already knew them. We stood to leave.

"Corporal, a moment," Cortez said.

Krista left, leaving me alone with Monroe and Cortez.

The screen changed again, now showing Meyers' information. One of the graphs labeled "relationships" was red.

"Private Meyers is going to be an issue," Cortez said. "We do not think that he will cause problems actively for your team, but he will, to an extent, hold it back."

"How do I handle it?" I asked.

Monroe shook his head, "The way you have so far. There's a chance, albeit a small one, that he will improve. His personality shows that once he becomes loyal to people or groups, he is extremely dedicated to them. As for now, he is ranked well, as is your team. We can't remove someone who is doing their job effectively."

Cortez spoke, "That said, he will always be abrasive at best. With luck, he will get on the same page as the rest of you. Also, do not forget that you can never put him in command. We will watch him over his term, but if he starts to become an issue, or you think he will, bring it to my attention. You also need to keep this to yourself; you are in command now and will be privy to confidential information that needs to stay that way, even with Private McLeod."

"I understand," I said.

They dismissed me. When I got into the hall, Krista was waiting for me. As the door closed, she wrapped her arms around my neck as I wrapped mine around her waist. I leaned down and kissed her.

"We don't have to hide this anymore," I said.

She kissed me again, "And I don't need to wake up at the ass crack of dawn to go back to my bunk anymore. Congratulations on the promotion, by the way." We started to walk down the hall. "Do you have any orders for me?" she asked with a mischievous smile.

I took her hand, "A few," I said, giving her a glance.

She laughed, "I can't wait to fulfill them."

Today had been a good day. I was now a Fireteam leader, and Krista and I would get to stay together. Now I just had to figure out this whole being in command full-time thing.

NINE

The showers in the training base might be efficient, quick, and effective, but they lacked one crucial thing, in my opinion: comfort. At home, I would stand in the shower forever, letting hot water cascade over me. It was relaxing and a time to think. In the HFDF, however, those showers would have to be saved for times when I was on leave.

I stepped out of the shower cylinder, dry and clean. In a bin next to me was my suit in a block with two handles on it, and next to it lay my sidearm. I grabbed the handles on the suit, and it flowed over my body. Although I still had years left in my service, I sometimes wondered what it would be like to no longer have the suit. At first, I wondered if it would bother me never having a choice in what I wore and if the suit would become uncomfortable over time, with its helmet making me feel claustrophobic.

So far, it had been just like Cortez had promised. My suit was like a second skin to me now. Even after a few days in the service, I had grown attached to it. It kept my body temperature and overall comfort regulated in a way I wouldn't have thought possible. It moved in subtle ways, ensuring that my foot or any part of my body didn't fall asleep if I was in some awkward position. It stabilized and squeezed me, ensuring that my muscles rarely felt fatigued. I was stronger and faster, and with it being made of nano-material, I could attach almost anything I wanted to it. When it was on, the helmet didn't make me feel like I had anything over my head at all. If anything, the world seemed bigger and more open.

I could remember Cortez showing us how to look at the stars. With the front of our helmet covered in light sensors, we could zoom in on objects kilometers away, or, in the case of stars, make our faces a light bucket catching the light of the heavens. I was breathless as I'd taken in the Milky Way as only previously seen in images. Cortez sent us overlay settings for the helmets, combining several different light wave intakes, making it so that we could see the stars like never before. We could zoom in on Arrow Station, making out ships coming and going. In that, there was a military lesson. If we could see the ships in orbit above us with the relatively small amount of light our helmets could bring in, those ships with far better optics sure as hell could see us on the ground.

I stepped out of the changing chamber and went down the hall to the mess. As I walked, I met up with Royle. After becoming Fireteam leaders, our teams were paired with other Fireteams in the platoon to make squads. My team worked best with Royle's, and she and I clicked wonderfully. When placed together, we consistently scored the highest in the platoon. I was a little worried that our squad would be broken up to allow the platoon to be more balanced, but in less than a week, our two Fireteams were the first in the platoon to be placed in a permanent squad. And the other squads had been left playing a seemingly impossible game of catch-up.

We sat down at a table, and I brought up a list in my CCPU, sharing it with Royle. In it were each of our team members' names and what they had accomplished. Our squad, Fireteams, and individuals had completed everything they needed for graduation minus the last exercise, which was our first and only live training jump from space onto a planet. I was only slightly worried about it. I knew I shouldn't be; it should be kind of fun, and the tech we had seldom failed, but there was always the knowledge in the back of your head that if the entry pack or space anchor failed, you'd burn up in the atmosphere.

The exercise was the last thing we would do in training. We had done simulation after simulation of it, not to train us, per se, but to get people comfortable with it. Cortez continued to point out that gravity, our suits, and packs did all the heavy lifting. All we needed to do was fall. Well, fall and not panic, but even our CCPUs helped with that if needed.

Royle's eyes seemed out of focus. She was probably looking at the same list as me. She and I had made quick work of getting our people trained. But that gave us several weeks of squad training time to fill, weeks that provided us the opportunity to further improve our squad. It shouldn't have been as stressful as it was.

"So, I think we should start working on more hand-to-hand combat. I know we aren't supposed to get into much of it, but you never know when we'll be called to deal with a human terrorist group or find ourselves needing it while fighting some alien that's close enough to us," she said.

"I agree. Our squad's marksmanship is overpowered compared to hand-to-hand. I was also thinking of working on stealth. I'm not sure there's been a military unit that was pissed that they were too good at hiding from the enemy," I replied.

She looked thoughtful and then nodded in agreement. This was the joy of working with Royle and the genius of how Cortez and the HFDF built Fireteams and squads. They tried to put you with people you worked well with. In the case of Royle and me, it was great. We thought the same way, and in combat, we worked more like one person rather than two. We spent our days in constant communication, and that was not a bad thing. We didn't always agree, but we resolved those disagreements quickly and efficiently. I couldn't think of a time when she'd gotten on my nerves, and she was pretty open about the fact that I'd never gotten on hers either.

Our training squad leaders told us that was important. The role of the squad and Fireteam leader had changed over the years. Whoever our squad leader would be, they would never be in combat with us. Their job was to direct and provide us with what we needed. Monroe pointed out that the squad leaders could be stationed on Arrow and be almost as effective as when in the field.

We continued to talk about the squad for a while before the conversation turned away from the HFDF. Working the way we did, it was easy to start becoming friends. We were discussing some of the dynamics in her Fireteam when we were pinged by Monroe.

"What do you think he wants?" she asked. "I hope they aren't planning on splitting up our Fireteams."

"Do you think they'd do that? Everyone works so well together; even Meyers found a friend," I said, referring to Patrick Retz on her team.

We walked to Monroe's office to find him sitting behind a desk. He motioned for us to take one of the two seats in front of him. Behind us, the door automatically closed. Monroe looked at us with a friendly expression.

"I've got some good news and bad news for you two. How do you want it?" he asked.

"Good first?" Royle suggested.

"Okay," Monroe said. "The good news is that your entire squad is at graduation level weeks ahead of the rest of the platoon. Don't worry, we aren't going to break you up to even out the platoon."

"And the bad news?" I asked.

Monroe's smile deepened. "The bad news is that squad leaders have been, and you two get to be stuck listening to me for the next five years."

I couldn't help but smile, as did Royle.

"Is it too late to transfer service jobs?" she asked.

Monroe laughed. "Good try. Honestly, I'm really looking forward to working with you two. I've been impressed with both of you for a while, and I think you're ready for the next level."

"Next level?" I asked.

Monroe grew serious. "Yes. As you've probably noticed, up to this point, we have been trying to keep the platoon at an even level. You've probably also noticed that the three other platoons in the company are scoring about the same as ours. What you might not have noticed is that in each platoon, there is a squad that is always on top. In our platoon, that is our squad. That's why you get me as a squad leader. The squad I oversee in our platoon is a member of a group called Special Teams. Don't mistake this with Special Forces; those people could run circles around us. But each Spaceborne platoon has an elite squad, a squad that gets extra training and is pushed a lot harder than the others. That's you guys."

He let that sink in for a moment.

"You will have much harder missions on the ground and be more isolated. That also means you will be in accelerated training programs over the next few weeks. Programs that will remain accelerated for your time in the service." He took a moment to look at both of us. "I was in Special Teams during my first term. Let me tell you, it's not going to be easy. You won't always be on more important missions than other squads in the platoon, but you will see a lot more intense action. You need to be ready for it. What you do will be important. The three of us will be working together a lot, every day in fact. Can I count on you two?"

We both told him he could. I should have felt intimidated, but I didn't. This was why I joined the HFDF: to prove that I could do something. That opportunity was here now, and I was looking forward to it.

"Good," he said. "Like I said, we will be talking a lot. I find it helpful to get to know each other better, so tonight I want you to come have dinner with my fiancé and me. She's in charge of the Special

Teams squad in third platoon, and they'll be there. It will be good for you to meet them."

"Were you and her on the same team together?" I asked.

He shook his head. "No, we met in our first terms, but it was during a training exercise in another system. We kept in touch until the end of our term. We both went down the command route, and here we are."

"Was it a pain to get transferred with you being from different systems?" Royle asked.

"Nah, it was pretty easy. We kind of thought that it would be difficult. Thankfully, neither of us really cared about which system we were assigned to, and Hunter had openings. That said, from other people we've talked to, it's not uncommon that there's some shuffling around between the systems," he said.

We got up to leave, making our way back to our respective rooms. Most of my team was gone when I got in; Meyers' bunk shade was closed, and Krista was lying in hers, her eyes out of focus. I sent a message to the team telling them to meet back in the room in five. As I walked up to Krista, she turned to look at me.

"How was your day?" I asked.

"Fine. We spent it in VR pods doing one-on-one simulations. How was yours?" She asked.

"Good. Royle and I have a plan for training, but I have some news. I also have dinner with Monroe tonight."

The team started to file into the room. Meyers' bunk opened.

"So, what could have been more important than me schooling Betts at the firing range?" Sweeting asked.

I snorted a laugh. "I'm sure you were smoking him."

Betts laughed. "He did, honestly! I didn't know we were competing to see who was the slowest and least accurate."

"That's cold, man," Sweeting said.

I cleared my throat. "I had a meeting with Monroe today. He

informed me that he will be our squad leader permanently after today."

Everyone but Meyers looked happy about that.

"He also said that we have completed everything we need for graduation and that we are the top squad in the platoon. This isn't news to us. What is news is that we are no longer going to be normal Spaceborne." This got their attention. "We are now going to be Special Teams. Each Spaceborne platoon has a squad like this. We are to be an elite unit, and our training will ramp up considerably. In combat, we will have harder, more demanding missions."

Betts nodded slightly with a smile, and Meyers looked happy now. Krista appeared a little apprehensive, while Sweeting, well, he always looked happy. "I don't know more than that right now. Tomorrow we will begin a new training regimen that I suspect will be exhausting. So get some rest tonight. That's all."

Betts and Sweeting left, and Meyers went back into his bunk, leaving me with Krista. I put my hands on her hips.

"You're going to do fine," I said before she could say anything.

"Thanks." She sighed. "So I don't get you tonight, and we have crazy training starting tomorrow?"

"Sorry," I said. "Maybe dinner won't be long."

She shrugged. "Nothing to be sorry about. This is the job. I doubt it will go late."

I leaned down, kissing her. My CCPU pinged, letting me know Royle was waiting for me outside. I kissed Krista again. "I've got to go," I said.

"Have a good dinner," Krista said. "And I expect a report on what Monroe's fiancé is like."

———

DINNER HADN'T BEEN BAD. IT CONSISTED OF SANDWICHES AND STORIES from Monroe and his fiancé about their time in the HFDF. I liked the

Fireteam leaders from the other platoon and was looking forward to getting a chance to work with them. After dinner, the two people from third platoon left, leaving Royle and me with Monroe and his soon-to-be wife, Sergeant Terra Bramley. She was blonde with a thin build and carried herself in the same controlled way that Monroe did. Their quarters weren't much larger than the squad room Royle and I were used to. It was a single room with its own bathroom and shower. Near the front was a small kitchenette and table. We'd had to sit on the bed, which was normal-sized, and against the far wall.

We sat at the table, sipping cups of coffee. "So, are the two of you looking forward to Special Teams?" Bramley asked.

"Yeah, I think it will be good," Royle said.

I echoed her. "It hasn't always been easy so far, but I'm looking forward to more challenges."

She smiled knowingly. "That's good. They'll come your way."

I couldn't help but notice their room and how small it was. Monroe caught my gaze.

"What, Taylor? Do our spacious accommodations not impress you?" he asked with a laugh.

"Sorry," I said. "I'm sure you get used to it, but I kind of thought that non-Service Term people would have a little bit...."

"Better?" Bramley finished. "This is just for when we are planetside training Service Term troops. On whatever ship we're assigned to, our quarters will be more comfortable but not large. There's enough room to eat, sleep, shower, and relax a bit. I wish I could say that the accommodations got better with rank, but they don't. Though the higher you go, you get access to more shared space aboard a ship." She finished with a shrug.

Monroe smiled at the room. "When on deployment, we spend most of our time in modified VR pods. We have access to everything in them, including food and waste systems. We each have fully customized interface systems in them. It makes the information dumped on you when you first got your suit seem small. Trust me, after you've spent a few weeks in one, you'll think a room even this size is massive."

I thought about that for a moment. I'd always wondered where our leaders were when in command. VR pods made sense. I could see the advantage of being in a fully immersed world as you commanded troops planetside.

Shortly after we left, I met Krista back in our room. We slipped into my bunk, shutting the screen. For a while, we'd tried having the walls make us feel like we were in the forest or even a regular bed, but that had only managed to remind us of how small an area we could lay in despite what our surroundings were. We'd finally settled on soft white.

"How was dinner?" she asked.

"Fine. The room was tiny. I was a little worried that was the norm for couples, but they said it wasn't." I sent a picture of the room to her. "I'm glad it gets better. It'd suck if we had to live in a little room forever."

She smirked. "So you're already thinking about *our* living quarters for the next term, huh?" She emphasized the word "our."

I laughed. "Just curious. Why, are you not? We do have an eighty-seven percent chance of another term, you know?"

She kissed me. "No, we don't," she said. "After they placed us in Special Teams, I asked one of the trainers if that impacted you and me. The HFDF gives us a ninety percent chance now, something about the demand of the job reinforcing bonds."

"That's impressive," I said, smiling.

"Do you find it a little creepy how the HFDF can do that?" I asked.

"You have no idea," she said.

I laughed. And while I found it a bit creepy, I was hopeful that they were right. I hadn't even really cared for the prospect of being in a long-term relationship, but with Krista, the idea sounded nice.

TEN

I stood looking over my gear one last time. Around me, the rest of my squad was busy with theirs. To my right, Krista secured her pack to the back of her suit and looked at me with a small smile. It had been several weeks since we'd become Special Teams—weeks made up of days and hours that had melded into one seemingly long day. Our training schedule kept us separated from the rest of the Company, except for the other three Special Teams squads. Our training had turned into custom-made lessons that pushed all of us to the absolute edge of what we could mentally, physically, and emotionally withstand.

We were all together—different soldiers and, in many ways, different people. Our scores showed it. Even the seemingly weakest among Special Teams dominated the strongest of the regular units. I had watched Krista go from being near the bottom to consistently placing in the top five in the platoon. In a way, it was frightening, and I could only imagine what the HFDF's Special Forces units were like. Within weeks, we had surpassed our fellow recruits, but the true elite of the HFDF had decades more training and experience than we did.

I flashed Krista a smile as we wrapped up prepping for our final exercise, which would be with the entire platoon. We were working under our graduated organizational structure, putting us in F Company, Second Platoon, First Squad. I commanded Fireteam Alpha, and Royle commanded Fireteam Bravo. We would jump into the exercise zone from a shuttle in low orbit. The birds would be in tight formation when they dropped us out towards Arrow.

I called our squad to attention, and we formed into two lines—one led by me and the other by Royle. Our teams moved quickly and professionally, the routine of prepping for a mission having been drilled into us to the point where it was second nature. We walked out of the prep room and down a gray metal hallway into a massive hangar that housed the shuttles.

The shuttles were large, resembling a flying wing shape with bulges on the top where the pilot's cockpit was. There were no windows on the shuttles, their skin a smooth matte black nano-material that could toggle between several color profiles depending on their environment. The nose of the crafts opened to reveal a big cargo hold where we'd be riding. Already in the back of the space were the folded forms of the Heavies and Mortar Drones. Our BIs and BBALLs would join us shortly. First Squad stood at strict attention as the other squads in the platoon entered the hangar.

For them, today would be their first and last training jump outside of simulations. For us, it was number twenty. Second Squad lined up next to us, one of their Fireteam leaders standing next to me. He stood at attention, but it wasn't like ours; it seemed to lack some of the discipline that First Squad had. It was, by and large, better than that of new recruits but somehow seemed incomplete or lacking in conviction. From the corner of my eye, I could tell he was nervous.

"It's not as bad as you think," I said softly. "Your suit and CCPU do all the work. That's why you only have one jump to graduate."

He nodded slightly, breathing out. "But why have you guys jumped so many times? And what have they been doing with you? We never see any of Special Teams anymore," he said, just as softly.

I couldn't help but smile. What had they done to us indeed?

"This jump is to get your nerves out, or at least that's what we were told. We're here to learn to integrate with the rest of the platoon and you with us. As for why we have jumped so many times, it was mostly in bad weather, so we could learn how to deal with that. We have to be more accurate with jumps and not freak out jumping into a storm or landing in heavy fire. As for training, it's…been intense, let's say that."

He didn't comment.

The rest of the squads entered the hangar, all displaying the same lack of composure as Second Squad. We stood in a block, our squad leaders coming to stand before each squad facing the shuttles. They would not be joining us in the drill, just as they wouldn't in actual combat, but would be guiding us from afar.

Cortez entered, standing before everyone. "Today is your last exercise as trainees. Each and every one of you and your squads has hit their graduation goals. But do not let that lull you into apathy; today, you fight as a complete platoon for the first time. Today, you will distinguish your platoon and Company for the rest of your term. Take today lightly, and in the future, generals and other companies will know what manner of soldiers you are!" He smiled at all of us, but it wasn't an overly kind smile; more like he was in on some joke that the rest of us weren't. "Some of you might think that I will not be part of your life after today. I know this must be a sad thought," he said sarcastically.

I restrained a chuckle. Cortez was a hard ass, but he did it for the right reasons. First Squad, along with the rest of the Special Teams squads, knew that firsthand. Most of the Company had a grudging respect for their head trainer, but for me and mine, we'd learned what we could do if we took his as the word of God.

The HFDF had instilled in us a type of masochistic joy at being pushed to our limits. I was proud of who I had become in a short time under Cortez's training. I could only imagine who I would be five years from now.

"My team and I will be monitoring and working on training programs for each of you and your units for the rest of your terms. Trainers such as myself handle only a handful of companies, so don't worry; I will continue to be a part of your life," he said with a wicked grin. Then he laughed. "I can see from your faces and from my CCPU notifications that all of you, save First Squad, aren't happy about this! In fact, each one of them feels happy and excited about that thought. Do you think they are all sick in the head? First Squad, are you a group of sick masochists?" He barked at us.

"SIR, YES SIR!" we all shouted without hesitation, and we meant it.

Cortez walked up to us. "You like training and pushing yourselves, don't you, First Squad? You like taking on the hardest missions, don't you?"

"SIR, YES SIR!" we replied again.

"You know we are going to drop you into the deepest shit on deployments, and you know you will face the biggest risks. Do you like the idea of this, First Squad?" Cortez asked, his grin widening.

"SIR, YES SIR!"

Next to me, the guy from Second Squad shifted, glancing at me like I was a bit of a nut along with the rest of my team. I couldn't help but smile just a tad.

Cortez smiled genuinely, speaking to everyone and pointing at me and my squadmates. "These crazy sons of bitches will do your platoon proud! They have been taught not to know how to fail! If the time comes that you and your team are in danger, these will be the people that save your asses! I would recommend following their example! Now let me introduce you to your new CO for the duration of your service, Major Steven Breeze."

A man with short black hair and tan skin stepped forward, inspecting the platoon. "Good morning, ladies and gentlemen. I am your commanding officer. None of you, save your squad leaders and platoon leader, have met me, but I have been watching all of you. I am pleased with what I have seen. After graduation, your training company will become Foxtrot Company on the dropship Arbiter. You will be joining five other companies on the Arbiter, along with her general crew, command crew, and air wing. Yours is the only space-borne Company. The Arbiter will be your home for the rest of your Service Term. It is my expectation that you serve your home well." His voice echoed with the smooth control I had come to expect from command.

As he finished speaking, there was the clank of boots on the floor, and my CCPU notified me that eight BIs, along with two BBALLs, were integrating with me.

Cortez moved forward again. "Your drones are here; load up!"

With that, the squad leaders turned and began issuing orders.

"First Squad, move out!" Monroe ordered.

We all engaged our helmets and ran forward. Royle and I stopped at the door; she hustled her team in and then their drones entered, with her standing before her team. I then ordered Fireteam Alpha into the shuttle in the same fashion. I entered last. On either side of me were my BIs, four on each side, with the BBALLs attaching themselves to the ceiling. A nano-material rod extended from the ceiling above each unit, attaching to us at the base of our necks. As it attached, my suit went rigid, holding me in place. I relaxed my muscles. The rest of the platoon was still loading up.

As soon as they were done, command left the room, and the doors to the shuttle closed. I brought up a feed from the outside of the shuttle as the air was purged from the hangar, and the shuttles backed out. The tarmac outside the hangar was bathed in Arrow's persistent red light, and I couldn't wait to leave the planet. I knew the cities were nice, but after spending time in Arrow's wonderful outdoors, I was looking forward to new scenery. Our shuttle taxied to the take-off area ahead of the rest of the platoon. The pilot came over our comms.

"Good morning, First Squad, this is Captain Goldberg. Our call sign is Trainer-358," a cheerful female voice said. "Last training jump today. You excited?"

"Roger 358, thank you for the lift," I said. "It will be nice to be done with training."

"You gonna miss us, Goldberg?" a woman named Janet Kwasny from Royle's Fireteam asked.

"Nah, I'll see you on the Arbiter," Goldberg said.

"You're going up with us?" Royle asked.

"Yep, ships train together. Every Company aboard the Arbiter is at the beginning of their term—well, minus career people like us shuttle pilots. But I won't have the pleasure of shooting any of you into space again, sadly; I'll just be picking you up planetside and bringing in infantry," she said.

"So you're who we'll be taking anti-aircraft measures out for in combat, is what you're saying?" Kwasny asked.

"That's right, so try not to suck at your jobs, alright," Goldberg said. "Hold up; I've got to talk to Tower."

I felt, as well as saw, the shuttle start to move forward and up. As it gained speed, it tilted skyward until the nose pointed to space. Magnets in my suit's boots activated, keeping my feet comfortably planted to the floor while my rigid suit connected to the ceiling, holding me in place. I relaxed as best I could as the shuttle accelerated in Arrow's thin atmosphere. My CCPU had already made it so that my body couldn't feel sick, and the biotech in my stomach kept my breakfast from being forced out. All in all, what was supposedly once a very unpleasant experience wasn't all that bad.

My CCPU downloaded our mission for the day. We were to jump onto the planet's surface, take out any anti-aircraft emplacements, then take and hold a staging building. Well, First Squad was to take the staging building while the rest of the platoon dealt with anti-aircraft. For today's purposes, the staging building was an ammo depot that would be fortified. On the way, First Squad was to deal with any anti-aircraft emplacements we encountered. The forecast showed that the weather was going to turn to shit about an hour after we jumped in, with moderate winds upon our arrival. I sighed. The weather was undoubtedly part of why our platoon's final was so easy. We didn't have a lot of time. For First Squad, we'd spent a lot of time in Arrow's storms; I'd even had the pleasure of spending a night in one. I'd laid on the ground using my multipurpose block of nano-material for shelter, along with drones and their blocks, for a whole night while the shelter was buffeted by wind and rock. The entire thing had been held down by running nano-material cables into holes we had drilled in the rock. It had been peachy. It wasn't the original plan, but Arrow's storms got out of hand in a hurry.

I vowed that we would take that building before the weather went south, so we didn't have to spend another night like that. I sent a message to my squad to that end. Royle reminded me that the whole platoon needed to be safe and sound to pass the final. I sighed again.

I toggled from the bird's exterior cameras to a map of the drop zone. The DZ was wide open plains leading up to the objective, nestled at the bottom of a cliff. When the storm hit, the wind, sand, rock, and whatever else the storm grabbed hold of would whip around the objective area. This could give us an advantage holding the building but would make for a terrible night.

I pulled up the drop vectors for the rest of the platoon and their expected targets.

"Alpha Team, this is Charley Team," the guy from Second Squad said over a private channel.

"This is Alpha; go ahead," I responded.

"Is that weather going to be a problem?" he asked.

"Negative, the brunt of the storm shouldn't hit for about an hour; we will be dropping into moderate wind." I paused, trying to decide what else to say. "Charley, once you are planetside, take out your objectives as quickly as you can and get to the depot for cover. Trust me when I say you don't want to spend the last night of our training sleeping under a pile of drones."

"Will you guys be done taking the depot in time?" he asked.

I merely laughed over the comms. As the connection cut, I opened a line to the entire squad. "First Squad, I just had a conversation with Second. They seem skeptical of our ability to take the objective before they are done with theirs."

Sweeting barked a laugh. "How much you wanna bet we have to take out at least one other Squad's targets?"

The pilot came on, her tone professional. "First Squad, we are two minutes to drop."

I addressed my team directly. "Alpha Team, we are two out; last checks confirm."

The chatter stopped, and everyone confirmed their final checks. The shuttle's interior went dark, and then a red light came on. In front of me, the door opened slowly, revealing Arrow in front of us. I checked my equipment one last time and ensured my SIR was correctly situated on my chest in its compact setting. My CCPU ran a check on the twelve mini thrusters placed on my shoulders and lower legs. These were the only extra gear we carried into a jump compared to that of regular infantry; even they had entry packs. But unlike us, if they found themselves falling to a planet, it was because something went terribly wrong, and the goal was just to get them on the ground in one piece. The thrusters were low-powered and small, but they maneuvered us as we dropped in the vacuum of space. They couldn't really change much of our trajectory, but they could help a bit and keep us from running into objects.

Our ceiling tethers retracted, and Goldberg came on the general comm line. "Drop in 5... 4... 3... 2... 1, go go go!"

The lights changed from red to green, a buzz went off in my head, and my body responded in the way drills had taught it to. I took a few bounding steps and leaped without thinking about the fact that I was jumping out of a shuttle into space. I crossed my arms over my chest and straightened my legs. My suit locked me in that position, and the thrusters started to work, facing me toward the planet and into the correct formation with the rest of my squad and drones. It was oddly comforting seeing the planet rush towards me. Arrow was bland and ugly on the ground, but from space, it was actually kind of pretty.

I fell through the silent expanse, using the optics on my helmet to inspect my POD, team, squad, and platoon. Everyone looked the same, their suits forcing them into the proper position, but I couldn't help but wonder how badly they were freaking out. I sure did the first time I jumped. My CCPU beeped, notifying me that we were about to hit the atmosphere.

My suit forced me into a ball, my Space Anchor turning on just a bit. As it activated, it felt like someone was tugging on the back of my neck, where my neck and shoulders met. Underneath me, my entry pack expanded into a disk that would provide drag and convert the heat of entry into power for my anchor.

This was the most exhilarating and frightening part of dropping in. My anchor was the only system I had that didn't have a redundant counterpart. If my anchor malfunctioned in the atmosphere, one of my BIs could probably grab and hold onto me until we were on the ground. If it failed on entry...my entry pack and suit could only handle so much heat. I tried not to think about becoming a comet to the people of Arrow.

I started to get bumped and rattled as I hit the atmosphere, gas streaking in my field of view. My anchor hadn't fully engaged yet. My pack's readouts showed quickly rising temperatures. When the thin disc I was sitting on hit three hundred degrees, it started converting heat into power that ported to my anchor. All at once, I felt like I was being compressed into the entry pack as the anchor ramped up, its output getting more powerful with each degree of heat. I slowed rapidly. Outside, there was a rushing sound of air, and I was jostled about uncomfortably. It was what I imagined it would feel like to sit on a jackhammer. My helmet had a bit of material in my mouth to keep my teeth from clacking together, and I felt my spine compress with the deceleration.

I tried to tell myself that it was actually worse for the regular infantry. The shuttles could take a lot more heat and made a bigger target, so they came in fast, the infantry inside pulling 10 g's before nose-diving to the ground where the shuttle stopped right before gears down. Fuck that.

The heat on my pack died down, and it folded back up. I was in the air now and maneuvered myself around. My display brought up a glide path, and I followed it. Below was the red barren land of Arrow, wisps of wind blowing dirt and sand about. My anchor activated again right before I hit the ground, slowing me down. My feet hit the ground, and my legs and suit absorbed the impact in a crouch. As my feet touched down, I deployed my Whiskers and released my SIR, its barrel and stock extending. I found a large rock and moved to it, shouldering my rifle.

———

GRADUATION CAME WITH ALL OF THE POMP AND FORMALITY THAT YEARS OF movies had trained me to believe it would be. What the movies didn't show was just how boring the whole affair could be. By the end, I had decided that I hated all graduations and never wanted to hear another speech again in my life.

Back in our room, I did one last check to make sure I hadn't left anything behind, which was pretty easy considering I had never opened the case I had come to training with. Our packs and SIRs would be meeting us on the ship. Still, we had our sidearms on us, and I quickly checked how much ammo I was required to carry. We had two choices. Besides the ammo block in our sidearms, we could bring one block with us or our Reloaders. The latter were small and blended in seamlessly with our suits. I chose that option.

I took Krista's hand as we exited the room for the last time. We passed trainees in the halls as we headed for the shuttle that would take us to Arrow City. My team all flopped down in seats in the center of the shuttle. I didn't care if I had a window seat or not; I knew precisely what Arrow looked like.

Krista squeezed my hand as the shuttle started to move. "Are you looking forward to leave when we get to Orion?"

I smiled. "I am. Are you looking forward to meeting my friends and parents?"

"Yeah, no pressure," she commented dryly.

I leaned my head back and closed my eyes. "Come on, there really isn't any pressure. They just know that we'll be fighting alongside each other for the next five years and living in tight quarters, which is a huge commitment for a new relationship. So, you know, they're just a little curious." I couldn't help but smile.

"That's fucked, man," Sweeting said next to me with a laugh.

"Ass," was all Krista said.

Arrow City was just as busy as it was the last time I'd been there. It was jarring being around ordinary people after weeks on base. I'd gone from a world of slate gray to every color imaginable, along with everything else society had to offer. As we entered the main terminal, we found a food court. We had about an hour before our car would head up the Shaft to Arrow Station.

My mouth watered as I took in the array of restaurants before me. The food we'd had in training was good but limited. I was done with meatloaf. I found an Italian place and ordered more food than I could possibly eat. I got a few questioning looks from other people, but any shame I felt about my order disappeared when I found my squad. I wasn't in the minority. I grinned, taking a place between Royle and Betts.

"We're gross," Kwasny said with a grin as she looked at the tray of BBQ in front of her.

It was true; we were gross. None of us finished our meals, and I felt like I had a bit of a waddle as I made my way to the gate. I sat at a window seat this time. While I didn't care for Arrow on the ground, I'd learned that I loved seeing it from space. It hit me in that moment—I no longer lived on a planet. None of us did. Our homes were the stars now.

That was the thought that held me as Arrow dropped away, revealing the view of the massive city stretching from horizon to horizon. As we ascended, the planet's ruddy landscape appeared, contrasting with the city—a view that soon turned to the black of space.

After arriving at the station, Krista and I found our way to our new home. We walked up to a large viewing window, looking out at the bow of the dropship. My mouth fell open with a plop. Before me was the hulking form of the H.F.S. Arbiter. Her main hull was an oval that was wider than it was tall, the top and bottom flat, the nose rounded. Sensing my question, my CCPU brought up basic schematics of the ship. She was long, with the back fourth of the ship dedicated to engineering and the Arbiter's main particle cannon and lasers. Forward of engineering, there were extensions that held shuttles and other crafts on the sides and bottom of the ship. The top bridge went up several levels in a block. Right now, she was slate gray, the skin of the hull set to docking colors. This made the Arbiter easy to see for anyone at the docks. Every military ship had several color schemes—one for in the dock that was gray, a bright orange one for search and rescue, and combat black. When a ship went to black, its skin changed to absorb light, catching 99.9% of it. Couple that with a ship's jamming measures, and the Arbiter was hard to find and hit despite the fact that it was the size of a couple of skyscrapers.

Krista and I smiled at each other and boarded our new home. There was a time when manufacturing was expensive, and ships as nice as the Arbiter would have cost a fortune. With modern mining, fabrication, and reclamation tech, the HFDF built and maintained ships at a fraction of the cost and could build a new battleship in less than a week. Every five years, a ship was refurbished to the point where everything was all but new. And even though the Arbiter had been in service for thirty years, she was just as nice and new as the youngest ship in the fleet when Krista and I stepped inside.

The passages were wide enough for several people to walk side by side, and when we got to our room, our whole squad was housed together. Our room was a larger version of what we had on Arrow, the main difference being that it held a squad instead of a Fireteam. By the back wall, there was also an automated bathroom that cleaned itself after each use. The back wall above the desk was a vid screen that went up and turned into the ceiling, showing a feed from the exterior cameras. There was a table with benches as well, though they were secured to the floor lest an enemy attack send things flying about our room. Our bunks had been assigned with Royle and I by the door on the left-hand side. I had the bottom.

The rest of our squad had already stowed their gear and was exploring the ship. Krista and I took advantage of the rare moment of alone time to check out the bunks. They were wider than those on Arrow, which was a nice change. At the base of the mattress, there was room for two suits to fit comfortably, proving yet again that the HFDF's attention to detail wasn't lacking. There was a small shelf at the mattress level and space to sit inside the bunk.

"So, what do you think?" I asked her.

"There's a lot more room than on Arrow." She looked at the vid wall and ceiling. "And the feeds will make this place feel nice. What do you think?"

"I like it," I said.

Midway through dinner, there was a ship-wide announcement informing us that we had left Arrow Station and were heading to Orion. The Skipper came on and welcomed everyone aboard, as well as all the new troops into the HFDF. I joined everyone in the hall with a cheer, excited about whatever adventures would come our way.

ELEVEN

I opened my eyes to pitch-black darkness, my CCPU lightly buzzing in my head. The walls of my bunk began to slowly brighten, casting a warm, honeyed glow over Krista and me. I activated my suit, feeling it slide its way up my feet, legs, and body. Krista was on the side of the bunk closest to the wall, sound asleep. I slid out of the sheets, trying to keep her covered and avoid waking her up. I opened the screen and rolled out of the bunk. From the bunk above mine, Royle dropped down. The rest of the squad was still asleep, but Royle and I, being Fireteam leaders, had an appointment this morning.

"McLeod in there?" Royle asked.

I nodded. "Yeah."

She looked thoughtful. "Are those bunks better for couples?"

"A bit, but they still aren't as comfortable as a normal bed." I chuckled. "Honestly, I hadn't thought much about getting out of bed this morning with her still asleep."

It took her a moment. "Oh yeah, in the buff, huh? Shit, that could be a pain if you needed to hit the head at night—having to make sure she's covered unless you want to risk the squad catching a glimpse."

We didn't say much else as we left the squad room and walked down the Arbiter's passages. We were a few hours away from pulling into port at Orion Station, and technically the Arbiter wouldn't be on active duty until it left the station. So, this early in the morning, there wasn't a lot of activity. I was sure that would change as soon as we were on active duty.

Our early morning meeting was with the ship's chief medical officer and the ship's psychiatrist. When Monroe had informed Royle and me of this, he'd said not to worry and that they met with every Fireteam leader. He'd then given us the choice of meeting with them before the Arbiter arrived at Orion Station or in the evening after the ship had docked. The latter would have meant less time planetside, so Royle and I opted for the morning.

The Arbiter, like all troop transport ships, was vast, and it took Royle and me a decent amount of time to make our way to the sick bay as we followed our CCPUs' instructions through the never-ending maze of passages. When we entered, we were met with an altogether different feeling than the rest of the ship. The Arbiter's passages were matte gray metal, whereas the sick bay was a glossy white. Inside the main entrance were two rounded terminal stations with people sitting at them. Their suits were white with a thick red stripe running from under their arms down to their boots. On the left side of their chests was a red dot with a white medical cross inside.

The two people rose. One was a man with short dark hair, and the other a woman with long blonde hair. They extended their hands to shake ours. We took them, and they introduced themselves, explaining that they were part of the ship's medical crew and that the doctors would be with us shortly.

"Are you HFDF?" Royle asked, slightly confused.

It was a valid question. Their suits appeared to be slightly thinner than ours, and they didn't carry sidearms, nor did they sport any of the slate grays the military seemed obsessed with.

The blonde smiled. "No, we aren't. We are doing our service for the medical corps; we are here as staff for Dr. Albright."

"I have a friend who's in the medical corps. How'd you get stationed here?" I asked, wondering if Liz would ever be assigned to an HFDF ship.

"When we are in our third year of service, they start assigning us to posts like this. We'll only be here for six months to a year before being reposted," the man said.

"Corporals Veronica Royle and Alexander Taylor, good morning," a woman's voice said from further back in the room.

I looked up to see a woman with red hair tied in a tight bun, her eyes a cool blue. Her suit was the same as the other two's, except that instead of a red stripe going down her side, it was military gray, and she had a gun strapped to her leg. From across the room, I couldn't tell if the suit was thicker or not. As all of this registered with me, my CCPU informed me that the woman before me also outranked me. I snapped to attention.

"Ma'am!" Royle and I said together.

The two medical corps people flinched just a bit.

"At ease; there is no need to be so formal with me. You can call me doctor or Doctor Albright."

We relaxed a little. "Yes, Doctor," we said, again together.

This elicited a bit of a smirk from the medical staff.

Dr. Albright smiled warmly at them. "The Corporals are Spaceborn Special Teams; their discipline is slightly more strict than most personnel you'll meet, but I'm afraid you will have to get used to a lot of sirs and ma'ams coming from them, and all of the crew," she explained.

She shook Royle's and my hands, then beckoned us to join her as she walked. We did, passing medical beds with white drones next to them that looked similar to our BIs but with faces wearing calm expressions. To be truthful, I thought they looked pretty creepy with the face and all, but I'm sure someone at some point thought they'd comfort patients. Albright led us into an office with a desk, several chairs, and a couch with a man sitting on it. His suit was pale blue with gray stripes like that of Albright's. He rose, introducing himself as Dr. Philips.

Dr. Albright asked us to sit in the chairs while she sat on the couch.

"How are the two of you this morning? Do you know why you are here?" Albright asked.

We said we were fine.

"Sergeant Monroe told us this was standard procedure. Though he didn't go into great detail about it, ma'am, uh, doctor," I supplied awkwardly.

Albright smiled a bit at my slip-up. "We make it a point to meet with Fireteam leaders. If one of your teammates is hurt or having problems, you are the people who are closest to them in the chain of command. It is beneficial for you to have a working relationship with us and vice versa. Both Dr. Philips and I are HFDF. We received schooling in our respective disciplines after our initial term of service."

"Armored company," Philips said.

"Spaceborne," Albright said.

I liked her more already.

"So, we understand your situations and what it's like to be a soldier," she went on to say.

They talked about our role in keeping our people healthy mentally and what to do if they had any medical problems. They also explained what happened after combat and that we were to give a full report of how our people were doing after an engagement. Philips told us that he met with troopers all the time and that everyone had a mandatory session with him at least once a year. None of this was a surprise to me. The HFDF was built on having its people come home in one piece, physically and mentally, so that we could be productive members of society. This theme had been notably absent from other Human armed forces throughout history. In the HFDF, the brass actually did care about us. None of us were expendable cogs.

The meeting was brief, and we were dismissed after a little while. When Royle and I made it back to the squad room, our CCPUs notified us that we had docked at Orion Station and that the ship would stay docked for four hours while being supplied. We were all free to come and go via the main hatches during that time, but after that, we'd need to wait for scheduled shuttles to come and go from the ship.

As we entered the room, I found Krista waiting for me, sitting in one of the chairs around the table in the middle of the room.

"How was your meeting?" she asked.

"Fine, nothing all that special. Hungry?"

We went to the mess for some breakfast before going planetside. I pulled up a list of contacts in my CCPU and sent a message to Liz and Jon, asking if they were at the station on leave. Liz was on leave for two days and then was to report to a hospital ship. Jon was not on leave and working on one of the Lift crews, but his shift didn't start until the evening, so he was free. I also sent a message to Monica, and she said she had a few hours off that afternoon. Jon, Liz, and I decided to meet and ride the Lift together. I was going to be meeting my parents for lunch, but after that, we were all going to get together. Sadly, Charles was in some deep space observatory, so we wouldn't be seeing him.

I was looking forward to showing Krista around. She'd never been on a planet other than her homeworld or Arrow, and as a result, hadn't been outside unless it was in some type of suit.

After breakfast, Krista and I walked off the Arbiter into the main space terminal. HFDF ships had their own section of the terminal, so we walked into a sea of gray military suits, save for two.

I strode up to Liz in her white and red med suit, pulling her up into a hug. She squeezed me tight, released me, and took a step back, brushing some of her long bronze hair out of her face. She looked me over in my HFDF suit with my sidearm. "You know Monica is going to act all tough when she sees you, right?"

I just laughed. I turned to Jon, whose suit was day-glow orange and looked thicker than mine. Each of the suits was made of nano-material, and I wondered why Jon's suit would require more material than a military one. After all, mine was designed to make me faster, stronger, and a whole bunch of other stuff while stopping enemy fire. He did what? Lift shit? We greeted each other, and I motioned to Krista.

"Krista, this is Liz and Jon. Jon and Liz, this is Krista."

They both smiled warmly.

"So, did they give you a medal for doing this?" Liz asked her.

Krista blushed a bit. "One for bravery," she said.

"They should have given you more than that," Jon said.

"I get a little hazard pay too," Krista said with a shrug.

I rolled my eyes. "Ha ha, funny funny," I said. I looked at Krista. "And see, you thought they'd pepper you with questions."

Liz scoffed. "Why would we want *her* to be uncomfortable?"

"Yeah, we're all pretty aligned on messing with you, man. I'm sure Krista's great," Jon said.

Krista perked up. "You were right. I do like your friends."

Once in a Lift car, I learned more about Liz and Jon's suits. It was impressive how specialized they were. Both could handle being in hard vacuum, which was common among all government-issued suits. Though in the case of Liz, she couldn't spend near the amount of time in space that Jon or I could. They also all had helmets that came on, but Liz's suit was lighter-weight as she wasn't as likely to put heavy strain on her body. It gave her a little more strength, but mostly it protected her from the almost nonexistent chance she came into contact with some sort of pathogen that our bodies couldn't handle. It also gave her incredible fine motor control. She had a utility belt with various medical supplies on it and a space anchor in the same place I did. Hers was for if she needed to get someplace to find a hurt person or when she was aboard a ship. However, she didn't have an entry pack unless stationed in space.

Jon's suit was slightly thicker than military ones and was designed to spend large amounts of time in hard vacuum or any other harsh environment. It made him significantly stronger than my suit, so he could work with heavy loads and had all of the long-term survival gear mine had, such as water filtration and all that built-in, so he didn't need a pack. He also had a space anchor that was three times larger than mine. Jon explained that people in logistics often spent significant amounts of time outside and used the anchor to help them work. Part of his suit's bulk came from a full-time entry rig. Mine came off, and we only wore it on the ship. Jon always had his on, lest he be screwed should he somehow get dislodged from a ship or space station. He was far more adjusted to the harshest environments for long periods of time. I suspected he could spend weeks, months, or even indefinitely in the cold vacuum of space or an equally hot and pressurized environment without issue.

"So, have you guys entered an atmosphere?" Krista asked.

Liz's eyes widened just a bit. "No, thank goodness! We had a thirty-minute lecture on it when I was in training, but they told us the suit does all the work."

"Ditto," Jon said. "What's it like? I know you guys did it a lot. Was it freaky?"

I pulled up my CCPU's memory banks and found a video clip I'd taken. It was common to record every drop so you could learn from it, and there was nothing secret about the footage, so we were free to send it to friends and family if we liked. The one I sent Jon and Liz was a cut-down version from a drop we'd had into one of Arrow's shitty storms.

Krista and I watched their expressions as they watched the video. Liz looked a little sick. "God, I hope I never have to do that. It looks so much more violent than what we were shown."

"Yeah, while you guys were watching, I pulled up some info about your suits. Our entry is a lot more violent than yours," Krista explained. "Apparently, your entry shield starts transferring heat into energy for your anchor sooner than ours, and your anchors use more of their own power to slow your entry before excessive amounts of heat are produced. Your entry is softer than ours but must take longer. Our suits slow us down as fast as they can before letting us free-fall. I bet it's so enemy ground surveillance has less time to get a thermal lock on us." She mused.

Liz laughed. "And another check in the 'hell no' column. Turn into a comet in some planet's atmosphere and then get shot at while you fall to the ground? No thanks."

"I don't know. The entry doesn't sound as bad as the fall," Jon said. "I hear it happens every now and then to people working on the space elevators. Not sure I'd like falling." Then he launched into information about the elevators, getting animated.

I couldn't help but smile. It was good to see some of my friends again and see that they were happy. Liz talked about her training too, and what she'd learned about the human body along with all of the tech inside us. It was pretty interesting for sure. We'd come a long way since my parents' time. In many ways, I wasn't sure how human we were anymore. Now we were something… better.

Our favorite part was watching Krista look out the window. Her eyes were wide with wonder.

"You look like a kid in a candy store," Liz said warmly.

Krista blushed deeply. "Sorry, I'm from a dead world. I've wanted to see a planet like Orion my whole life," she said with wonder.

I squeezed her hand a bit. "So what do you think?"

She shook her head in amazement. "It's so… I don't know, blue and green. I know that sounds dumb, but it's all I see. My home is in pitch black, save for what light buildings produce. This… this is amazing! I mean, we didn't even have a lot of the stuff like Arrow City, where it made you feel like you were on a normal world. People work on dead worlds to see the emptiness of space. Don't get me wrong, it's beautiful seeing the stars all the time, but not like this."

I hadn't thought about what it would be like. I had never been on a dead world before.

At the terminal, we parted with Liz and Jon. We joined my parents for lunch. I worried it would be awkward, but it hadn't been. My mom was friendly, and my dad didn't bombard Krista with too many questions. I think it helped that Krista was so wholly overwhelmed with essentially being outside for the first time in her life that meeting my parents wasn't that big of a deal.

It made me appreciate my home world. I knew many people didn't want to live on Earth-like planets and chose not to, but seeing someone who'd always wanted to see blue sky for the first time was sobering. I'd never really appreciated a tree until seeing Krista tear up seeing one for the first time.

It was perfect that we were meeting Jon, Liz, and Monica at a local park after lunch. There was a small lake with a little pier going out into it for people to look into the water and trees scattered about. There weren't many people around, giving us the feeling of being on our own. Not being surrounded by thousands of people unless you were in a simulation was new for Krista and me. We loved it. We sat on the grass talking.

Liz was explaining that the nutrient packs we received—in Krista's and my case when on a mission, and for Liz and Jon when they had to work long hours—were actually not edible. I'd always found the softish blocks to taste salty and sweet. Liz explained that our CCPUs tricked us into thinking that, and if we turned that feature off, as she'd done once, we'd find that the blocks tasted like a cross between dirt, refried vomit, and a few other things I didn't want to think about. She also said that our bodies couldn't process them and that our biotech had to do it, and that we could actually get nutrients from dirt if we needed, though that would use more calories than we'd get from the soil. She was about to go on when Monica arrived. I'd never been so happy to see her.

She had her new boyfriend with her, a tall, muscular guy named Derek. His hair was cut in a buzz, and his neck was as thick as his chin. Both he and Monica wore suits of deep navy blue with guns in holsters on their hips. The weapons were slightly smaller than HFDF-issued sidearms and looked sleeker. They also looked a lot less sturdy than Krista's and mine. Monica greeted us and introduced Derek to us, and I introduced Krista to her.

"Wow, so this is like a triple date then, huh?" Monica said.

Jon and Liz looked awkward, backing away from each other. I shot Monica a sideways smile, which she returned with a wink.

> ME TO KRISTA: Jon and Liz have had a thing for each other for years but won't admit it.

She smiled.

> KRISTA: You guys are dicks.

> ME: Oh yeah!

"So Monica tells me that you guys are Spaceborne Infantry. What all does that entail?" Derek asked.

"We jump out of troop transport ships and free fall planetside. From there, we basically do what other infantry does. Though Spaceborne tends to be focused on dealing with anything that will slow or endanger landing craft. After the first few waves, we move to more support roles, putting out fires and plugging holes," I explained.

"They are Special Teams," Liz said with pride.

Derek looked at me and chuckled. "So you're some kind of tough one, huh?"

I shrugged. If Derek was anything like Monica, then he was a tough guy with a superiority complex. This was annoying in Monica, but I'd known her my whole life, so I put up with it. But this guy?

Derek pointed at my sidearm. "How are you with that?"

"Best in my squad," I said.

Krista glared at me playfully. "Barely. Betts and Royle will beat you on the next assessment; you got lucky," she said. It was true—well, at least about Betts; I could take Royle.

I just smiled. "Okay, sweetie, whatever you say."

"Mind if I take a look at it?" Derek asked.

"Sure," I said, unholstering my sidearm and handing it to him.

All government-issued weapons had both user and discretionary safeties. The user safeties were so no unauthorized person could use the weapon for anything other than a paperweight. Though when I thought about how heavy my sidearm was, you could also use it to prop a door open as well as it being a paperweight. The discretionary safeties were in the user's CCPU, making sure they didn't shoot someone by mistake.

Krista unholstered her gun and handed it to Jon, who looked curious. He took it in his hand.

"It's heavier than I thought it'd be," Jon said.

"Yeah, it's a gun, buddy," Derek said with a chuckle.

Jon made a face. "My CCPU is telling me that I don't have clearance for this, and all the safeties are engaged."

He handed it to Liz, who said the same.

"Nonlethal user safeties are disengaged, but our normal discretionary safeties are active. I can only see some of the gun's features," Monica said when it was her turn. She hefted it. "Jon's right, Derek; this thing is heavier than I thought."

He bounced it in his hand, inspecting it from all angles. "Yeah, it is. Dang."

Monica handed me her gun. My CCPU integrated with it.

**ALL USER SAFETIES DISENGAGED, ALL DISCRE-
TIONARY SAFETIES DISENGAGED.**

I could see twenty nonlethal rounds and a small ammo block that would be good for maybe another ten lethal shots.

"Shit, man, you only have three nonlethal rounds!" Derek said, amazed.

"I know they're kind of a waste. If we need to use our sidearms, we aren't using nonlethal force. Why do you guys only have a handful of lethal rounds?" I asked.

"Wh-what? You can see that?" Derek asked.

I shrugged. "Yeah, all the safeties are disengaged. I can do anything I want with the gun."

"That's crap!" Monica said. "We can't even use our nonlethals unless our CCPU deems it necessary, but you could just start shooting. And we can't even see what your gun can do!"

"Nah, my CCPU would shut me out if I was unstable like that. But otherwise, yes. I guess the HFDF has more discretion with their weapons," I said, smirking.

Out of the corner of my eye, I saw Liz and Jon suppress smiles.

"And ours can do way, waaayy more stuff," Krista added, still looking at Derek's gun. "I see why the HFDF gets called in when they think law enforcement is going to be getting into a firefight. You guys are seriously under-armed compared to us. Our sidearms can produce hundreds of different rounds, hold way more ammo, and have a lot more power." She said casually. Krista hefted the gun, looking at it and then at ours. I could see the wheels in her head turning. Our weapons looked more like blocks than guns. They were ugly as all get out, but they could get the shit beaten out of them and still kill stuff. "But I've got to admit," she finally said, "yours look a hell of a lot nicer than ours."

Monica's expression darkened, then she smiled lightly, punching my arm. "Well then, why don't you show me what you're made of, if you Defense Force guys are so tough?"

I rolled my eyes, and Jon and Liz groaned.

"Seriously, Monica, are you gonna try to get all macho?" I asked.

"What, you can't handle her?" Derek asked.

Krista glanced at him for a moment before shrugging at me. "I bet our suits have different specs; you might want to make sure you sync yours up," she suggested.

I sighed. "Fine," I said, doing as Krista said and telling my CCPU to have my suit match law enforcement's specs as best it could. Once my suit was sufficiently watered down, I nodded at Monica.

Monica grinned, stepping into an open patch of grass, looking cocky. Every group of friends had that person who thought of themselves as being tougher than the others. For us, that was Monica. She'd been trying to prove that she was a hardcore badass since I met her. She'd spent all her time watching how-tos on fighting and trying to pick sparring matches with all of us for years. But to my knowledge, she'd never taken more than an introductory self-defense course past the videos before her service began. Monica hated to lose. That meant no teacher that might damage her ego.

I followed her to the patch of grass. She bobbed around like she was warming up. "It's on now!" she said animatedly. "We spend one hour a week in training."

That gave me pause. "You spend an hour a week?"

She grinned. "That's right! What, you Defense Force pukes don't have that kind of schedule?"

I could see Krista repress a smirk. No, we didn't have that kind of schedule. We had trained almost every day with hand-to-hand combat. But unlike Monica, ours was always with a new opponent, or I should say, type of opponent. You never knew what the physiology of the enemy would be, so we trained to fight a whole array of body types. We also put time into learning how to beat other humans too.

"Yeah, something like that," I responded to her. "Alright, come on."

Monica got into a fighting stance, her fists up. I did likewise, though my stance was more open than hers. My training kicked in, and my eyes focused on Monica, not looking for her to punch or kick but for indications of her body moving. If you knew how an opponent's body moved, you could see an attack coming. You could also use their body's limits to your advantage.

Monica took a swing at me. I saw the hit coming and knew what direction her fist and body would be going in. I dropped down to the side, letting momentum carry me. Her fist slid by me, her body moving forward. I pressed my hand to her neck while placing my foot behind hers. I pushed, sending her toppling. In the span of a punch, Monica was on the ground, my knee at her neck, and my hand holding her arm.

She looked up at me with wide-eyed amazement that turned into agitation. "What was that? That wasn't fair!"

I couldn't help but laugh. I stood, offering my hand to her to help her up. She took it grudgingly. "We don't fight to be fair. We fight to win. Surely you learned that in your one hour a week of training," I said, slightly sarcastic.

Monica glowered at me. "Yeah, we did. Geez, man, how did you get so good?"

"We train every day," Krista said simply.

Derek and the others looked at her. "Our job is to kill hostile aliens. We spent a lot of time in classrooms, but we spent even more time on the range and learning how to fight and use our drones. Heck, Alex and I are Special Teams; we trained from the time we got up until we passed out at night. Our CCPUs stimulated the hell out of us in training; sixteen-hour days were the norm." She chuckled but got serious. "We don't have backup. We are the backup. We will spend most of our time outnumbered by races we don't even know about right now."

"I guess your job is a bit different than ours, isn't it?" Derek said thoughtfully. "Most of our training is classroom-based, and we spend a lot of time in the field. We're supposed to keep violence from happening. Your job is to be violent."

"Pretty much," Krista said.

Monica looked over at me and smiled a bit. "I guess when I think about it, I wouldn't want my friend going up against some crazy alien if he didn't know how to kick a little ass."

We all sat around talking about our various training, and in the case of Derek, his day-to-day life, for a while, then decided to go to dinner before Jon had to go in for his shift. As we got up from the grass, my CCPU flashed a message making me pause.

ATTENTION ALL ARBITER CREW. REPORT BACK TO SHIP IMMEDIATELY FOR COMBAT DEPLOYMENT. THIS IS NOT A DRILL. ALL CREW ARE TO REPORT TO THEIR POSTS IMMEDIATELY. REPEAT, THIS IS NOT A DRILL.

"Hey, you with us, army boy?" Monica asked.

I looked over at Krista. Her expression was concerned.

"The Arbiter?" she said.

I nodded.

"I just got a message from my ship telling me to report. That we are being deployed to help the Orion Fleet," Liz said, sounding shaken.

"Yeah, that's us," I said. "Krista and I just got orders to report back to the ship. We have a combat deployment. So much for leave."

Jon looked worried, as did Liz.

"What, you're going off to war or something?" Monica asked, surprised. "With who?"

"The Erie," Krista said after a moment. She looked over at me. "I opened the message's corresponding document. It looks like we are going to Erie Prime."

TWELVE

The trip to the Lift was short. Jon was going to accompany Krista, Liz, and me up to Orion Station, but we'd be parting with Monica and her boyfriend planetside. Monica had lost a bit of her normal bravado as we made it to the gate for our Lift car.

I shook Derek's hand. "It was nice meeting you," I said.

"You too. Good luck up there, man," he said sincerely. I was reminded that while Derek might have seemed like a bit of a jerk, he was human, and I was going to go deal with something that wasn't. That put him and me on the same team.

I turned to Monica, and she hugged me tightly, dropping her tough-girl act. "Don't get yourself killed, you hear me?" she said. I squeezed her back. While she came off hard, Monica was actually a deeply caring person, which was why we all put up with her. While she'd been a pain growing up, she'd also looked out for all of us in many ways. Being a cop, I thought, was her way of protecting those she cared about. "You report back to me every day. Just a ping is fine; you can do that. Alright?"

"A ping every day," I said.

She nodded, satisfied. She told Liz to watch herself and Jon that she'd see him later. Her last words were to Krista, telling her that I was kind of a moron and to not let me get myself killed. With that, we got in our car, heading back to the station.

We sat in the front corner next to a large window, watching as Orion vanished below us. Jon and Liz seemed on edge, but I wasn't feeling that. I opened a chat with Royle.

> ME: You worried?

> ROYLE: Nah, not really. Our fatality rate is really low. I'm a little nervous but also kind of excited. You?

> ME: SAME. Same. I'm sure it will be freaky once we hit atmo. If we're dropping in, that is.

FOR HER PART, KRISTA LOOKED LIKE SHE ALSO FELT FINE.

"You good?" I asked her softly.

"Oddly, I am. This is what we do," she said with a bit of a shrug.

I smirked. "You gonna get stressed when we hit atmo?"

She looked at me like I was crazy. "Hell yes I am."

I kissed her. "Me too."

As we entered space, ships came into view. To my right, I could see a bright white one with a red stripe running along it. It was nowhere near the size of the Arbiter, but the hospital ship wasn't the size of a tug either.

"The Healer's Touch," Liz said, looking at the ship. "That's mine," she sighed slightly.

"Hope there's more than one hospital ship going. No offense, but it doesn't look overly big to me, and while HFDF doesn't take a lot of casualties, we do take injuries," Krista said.

Liz perked up a bit. "Oh, there will be others, I'm sure. Probably some from Alpha," she said, referring to Earth's system. Alpha was the most populated system in the Human Federation by a considerable margin. Earth itself still boasted a population of around eight billion people, with another twenty billion in the rest of the system. Humans had built and colonized every planet and moon with a solid surface along with building who knew how many satcities. As a result, Alpha had more people in its service than any other system. All major operations had people from Alpha participating.

"But our ship's size is deceiving," Liz said. She pointed at the ship. "The flat sides along her hull expand out. Most of the time, ships don't need that much space, as human biotech has come so far along that we are really only needed in emergencies and basic checkups. But when needed, the hull expands out, giving it more room on the inside. There are also loads of beds and drones that are kept in tight storage aboard the ship. The Healer's Touch can more than triple its bed count this way."

"That's pretty nifty," Krista said.

I could see other ships leaving Orion orbit now. Massive military cargo ships were departing, their engines glowing brightly. I watched them, wondering why they were already leaving. A hand clapped my shoulder. "Just the man I wanted to see," Monroe's voice said.

Krista and I turned to see our commanding officer. We shot up, saluting. He returned it. "At ease. Sorry, our downtime was cut short."

"Sorry we didn't see you on this car," I said, then pointed at the cargo ships. "Why are they leaving already?"

"Cargo ships aren't as fast as transports or combat ships. It takes them longer to reach jump range. We normally give them a day or two's head start. Also, we have more coming in to be loaded up. Those things have to move a lot of equipment and ordnance to keep us going. Who are your friends here?"

I introduced him to Jon and Liz.

"Pleasure to meet you two, and thank you," he said.

"For what?" Jon asked, confused.

Monroe looked at him. "Not sure if you're working anything for this op, but you will work on an HFDF op at some point. Without logistics people, the HFDF wouldn't move. Our tech would mean nothing without food, ammo, and other supplies. We'd be sitting ducks without you guys; no war effort would be possible. And you," he said to Liz, "a ship's sick bay can take care of lots of wounded people, but hospital ships are truly what keeps us in the fight. I know modern humans don't think much about injury. I mean, hey, we can heal just about anything, right? And our CCPUs shut off pain receptors to keep us from feeling the effects of those injuries. But you guys are the ones who do the healing. Our bodies can't grow back limbs and stitch up holes nearly as fast as you lot can. Do you know why the military doesn't give out commendations for getting wounded in battle anymore?" he asked her.

"Um, ah, I don't know," she admitted.

"Because everybody gets wounded at some point. It's just a fact of life. Not bad usually, but I've been shot by enemies before. If everyone gets hit, there's no real point in making a big deal about it, is there? Point is, when we get hit, we go to you. If it's bad, we go to a ship. If not, then we go to a center you all set up planetside, and you fix us up. Logistics and healers make the military go round and round. And after an op, you lot will get bought more drinks than you could have in a lifetime, trust me on that."

The Lift car made it to the station. Jon, Liz, and I said our farewells as Liz headed off to a shuttle that would take her to the Healer's Touch, and Jon went to see if the station crew needed help. That left Krista, Monroe, and me to head to our own shuttle. Our ride back to the Arbiter was packed with other crew members, and the ship's corridors were thick with people.

"Go to your room. I'll let you know when the briefing is," Monroe said.

Krista and I made our way back to our room. When I got there, I did an inventory of my Fireteam. Betts was still on the Lift, but the rest of the team had made it back already. When we entered, Sweeting jumped down from his bunk.

"Do you know what's up?" he asked.

"Probably not more than you do," I said as Royle tended to some of her Fireteam. "Just that we are going to war."

Sweeting seemed amped up. "So this will be it, huh?"

Royle's people also seemed a little on edge. Our first mission in active duty was not going to be a training exercise with some other human planet. It was going to be actual combat.

"Listen up!" I said, deciding to nip any uncontrolled emotions in the bud. Everyone in the room turned around, giving me their attention. "I know everyone's on edge, but remember what we are. We don't lose our cool. We don't get over-excited or worried; we're elite, remember? Whatever the mission is, we'll go and do our job better than anyone else, and then come home."

The squad relaxed somewhat, with Sweeting's expression shifting from slight excitement to controlled calm. A few of the squad members nodded to themselves. I could see it took them a little effort, but they managed.

Royle came up next to me. "We don't have orders yet, but we know we're going into combat. I suggest you rest, clear your heads, and go over jump protocols."

People went to their bunks, while a few others sat at the table in the room.

"Nice," I said to her softly.

She nudged me. "Nice yourself," she replied.

A few hours later, our squad gathered in one of the Arbiter's briefing rooms, with Monroe at its head. Behind him on the vid screen was the image of a planet with vast oceans and one large landmass surrounded by sizable islands. Above the planet, the words "Erie Prime" were displayed.

Monroe waved his hand at the planet. "This is Erie Prime, formerly known as Orion 234rb, or our first mission," he said.

Once humans truly made it into space, they quickly changed much of how they named and labeled things. One of the biggest examples was renaming Earth's sun; the star had been renamed from Sol to Alpha. For better or for worse, everything was based around Alpha. On Earth, we had a very limited view of the cosmos, and many of us had wondered what alien planets and races would be called if we ever encountered them. Once we did, it became apparent that language and culture weren't quite as translatable as we'd once hoped.

So we, like virtually every other sentient life form, adopted a method of naming. We used our own language. But even with this, there were a lot of stars and planets, and new races were always being discovered. The newly formed Human Federation decided to name stars based on their corresponding Earth constellation and use names associated with that constellation when convenient. Other stars got numbers. If a race was found on one of those stars, a name from a list would be applied to it. There was also a naming convention for planets as well. It made explaining systems much more straightforward and rid society of having to debate over them.

Thus, Erie Prime was part of the Erie System, and the race was accordingly called the Erie. Using Earth as the center of everything had received some flak, as did changing the sun's name from Sol to Alpha. But as we started to glimpse the true vastness of the galaxy and the numerous races, we moved on to better arguments than the labeling system we'd come up with.

"We have known about the Erie for two years now," Monroe was explaining. "They were first discovered by one of our allies, and we and our allies have been studying them ever since. Shortly after their discovery, they were deemed a potentially hostile species, but it would be another year before we'd know if we were correct or not. A year ago, the Erie attacked one of the known Ageless races, one of our allies. Lucky for them, it wasn't the Quiver, or we wouldn't be talking about this today. Then, six months ago, they attacked one of our dead worlds."

Krista shifted at that. I placed my hand on her knee.

"We did not sustain any losses, and the attack was seen as more of a scouting exercise. The planet's defense grid took care of the Erie ships quickly. We contacted the Erie and informed them that if they attacked us again, we would destroy them."

This, I knew, was not an uncommon practice. While war had become relatively inexpensive and easy for humans, we and other races tried to avoid it. It was easy to spread yourself too thin, and with all of the massive expanse of space, there was really no need for territorial disputes. Namely, because space exploration was even cheaper than war. In the case of humanity's expansion, it was also far more economical than war, as it engaged more of society. It wasn't that we couldn't wipe out enemies with ease, but that usually, to completely kill off an alien race required doing significant damage to the planet or planets they inhabited. It was wasteful. Make a habit of that, and the interstellar community would frown on you and eventually wipe you out in turn to protect themselves.

Therefore, the Human Federation had a two-strike policy. Strike one, we warn you; strike two, we do serious damage to you. Should your society recover and come after us again, then we wipe you out. In those cases, we tried to do as little damage to the home planet as possible, but the HFDF would sterilize the planet or planets in question if there wasn't a way around it. Our policy actually made us quite humane, for lack of a better term. One of our closest allies, the Quiver, valued their citizens' lives so much that their military was frighteningly good at finding ways of removing a planet's population without causing vast amounts of damage. And if you messed with them, they went right to wiping your ass out. For races that were on par with the Quiver, they had strong diplomatic ties in an effort to avoid conflict.

Monroe went on. "One week ago, an Erie warship attacked an observatory studying a Red Dwarf. When the Erie arrived and fired on the observatory, the staff rabbited using their shuttles, jumping back into HFDF space. When they did so, the Orion Constellation Emergency Fleet dispatched the HFS Nairobi, a Flair-class battleship. The Nairobi took out the Erie ship quickly. Now, everyone knows our two-strike policy. So here's the simple rundown.

"The Erie attacked us, and we responded by saying, 'don't do that again, or we'll hit back.' The Erie responded by attacking an unarmed science station, and now the HFDF is being sent like the all-powerful hammer of Thor to bitch-slap them back into the Stone Age." His voice started taking on its normal commanding tone.

"Here is the deal, people. Our mission is to take out any and all Erie tech. When the HFDF is done, they will have no infrastructure, no transportation, and sure as hell no way of getting off their home planet."

The screen behind him changed to a diagram of Erie Prime. Space, the planet's atmosphere, and part of its landmass were visible. Monroe pointed to the section representing space. "The fleet will take out everything in Erie Prime orbit. Once that is underway, ships will begin creating corridors on Erie Prime." A red column appeared in the section marked atmosphere when he said this. "These corridors will be what our forces use to deposit air, land, and sea units on the planet's surface; these are our beachheads, and they have to be secure. Once the corridors are opened enough for ground troops, the Arbiter, along with the rest of the transports in the fleet, will jump into Erie Prime space, and the Spaceborne will do its job." He looked at us all. "Our job is to take out enemy anti-aircraft entrapments and secure landing sites for the rest of the army to land. As Special Teams, our squad will likely have some other job with, or on top of, that basic mission. You will find out that job if we have one prior to jumping into Erie space. It is the job of the Service Term infantry units to secure landing sites and set up reclamation and manufacturing locations so that when the career infantry and armor lands, they have drones to work with.

"Never forget. We, as a Service Term Company, are not here to win the war. That is the job of the career troops. We are here to prep and maintain until the career troops can take over. Once the situation on the ground is fully in the hands of the career troops, the Arbiter, along with every other Service Term ship, will leave the area," he said with emphasis.

This was something that Cortez had tried to drill into us. In so many ways, Service Term units were a blunt instrument. We had the training to be able to make advances on a wide variety of worlds. We could do that because we controlled small PODs of drones and used heavy operator oversight in those PODs. But those small PODs were lacking when it came to what was necessary to subdue a planet, as was our jack-of-all-trades training. For one thing, though a Service Term invasion force might be massive, it was still only a fraction of the size required to control a planet. We didn't have the necessary bodies for managing that many small PODs. Career units had more specialized training, and their large PODs leveraged the lessons that Service Term units gained at the beginning of a conflict.

The screen changed again, this time showing a spinning creature. It had a short stubby tail and was bipedal with a bulbous head. Its legs were thick and athletic-looking, resembling those of dinosaurs. Its arms were long with clawed fingers, and its upper body looked sturdy. Monroe pointed at the creature.

"This is an Erie," he said. "We have genetic samples and have extrapolated their base physical and mental characteristics." He circled the Erie's center mass. "From what we have gathered from observation and collecting years' worth of media and other communications, the Erie prefer close-quarters combat. Their culture has a strong sense of pride when it comes to combat and how powerful a warrior is. Their bodies are built for fighting. Their ribcage is very dense, protecting most of the Erie's vital organs. They have dense muscles as well, and the circulatory system dips in and out of the ribs, meaning that they can take a lot of superficial damage without dropping. We think this is part of the reason why the Erie don't seem to believe in body armor. Yes, you heard it; they do not use body armor, but like I said, their bone and muscle tissue aren't light. Command is recommending using

High-Density Flesh rounds on the center mass with your standard armor-piercing for headshots."

I took mental note of that. My CCPU would assess each shot and pick a round for it from a list I defined, but it was always good to know what you were using. The flesh rounds were a category of nasties that, in the case of the high-density version, were comprised of a dozen or so flechettes packed together. Our SIRs would fire the round at high velocity, giving it the energy needed to punch through the Erie's ribs. Most hollow points and flesh rounds would either not make it through the Erie's ribs or lose too much energy, but not the high-density round. The Erie's bone would cause the flechettes to break apart, going in different directions and creating a dozen wound channels inside the Erie's vital organs. And I'm sure causing a tremendous amount of pain.

"Based on their history of close-quarters fighting, they should have poor accuracy over long ranges. Your camo patterns will be optimized for the Erie's visual acuity," Monroe went on.

Betts raised his hand. "Sir, how far along are they on biotech?"

"Good question. The answer is not very far. The Erie are a very survival-of-the-fittest type culture. They have a grip on common diseases and wound treatment, BUT they do not have any rapid healing tech, nor do they have any nanotechnology that we can find. That brings us to the inevitable question of what happens if we can't beat the Erie." Monroe paused for a moment. "The brass has a casualty count. I don't know what it is. But if we reach that amount, we will move over to our secondary plan."

He went on to explain that Plan B, so to speak, was a nano-virus provided to us by the Quiver. Apparently, as soon as the Erie came on the scene and proved that they were probably hostile, the Quiver started working on an action plan for them. Since the Erie didn't have nanotech, that meant that a nano-virus was the perfect solution. Monroe explained that the virus would shut down the Erie's higher brain function and eventually stop their hearts. It was supposed to be painless and would keep Erie Prime from suffering any adverse effects of the death throes of its former tenants. This was also the HFDF's last resort, shy of sterilizing the planet. If it looked like we were going to lose or sustain unacceptable casualties, pods of nanobots would fall on the Erie, and our forces would sit tight and wait. Monroe explained that our casualty count didn't have to be high for command to choose this option. He also said that option B would be employed if the Erie showed they were going to try to go out in a blaze of glory, killing themselves and messing up the planet at the same time.

I thought about that. There had been a few engagements like this one as I was growing up. From my understanding, we hadn't wiped out any of those races, but as my mind wandered, so did my CCPU. It brought up search results of several alien races we had killed off. They were the minority by far, but still there. A chart came up in my field of view showing the dominant races that we knew of, and I was happy to see that Humanity had killed off the least amount. Indeed, brutal though this campaign sounded, our overall enemy casualties were lower than most of the other top races.

Monroe was going over mission specs that were also downloading to my CCPU. I paid attention to the rest of the briefing, creating a separate file for questions I had about the mission and stellar history. There had been races like the Erie that had been either ignored or snubbed, as opposed to what we were doing now. Of those, all had become larger problems. Many gained new technology that made them harder targets. A few had been killed off eventually as a joint effort by several races. In each case, the costs of those wars had been high. Most of those races finally proved to be too high of a risk to ignore. Many outright attacked allies or, in some cases, had killed off many other species, destroying worlds as they did so.

My search pulled up a particularly distasteful race called the Venom, whose home system was in the Hydra constellation. One of our allies had only semi-dealt with them years ago. In the process, the Venom managed to acquire new tech. To date, they were responsible for the deaths of several races and had engaged in minor conflicts with another twenty. They were currently entrenched in wars on several different worlds—worlds they'd likely win on. The Venom weren't alone, of course. There were a few others. Most of these races had just enough tech to make it hard to scrape them off a world, but not enough to pose an actual threat to us. For the most part, these other races had the sense not to pick fights they couldn't win.

We were to start working on hand-to-hand combat designed for the Erie's body type and suspected fighting style. While most of the infantry wouldn't see any hand-to-hand combat, that was not as likely for us. We'd be going on missions where destroying the target might not be an option. That meant close-quarters fights, which meant learning how to get the beat down on.

The following day we began our new training. The Arbiter was still in port and would remain so for the day before starting her journey to jump distance. It was estimated that we had three to four days before deployment. That was going to be an intense three to four days, but not exhausting. We needed to be fresh when we hit the ground.

No alien was exactly like humans. They varied in almost every way imaginable. Some were big or small, had carapaces or thin skin. Their fighting styles and technology were as vast as the races, as well as the terrain. This was the great danger in interstellar war. It was also a significant deterrent. With so many unknowns, most races knew they would sustain serious losses if they didn't know what they were getting into. They could also just as easily get their asses handed to them. It's another reason why drones were popular with ageless races and why we had people on the ground to control those drones.

The HFDF, along with many advanced races, learned long ago to start training their troops in disciplines, as we called them. Like a genre of book, they are all a little different, with the end goal being that the enemy is dead, and you are not. In training, we had to attack an ever-changing array of enemies, teaching us how to be adaptable. We learned the basics of many different types of combat, terrain, and enemies, and then learned how to adapt them for every situation. Our forces would do this on the ground as well. Our drones, along with us, would learn how to best take out the enemy and, in turn, pass that info on to others. As the Erie took losses, we'd learn and replace drones.

For now, I was in a VR Pod working on a hand-to-hand combat scenario. Before me was an Erie. I was working on how to read its movements. We had some of their DNA, and computers had rebuilt their bodies and used models based on those bodies and information gathered by us and our allies on how the Erie fought. Knowing how their bodies moved was huge for us. We might be slightly off about their fighting style, but knowing more about their physiology than they likely did meant that no matter how they fought, we'd be trained to see it coming. Our CCPUs were also continually assessing what they thought the Erie might do, helping us to read them and stay one step ahead.

The Erie was taller than I was by about half a meter. Its center mass was protected by thick bone that I could shatter with the help of my suit's extra strength, but that wasn't the recommended fighting style. We were smaller, faster, and with our tech, stronger. Instead of going fist to fist, we were to use our suits' vambraces, having the vambraces fashion stilettos and hooks out of the nano-material within them. The Erie's claws were thought to be unable to effectively penetrate our suits, and their arms were long. This meant getting in close and personal, using a hook to grab onto an Erie, and then using our other arm's stiletto to stab them. In the simulations, it was effective, if not a little difficult to master. Depending on the terrain, the soles of our boots could grip the ground better than the Erie, giving us much more solid footing. Our job was to keep the fights as one-sided and unfair as possible.

After a simulation, Betts, Sweeting, and I sat waiting for the rest of the team to finish up.

"Brutal, man," Sweeting said. "How are you guys doing at it?"

"By my last cycle, I was ten for ten," Betts said.

Sweeting and I nodded. "Regular infantry isn't doing as well. They lose as much as they win," I said.

The regular infantry was also getting this training. They weren't supposed to get themselves in hand-to-hand scrapes at all if possible, but they were trained just in case.

"Good thing they just blow buildings up and don't go in them, huh?" I said.

Sweeting laughed. "Where's the fun in that?"

Krista and Meyers were out now. I looked up their scores, seeing that both were ten out of ten in their last cycle. "Good work," I told them.

Meyers shrugged. "Anyone else as creeped out by how good we are as I am?"

"How so?" Krista asked.

"In basic, we learned way more disciplines than other Fireteams, right? I'm just creeped out to see how well that gave us the base to throw down with almost any alien race out there, is all. Not that I'm bothered by it, but…." he said.

"Yeah," I agreed. "I kind of thought it would take us years to be like this."

"How freaky are we?" Betts said, nodding, and then, "Grub?"

We headed to the mess. It seemed that our CCPUs kept us in a constant state of hunger. We weren't burning calories but putting them on. Once planetside, we'd have nutrient packs to eat, but that was all we'd have for weeks or maybe even months. They could completely sustain us but were cargo that had to make it planetside. The mess of the Arbiter was about to have a lot fewer patrons but was still full of supplies. Our CCPUs ensured we were stocked as possible for healing, growing, and all the normal bodily functions that didn't involve energy. I wasn't going to complain, though. Five meals a day? Count me in.

THIRTEEN

After a final equipment check, I filed into the launch tube with the rest of my squad. My POD for the day consisted of eight BIs and two BBALLs. One of the BIs had their usual SIR and a Heavy Infantry Rifle, or HIR. They were fantastic against light armor or vehicles, though a bit of a pain in the ass in tight places.

I divided the BIs into three groups. BIs 1 and 2 stayed with me in group one, labeled G1. G2 had BIs 3, 4, and 5, while G3 had BIs 6, 7, and 8. As a fireteam, I also commanded two mortar drones, each with its own escort of two BBALLs and six Whiskers. I had no control over the BBALLs unless a human operator was about to die or if the mortar drone was incapacitated. In short, you didn't want control over the escort BBALLs because it meant you were in a world of hurt. I also had two Heavies, each with five Whiskers.

The Arbiter had four tubes designed for launching personnel. Each could hold an entire platoon with its BIs and BBALLs. Our Heavies and mortar drones would be launched from other tubes. I stood at the head of Second Platoon. Three meters before me was a door, on the other side of which was space. On either side of me stood my BIs, packed closely together. When it came time to jump, they would move into a shoulder-to-shoulder line, but for now, having them like this allowed some movement up and down the tube.

The tubes weren't so much tubes as they were hallways leading into the void of space. The perk of being the first one out was that I was at the front. There were about three meters between me and the doors. I walked in front of my drones and sat against the wall. The rest of the squad joined me, while everyone else had to sit in the space between their BIs.

The launch tube was still pressurized, so I didn't have my helmet on, nor did Krista, who sat next to me. But we might as well have had our helmets on. I could hear the chattering of the rest of the platoon, but First Squad was silent, each of us appearing to stare off into space. In reality, we were looking over materials about the Erie or checking our drones or equipment. Once the fleet launched, we would start receiving real-time information.

I looked at the door, having my CCPU overlay the exterior feeds. There were hundreds, if not thousands, of ships around us, but all save the Healer's Touch had their color patterns switched to combat black. My CCPU overlaid the ships in my field of view. Sweeting, sitting across from me, was looking at the door too.

"What you looking at?" he asked.

I glanced back at the door and space. "A battleship, Juggernaut-class, centipede design."

Sweeting nodded, and Betts whistled, "Mean those are."

The ship was a long cylinder with a cone at the bow. It was absolutely massive and simple, giving it an almost alien appearance. I tried not to laugh as I realized that it had the silhouette of a vibrator. I could have had my CCPU tell me everything about the ships, but instead, I asked Betts.

"That one people call Pedes, for the centipede in their name. They are built in segments; each one can function completely on its own. You see the outside of it? Each segment can rotate its outer layer, moving weapons and undamaged sections to face the fight. They are

Juggernaut-class ships, so they're damage takers, and there's none better than the Pedes." Betts pointed at the door. "That one has twelve segments. The crew will be in a center shaft; everything is self-contained and mobile. If a segment gets too messed up, the rest of the ship separates from it and then reforms. The damaged segment will move unmanned and blow up like a big frag grenade. Each segment has a jump drive and propulsion." Betts shook his head. "We haven't lost a crew from one of those in fifty years. Man, they take a lot of hits and dish out plenty of their own."

The mission plan showed that the Pedes would be the first in, drawing fire. Also floating around were large spherical ships called Drone Stars. In their center was the ship with people in it. On the outside were a thousand drones that interlinked until deployment. When separated, they worked like a swarm of insects. They'd also be part of the first wave. Then the damage-dealers would roll in: the comet and, of course, flare-class ships would jump in, along with carriers and bombardment ships. That would be what truly messed up the enemy.

I spotted a flare-class cruiser. It was nowhere near as big as the Pedes but could deliver a lot of punishment. I marveled at the fleet. There was so much specialization in it, but also a lot of generalized ships. The HFDF had built an almost infinitely adaptable military that was also capable of specializing in virtually anything at the same time. It was remarkable and frightening.

Groups of ships outside began to wink out of existence. The invasion had begun.

We stopped talking and waited for intel to start coming in. It didn't take long. As soon as they reached enemy space, shipboard sensors began sending copious amounts of information back to the rest of the fleet. The data was analyzed and sent to other ships for further analysis, working its way down the chain of command and eventually reaching us.

I brought up a map of our team's corridor. I noticed details changing as the battle progressed. None of the fleet was hitting the surface yet, but ship sensors noted surface activity. The map shifted, updating with landing zones.

"LZs are up," I said.

I zoomed in on the area we were anticipating landing in. The topography hadn't updated, but some of the enemy info had. Looking at the map, it was easy to see where the fleet planned on landing troops. As soon as I thought that, shuttle landing zones lit up on the map. Monroe pinged Royle and me.

"Orders are in," he said. "Our squad is to escort two intel drones to an enemy command center. Once you get to the center, you need to take it and hold it without inflicting significant damage to the building. You will have movement control of the drones until you reach the center, at which time their operators will take control. Each fireteam will be assigned its own drone."

A waypoint appeared on the map. I inspected it. Next to me, Royle perked up.

"I will work on a route for you," Monroe told us.

"Any idea how much of the enemy will be taken out by orbital bombardment?" Royle asked.

"Negative, but I wouldn't count on a lot. Erie history shows that they had a lot of little spats with each other. They've probably been using this center for some time. When the fleet came in and started lighting them up, they moved to historical ground tactics in anticipation of our attack. They are going to be close to that center. Command won't risk it."

"It's in a heavily wooded area," I said to Royle. "Looks like lots of cover for them and us."

We shared our map displays, both of us working on the same one.

"You breach; I'll hold," she said.

I nodded. We started planning possible attacks, time losing its hold on us. As we planned, the situation on Erie Prime changed. The planet, being new to interstellar war, had little in the way of a defense grid, and the periodic reports we saw from the ship-to-ship battle reflected that. The Erie were getting the tar beat out of them. The planet's largest station was pulverized and entering the atmosphere. It would hit an area several thousand kilometers from our landing site.

My CCPU pinged me. I'd set up notifications for different waves of the invasion. Wave one had been the Pedes and Drone Stars. Shortly after, the second wave started with the flares and main damage dealers. Now we were onto wave three. Bombardment ships were jumping into orbit. This would be the wave that would start the process of softening ground targets and securing corridors.

"Bombardment wave!" I said.

Our squad rose, taking our places next to our BIs and conducting one last physical inspection of them. The rest of the platoon looked on, confused. It wouldn't be long before the Arbiter initiated the jump countdown. Moments later, the ship notified the platoon that we were ten minutes out from the jump. The rest of the platoon began scrambling to their feet. Monroe, Royle, and I had our plans A, B, and C locked and loaded. I sent them to my fireteam so they could familiarize themselves with them. Eight minutes later, my BIs moved shoulder to shoulder next to me.

I felt a buzz of excitement as everyone got into place. I took a few breaths to calm my nerves.

Before the jump, every team member reported that they understood their jobs and asked any questions they had. All we had to do was monitor the incoming intel for changes and wait.

"Be careful," Liz said to me over a commline.

"I will," I replied.

I brought up my CCPU's recording options. Command could see every moment of an engagement from our suit feeds for training purposes, but we could keep our own copies. I wasn't about to forget my first combat jump. My helmet wrapped around my head as the Arbiter decompressed the launch tube.

The lights went out in the tube, its walls turning black. The lights on the entrance's floor turned on, little red dots blinking in a forward motion. The door at the end of the tube opened to the blackness of space. A small, excited, and nervous pit formed in my gut.

The ship started its countdown to jump. 5...4...3...2... I looked to where Liz's ship was and smiled. 1. The blackness before me was replaced with the blue, white, and green of the surface of Erie Prime. The lights on the floor turned green, and a buzz sounded in my head. I ran forward, hurling myself into space.

The Arbiter caught me in a gravity well, pushing me on course towards Erie Prime. My suit went rigid as I left the safety of the ship. Maneuvering thrusters kicked on, carefully arranging me amongst the platoon and drones. Once on course, I could move my head around and observe the battle around me—or what was left of it. The space around the planet sparkled with explosions that only had form or detail when I zoomed in on them. When I did, I could see the wreckage of ships and the occasional body floating.

My view returned to normal as ordnance and drones from the Arbiter passed by me. A missile pod as thick as a house streaked by on its way to the planet, along with several others. The pods were long tubes with a thruster, space anchor, and hull that would transfer heat to the anchor. Inside the vacuum-sealed pod were dozens of missiles and bombs, each with its own target. The pods were moving much faster than we were, and I watched as some began to hit the atmosphere, followed by columns of drone aircraft sitting atop heat shields.

The battle in the atmosphere wasn't optimal yet, as the Erie still had a lot of land-based defenses and aircraft to deal with. The drones that passed me would be dealing with Erie fighters and occasionally coming down to lower altitudes to distract the Erie from us.

My CCPU pinged me that we were about to hit the atmosphere.

"Final checks," I said to my team.

I did my own check, ensuring that I was falling along the proper vector, my equipment was ready to go, and my drones were all online and fully integrated with me. As I did this, my CCPU pinged me with a new drone. It was the intel drone I was in charge of. I integrated with it, noting it was behind us and wouldn't hit the planet until a few minutes after us. My anchor activated, rolling me feet-first. My entry pack fired up, and I curled into a ball as my heat shield formed below me. My heart started to race, and a moment later, I began to bounce around as I hit the atmosphere. My anchor kept me upright, and I felt more turbulence. This air would be much thicker than that of Arrow.

At three hundred degrees, my heat shield started transferring power to my anchor, and I felt as if I had slammed into the ground. My anchor fired, using all the energy it could from the shield. My heart raced even faster, and I tried to relax. I took my mind off the entry, looking at a missile pod in the distance. It was moving quickly, the air around it ablaze. I also saw several fighter drones' heat shields as they burned bright. Oddly, this calmed me, and I realized it wasn't the entry that had me overly worried but the fact that my heat shield would look like a prime target for enemy thermal imaging. The missile pods were pushing around four thousand degrees. Compared to them, I was an ice cube; my anchor was slowing me down much more gradually, and I'd hit at a much lower speed.

The ride became bumpier as Erie Prime's atmosphere thickened and my heat shield's temperature rose quickly. It sent more energy to my anchor, which in turn exerted more effort, slowing me down faster. I was compressed by the force of deceleration, my suit squeezing me tightly. Soon enough, the outside temperature dropped, and my bumpy ride subsided. My shield collapsed back into a small block on my back, and my anchor stopped trying to slow me down. I righted myself, pointing my head down towards the ground, keeping my arms and legs together, trying to be as aerodynamic as possible.

I received a notification that my Heavies were in the atmosphere and unfurling themselves. Below were clouds, the deep green of the forest and grasslands, along with lots of smoke. There were flashes on the ground as missiles and bombs hit, along with explosions in the air from aircraft engaging. I zoomed in on a large drone hovering high in the sky. It was an air platform that could be configured into whatever was needed. Sometimes, they were autonomous troop transports, floating gunships, or rearming platforms for fighters. The one I saw now was covered in missile pods, along with a complement of missile defense systems that were presently taking out incoming threats.

My CCPU pinged me, and I looked at the ground, a map overlaying it as I fell. We were almost there. My BIs and other drones began to scan for enemies. Monroe sent the squad a waypoint to form up at. I added my own for my fireteam. Moments from impact, I flipped, and my anchor activated, slowing me rapidly. I landed in a crouch, my Whiskers deploying as my SIR came to my shoulder. My suit's pattern changed, matching the tall grass I landed in.

At once, my POD and I were fired on. We'd dropped in or near a group of Erie. In front of me, three creatures ran into the grassy field I was in. They were tall with lean muscles. Two of them were purple, and one was a muddled greenish-yellow. They were holding and firing what looked like an approximation of a rifle. Rounds whizzed by me in the grass, but the Erie obviously didn't know exactly where I had landed. I cursed to myself and took quick aim, my SIR set to burst mode.

I squeezed the trigger, aiming at the center Erie about fifty meters away. My SIR fired three rounds. The Erie thrashed backward as the rounds hit it, sending a cloud of flesh and fluid from the exit wounds. As its companions turned to it, I dropped the next one and then the last. The entire engagement was over in a few heartbeats. Around me, my BIs and BBALLs took out their own groups of Erie. I heard the occasional sound of enemy fire, but it stopped quickly.

I moved forward, my training guiding me, my mind not even registering that I had just killed three sentient beings—and I couldn't care less about it. My POD of drones formed around me, each looking for trouble, allowing me to focus on my fireteam and the status of our

Heavies and mortar drones. The team was fine, all heading to rendezvous waypoints.

I moved through the tall grass, keeping low to the ground. I'd move and then pause to assess my surroundings. I took a knee to check the feeds from my drones and Whiskers. While I'd landed in grass, our rendezvous point and objective was in dense forest. I looked ahead, seeing the tree line... plant line? Erie Prime didn't have trees like I'd grown up with on Orion. Instead, as I approached the forest, I saw tall... well, trees? Let's go with trees for the sake of ease. I saw tall trees with thin trunks that were muddled gray and black. Wide green and purple leaves shot out from thick stems.

I moved forward into the trees. Sound all but stopped as I entered, the dense foliage absorbing it. I looked at my HUD, seeing the Heavies' vectors as they headed towards me. The ground was soft and squishy, allowing me to move faster while keeping quiet. I kept my SIR raised as I moved.

"G2, stay forward and to my left. G3, stay forward and right," I told my POD.

I had the BBALLs at the rear.

Above me, I heard clicking and rustling. A Whisker checked the source of the sound, finding a group of six animals. They were small with gray and green fur that blended into the trees. I stopped for a moment to look at them. Large green eyes looked at me curiously. They had six limbs and a long tail that wrapped around the trees. Large ears swiveled around as they listened to my POD. Charles would be losing his mind. I started to move forward.

The light dimmed the deeper I got into the trees, but my helmet kept up without any issues. In training, Cortez had us do countless exercises in VR on numerous alien worlds and environments. I'd always thought the animals in the simulations were just there for background effect. Now I saw they were part of the lesson. A bug or something bounced off my arm, but it didn't even faze me. It should have. Before training, it would have, but I'd gotten so used to strange sounds, random critters popping out, and some creepy-ass shit that I was okay. Cortez was a sneaky one.

At the rendezvous point, we waited. Betts and Krista took a little longer to reach us as each landed closer to whatever Erie was in the area. Krista had found a gun emplacement and what looked like some handheld anti-aircraft weapons.

I looked skyward as we waited, my CCPU overlaying what I was looking for. Above me, I saw an icon indicating a drone and a vector for where it would fall.

"We're right on target. Intel drone inbound," I said to my team.

We were located in more tall grass, which seemed typical in this area. There would be dense forest broken up by patches of grass. It didn't provide the best cover, but with Heavies in tow, there was little we could do to hide from the enemy anyway. A blur fell from the sky not far from me. I moved to it, finding the intel drone.

It was about the size of a person, with a casket shape. Its exterior had taken on the same camo pattern as the rest of us, along with a texture that almost looked like it could be covered in grass. It hovered just above the ground, awaiting my instructions. My CCPU showed that I could only make it move and follow me around, but its higher functions weren't under my control. Its programming indicated that it had advanced evasion and detection capabilities, which was comforting. I didn't fancy being on the ground with a moronic drone that couldn't hide itself.

"We've got the intel drone, and the team is here," I said to Monroe.

"Roger that, Alpha. Meet with Bravo at waypoint one. Be advised there are enemies on the path," Monroe replied.

"Fireteam Alpha, clump up and head to waypoint one," I instructed the team.

My POD formed up around me, my BBALLs pushing ahead of us. I placed the Heavies in the center and positioned my Mortars in the back of our formation. The intel drone was right behind me. Our fireteam moved out, Betts taking point with Sweeting and Meyers on the sides. Krista brought up the rear, while I stayed centered, protecting the intel drone.

We moved silently, our Whiskers constantly scanning. Our training scenarios had been executed so well that, in many ways, this felt just like another training exercise, but I knew it wasn't. Low though those odds might have been, I could actually die out here today. And the targets I hit were actual living beings.

We entered a dense forest with tall trees and bugs the size of dinner plates flying around. In the distance, I could hear the concussions of explosions going off. Above us, the occasional fighter passed overhead, its engines screaming. Betts paused.

"Hostiles ahead," he warned.

I pulled up what he was looking at. Sure enough, there was what looked like an anti-aircraft emplacement ahead of us.

"Fireteam Bravo, be advised we will be running behind," I said to Royle.

Our Whiskers quickly surrounded the enemy, gathering information. There were five ground-to-air missile pods spread out over about one hundred meters. They were connected by trenches, with two gun emplacements around each one. In the center of the trenches were several holds, which I presumed were rest areas for the Erie. My CCPU counted eighty-five Erie.

I came up with a quick plan. I set up waypoints and sent them to the team.

"Meyers, you are going to take the rear, kill anything that comes that way. Betts, you'll be the assault team. The rest of us will be sniping. We are going to sync our shots: two main salvos, one on the guns, the next on gun support, and on the Erie working the missiles. BBALLs deploy after the first shots, focusing on the trenches. Move out," I ordered.

I moved to my own waypoint, staying out of the Erie's sight. I lay in the grass next to a tree. A brown, slug-like creature climbed the bark, leaving a streak of slime behind it. I pushed the slug out of my mind and focused on sighting my SIR. My vision narrowed as I turned on auto-zoning. Before me was a gun emplacement. I picked a primary and secondary target. I could see my BIs' targets, along with everyone else's, as they moved into position.

I kept the Heavies back and well out of sight. Handy though they were, we could end this much faster by being smart. If we executed this right, it might take the Erie a while to realize we'd taken out one of their defenses. I monitored my assets panel in my HUD, seeing each unit get in place, and then selected targets. In front of me, an Erie was sighting down the barrel of a gun in my general direction but didn't seem to know I was there.

Once in position and ready, I set my POD to sync its first volley with me and opened a line to the team. I sighted the Erie, its head taking up a large part of my field of view. I could make out the color of its eyes and the expression on its face.

"Fire on my mark. 3... 2... 1... fire," I said calmly.

I squeezed the trigger. My SIR thumped softly against my shoulder. The Erie before me's head snapped back, bits of bone, blood, and tissue filling the air in a mist. I moved my SIR to the next target and fired again. It too dropped.

As the first salvo fired, BBALLs shot forward, covering half the distance to the enemy before the first body hit the ground. Forty-five guns fired at once, and forty-five Erie died simultaneously to armor-piercing rounds to the head. Less than a second later, another thirty went down. The rest weren't in optimal lines of fire unfortunately. Some of them tried to move as what was happening registered. The BBALLs were there now. Most of their victims were unaware that they were above them. The BBALLs began to quickly and systematically kill the Erie in the trenches. Most only had the chance to take one or two steps before being pelted with rounds.

Betts and his POD sprinted forward to the center of the trenches. They dove in, hunting down what few Erie had taken cover or were inside little dugout rooms. It was over so quickly that the Erie never returned fire.

"Clear," Betts said.

"Only two thought about running," Meyers noted. "They didn't make it out of the trenches."

"Roger that. Fireteam Alpha, move to the enemy position. Place charges on the missiles and prepare to move out in two." I moved forward to the Erie I had killed, hopping down next to it. I looked down, seeing blood turning the dirt to mud. The back of its head was blown out. I tweaked my SIR's settings. In a perfect world, the bullet wouldn't have exited the other side of the Erie's skull. A small part of me noted again that I should be experiencing more emotion about this than I was.

I ran up the trench, placing a charge on one of the missile pods.

I paused to take an inventory. We hadn't lost a drone or a person. We'd fired one hundred and ten rounds in total and killed eighty-five Erie. When the charges were placed, I gave the order to move out. At a safe distance, I detonated the charges. I checked my CCPU. We had slaughtered the Erie in just under ten minutes, including our time moving into position. We reached Monroe's waypoint at about the same time as Bravo team.

FOURTEEN

Our squad moved out northeast in the direction of the target building after Royle and her team arrived at the waypoint. Royle and I each took the safest part of the formation, as we had the intel drones with us.

"Sorry we were late," Royle said as her team arrived.

"No worries, we just got here. We found an anti-aircraft emplacement. Did you guys hit any snags?" I asked.

"Armor," she said. "We didn't engage; there were a lot of them, and no way we could take them. We hid in the forest, waiting for them to pass."

"Armor, huh? That's not good."

Royle's response was slow to come. "Yeah, I'd say. I'm not really interested in dealing with that today."

Around us, the forest was dense, with trees rising high above, limiting the amount of light that could come down. Our suits compensated for it without us having to make any adjustments, but I could see where a campaign on a planet like this would have been brutal without our tech. The terrain was relatively consistent on Erie Prime, leading HF biologists to conclude that this was a leading factor in the Erie's visual acuity. From DNA and Erie bodies recovered from our few encounters with them, we knew a great deal about their biology. Their eyes could not see the full hue spectrum that humans could naturally, but their low-light sensitivity was much greater than that of normal humans. They could also see part of the infrared spectrum, making them ideally suited for thick, dark forests.

The Erie we had encountered wore minimal gear and did not use helmets. The HFDF had anticipated this. It seemed that the Erie weren't big on using technology to protect themselves, something that tied into their culture. Thus, no helmets that allowed them to see in other light spectrums or anything else that would give them a clue as to where we were. Our suits were doing their damnedest to keep our heat levels in line with that of the environment around us, and displaying a color pattern that the Erie would have a hard time making out. We weren't invisible, but unless the enemy was paying extremely close attention to where we were, they'd have difficulty finding us. This had allowed Royle's team to go unnoticed, and now the squad as we crested a hill.

Ahead of us stood a squat gray building. Its smooth surface showed little in the way of entrances or windows. We paused to look at it. I zoomed my view in, seeing plenty of places for cover along the outside. It appeared to be made of the Erie version of concrete. The data we had on the Erie suggested that the top level would be hardened and easy to defend, with the levels underneath much softer. I tried to toggle view modes to see what I could see inside, frustrated to find nothing.

"I'm seeing a lot of heat coming from that doorway," Betts said, sending an image of what he was looking at to the squad.

"They see heat, though, don't they? It looks dark too. So that makes sense; they can see out, but nothing can see in. I bet that top level is one trap after another," Chad Brown from Royle's team said.

"The building is dense too. I can't see anything through the walls. We're gonna have to take our time clearing it," I said.

"Too bad we don't have a lot of that," Royle noted.

"Royle is right. We are twenty minutes out from shuttles hitting atmo. Most of the anti-air is down, but we need that comms center mopped up," Monroe said.

Royle and I took a moment to confirm our plan of attack that we'd come up with on the Arbiter.

I opened a line to my Fireteam. "Here's how we're doing this. Alpha is the main assault force. We will breach from the south. Betts, you and I take point. Sweeting and Meyers, you two circle around the building and take care of anything outside. Krista, I'm going to leave the drone with you. You cannot control it, but I will tell it to follow you. Watch our backs. When Betts and I have the top floor secure, we will all move in and down, securing the rest of the building. Fireteam Bravo will hold the area around the building," I said.

We moved down the hill. I assigned my Heavies to Royle to secure the perimeter and had my mortar drones zero in on the few targets we could see. My team crept up to the building, stopping right in front of the doorway. It was small for an Erie, which would slow any infiltrating Erie down. Unfortunately for them, the opening was about the size of a standard human version.

I waited for my team to take position and then loaded a frag grenade onto my SIR. I took aim at the doorway, my suit steadying me. Two of my BIs did likewise; our combined grenades in the tight space should prove effective. Once set, I sent the order to the mortar drones to fire.

A moment later, the ground shook, and my suit registered explosions. Dirt and flames filled the air around the building, along with several Erie. I held my fire.

BOOM, BOOM, another volley. Still, I held. My helmet overlaid the UV spectrum into my view. There wasn't enough light spilling into the building from the sun to see far, but I could see the entrance just fine. Once we got inside, we'd turn on small UV lamps built into our helmets to see. For now, though, I could easily see a group of Erie coming to the doorway and taking position.

"Do they think they're going to catch us off guard when we come in?" Meyers asked incredulously.

"Looks like it," Sweeting said.

"This is gonna be fun," Meyers said with a chuckle.

"Keep the chatter down...but yeah, this isn't going to go well for them," I admitted.

A few more Erie were coming up behind the others. I waited a few moments longer for them to settle. Then I fired along with my BIs. Three small grenades arched across the distance, separating us from the building and flying through the doorway. Each detonated mid-air behind the first set of Erie with a flash of light and sound. Several Erie flew from the entrance, while others were pushed back.

"MOVE MOVE MOVE!" I ordered.

I stood up, moving forward, my POD and fireteam joining me. Four of my BIs moved ahead of me, each jerking their SIRs down, firing single shots at the Erie's heads, lest they weren't dead. There were groans and shots that could be heard as we approached the building and slipped inside. Four BIs ahead of me moved quickly down the hall towards an intersection. My UV lamp switched on as I entered, bathing the hallway in light. Erie bodies were all over the floor from the frags, and I tasked a drone to pull them out of the way. At the first intersection in the hall, my BIs stopped. One lowered its SIR and took out its sidearm. I did likewise. With my sidearm gripped in my right hand, the nano-material in my left vambrace expanded into a long, thin blade. I moved forward. My BIs opened fire at an enemy I couldn't see. I switched my view to one of theirs, seeing the BIs shooting at two Erie who were returning fire.

The wall next to me flew apart, and clawed hands reached out at me. My helmet's proximity sensor buzzed. I let go of my sidearm, the material on my hand flipping it back along the inside of my forearm. I fell back, avoiding the grasp of the Erie. I caught myself in a crouch. My right vambrace extended into a long shaft with hooks on the end.

The Erie spilled out into the hall before me, its arms swiping where I had just been. Its head turned to look at me. I reached out with my right arm, the hooks sinking into the Erie's arm just above its elbow joint. I pulled its arm out of the way, leaving its ribs exposed. With my left vambrace, I stabbed the Erie in the ribs, the blade sliding between them smoothly. It gasped, and then a moment later, its head jerked as a BI shot it. My right vambrace retracted, and I stood fully upright. My sidearm moved back into my right hand. I gripped the weapon with both hands, sweeping where the Erie had come from.

"Watch the walls; they are hiding in them," I warned the team.

I moved forward slowly as my BIs took the time to check the walls as we went. Other PODs were reporting similar events, and I pinged Monroe so he could warn the rest of the invasion force. We cleared the floor we were on, stopping before a passage that led underground. I sent a whisker down the passage to check it out. It got shot at by an Erie, but the Erie only succeeded in giving us its location. Our intel had been correct. The lower levels appeared to be a much softer target, the walls thin enough to shoot through and for our density view to see through. I gave the order to move out, and one of my BIs popped the Erie that had shot at the whisker.

We moved much quicker this time as soon the shuttles would be hitting atmo. I stayed low, using my density view to find Erie and shoot them through walls and doorways before they had a clue where I was. When we reached the central computer room, I waited outside as the rest of my team formed up.

"Remember, we need the computers to be functional," I reminded my team. Also, for good measure, I sent a command to my team's drones telling them to avoid damaging the equipment in the room. I wasn't keen on my first real mission hindering the invasion force.

I set my sidearm to not shoot at anything metal and to frag rounds.

On my order, BIs broke down doors and swept into the room. I followed two of mine, shooting at three Erie. Betts on the other side of the room did likewise. The frag rounds were not as effective against the Erie, so we drilled them with fire. A few rounds missed, and I felt a plop on my suit as one broke apart. A voice in my mind noted that never in the history of war would getting caught in a crossfire with your own side be considered a nonissue. As we pelted the Erie, our BIs moved quickly, killing others with hand-to-hand techniques. In under a minute, a dozen Erie were dead on the ground.

"Secure the building," I ordered.

My BBALLs were critical in this process as they could move faster than the BIs and went from room to room, as did the Whiskers. When everything came back all clear, I took control of the intel drones and guided them into the computer room. Once inside, a voice buzzed over the comms.

"Fireteam Alpha, we have control of the drones. Please do not interfere," a male voice said. There was no corresponding ID tag with the comm line.

"Roger that," I said.

"Hold tight while intel does its thing," I said to the team.

My CCPU alerted me to danger outside the compound. The Erie had arrived.

The intel drones stood vertically in the middle of the room. Compartments opened, and then other smaller drones that looked a bit like crabs and spiders started coming out in an orderly fashion, making their way to the Erie's computers.

"Companies here," Royle said.

My Heavies, still under Royle's command, alerted me that they were being engaged. I pulled up a map of the area, seeing hundreds of hostiles. My CCPU pinged me.

ALERT-MESSAGE: ADVISE - ENEMY IS BOMBARDING YOUR LOCATION.

The ground shook a bit as what I assumed to be artillery hit the building above. Heavy number two's missile defense system activated shortly after.

"Could use some assistance," Royle said.

"Betts, Meyers, Sweeting, go topside and assist Bravo with defense. McLeod, hold the upper level," I ordered.

The team moved out, and I sent all but two of my BIs and my BBALLs with Betts.

The building shook again. *God, what's it like up there if it's shaking down here?*

I got on the comm line with intel, "Do you have an ETA?"

The little drones were gone, now working inside the computers.

"Hang tight, Alpha, just a bit longer."

"Roger that," I said, trying not to sound irritated. I had no clue what was involved in hacking alien tech, so I tried not to get put off by having to wait. This, after all, was the job.

I pulled up a feed from one of my Whiskers outside.

The comms building was surrounded by dense forest, a forest that was erupting with enraged Erie. I could see rocket trails and what must have been the Erie equivalent of tracer rounds screaming from the tree line at our perimeter. It appeared that most of the fire was being concentrated on the Heavies, their large armor-clad bodies sparkling with impacts, and missile defense systems spraying clouds of shrapnel in the air, ripping the Erie's rockets to pieces and causing them to explode.

The Heavies weren't just taking a beating, though; they were dishing out plenty of punishment. Their large caliber guns burped out round after round, breaking apart trees and Erie alike. Their own missiles were fired at groups of Erie, sending limbs and chunks of flesh skyward. It was easy to see why the Erie were so focused on the Heavies. Heck, in training drills, I'd concentrated on them too. On top of the comms building, our Mortar Drones, under the direction of Royle, were preparing to shell the areas where Erie were clumping. BBALLs were zipping high above the trees, firing down on the Erie, not really hitting any of them but generally herding them together.

It was nerve-racking not being able to do anything. Just sitting there babysitting the intel drones was far more difficult than I could have imagined.

"What's up, Taylor? Your stress levels just went up," Monroe asked me on a private line.

"Don't like my team being out there without me, that's all," I said.

"Welcome to my life; it sucks, I know. Sit tight."

"Roger that," I said.

The lesson for the day? Sit tight.

The BBALLs and Heavies had done their jobs well. The Erie were packed in nice and tight, putting all their attention on the Heavies, not noticing our BIs taking up position. I couldn't see the commands Royle was sending to her drones, but I could see the ones she sent to mine. She gave the command for the Mortars to open fire. My Mortar drones acknowledged and started pre-defined sets of volleys. It appeared as if nothing had changed for a moment, and then... BOOM! The trees exploded as shell after shell hit home. Seventy or eighty Erie died in a matter of moments, others were maimed, and still, others left cover, running away from the shelling. As they did, the waiting BIs opened fire, starting what looked to be an intergalactic turkey shoot.

Again, waves of Erie went down, some more or less gracefully than others. They reorganized surprisingly quickly, finding cover and shifting their focus from the Heavies to our BIs and troops. Though they still kept just enough attention on the Heavies to keep them from tearing apart their lines.

"Please place the charges," the Intel tech said on the comms.

I turned to the intel drones, seeing a drawer in their sides open, exposing several sets of explosive charges. I started placing charges with my BIs, where the intel people indicated. From the Erie computers, there was the sound of keening metal. Apparently, the little spider-looking bots were done with their thing and were now destroying the computers.

While I had no control of the intel drones, I could see basic updates that they were making. A message in their queues changed to UPLOADING DATA. After I placed a few more charges, the status changed to UPLOADED.

"Charges placed," I said over the comm line.

As I said this, a status from the Arbiter came down the line.

ARBITER: ATTENTION - COMMENCING KEY BOMBARD-MENT OF ERIE PRIME.

ARBITER: ATTENTION - LANDING SHUTTLES INBOUND.

The intel drones were queued up by the door and were now back in my control.

"Heading up," I said.

"Good, we need you," Royle said.

I checked the action up top, startled at what I saw. In the few minutes I'd been setting charges, the situation up top had gone from us dominating the Erie to us losing ground. I inventoried my fireteam and equipment as I started to run up to the top level, my two BIs with me, followed by the intel drones. My mortar drones were in tip-top shape, but the Heavies were starting to take damage, the Erie switching from missiles to explosive rounds on them. I watched as one Heavies missile defense system ran out of ammo, and the Heavy was tagged by three consecutive missiles. Its status dropped from Active to Inactive. *Damn it.* The rest of the team was running low on ammo despite having reloaders placed on walls and nearby metal.

As I reached the opening of the building, the whole thing shook with impacts. I stumbled as I came out, and a moment later, there was a flash of heat, and the wind was knocked from me as something large hit me, sending me into a nearby wall. I was disoriented for a moment.

I looked down to see that I was covered in concrete. I pushed it off me, my BIs coming to my side, helping me up. There was another impact, and more debris pelted me, but not as badly this time. I took cover behind some more concrete. In that short time, the Erie had advanced quickly.

I shouldered my SIR and fired, dropping an Erie.

"Monroe, we could use some air support," I said.

"Already working on it," he replied.

I took out another Erie. They were moving slower now, and their artillery had stopped. They had this location zeroed but didn't seem to want to risk firing with friendlies so close. That worked fine for me. From what was left of the tree line, heavy caliber fire started, kicking up bits of concrete that bounced harmlessly against my suit. They started firing on us with what seemed to be about the equivalent of a .50 cal. I ducked behind my cover. My suit would stop a lot, but not that.

My display pinged me. Krista was WIA.

"Krista, talk to me," I said, worried.

"I'm hit. It only hurt for a moment; my CCPU is stopping the pain," she said, sounding a little shaken.

Her BIs were tending to her, and my display showed that her right shoulder was hit and unable to function.

"Help is on the way," Monroe said calmly.

ARBITER: ORBITAL ASSETS INBOUND. BUNKER BUSTERS THIRTY MINUTES OUT.
ARBITER: HOLD POSITION LASER FIRING.

My heart picked up a bit. First at the bunker busters, because I knew those were going to hit our current position, and then with the laser. It's one thing to logically understand that the particle cannons and lasers on the ship were not only really, really powerful but were also really, really accurate. But it's an altogether different thing to believe that when you hear to sit tight while someone four hundred kilometers above you zaps the area you're in.

ARBITER: LASER FIRING IN THIRTY SECONDS. TAKE APPROPRIATE ACTION.

"TAKE COVER!" I yelled at the squad.

I, like my squad and BIs, took cover. I patched in a feed from my Whiskers. It took us all of a second to get down. Not that the laser would hit us, but from any debris from Erie munitions it set off might, and oh yeah, because the atmosphere and everything else around us was going to get superheated and expand. Two seconds after we took cover, the Erie started forward. They made it a step or two before some realized something bad must be about to happen, and then the world got very bright and very hot. My feed from the whisker lit up as the forest exploded in fire, the blaze quickly engulfing the Erie.

Our position was hit with a wall of heat. The Whiskers' thermal sensors measured the blaze to be around 800 C. That would have been too hot for even our suits to handle. I could feel the heat through my suit, something that was entirely new to me. My gut clenched with nerves, and my skin prickled involuntarily. The Arbiter was hundreds of kilometers above us. If its lenses were off in the slightest, we'd all be vaporized. The fire around our egress route cooled down the fastest, the blaze quickly burning itself out, cooling down to a temperature well within our suits' tolerances.

"You're clear. Get out, and fall back to LZ Alpha. McLeod, you good to move?" Monroe asked.

"I'm good," Krista said.

Krista was able to move, but she couldn't use her right arm, which meant no SIR. We put her in the center of the formation with the intel drones while she carried her sidearm, her suit holding her injured arm still. Our exit was not all that dramatic. Thick, hot smoke filled the air all around us. The Erie would be unable to see through it... if there were any Erie left in the area, which I doubted. A few hundred meters away from the building, we lay down on the ground, taking what cover we could from our drones as the bunker busters pulverized the comms building. The concussion shook the ground like an earthquake. After that, we continued our retreat to the landing zone. That was a bit more of a sight.

Shuttles streaked down to the ground, their noses opening up as they touched down. Troops and drones stormed from them. Once the last boot had left the shuttle, the crafts jerked up in the air, their main engines rumbling to life, and they screamed out of the area, firing missiles as they went and eventually pointing themselves skyward. Spaceborne's primary job had been to secure landing sites and take out anti-air. Now the company was to hold the area, allowing regular ground troops to start their advance. Within the hour, armor would be touching down. Shortly after the armor touched down, logistics crews would begin setting up shop, and the HFDF would begin slowly expanding in the area like an unstoppable force.

We reported to medical to get Krista taken care of. Her injury was not serious enough to move her off-world, but medical personnel hadn't been brought planetside yet. So instead, Krista had to use an MHU or Mobile Hospital Unit. MHUs were boxy, looking to have more in common with a crate than a bed. You lay down inside them so they could work on you. There was a small line Krista stood in until her turn.

It was a mark of our training and conditioning that I wasn't more worried that my girlfriend had a hunk of alien metal in her shoulder. I wasn't happy about it, but I wasn't as bothered as I would have been before basic.

Once Krista was inside the MHU, I took an inventory of what we had. We'd lost a Heavy and three BIs. My other Heavy was damaged, and so were several other drones. We were also pretty much out of ammo, but that was easy to fix. I wasn't sure how long it would take to get new drones.

I organized the drones needing repair, along with ammo in my CCPU, and sent it to Monroe.

"Thanks for the list. Ammo should be easy. I'll get that to you first. A few cargo containers are in the LZ. You can rest next to those while I get you re-fitted."

I found the containers on the map and sent them to my team while I waited for Krista.

"ETA is three hours on the drones. You'll have to hang out until then," Monroe said.

"Bummer?" I said.

He laughed, "try not to get too torn up about it. Good work today. You seem to be fine with McLeod."

"Yeah, about that, is that my CCPU?" I asked.

"A bit," he admitted, "most of it is training. You didn't notice it, but you've been being conditioned for days like today. I'll let you know more about the replacement drones when I have more updates."

I started pulling up action reports from my team and drones. I'd have to get those compiled and sent to command. My CCPU would do an auto-summary for me to inspect for everything from the mission. All I had to do was wade through the report highlighting what I thought was important.

Krista came walking up to me.

"Aren't you supposed to be getting fixed?" I asked.

"Yeah, I was in there for a half hour. The MHU repaired the bone and put in synthetic muscles until mine can grow in. The round didn't break apart." She said, tossing a bit of metal in her hand.

I pointed, "that it?"

"A souvenir from Erie Prime," she said. "So, have you just been standing out here like a weirdo?" she asked.

"Reports," I said.

"Ah, so yes, you were just standing around like a weirdo."

I laughed, "fair enough, let's join the rest of the team."

We went to where Monroe had told me. There we found plenty of ammo and a few parts to fix up some of the BIs. If the Erie came at us, we'd be able to hold our own, but we were far from full strength.

I sat down against one of the crates, two of my BIs joining me. I wanted to sit with Krista, but that was a bad idea. Right now, to an Erie, my drones and I looked like three bad guys that they could take out with a single rocket. As a result, none of the human operators sat close to one another.

"How are you?" I asked Royle.

She shrugged, sitting a ways away from me. "Tired but fine. You?"

"Just tired. That was a little bit different from training, yet somehow it felt like something we'd done a thousand times."

"Something like that crossed my mind. It's a little different when you know things are real, isn't it?" she said.

"That it is."

I checked my CCPU notifications to find a list of available updates. They ranged from SIR settings to BI behavior. I checked the SIR updates. As I'd expected, they were lowering the amount of power the SIR was using.

Some of the updates were informational for human operators, each giving us more intel on the Erie and how to better kill them. The updates wouldn't load on my drones until I told them to. Useful, though they were, you didn't want your drones changing mid-fight if you could avoid it. I processed the updates and sent them to my team.

After I did that, I sent a ping to all of my friends and family, saying I was okay. A ping was all I could do, and I knew that I wouldn't get a reply for days as communications were being limited. But I'd promised Monica I would ping her every day.

"Fifteen percent," Sweeting said to the team after a moment.

"What are you on about?" Meyers asked.

"Read your updates, man. New troops are hitting the ground with these settings. They are fifteen percent more effective than when we hit the ground," Sweeting said.

"So we're better killers," Meyers said. "Isn't that the idea?"

"Dude, we've been here for three hours; we've gotten fifteen percent better in three hours!" Sweeting said.

There was silence on the comms as what Sweeting was saying registered in our minds. What was there to say? Apparently, we were the stuff of nightmares.

FIFTEEN

I awoke to a ping from my CCPU. I shifted in my bunk, or what passed for a bunk on deployment. In reality, the space I had been sleeping in had more in common with a shelf or shoebox. I was still in my full combat gear, with my SIR and sidearm next to me. My pack was just above my head near the small square door to the bunk. A thin line ran from it, attached to the top of my head, so all of my suit's life-support functions were uninterrupted. There was no padding nor room to move around. While the bunk wasn't what most would call nice, it was more than the HFDF needed to give us, strictly speaking. We could have just slept on the ground, our suits being more than up to the task. But that would also lead to random groups of troops lying around the base, getting underfoot.

I reached up and pushed open the door. Bright light flooded in. I snaked my way out of the bunk, putting my pack on and securing my weapons. The bunks were stacked five high and arranged in a block that was about twenty long. Each of the bunks was made of thick armor, with the top being several times thicker.

Other doors were opening now as members of my squad woke up for chow. It was slightly odd watching my squad come out of the

bunks—it was like a group of insects whose home had been threatened. But I had to marvel a bit at the bunks, simple though they were.
Every troop on base could mobilize in a matter of a heartbeat.

Krista came out and stood next to me, accompanied by her two
mandatory BIs. We greeted each other as warmly as possible in suits
and helmets that kept us completely contained. Around us, the base
was abuzz with motion. Two months into our occupation on Erie
Prime, and we already had several bases of operation. The bases oper-
ated almost like factories, each with power production along with full
complements of reclamation and mining drones—drones that were
busily gathering raw materials from the surrounding area so that the
rapid manufacturing units could produce everything the HFDF
needed, from ammo to aircraft.

This infrastructure was crucial to swarm warfare. It took a Rapid
Manufacturing Unit or RMU only a few minutes to build a BI from the
ground up, and it took a reclamation drone even less time to gather the
needed supplies. This speed was what made space warfare economical
for the HFDF. Other than the initial supplies we brought with us to
Erie Prime, the Erie system would be providing almost one hundred
percent of our materials. Heavy space mining operations were underway, fueling the fleet with orbital assets. Our core ground and air
strategy was pretty simple: build more drones than we lost.

This was what would eventually lose the Erie the war. With each
drone lost, we learned something that was applied to every combat
unit in action. As we learned, we lost fewer drones. At the same time,
we'd taken resource-rich areas, making our manufacturing fast and
easy. As it currently stood, for every drone we lost, RMUs were
producing two. These were luxuries that the Erie did not have.

This was compounded by the fact that the Erie were starting to lose
some of their best troops, forcing them to use ever more ineffective
units and pulling those units from support roles. They got weaker as
we got stronger. And like a constrictor, we'd eventually crush them.

Our career troops were planetside now, each trooper controlling over fifty BIs. With so many drones to tend to, the career units tended to lose more drones than we did, but the trade-off was that a fireteam of five humans could effectively take out a medium-sized town on their own.

So far, I'd liked all the career people I'd talked to. Like most of us in our Service Terms, I had assumed that the career troopers would be dicks to us and look down on us for being new. They hadn't. They'd taken the time to ask how the fighting had been and general questions about the enemy. When we talked, they listened intently. Monroe told us that career troops talked to service troops because we had firsthand experience with the enemy and could communicate that experience better than any report could. We couldn't win the war without the careers. Controlling a POD of eight to ten drones was hard enough, and I couldn't imagine trying to keep track of fifty of them. Conversely, the careers couldn't win without us.

Service troops were the first wave. Career formations weren't effective in the close-in fighting needed when establishing a corridor and locking down resources. While great in one-on-one combat, the drones started to struggle with strategy in large groups. There were limits to just how powerful we could make them. Plus, most of the career drones were built on the planet and not brought from home. We'd landed with a fraction of the drones needed to take Erie Prime. To bring an army big enough would require thousands of ships and shuttles.

Krista and I started toward the mess hall, one of the few places we could remove our helmets. Amenities like the mess were new. It was nice to actually see my girlfriend's face and not just the front of her helmet. Also, planetside was the medical staff from the Healers Touch, including Liz. We saw her standing outside the mess; her white suit stood out among the figures in gray. She greeted us quickly and then stepped inside. We joined her in an airlock that purged the air and replaced it. The atmosphere on Erie Prime was breathable, but as it was a war zone, no one could be outside without being fully suited up.

That went for medical staff, too. The moment she was allowed, Liz disengaged her helmet, her bronze hair in a tight bun.

"God, I don't know how you guys stand that all the time. I just want to breathe fresh air!" Liz complained.

I smiled. "You say that now, but you wouldn't feel that way if the Erie gassed us. And the air in your helmet is fresh," I pointed out.

"I know, I know. Has anyone been gassed? And your air is fresh; mine, not so much. Your air processors are better than ours. We really don't spend the time you do with them on."

"Yeah, corridor four had an LZ that got gassed," Krista piped in. "Obviously, no one was hurt by it, but I guess it covered everything in this yellow junk. From what I've heard, it's been a pain to clean up."

We walked over to one of several food lines. I was excited. Today the mess would be serving real food. Every day up to this point, they had just handed out nutrient packs, but the food processing units had landed last night.

Almost every advanced civilization had developed superfoods that could be grown quickly and feed an entire population. The Erie hadn't gotten that far yet, as they had never had the population to push their planet's resources, nor had they tried to leave Erie Prime until recently. Humans had done both. Thus, the Plump Grain had been developed. It had everything a body needed and could be made into almost anything.

The texture could be a little sketchy for some types of food, but for the most part, I didn't mind plump grain-based food. Honestly, after two months of nutrient packs, I didn't care if everything had the consistency of snot. I approached a machine that spat out a tray with food on it.

"Mashed potatoes, teriyaki chicken, and scrambled eggs with cheese?" Liz asked, disgusted.

I grinned. "I haven't had anything more than nutrient packs for two months," I said.

"But that combo?"

I laughed. "Judge me if you will. I told my CCPU to order what I've been thinking about the most, and I guess this was it."

We found a table and dug in. My eclectic plate wasn't unusual. Krista's was a sandwich, a chunk of steak, and some sort of snack cake. Say what you will about plump grain food, but when I bit into those mashed potatoes, I had never tasted anything better in my life. I couldn't help but sigh just a bit. Krista groaned, biting into her sandwich, and Liz looked at us like we were nuts.

"You know your body couldn't even digest that if it weren't for the biotech in it," Liz said conversationally.

Liz and Krista could have been getting it on in front of me at that moment, and I wouldn't have cared, but I didn't want to be a jerk and sound uninterested.

"No kidding?" I said.

She shook her head. "Nope. Pre-ageless humans couldn't eat it. In fact, they couldn't eat the bulk of the fruits and vegetables we eat on the different worlds we live on. Technically, we could eat dirt and live," she reminded us.

"I'm gonna remember that the next time I haven't eaten anything other than nutrient packs in weeks," I said.

Nice though breakfast had been, Krista and I had to hurry. We had a patrol scheduled for that morning. After we ate, we met up with our squad and drones in one of the base's staging areas. There were two of the Arbiters' heavy lift transport ships waiting for us. They weren't anything to look at. Unlike the sleek shuttles, the transports were modular and could carry troops or heavy armor. They had four large, heavily armored engines: two attached near the rear and the other two closer to the front. The engines moved around, giving the transports complete freedom of movement. In their current configuration, the rest of the transport was very boxy, allowing for a whole fireteam of troopers and drones to fit, with two carrying clips for the Heavies underneath. The front and sides boasted turrets and several rocket pods.

We all loaded into the transports, with cables from the ceiling securing us like in the shuttles. The pilot told us to prep for take-off, and the engines wound to life. The transport lifted into the air high enough for the Heavies to take position and clip onto the belly, and then we were moving. My helmet ported video feeds from the exterior, so it appeared to me as if the transport had no floor or walls. I saw forests and fields passing below us as we went. After a few minutes, the scenery changed to an urban environment, though not a happy one. There were no life forms below us, just burned-out buildings. The transport slowed, hovering fifteen meters or so above the ground.

"We are on-site; you are clear to deploy," the pilot told me.

I instructed the Heavies to disengage, then gave the order to unload to my team. We jumped out of the back of the transport, our anchors slowing us down and keeping us from running into one another. As my feet hit the ground, I shouldered my SIR and fanned out with the rest of my team, securing the area immediately around us.

My drone configuration was the standard of eight BIs, two BBALLs, and then the fireteam Heavies and mortars. We were in the Erie's version of the suburbs. In front of us were domed purple buildings. Behind us were burnt-out charred remains of what were once domed purple buildings. The unburned ones had no windows and were much larger than average human houses. The Erie lived in big family groups, with homes that had halls spiraling into a central living chamber, the top of which normally boasted an impressive skylight. The outside walls were a thick plaster-type material, and the homes would be easy to defend. Our intel suggested that with how violent the Erie's history was, it was likely that fighting among community members was commonplace or had been. Their culture also heavily emphasized hand-to-hand combat and taking on your opponent in person. It was a very macho mindset, if an alien race could be macho. The thought of climbing up a home and coming in through the skylight to kill everyone inside silently or by surprise was not something the Erie generally did.

What the bastards did, however, was hide weapons inside those homes and pop out, shooting reclamation drones. There wasn't much in the way of materials we needed in the houses, but in the center of each little community, there were resources. And our units had to traverse these areas. So we had several choices. We could post more security around reclamation units, but we were already spreading our troops thin, or we could make it difficult for the Erie to sneak into town, try to hide, and attack those units. We went with option B.

Honestly, I couldn't blame the Erie. We were the invaders, after all, and it wasn't like they were going to just leave us be as we turned their homes and communities into drones or whatever else we needed to kill more Erie. That said, knowing the Erie's temperament, it did seem like kind of a cowardly move hiding around, waiting for reclamation drones. But whatever.

We were here to secure the area, allowing reclamation security to be more localized and effective. The Erie would try to pick fights with us and draw us back to a dwelling to force us into close combat. Unfortunately for them, we didn't want to play that way. It would have also been a pain searching dwellings for weapons and Erie, not to mention you'd just have to do it again if the Erie tried to come back. So our orders were to burn the houses.

This was probably going to happen anyway, as our strategy was knocking them back to the Stone Age. And while I thought the plan was a good one, I did feel a little like an asshole burning down something's home on the off chance they might put guns in it. If the Erie were inside a building, they'd come running out, and we would shoot them if they were armed. If we knew they were inside before we set it on fire, we would task Heavies to the house, light it up, and then the Heavies would deal with anything fleeing the building—again, if they were armed. A lot of non-combatants had died and would die in this war, but we weren't going out of our way to do it.

Our jobs were easy. They consisted of walking down the street, stopping in the middle of the road, pointing our SIRs at a building, and shooting it with a small sticky charge that blew a hole in the wall, then shooting a special incendiary dart inside. This last part would have been hard if our suits didn't make shooting effortless. Then you walked to the next house. We could, of course, task our BIs with this task, but they didn't suffer from the boredom we did.

After a few minutes, the street behind me was thick with smoke as the buildings started to blaze. Each trooper took a street with his or her POD. Occasionally, small resupply drones would come by, keeping us all stocked up on charges and darts. We also kept various comm lines open, talking to one another.

This patrol was not a high priority and was considered more of a housekeeping item, which was why we pulled it. If there was a downside to being Special Teams, it was that you had to be ready to go take care of an urgent or priority op at any given time, but it wasn't like the HFDF was going to have us sitting on our thumbs the rest of the time. With this mission, if and when something came up, we'd be fully armed, rested, and ready to rock. Hell, we'd be eager for it. This made the day's roller coasters of semi-boredom interrupted by intense fighting and behind enemy lines missions sometimes lasting over a day.

I was burning another building when my CCPU pinged me. It was Monroe.

"First squad, we have a priority mission. Prepare for pickup," he said.

"Fireteam Alpha, prep for pickup for priority mission. Rendezvous at waypoint Alpha," I said to the team.

I disengaged my POD, making my way to Alpha, meeting up with the rest of the Fireteam. Royle's team was gathering there too, and we soon heard the roar of two transports coming in overhead, their backs opening up, turrets on the undercarriage swiveling, looking for targets. The ships hovered ten meters off the ground. I gave the order for my team to load up, making sure everyone was on before I was. As Krista loaded up, I took three running steps and jumped. My suit boosted my jump, and my anchor jerked me up to the transport.

Once inside, two of the BIs that were always with the transport herded me to the front while all of my team's drones leaped in. The ship bounced a bit as the Heavies latched on, and then it tilted forward, starting to move, cords coming from the ceiling connecting to my suit. An indicator on my display showed my anchor being charged by the ship.

Monroe opened a comm line to Royle and me. "We have a downed shuttle thirty clicks from your position. The pilot's ejection pod was unable to eject, and the pilot is trapped. You are to set up and hold a perimeter while maintenance and medical drones extract the pilot. You will have transport air support along with four mini gunships."

I felt anxious at once. Humans could take a lot, and with our tech, we were faster and stronger than the Erie. Even well behind enemy lines, a pilot could hide relatively easily for days waiting for EVAC. But not when they were pinned down. The Erie could kill them with a single missile or just walk into the downed shuttle and shoot or stab them.

"Roger that," Royle said seriously. "What's the situation like on the ground?"

"There are hostiles moving into the area; the Minis are currently holding the area immediately around the shuttle, but recon shows large numbers of enemies en route."

My display showed a stream of data coming in as I relayed our mission to my team. I found it unlikely that the Erie had just managed to get lucky taking out one of our birds. They'd probably spent a few days planning the mission, which meant they would be ready for a fight on the ground. Missions like these were always stressful. You couldn't be sure how prepared the enemy was going to be. The stress was also compounded by the fact that you couldn't just retreat if the shit hit the fan too hard.

The back of the transport was still open, and I could now see two medical drones coming up behind us. Now that the pilot was part of our mission, I could see everything about their current situation. I pulled up their vitals, seeing that they had a broken spine and that their CCPU was keeping them unconscious. I checked their ID, seeing it was Captain Goldberg from the Arbiter. That it was someone we knew would make the team that much more on edge.

"Goldberg's our mission; let's get this done quick and get her back to the ship!" I said.

I could see my team shift at the name, each of them disquieted by the knowledge that it was one of our own shipmates and someone who we had come to see as a friend during our many training missions.

"Can we move any faster?" Sweeting said.

Sweeting's thoughts were echoed by others. As we flew, I pulled up feeds, watching the enemy streaming into the area. While they had probably worked hard to bring the shuttle down, there was no way they could have planned where it would crash. That was good. If they had artillery in the area, it would take time to zero it.

When the time to drop came, it was all I could do to keep from pushing my team out the back. I jumped out, falling around a hundred meters; my anchor stopped me right before I hit the ground. The Minis were circling the area, their guns buzzing here and there. To my left was the smoking form of a shuttle, one wing up in the air, the other completely missing. At once, the maintenance drones started work on cutting their way to the pilot.

"Perimeter up," I ordered. For all of the angst and nerves I'd felt on the flight, my mind and body calmed as soon as I'd landed. My training and conditioning took control.

My POD and team spread out, covering the exposed belly of the shuttle, while Royle's team covered the other side. I directed several of the BIs to dig fast impromptu foxholes. The machines started on the task, working at a speed that would make it very obvious to even the Erie that they weren't human. As they dug hole after hole, other drones and my team took position. As I looked at the map and the enemy's movement, I adjusted zones, trying to optimize them.

"Contact," Meyers said, his voice calm and controlled.

I shouldered my SIR, scanning ahead of me. The Minis opened fire in the near distance.

"Confirm you have hostiles inbound. Minis moving back for close-in support. No ETA on pilot extraction," Monroe said professionally as ever.

My display showed the progress the drones were making on Goldberg. They hadn't reached her yet, and from what we could tell, her legs might be pinned in the cockpit. I toggled my display to the battle map, and my heart skipped a beat. Hostiles inbound was an understatement; my map was popping with close to a thousand contacts.

"Fireteam Alpha to command, requesting additional aerial or ground assistance. Monroe, we have a lot of bad guys closing on our location," I said.

"Negative on the additional support, Alpha. Ground artillery is zeroing in on your location, but you are too close to the enemies for safe bombardment. The transports and Minis will try to hold anything fifty meters or more away. Hold your perimeter as long as you can. If needed, the MEDI drones will execute a surgical extraction," Monroe said.

I cringed. That would mean that if we were starting to lose the line, the drones would merely cut off anything on Goldberg that was pinned down. Sure, she'd live, and those parts of her body would be regrown, but I didn't like the idea of a team member getting chopped in half because I couldn't hold the line.

The Erie were still closing fast. On the other side of the shuttle, I heard gunfire as Royle and her team engaged, along with the buzz of auto-cannon fire from above. I hunkered down, waiting for an enemy to come into my zone. I didn't have long to wait before I saw movement in the trees ahead of me. Flashes of purple came into view. All of the information from my Whiskers and drones, along with the data from every other unit in the area, was being piped into my display. I deployed the Heavies, telling them to funnel the Erie into columns at the head of which my team and I took aim.

The first Heavy started firing, its large caliber guns burping out rounds that sliced through the forest, making bits and pieces of foliage fly. The random blobs of purple came into sight. I drew a bead on one and fired a single round. The Erie jerked and dropped, falling backward. I drilled two others behind the first. Every member of the team was firing now, along with all of our drones. The enemy was using the area's thick, heavy trees for cover, popping out and firing back at us. Little puffs of dirt rose up all around me. The nano-material on my SIR formed into a T-Pod, giving me more control as I started taking out Erie.

The Erie were doing a pretty good job of using cover. They'd pop out, take a shot, and duck back behind the trees. Slowly, they'd creep up on their bellies to the next tree and start the process over again. I tasked my BBALLs with targeting them from above, but the dense foliage obstructed most of their shots. This was going to end up turning into a close-quarters fight. I pulled back from the fighting, connecting with Royle.

"These bastards are getting too close," I noted.

By all appearances, they were going to employ tactics that we used. They had more numbers, and they were fighting in a way that said they weren't going to be dumb but knew that if they pushed enough troops at us, they'd be able to win.

"Options?" Royle asked.

"Incendiaries? I'm worried we are too close to use them, but we might be able to use a few small fires to clog the area with smoke," I said.

"Let's see what the ETA on Goldberg is," she said, not sounding like she liked the idea.

I refocused on the fight to check in with my POD and Fireteam. The Erie were still advancing closer and closer to us, though they were

starting to slow down as the gunships took shots. I pinged the maintenance drones to see where they were with Goldberg. They were not
moving as quickly as one would have hoped.

Each Fireteam had a dedicated computer aboard the Arbiter to
handle any kind of analysis that we might need. I tapped into mine
and started it working on whether it thought using fire for defense was
a bad idea.

Some more dirt exploded by my head, and I focused on where a
group of Erie were and launched a grenade at them. It blew, sending
dust and rock flying, but my Whiskers noted that the Erie had taken
cover under some roots. The Arbiter pinged me with the report.

"Looks like it's a bad idea. We have a high chance of the fire
hampering flight ops and pinning us down. It's a last-ditch," I said.

"Got it," Royle said.

There were a few more booms from grenades. Two of Meyers's BIs
went up as their foxhole was hit. Then there were several more large
explosions. The Erie had zeroed small artillery on our location. The
gunships fired rockets, and two of them zoomed off, looking for the
Erie's guns.

In my HUD, I could see G2's foxhole taking fire. A quick check
showed BI4 and BI6 had sustained minor damage, with BI5 having
been grazed on the head. There were more deep booms as more
artillery hit our area. Debris filled the air, and I tried to duck down, but
too late. I felt my head wrench to the side, my CCPU alerting me that
I'd been hit, in case I needed the notification. At my feet, a large chunk
of stone lay. My suit didn't register any major damage, so the rock
must not have been going that fast, but it's still never good getting hit
in the head with a big rock. This firefight needed to end swiftly. I
toggled my display modes until I found one capable of seeing through
the dust in the air.

The Erie, assuming that we could no longer see, were ditching their
cover, rushing our location. I sighted my SIR and gave the command to
hold fire until the Erie were mostly out of their cover. Once they were,

we opened up. Our shots took the Erie off guard as we downed the ranks closest to their cover, leaving the forward units to the Heavies. Above, the gunships lit up the enemy as well. In the tree line, what Erie hadn't made it away from cover were retaking it, prepping for another slow push forward.

I did an ammo check, seeing that my units were doing fine in that department. On Royle's side, the Erie were trying to push their way forward much in the same way they had with my side, but not making the same mistakes.

"They are getting smart fast," Royle said.

"I see that."

"Shit, this must be kind of what it's like fighting us," Retz in Royle's team said.

"Shut it, Retz!" Royle said, and then just to me, "he's got a point."

Above me, one of our gunships exploded. That was less than a good sign. Its wreckage fell onto one of Sweeting's foxholes, taking out three BIs.

I opened a channel to Monroe. "This isn't going well," I said to him.

"Affirmative. MEDI drones are with the pilot and are commencing emergency surgery. EVAC in five," Monroe said.

My anger flared up at the news. We'd failed. Right now, the drones in the shuttle had gone from trying to remove all of Goldberg to cutting her in half. A few short minutes later, the drones notified us that they were done.

"Leave your drones. They will cover your EVAC. Get moving!" Monroe ordered.

"Ditch drones and load up on the boat. We're out of here!" I said to my team.

I received a notification that Monroe was taking command of all drones as the transports approached the ground. As they did, our drones sprang up, unloading everything they had, pushing the Erie back. Training kicked in, and I trusted the drones to do their jobs as I ran and then jumped, feeling my anchor hoist me up. BIs on the transport pulled me in, followed by other team members. A flying MEDI drone with Goldberg lifted off. It all happened so fast that the enemy didn't have time to respond.

As we climbed, I couldn't help but feel a little guilty watching what was once my POD of drones on the ground. Though another part of me was impressed to see the progress they were making under Monroe's command. It wasn't a sustainable fight, but he was certainly making our drones a much larger threat than the transport.

As we left the area, missiles flew past us, hitting the area around the shuttle, destroying it, our drones, and anything alive in the vicinity. The exterior feed showed a massive rising column of smoke and flames as the forest burned. I watched the air shimmer with shock-waves as more ordnance hit the area. A moment later, the transport rattled as the sound of the bombardment reached us. I felt it thump in my chest.

I pulled my attention from the crash site and checked on Goldberg's status, seeing that she was stable and still asleep. Everyone was alive and headed home, which was the mission, but I couldn't help feeling like we'd somehow failed. From the postures of my teammates, I could tell they felt the same. I tried to distract myself from our failure by looking over my CCPU's auto-generated report of the mission. It didn't work.

Monroe was there to debrief us when we landed back at the base. We walked with him to a building, allowing us to remove our helmets. As I looked at the faces of my squad, no one other than Meyers seemed to be in a good mood.

It was odd seeing Monroe. I could count on one hand the number of times he'd been planetside since we'd arrived at Erie Prime. For the most part, command spent their time in VR pods controlling and supporting their troops from the ship. *Is he here because we fucked up?* I wondered.

Monroe looked us over. He didn't appear upset at all. "You feel like you've lost today, haven't you?" he said, and then, without waiting for a response, continued, "You didn't. You did your jobs, and you did them well. I know it doesn't feel that way right now, but trust me, today was a win. Our pilot will make a full recovery, and believe me, she won't hold this against you. I assure you, Captain Goldberg will be extremely thankful for what you did today—a sentiment that will be shared by her spouse and children," he said with warmth and firmness.

"This is the shitty part of our job. Sometimes you go into a losing situation. You've been in these in training. The Erie planned the hell out of this op. Give credit where it is due. They did a good job today. But we didn't lose a single person; they lost over a thousand units. And for what? For a shuttle that will be replaced by the end of the day, one hundred and fifty-two basic and heavy infantry drones that *have* already been replaced, and a gunship that will be replaced within the hour? The Erie do not understand how little today's losses mean to the HFDF. They paid a heavy price for today's perceived win."

He was right, and I knew he was. Our chances of holding that area for long were slim. Had the Erie pushed their luck more, or had they not jumped the gun when they thought we couldn't see, they could have advanced a whole lot faster. The reality was that we could have just as easily not gotten Goldberg out at all. But knowing something and feeling it were different.

His expression changed. "I'm down here for different reasons today, though. Our initial deployment for Erie Prime was set for three to four months." There were a few looks of surprise at this. When we'd left for Erie Prime, none of us had thought to ask how long we'd be gone, but I would have assumed it would be longer than a few months.

Monroe smirked a bit at our expressions. "I see none of you looked up average deployments for Service Term troops in your CCPUs. You need to remember that we are service troops. Our jobs are not to win the war. We are here to make it so that career units can get a strong foothold so they can spend the years it will take winning the war. It will take them the better part of a decade to complete the mission here.

"The Hunter fleet is being called back in preparation for a possible major deployment. Career forces are well embedded here and can handle losing our support. We were only about a month out from being recalled as it was at the most. I do not know what our mission is going to be or if it will happen at all. This might just be precautionary. But we and all support staff will be leaving Erie Prime within a week."

He looked at all of us. "We've done good work here. Today has been a hard day. Get some chow and try to get some rest."

SIXTEEN

I walked up the ramp of the shuttle alongside the rest of my squad. The only drones with us were our two mandatory BIs. The rest of our PODs would be staying here on Erie Prime, where they could be put to use. I'd managed to shake off my frustrations with what happened to Goldberg. She'd messaged all of us, saying thank you a day after we'd rescued her. She'd be fine by the time we deployed to wherever we were going next.

While I wasn't weighed down by the experience anymore, I was determined to avoid similar situations in the future. The reality was, in situations like that, time was all that mattered. Royle and I had several conversations about the mission, and others like it. We'd always been too focused on other objectives, like how to best hold our perimeter or taking an objective. While that wasn't a bad thing, it wasn't what we needed to be keeping an eye on. Both Fireteams had reviewed mission logs and identified areas where we could have slowed down or hampered the Erie before they reached our perimeter. Fifteen minutes. That's how much more time we could have bought the maintenance and repair drones with Goldberg. In the end, it wouldn't have mattered. Data showed that a surgical extract would be the best, if not the only option, no matter what we'd done. But fifteen minutes could mean life and death. We weren't going to give another second to any enemy we encountered. Monroe and our Lt., Lisa Middleton, had reviewed our findings and agreed with our assessments.

I turned, taking a last look at Erie Prime. All around were drones and people moving about. In my hand, I held a rock. It was customary to take one with you when you left a world. There was a wide range of display boxes that I could get to keep it in. This way, a piece of Erie Prime would always be with me. It seemed fitting. I bounced it in my hand a few times and then walked to my spot in the shuttle.

The cord from the shuttle secured itself to my suit, and I tapped into the shuttle's external feeds by habit, making the walls and floor seem to vanish. There was a thrum and a slight vibration as the shuttle lifted from the ground. It turned in the air and started moving forward. As it sped up, its nose pointed up, and the engines roared. I was pressed back in my suit as we accelerated. I switched views through the external feeds, watching the horizon of Erie Prime expand. All around us in the distance was smoke adding to a dark haze that had persisted since the fourth day of the campaign.

There would undoubtedly be an ecological impact on Erie Prime due to this war. Aside from the smoke of millions of structures being burned, there was the displaced population and the smoke from the dead as they were cremated. Erie Prime itself would recover in a few years from our encounter, though. But decades from now, the Erie would still be reclaiming ruined cities and rebuilding what was once a vast civilization. Unless, of course, they did something in the mean-time to provoke the Human Federation again. In which case, the Erie would succumb to a nano plague that would blot them out of history. And they would be replaced with Humans instead. More likely, the Erie wouldn't recover from this on a societal level.

It was almost a fluke they'd managed to come together in the first place. Now there would be years of blame and infighting, along with a long-lasting memory of losing so badly that they almost died out. Add to that, they were losing centuries worth of technological knowledge and achievements. I could see the war of today turning into the wedge of tomorrow, and the memory of a past time; in a few generations, it could become a legend or a religious event that would haunt and keep them on Erie Prime for centuries to come. But I could be wrong. The Erie might just dust themselves off and come at us again. For their sakes, I hoped they didn't do that.

The roar of the shuttle died down some as we entered space, and the vibration from speeding through the atmosphere calmed. The space around the planet was not strewn with debris like one would assume after a major conflict. Instead, fleet clean-up drones had cleaned up the space around the planet, helping to ensure that small bits of the battle didn't slam into ships or shuttles.

Below, the once blue and green planet had taken on a brown tint, so ever-present was the smoke of their dying civilization. I could see great pillars of it rising from the ground where our army had been and where the front line was. Seeing it on such a large scale darkened my mood a bit. Necessary though the war had been, we were responsible for the destruction I observed now. In all of Earth's history, there had never been a genocide on the scale of which I'd taken part in on Erie Prime. Yet history told me that the genocide of today would be small compared to the inevitable one had the Erie not been struck down. I turned my attention away from the planet, shaking off the dark feeling.

Before us was the Arbiter. I couldn't see it, of course. Not only was it far away from us, but its hull was coated in a black material that absorbed almost all light. However, my CCPU was in communication with the shuttle, and the shuttle knew where the ship was, so I could see an icon for it fast approaching.

The shuttle turned, facing away from the ship, and fired its engines, slowing us down rapidly. Then it flipped back around before it reached the ship, letting its space anchors slow us down the rest of the way. We docked with a slight thump, and the ramp to the shuttle lowered. I walked out with the rest of my squad, making for an airlock. Our BIs left us, going to wherever they were stored on the ship. Once we were out of the airlock, I disengaged my helmet.

"It's going to be nice not having to wear that all day," Krista said.

"What are you talking about?" Meyers asked, sounding irritated. "It doesn't feel any different with our helmets off. Besides, now I can't ignore you people."

Before any of us could say anything, he stalked off down a passage. I thought about talking to him but decided better of it. Meyers was a prick, and there was just no changing that.

"I agree with you, McLeod," Betts said. "The suits feel natural, but there's just something about having that helmet off."

"I'd say," I said, walking up to Krista and kissing her.

She leaned into my ear. "And think about how nice it will be not having the suit on at all."

We laughed, and our squad pretended like we weren't there. We weren't alone, though. Sweeting and Kwasny were in the middle of a long, deep kiss. We all made our way to the showers. When my suit flowed off my body, I was surprised that I wasn't assaulted by the smell of months-old BO. Our suits had minor cleaning functions that seemed to keep it at bay. That said, I was thankful to see that the shower would run several times before letting me out. I also appreciated the fact that the thing was like a car wash and did a very thorough job. I doubted the showers needed to run more than once but likely did so for our emotional rather than physical needs.

I stepped into the shower and held my hands up. As soon as the water started hitting my skin, I felt like I was in a kind of paradise. I felt like months' worth of dirt and debris was being blasted off my body. I knew this was nonsense, of course. I'd never come in contact with dirt on Erie Prime, and I knew my suit kept me clean. But knowing, and *knowing*, aren't the same thing, are they? I breathed in the thick steam as the water ran and felt my muscles relax. It was good to be home.

I returned to our room, where Krista and I slid into my bunk and didn't come out until breakfast the next day.

It took the Arbiter several days to reach jump distance from Erie Prime. Days that we spent sleeping, eating, and for Royle and me, going over reports from our time on Erie Prime. After the constant rhythm of war, it felt odd to do nothing. Or to mostly be doing nothing. We spent some time in the medical bay with the medics, checking over all of our vitals and seeing how well our bodies were performing. They ran every analysis that could be run on a CCPU and biosystem, along with fine-tuning them. Sitting with them as they discussed results made me appreciate what it was like for our drones.

After that, I met with Dr. Philips, the ship's psychiatrist. I sat in his office as his eyes were out of focus. I'd been in relatively constant contact with him on Erie Prime, sending reports about my team and myself.

He focused on me. "How are you feeling?" he asked.

"Fine. Better after the shower," I laughed.

"I can understand that; those never get old after a deployment, by the way. Just wait until you take a real one on leave after a long deployment." His tone became more business-like. "Any concerns with your team? I see that you had a few with Private Meyers, but nothing out of the ordinary with him, and I suspect that's not what's on your mind."

I thought for a moment. "Shouldn't I be more bothered about killing as many Erie as I did?" I asked.

"How bothered are you by it?"

I thought again. "On a logical level, I'm disturbed that we had to do what we did in the Erie system. But emotionally... I'm not that bothered by it. I was more upset seeing the planet than thinking about the Erie. Why is that?"

"They aren't human or anything that humans are supposed to care about. Erie Prime is a life-bearing planet, which is something we care about deeply. But that's just because it's life-bearing. If it were a dead world or even one like Arrow, you wouldn't worry about the damage our time there caused," Philips said frankly. "I wish I could say that there was a better answer, or that in the years since finding other intelligent life, humans would have emotionally evolved to care about life other than our own. But we haven't. In a way, I suppose it shouldn't be a surprise. After all, it was finding other intelligent life that made us start caring about not killing each other. We can show empathy for an entire race or for races that we find ways to connect with. But in the case of the Erie, there aren't any real connections we can make.

"This is compounded by the fact that humans don't have to deal with death the way we did in the past. Death is still a certainty for all of us, but it is potentially thousands of years in the future. For our minds, it's not quite real. So part of your lack of concern is that you don't know how to be concerned about the Erie dying. Humans are supposed to live for millennia, not hostile aliens."

That I could start to wrap my head around. He gave me a few books to read before sending me on my way. As soon as I was out of his office, I tried to push the Erie from my mind.

We all understood why we were to rest as much as we were. We would have a short leave once back on Orion while the Arbiter was prepped, and then it would be off to some other system. Where and what we were fighting was still unknown.

Our squad's room wall was displaying one of the ship's external feeds when we made the jump back to Orion. One moment there was nothing but stars, and the next, the bright blue and white of Orion. The number of ships floating around the station was incredible. Not just the numbers but the types of ships. The station didn't specialize in any one kind of industry or function, but to look at it now, you wouldn't know that.

What looked like most of the Hunter Armada was either at port or floating around the station. With them were several hospital ships, including Liz's. But the biggest thing that I noticed was the cargo vessels. Not the typical commercial type, but the military variety. The

HFDF had its own cargo fleet. Ships that were a little tougher and faster than their civilian counterparts. Each had a complement of automated drones and defense systems built into them. They had large bays and small cargo drones by the hundreds that could launch and make their way to whatever planet or object they needed. They could quickly load and unload, and the cargo drones could deliver cargo to ships positioned within fleets.

We docked at the station, and I didn't need any encouragement to leave the ship. Krista and I walked hand-in-hand with the rest of our squad off the Arbiter onto a busy terminal. Several of the squad members made their way to a group of very attractive drones that were affectionately called Bone Drones.

Krista bumped my arm. "Have you ever used a Bone Drone?" she asked.

I chuckled. "Yeah, once," I admitted. "You?"

She raised her eyebrow. "Really now? What did you get?" she asked, teasing.

"Nope, you first."

She smiled. "One time. I was curious what it would be like, and I have to admit it was fun. I can see why people use them."

A voice came from behind us. It was that of Monroe. "The HFDF almost put them on ships and on the ground, you know?"

"That would blow off some steam," Krista said with a smirk.

"In the tests they ran, it did. Bone Drones changed sex work when they were invented. But despite the positive impact they had on morale, it's not like you're going to stay in your suit when you're doing the deed. That meant a higher chance of death, and it also meant having to take up more space in a base," he explained.

"Yeah, and God knows we don't want to take up space. You know, I honestly thought the recruiter was BS'ing me when he said I'd sleep in a box on deployment?" I said.

Monroe laughed. "Didn't we all!"

We found Liz looking out of one of the many large windows at her ship. When I came up next to her, I could see what she was looking at. Yard crews were installing two long black rectangular pods on the sides of the ship.

"What are they doing?" she asked no one in particular as we approached. "My CCPU can detect that whatever they are is attached to the ship, but nothing more."

On the other hand, I could integrate with the PODs as they were HFDF, but Monroe answered, sounding concerned. "Those are defense measures. Several fighter drones and a complement of anti-missile batteries. If your ship is about to get into trouble and your escort can't help, they'll take control of the helm and rabbit out of the area. If that is not an option, they will emergency jump you someplace safe."

Liz turned to him, looking irritated. "Why would a hospital ship need defenses? Those things will take over? And what do you mean, escort?"

I answered. "Whoever we are fighting is another race. They aren't going to care what kind of ship they are attacking so long as it's one of ours. The Healer's Touch can't take the damage a military vessel can. Think about it? You'd be defenseless and an easy target."

Liz didn't look happy.

Krista's eyes had been out of focus and came back in. "You will have a Comet-class destroyer as an escort. I don't think a ship has been assigned yet, or at least I can't see her name."

Liz looked at Krista, me, and then to Monroe. "What are we going into?" she asked.

Monroe looked somber. "Nothing good if you need a dedicated escort. Normally, there's just one for a group of support ships. Come on, this terminal is busy. Go enjoy your time off. It might be the last you get in a while," Monroe said and walked off.

Krista, Liz, and I made our way through the packed corridors to the Lift. Liz didn't seem overly talkative as the Lift started down.

"I'm sure your ship won't be in any danger. You know how the HF is with safety," I tried to comfort her. It didn't seem to help.

She sighed. "It's not me that I'm really worried about. I'm sure our ship will be with a small group of other support vessels like it was over Erie Prime."

"So, what's bothering you?" I asked.

She looked over at Krista and me and then back out the Lift's window. "You know... all of you on the ground."

"We'll be..." I started but was cut off.

"How do you know that?" Liz asked sternly. "I saw lots of people from Hunter when we were on Erie Prime. I know humans can live through a lot, but there are limits. And if they think my ship might be in danger, that means we aren't facing some weak race like the Erie." She waved her hand at the window and the gathered ships. "If we were, do you really think the entire Hunter Armada would be here? And why did your commander look worried?"

I placed my hand on her arm, trying to calm her; others were looking at us. Most of them were HFDF. "Okay, okay, I see what you mean. You're right. If this much of the fleet is here and with how Monroe looked, I get it."

She looked like she wanted to argue more but instead just said, "You promise you won't get hurt... badly. I guess it would be dumb of me to ask you not to get hurt at all. You got shot what, four times on Erie Prime?"

"You looked at my medical records?" I asked.

Krista laughed.

"You got tagged five times, missy," Liz accused.

Krista stopped laughing. "None of them were serious. Only one made it past my suit." She held up a chunk of metal in her hand. "But on my first day, I did get this baby from the one that did make it past my suit." She looked at it intently. "Monroe gave me the name of a guy who can turn it into a pendant before we deploy."

"Nothing even made it through my suit," I pointed out.

Liz looked at Krista. "Is that the bullet that got lodged in your shoulder?"

"Yep," Krista said proudly.

"You're having it turned into jewelry?" Liz asked incredulously.

"What? It would be bad luck if she didn't have it!" I said. Another trooper next to us who'd been trying to pretend like he wasn't eavesdropping nodded his agreement. I pointed at him. "He agrees," I said.

Liz shook her head and muttered something about insanity.

At the terminal, Krista and I left Liz, heading for a train that would take us out to my parents' house. I was disappointed to find out that they were on vacation in another system. We only had two days on leave, and they wouldn't be able to get back in time. Though my mother was sure to remind me that had I been more prompt about sending notification, they could have caught a ship home. Which wasn't really something that hard to do because I had a computer in my head and I was a grown man who was capable of thinking ahead and some other things you could expect a mother to say.

We got off the train and caught a taxi to the house. We stood outside, Krista holding my hand, looking around the street.

"Nice house," she said.

The house wasn't large or fancy in any way, but I could see where it would seem that way if you'd grown up on a dead world. We walked in, the cat coming up to me and looking at me. It looked like he couldn't decide if he wanted to ignore me as punishment for leaving or to say hi. I walked up, petting him, and he purred reluctantly. Krista removed the thing of nano-material holding her hair in a bun. It poofed around her head, but the action seemed to relax her a bit.

I took Krista on a house tour, ending in my room.

"So this is my room," I said, walking in.

She looked at me with a smirk. "Saved that for last, huh? What do you think is gonna happen?"

I put my hands on her waist, smiling down at her. I leaned over and kissed her lips and then her neck.

"I just thought we might like being in an area that wasn't three feet tall, is all," I said.

"Ah, I see," she said, her hands running up my chest.

Her suit started to slide off her body, mine following just behind. My kisses moved from her neck to her collarbone. My hands roamed down her body, and all of a sudden, I was thrilled that my parents were out of town.

I felt Krista's fingers gently move up my arms. Mine went to her waist, and my lips found hers. We held the kiss for a moment, and I felt our bodies start to mold to each other. When we broke, I looked into her eyes, seeing a startling hunger in them.

She huffed, "Fuck this, I'm so not waiting. We can do the sweet lovey shit later."

I was confused for only a moment, then I felt her hands on my chest, and she pushed me onto the bed. I grinned, loving the sight of her as she climbed on top of me. I instantly felt myself getting hard as she straddled me. A wicked grin crossed her face, and then her hips were moving down.

"Oh fuck," I groaned.

I felt pleasure like fire run through my body. My hands slid up the smooth skin of her thighs and rested on her hips. My gaze moved up her belly and breasts to her face. Her expression was almost predatory, and it made every cell in my body pop to life.

"Christ, you're sexy," I commented.

Did you really manage to land this woman? a voice in my head said. That wicked and unimaginably sexy grin turned up her lips again. She leaned back slightly and began to move up and down, biting her lip and moaning softly as she did. I moaned and gripped her hips, guiding them as they began to rock. Her hair tickled my face as she leaned over me.

"We have been stuck in a box for months, and we are going to be on deployment for who knows how long. I fully plan on enjoying myself, *and* enjoying you on leave." Her voice had an edge I'd never heard before, and I absolutely loved it!

"Mmmm, that sounds good to me," I ran my hand up her side, "sounds like you best get to work then. That's an order."

At my words, I saw a flash of pure lust in her eyes. "Yes, sir," her voice purred.

She leaned back and began to move again. I guided her hips as she went up and down, making bliss rock through me as I went in and out of her. I thrust up, making her moan, and I cupped her breast. She leaned forward, and I took her perfect nipple in my lips, sucking and nibbling on it. This elicited more moans, and I felt her clench around me, her thighs squeezing me.

I felt like I would burst, but I wouldn't let myself. She broke away as she rode me faster and harder. Goddamn, I was glad we had the house to ourselves. I put all my focus on not exploding in the moaning goddess on top of me. I felt my self-control start to crack as she moved, making her breasts bounce in the most delicious way.

"Fuuuuck!" I groaned, unable to take it anymore.

I gripped her hips, rolling her off me. Surprise and confusion crossed her face. I rolled her onto her belly and hoisted up her hips. "My turn," I said. I drove into her, feeling my mind start to come undone. I was rewarded with a moan of ecstasy from Krista.

I gripped her hips and started to pump, feeling her tighten and flex around me. The sensation of it drove out what little sanity I had left. I sent a command to my CCPU, slightly desensitizing myself. There was no way I was finishing first, and this was not going to be fast.

"God damn, Alex!" she moaned.

I pumped harder, loving the feeling of driving into her. I pulled her up. One of my hands reached around to grope and squeeze her breasts. I kissed and sucked her neck as my hand shot down between her legs.

"Let's see how loud you can get," I growled in her ear, making her shiver.

I began moving my hips again, and my fingers found the tight ball of nerves at her apex. My fingers began to move, teasing her and coaxing pleasure from her with each movement. I was rewarded with moans that grew in volume with each motion of my fingers and body. Her hips rocked, and I felt her walls pulse and tighten as she went over the edge. I kept rubbing her as she rode out her orgasm, her body shuddering slightly in my arms.

She looked at me, her face sweaty, her eyes glazed with pleasure. "Did you...?"

I shook my head.

She smiled, her voice husky, "Mmmmm, we can't have that."

I'd never thought there were benefits to being with someone with extensive training in hand-to-hand combat. I mean, what use would it be in the bedroom, right? That had been a wrong belief to have. Krista McLeod had me on my back with her atop me in what felt like a nanosecond. It might have been the hottest thing anyone had ever done to me.

All of these thoughts left my mind, of course, as soon as they happened. With those thoughts, every other thought I'd ever had in my life left as well. A state I stayed in until I felt myself throbbing inside her and every muscle in my body tensing and shuddering. As I went, I felt her clamp down as she pulled every last bit of pleasure from me.

———

THAT EVENING WE WERE SPRAWLED ON AN OUTDOOR COUCH, LISTENING TO the wind in the trees as a fire in a small pit next to us crackled. We had to wear our suits while in public, but mercifully my back deck wasn't public. My parents had planted trees and shrubs around the property to give them privacy, and it felt like we were all alone in the woods. I was just in a pair of shorts, Krista in one of my old shirts and a pair of sweats.

She was looking at the fire, smiling.

She turned to me, "I like this," she said.

"Yeah, me too. Someday this can be our norm."

She smiled, "I like that too."

I sat watching her watch the fire, occasionally looking at the stars, smiling as if there wasn't anything else in the universe.

I noticed she was looking at me, her eyebrow raised questioningly.

"What are you thinking about?" she asked.

What was I thinking about? The coming war, the past war? Here sitting around with Krista, loving every moment of the evening. I really would be fine doing this every night. Not just sitting by the fire, but sitting with her.

"I'm thinking I'm in love with you," I said honestly.

She smiled broadly, crawling on top of me. She kissed me and looked into my eyes. "I love you too," she said.

I sighed in relief, pulling her in closer.

"Were you worried I didn't?" she asked.

"A little," I admitted.

She kissed me. "That's nothing you ever have to question."

SEVENTEEN

Our leave, while enjoyable, was far too short. I hadn't seen Monica because she was on a Satcity, and Jon had been transferred to a military cargo ship. He wasn't part of the HFDF, but like Liz, his branch of the government was there to help out. His schedule was packed as he helped prepare his vessel and several others for departure. Charles was in some distant corner of the galaxy, and Liz was prepping the Healer's Touch. Oddly, I felt like I was coming home as I stepped back onto the Arbiter. I hadn't thought it would ever really feel that way, but it did. This was my life now.

The external feeds showed that much of the fleet had already left Orion, heading for a staging area at jump distance. Ours and several other transport ships that had been at Erie Prime were the last to leave. Before Orion had even begun to fade into a small dot on the displays, we were in a briefing room with a calm and somber Monroe.

The vid wall behind him showed a planet labeled Pike Prime. Unlike usual, my CCPU didn't start looking for information on Pike Prime or its inhabitants. This was something that we all had set for when we were in this room. We didn't need to be inundated with stats about the planet. We needed to know whatever Monroe was going to tell us. We could research to our heart's content afterward.

"As you can guess, we are going to Pike Prime." He paused, collecting his thoughts, something I hadn't often seen from him. "But we aren't going there to fight the indigenous population. We are going to help them remove a race called the Venom from their planet, while Alpha's fleet, along with most of the rest of the HFDF's fleets, attacks the Venom home system."

I couldn't help but feel a slight sense of dread about this.

Monroe launched into our briefing. The Pike were our allies. They were mostly a pacifist race that had shown up on the intergalactic scene roughly twenty years ago. Their race's last war was almost five hundred years ago, and from what we could tell, their definition of war was nothing like what humans had.

However, they weren't exactly weak. Pike Prime also hosted a large predatory species that had plagued the Pike for their entire history. They were reluctant to wipe the creatures out but had managed to confine them to remote areas. The upside of this was that the Pike weren't lacking when it came to killing technology. They were just hesitant to use it.

When they had first made contact with us, they knew nothing of defense grids or space warfare, nor did they have any desire for it. The Pike wanted to learn about the rest of the galaxy but had no intentions of even colonizing the other planets in their own system.

It had taken them several years of observing the galaxy and our prodding to finally invest in defense. But they had been slow to learn and prepare. Three years ago, they'd been attacked by a locust race from the Hydra constellation called the Venom. The Venom managed to break the Pike's defense grid in under two weeks. Since then, the Venom had been taking more and more of Pike Prime. When the HFDF approached the Pike to remove the Venom, they were all too happy to let us do it.

"So why are we helping these helpless things out?" Meyers blurted.

Instead of looking angry, Monroe nodded at Meyers. "That's a good question, Private. Let me explain why. And for the record, usually, you'd be right. The HFDF defends humanity, not other races.

"We learned of the Venom fifty years ago. At the time, they were classed as a potentially hostile race, but they hadn't left their home system. Then that changed. They have attacked no less than thirty systems in the last fifteen years, none of them ageless, with most of them being mid-level races. For the first six years, they were consistently repelled. Even a few races tried to attack the Venom's home worlds of Venom Major and Minor.

"In each encounter, we have observed that they have progressed technologically and strategically. Four years ago, they achieved their first win. It took them several years, but they did it. And when they did, they wiped out a planet of nearly ten billion."

There was an eerie silence at that.

I raised my hand, and Monroe nodded at me.

"They sterilized the planet?" I asked.

His face turned grim. "No. They took it over, one meter at a time. They have done this on three other worlds. Four planets, including Pike Prime, are still holding out. They have several others where they have made probing attacks while in the middle of these other conflicts."

That wasn't comforting. I'd seen what it took to take on one planet, and we weren't even trying to wipe the locals out. To be actively engaged in four ground wars and still begin or look into beginning attacks on other planets seemed either insane or terrifying.

On the wall, a list of our ageless allies appeared, and I felt a pit start to form in my gut. Monroe continued, "We and eleven of our allies have determined that the Venom are a serious danger to ourselves and others. At their current rate of expansion, the HFDF will not be able to repel them in ten years without crippling ourselves. In twenty, we won't stand a chance. Our allies are in a similar situation." He paused, "Our government, along with our allies, have come to the conclusion that we will not be able to simply put the Venom back in the Stone Age. In fact, our chances of actually taking their home worlds are slim.

"We will go to Pike Prime and kill every last Venom we encounter until the planet is clear of them. Just prior to the Hunter Armada jumping to Pike Prime, fleets from almost every other Human Federation system will begin an assault on the Venom's home system. Our allies will be launching similar attacks on other systems. This will pull Venom ships away from Pike Prime. When they are midway to jump distance, the Hunter Armada will jump to Pike Prime. There they will actively engage the remaining Venom in orbit."

The screen changed, and my CCPU pinged with a request to dump information inside my head. I granted it. The Venom had not wasted any time on Pike Prime. They occupied a large chunk of one of the planet's two continents. Above which, they had been aggressively installing their own defense grid. The Pikes' grid, minus the area above occupied territory, was partially in place. Though it appeared that the Venom had mostly suspended attacks from space in favor of ground efforts.

It was assumed that part or all of the Venom ships that left to jump to defend their home system would turn back to Pike Prime. An interceptor fleet from Sagittarius would engage those ships. The main battle fleet hitting the Venom system would first target deep space anchorages. These were stations with munitions that were at jump distance from the Venom system. Once those were taken out, ships not close to a planet would be unable to resupply. The fleet from Sagittarius could take its time and run the Venom out of supplies.

"Sir, how are we going to wipe the Venom system clean if we can't take Venom Major and Minor?" Betts asked.

Monroe sighed. "It seems that no matter how advanced your race becomes, sometimes old methods still work the best."

Monroe explained that after the space around the two planets was sufficiently controlled, engineering crews would be working to do something that humans had been doing to kill things since the beginning of time. We would use rocks. Big ones, mind you. Venom Major and Minor would both be bombarded with asteroids. Listening to the plan, I could almost hear my mother getting on my case as a kid for throwing rocks. The planets' surfaces would be pulverized by asteroids that would break their crust to pieces, causing earthquakes and volcanic eruptions. Never mind what would happen to the atmosphere. Even the Venom's most secure underground bunkers would eventually be destroyed as the planets' surfaces became molten, a state it would remain in for several hundred years. The scale of an attack like that was way beyond my understanding. I couldn't imagine coming into work one day and being told to figure out how to smash not just one, but two planets so thoroughly with asteroids that not even bacteria could survive.

How does that conversation at home go? *"Hey, babe, how was your day?" "Meh, kind of boring; the coffee machine broke. Oh, and I guess I committed a little genocide."*

"But that's not our problem. That's the problem of the fleet engineering corps, and trust me, this plan isn't as easy as it sounds. Here is our concern," Monroe said.

The vid screen changed, showing an alien. Its body was a tube with spindly legs coming off it. At the front was its head, where mandibles jutted out slightly. I couldn't see eyes that I recognized, but I did note four smaller limbs. Two ended with digit-type appendages that my CCPU told me were the Venom's version of hands, and the other two ended in weapons. The Venom's weapons were literally a part of their body. Its hide looked like it was an exoskeleton.

"This one is a soldier," Monroe said. "As I'm sure you can see, its firearms are surgically attached to its body. They are controlled by the Venom's version of a CCPU. That's right, the Venom have CCPUs. I'm sure you can all guess what a problem that is going to be for us.

"They are a caste race with breeders that can change genders if needed and lay one thousand eggs a day. Next, there are five worker castes that range in size from a small dog to a small elephant. There are three soldier castes: a small version like the workers, one that is roughly twice the size of a human adult, and another that is much like their large workers." Monroe gave everyone a moment to think. "The Venom hatch after a week and are full-grown in two months. With the aid of their CCPUs, they are slightly more intelligent than our BIs. They learn quickly. These are some of the meanest, nastiest creatures in the galaxy. This will be nothing like Erie Prime. They have nano and biotech that not only helps them to mature quickly but, like you and I, keeps them alive. They are extremely hard-wearing; unlike the Erie, their entire body is armor," he said.

The Venom had made a habit of altering themselves for each planet they were on, tweaking their biology in a way that allowed them to consume and use the local flora and fauna, along with breathing the atmosphere. This wasn't unlike what humans did on each planet we went to. Though the difference was that humans used our technology to make it so we could go from world to world without issue, whereas the Venom customized their genes for each world.

Their CCPUs were located deep inside their bodies, along with their primary brain. They had several other nerve bundles that acted as brains, assisting with movement and other bodily functions. This made for a fairly small target for us to hit. The Pike had gotten around this by using large-caliber rounds that did enough damage to the Venom to kill them. Unlike humans, the Venom's enhancements did not keep them alive as well. Nor did they have medical groups to save the severely injured. The average Venom seemed to have a lot in common with our BIs when it came to society's views on their lives. I was sure if you could throw your citizens away like they were nothing, you were capable of doing truly horrible things to creatures that weren't your own species.

We'd be using a different tactic when fighting the Venom. Unlike the Pike, we weren't six tons and couldn't carry around the amount of ammo they did. Thankfully, we and our drones were good shots. The

Venom's armor was thickest on the front, where its mandibles and arms were.

We were going to start training on how to fight the Venom. We would be spending a large amount of simulator time in tunnels. The Venom were, by nature, subterranean creatures. Their ability to burrow and barricade underground was one of the things that made them difficult to get rid of. And as long as an underground bunker had one breeding pair, they could replenish their ranks quickly. They were everything that our swarm doctrine was. The difference being that humans had to learn swarm, whereas the Venom were its embodiment. They were scary, and they were going to be an absolute nightmare to kill.

Goodie for us.

I pulled up information on their fighting style. While swarm incarnate, the Venom had a different battle doctrine than humans. We tried to balance the line between being good offensively and defensively. For the Venom, that was different. Their offense was, in large part, their defense.

There were boring and digging units on the backs of each of the Venom. They were fast and could dig the Venom a burrow in stone in only a few minutes. They were faster in the dirt, or in the case of the Pike, flesh. They kept a block of some type of nano-material that could be placed over the hole's opening, allowing just their weapons to stick out and shoot.

Over time, a Venom would dig the burrow deeper and place a small cavern at the bottom where food and ammo could be stored. A small drone would tunnel from one of these burrows to another, allowing the Venom to share resources with the same drones that dug the tunnels, running as little subway trains for them. If one Venom was by a supply line, they could support hundreds of others.

I sighed as I saw that the Venom, if given enough time, excreted a liquid that would turn dirt and loose rocks into a sticky, rubbery glue that was great at absorbing projectiles that pierced the ground. This must have been commonplace on their home worlds, as from the Pike's accounts, the Venom were perfectly content to stay in these burrows seemingly indefinitely, all the while improving them with walls and stocking up on supplies.

That ruled out siege warfare. Also, a lesson the Pike had learned the hard way.

The Venom did not move across the battlefield quickly, strictly speaking. They were just fine taking some space and holding it, then moving just a little further. And as their slowly moving line progressed, they built vast supply lines behind it. Lines that were supplied by converting the areas they held into whatever they needed.

This also, by and large, ruled out insurgency on the part of the indigenous population. Our quick movement on Erie Prime had made insurgency a bit of an issue. We couldn't move as fast as we had and perfectly hold the line. But our objective also hadn't been to wipe out the Erie. Just their technology and civilization. We moved from objective to objective, putting little weight on the areas outside those objectives. Our army ignored the fleeing masses and focused on infrastructure.

The Venom took objectives too. But they didn't generally do so until they were close to them and could overwhelm the enemy. While this gave species like the Pike plenty of time to evacuate civilians and resources, with each successive loss, they were running out of room to run. Eventually, the Pike would have lost the continent. After securing it to their liking, the Venom would have started taking the other one.

———

TWO WEEKS AFTER LEARNING OF OUR MISSION, I WALKED INTO A TENSE mess aboard the Arbiter. People were hunched over food, eating quickly and silently. On occasion, you would hear someone or a group cheer. My CCPU had a running feed of the fleet's progress in the Venom system and over Pike Prime. I got some food and sat next to

Krista, her eyes out of focus. A moment later, my own slid out as I pulled up a live feed of the battle over Pike Prime.

The feed I was accessing was from the core of a Drone Star. All of its drones were busy engaging the enemy. I'd spent a lot of time watching feeds like this over the last few days. This war, unlike the last one, wasn't as one-sided. We were clearly winning. The HFDF had decades, if not centuries, on the Venom in fighting in space, but that didn't mean they weren't making us pay for every bit of it. The space above the controlled section of Pike Prime flashed with thousands of explosions. Streaks of debris burned up in the atmosphere. I could only imagine what the fight looked like from the ground.

Manned and drone fighters zipped around, chasing and being chased by the enemy. The Venom ships were blocky and utilitarian in design, most of them trying to stay clumped together above the planet. The Venom defensive grid, while not fully realized, was putting up a fight, trying to keep the Venom ships from being overwhelmed. I watched as a massive Centipede Juggernaut Battleship pushed its way toward the center of the Venom formation. I zoomed in, watching as every Venom ship in the area launched everything they had at the battleship.

The Pedes' defenses destroyed most of the incoming missiles, but soon I could make out impacts on its hull. The ship did not slow. The exterior batteries onboard the vessel rotated, pumping out ordnance that ripped into nearby Venom ships. The front of the battleship was taking copious amounts of damage, but the ship pressed forward unfazed as most of the bow became unusable. The bow section detached itself from the rest of the hull, and engines on it ignited, rocketing the bow forward. As it moved away from the ship, I could see the battleship's new bow. Not a cone like the last one, but a flat surface that had several missile banks that began to fire. I'd be lying if I said I wasn't in awe of the juggernaut-class ships. The old bow plowed through Venom, stopping when it struck what must have been the

Venom equivalent of a battleship. The bow exploded, sending its shattered decks flying into the enemy as shrapnel.

The Venom battleship began to disintegrate, falling to the surface. The Venom attacked our Pede with might, all the while ignoring two flare-class battleships and a host of smaller ships moving into position. They fired on the Venom, who didn't have the time for their own countermeasures, so fixated had their focus been. I couldn't imagine how many Venom were wiped out in a few short moments.

I refocused on my food and Sweeting sitting before me, digging into his meal. "How's the fight?"

"The Venom fleet over Pike Prime will break today, I think," I said.

Sweeting swallowed his food. "Well, I guess that means we'll be doing some skydiving soon then."

"I'm sure we will."

After breakfast, we spent some time in VR pods training. But we didn't spend too much time. We had to be ready to go within a few hours' notice, and command didn't want us tired. Instead, we spent our time trying to relax. Krista and I lay in bed together, messaging friends and trying not to think about the coming fight.

> JON: What's the fleet doing? I can't see anything.

> LIZ: Neither can I.

> ME: The fighting is intense. I think fleet will break the venom today.

> MONICA: What does that mean for you?

> ME: We drop.

There was a long pause. I decided to break it.

ME: Liz, how goes prepping the Healer's Touch?

LIZ: Nice change of subject. It's fine. We are ready for whatever comes our way... I think.

MONICA: Will you be dropping onto what's it called again? Pike Prime?

LIZ: No. We don't drop.

JON: Only crazies do that.

ME: Still on the chat.

CHARLES: We know. Truth is truth.

ME: Assholes.

CHARLES: Jon, what's your job in all this?

JON: Get shit to the planet. Alex, the support fleet is massive. What are we going into?

What were we going into? Hell? Probably, but they didn't need me saying that.

ME: Career troops are landing with us. We aren't going to be pulling resources from Pike Prime, so we have to bring them with us. Sorry, buddy, but you are going to be busy.

By three in the afternoon, the Venom fleet was pushed back almost completely against its defense grid. HFDF forces kept them hemmed in, trying to stay out of range of the grid. It was time for us to go to work.

I'd been amped up since returning to the Arbiter, but once the order to mobilize came, I calmed.

I rolled out of my bunk, the rest of my team sitting around with the squad.

"Fleet has pushed back the Venom. Get ready and move to the prep room!" I ordered.

Royle was right after me, ordering her team into action. There was a brief flurry of movement, and then all of us were out the door and heading down the hall.

EIGHTEEN

A s we prepped for our drop, other ships were jumping into the area, starting bombardment of Pike Prime. Once we'd attacked the planet, the Venom had begun a massive campaign to take more of the surface. Our initial landing waves would have the job of slowing the Venom advance so that other units could create a line to stop the onslaught.

Unlike Erie Prime, we would not be relying heavily on the surrounding areas for resources. Nor would we be staging for career troops. They would be arriving with us in the first waves. Service troops would be the ones slowing the line as cargo ships unloaded the massive amounts of drones needed to stop the Venom. As the army moved forward, service troops would plug holes in the line. The amount of materials that needed to be shipped in was staggering, and I wondered whether Jon or I would be worked harder.

Monroe sent our mission as I stepped into the launch tube with my squad. We were to land near the front and make our way to a town that was soon to be overrun. Our job was not to win the day, but to do our best to slow the Venom advance, giving the Pike time to evacuate refugees.

The Pike had been wholly unprepared for the sudden Venom assault. The Pike's army hadn't lasted two days, and as a result, the Venom had managed to move the front nearly eighty kilometers, killing tens of thousands in the process, along with wounding and displacing several hundred thousand more.

The launch tube was now sealed, and the air purged, forcing us into our helmets.

"Looks like we will be getting there right in time," Meyers said to the team.

"How so?" Krista asked.

"Are you dense? The Venom just broke those weaklings' backs! Without us, they'd be done in a few months," Meyers said.

"Don't be a dick, Meyers," Betts said.

"What? Telling the truth is being a dick?" Meyers asked.

"That's enough, Meyers! You are right about us getting here in time, however. When we get planetside, work quickly and efficiently. Remember, we are not to hold the line, just slow it down a bit. Most of the civilians will be cleared from the area. We just need to give what's left of the Pike military in the area time to get out," I said.

My CCPU pinged me that we were prepping for our jump. The lights in the tube dimmed and were replaced by red ones in the floor. The outer door slid open, revealing the calm and beautiful expanse of space. I formed up with my POD, gazing at the stars before me. My helmet gathered more light than my eyes ever could, showing me thousands of stars, nebulae, and other celestial objects. The support fleet was all around us. I opened a line to Jon and Liz.

"You guys try not to get into any trouble," I said to them as jovially as I could.

"Are you jumping already? Stay safe, man," Jon said. I could hear stress in his voice.

"Soon; we are prepping," I said.

"Stay safe," Liz said. Her stress was there as well, though she did a better job of hiding it than Jon.

"You too," I said.

I closed the line.

ARBITER: JUMP COMMENCING IN 5... 4... 3... 2... 1...

The space before me was replaced with Pike Prime, the little red lights in the floor turned green, and a buzz sounded in my head. I ran forward, my BIs keeping pace with me as I jumped from the Arbiter. She created a gravity well that shot me on a course for Pike Prime. My CCPU counted down as each of my squadmates jumped. I looked back to see the Arbiter firing long-range missiles heading in the direction of bright flashes. The fleet was pushing the Venom, ensuring they could not task ships to deal with landing parties.

I focused on the planet, pushing everything but my mission from my mind. We needed to move fast once on the ground. We didn't fall long, the Arbiter having jumped close to the planet. My space anchor jerked, and my knees came to my chest as my entry pack flung open. My suit got just slightly warmer as Pike Prime's atmosphere created friction. I was shaken and buffeted as I fell, and then I was free-falling in the air, pointing my head down at the mountains and forests below.

Forests and mountains soon resolved into rocky cliffs with a road running between them, clogged with little greenish dots. As the dots got bigger, they resolved into Pike. My space anchor jerked me upright and then slowed me down. My feet hit the ground hard, my legs and suit absorbing the impact. I released my Whiskers and brought my SIR up. The rest of my fireteam and I had landed on the side of the road in a close group. Several hulking forms on the road moved away from us as we landed. It's one thing to know that a Pike is the size of an elephant and another to see it for yourself. Before me was a procession of lumbering forms varying in size from something the size of a rhino to others the size of, well... elephants.

The Pike were utterly alien to us. How do I explain one?

Alright, think of a dinner roll. Not the ones you make, but the ones you buy from the store in sheets and then tell people you made. You know, the square-ish ones. Alright, so now let's pretend that golden morsel of goodness isn't so golden but brownish-green. Also, let's say that it's eight tons, give or take, and that the corners are really big legs. On the sides between the big legs are three smaller ones. Now, at the front, imagine a large triangular head. Under the head, there are two long arms at the end of which are eight digits. Also, the roll isn't smooth but covered in a wiry wool that can turn some sunlight into energy. And under the wool is skin that's more like shark scales. Their backs are bumpy, and all of that flesh is being held with a latticework of bones. Give it a belly that's almost on the ground, and you've got a Pike.

On the side of the road was a Pike that made a loud sound that my CCPU translated to: "These are our friends; they are here to help us; do not fear them and let them through."

I would have loved to have stuck around and observed the Pike, but as soon as my CCPU told me that everyone was on the ground and ready, I gave the order to move out. I started to jog, trying to stay on the sides of the road, dodging the occasional Pike. Ahead, smoke rose above the low mountains in the area. As I jogged, I took the chance to look at the Pike along the road. Their green woolly hides looked odd to me. They were so entirely alien that I hadn't been expecting it. The Erie had, in many ways, seemed almost human in appearance. They were bipedal with heads that had similarities to us. Not the Pike. They were anything but human. Many had dark gray blood oozing from injuries, others were limping, while others were around smaller Pike. One of the things that I knew our civilizations had in common was a similar family structure, and it wasn't lost on me how many hurt youths there were and how many were accompanied by only one adult or none at all.

On occasion, a Pike would move off to the side of the road and collapse; another Pike would help, or a youth or adult would stand next to them shaking. My CCPU told me this was the Pikes' version of showing extreme emotion, but I didn't need the translation to know that. For the most part, the Pike moved in an orderly fashion, none of them jostling to get ahead of the others. Some looked at us, but most plodded on as if we weren't there. The line of Pike thinned, and within a few more minutes, we turned a corner that led to a small valley, kind of. The map said it was a valley, but as far as I could see, it was a valley with many large hills. The hills were dotted with alcoves and towered overhead. They were, of course, buildings.

The Pike were a hardy race; their buildings had an open design that favored ramps over elevators, unlike human structures. Their size and bodies were well-suited for their environment, shaping their engineering. The buildings were separated by wide roads of smooth concrete. I could see large flatbed carts parked along the street. Lights shone through some of the alcoves, showing that many Pike hadn't even had time to turn off the lights; their escape had been so fast.

The streets were silent as we made our way down them. It was eerie, but not the first time I'd been in an abandoned city. The buildings resembled the Pike with the same wool-like texture on the outsides.

Intel said that a small group of Pike were rapidly retreating in our direction. They'd been told to expect us and not to stop their retreat or shoot at us. It's always nice not to get shot at by the species you're there to save.

"You have friendlies coming your way. They are not as fast as you are, and they have the Venom on their heels. Set up at these two buildings and provide cover for them. The Venom have not dealt with us on the ground yet, nor has this advance faced any real resistance. When you engage, this should temporarily halt their progress. Get them to hunker down and hold them for at least a half hour. After that, you turn tail and run," Monroe said to Royle and me.

Two waypoints appeared in my vision—one for Royle's team and the other for mine. Each building was on either side of the road we'd come in on. I deployed my two Mortar drones to the back of the building, having them zero in on an area on the road. I would have liked the buildings on either side of the road to be destroyed, leaving the Venom only the road and the choke point that it created, but my CCPU informed me that time was not a luxury we had much of. Also, it turned out, command wasn't likely to waste ordnance for my convenience. Dicks.

I ordered Meyers and Krista into the building to take sniping positions along with myself. Betts and Sweeting were going to take the ground levels, with Betts focused on keeping the Venom from flanking us in the little space they'd have to do so. The Heavies were taking slight cover on the ground level behind large chunks of concrete. They were to act as pillboxes, keeping the Venom pinned down.

I ran up to the building, going through an entrance that turned into a ramp. I ran up it with Meyers and Krista. There were lights above me, the walls were a smooth brown stone. I peeled away from them at an alcove, going in with my POD. The inside of the alcove had the same smooth walls. Above me, the room's ceiling turned into a dome with a light at the top. On the wall, a screen showed footage of Pike fleeing cities. The alcoves didn't have windows, instead opening to the outside. In the center of the room was a depression with an orange cushion of sorts. By the side of the depression was a bowl with little red berries the size of cherries. My CCPU informed me that the berries were the Pike's primary food. Of course, something that was eight tons lived on cherries.

I set up against the lip of the opening. My CCPU started interpreting the video playing in the background, but I stopped it. I didn't need the distraction, and I knew what they were saying. The Pike were running for their lives.

One of my forward Whiskers pinged a contact, and I pulled up its feed. Four Pike were moving as quickly as they could. A kilometer behind them, not firing, was the Venom. I saw hundreds of them pouring over the ground. Most were the standard soldier caste that we expected, along with a smattering of the larger Venom. My heart sank as I saw what was with them—a column of armor plodded down the road. The tanks were long and on many legs. Their fronts appeared to be highly armored, and with the legs, they could move around almost any terrain. For that matter, the Venom ground units didn't seem to care much about what was in their way; they crawled over the sides of buildings and vehicles, and I started to worry that the bottleneck we had planned wouldn't do anything.

"Advise we have armor," I said to Royle and Monroe.

"Roger that. The mission remains unchanged. If you lose your Heavies, retreat," Monroe said.

"Understood," Royle and I said.

"Be advised we have a large number of hostiles and armor heading our way. Be ready for action shortly," I said to my team.

I took position with my SIR's nano-material forming a T-pod that clung to the building. The outside of the buildings was covered in porous rock and green wool that looked much like that of the Pike themselves. Before I had too much time to think about the buildings, the Pike came lumbering into view. They didn't hold weapons in their hands but rather had a harness on top of their backs. On it, there were five turrets—one for each corner and one on top. The Pike connected with them with CCPUs, and each could target and fire at will. The turrets were large caliber. I knew all this, of course. I'd watched videos of those turrets shredding Venom, just like I'd seen videos of Venom being crushed by Pike as they lay or stepped on them. But again, seeing it in person is different.

"Jesus fuck, look at those things! It'd take a whole POD to bring one down. They have to have more firepower than a Heavy," Sweeting said, "do you still think they are weaklings, Meyers?"

"Yeah, they don't look so weak to me," Krista said.

Meyers was slow to respond, "well, shit! I guess give credit where it's due. Those things do look intimidating. And the Venom mopped the floor with them? Shit!"

Shit was right.

My CCPU pinged me with a message from the passing Pike, translating their language and giving a rough approximation of what it thought was the meaning behind what they were saying.

"Thank you and Godspeed."

Comforting.

I chose not to send it to the rest of the team. The gratitude was nice, but "godspeed"? Maybe that was the closest approximation my CCPU had for whatever the Pike's expression had been. Maybe to a Pike, saying something like that was the same as saying, 'fuck their shit up, guys! Don't worry, this will be super easy!' But I doubted it.

Soon after the Pike ran by, my CCPU notified me that the Venom were nearly on us. Their movements had changed, indicating they knew we were here. This didn't surprise me. The Venom were very close to being on par with us technologically. Still, it was unnerving. The Erie had been easy to hide from, but the Venom would be a different animal. It was likely that they were detecting the Heavies, not BIs and people, but I sent a message to my POD and then to the fireteam, telling them to make sure all of their camo was active.

Zones were popping up in my field of view, and I checked my teams. This was going to be the hard part. The Venom were going to run over the building. I could see that. The first wave might not, but the following ones would. What that meant was that our team of five humans and fifty-two drones had to cover a whole lot of area.

Between the buildings, several Venom started to scuttle into view, their two limbs with weapons scanning the horizon. *Good,* I thought, *at least they don't know exactly where we are, just that we're here.* It was possible and even probable that the Venom had hacked into the Pike's communications. Their standard units didn't use alt-comms like we did, making their signals easy pickings. This had hurt the Erie as well. We'd been able to track units and decode transmissions costing the Erie dearly. For the Pike, when they'd realized their misstep, it was too late to retool their entire military.

I told my units to hold fire. The Venom spread out, moving efficiently with more and more coming into sight. My Whiskers said that armor was about to come through. I tasked my Heavies with dealing with the armor and ensured that the mortars would take out plenty of Venom. The large blocky form of a Venom tank came into view. It walked on several legs with the front end thick and heavily armored. I told the Heavies to use missiles that would fly high in the air and come down on top of the tank in hopes that it was weaker there. I would time it with the mortars.

The Venom hadn't invested heavily in developing mechanized units. As it was, Venom armor had been limited on Pike Prime, as the Venom tanks weren't much larger than the Pike themselves but were much less maneuverable. Add to that the fact that each Pike was like a tank unto itself, and I could see why the Venom had gone with the less resource-heavy tactic of burrowing and fighting from cover or burrowing into the Pike themselves.

"Open fire in thirty," I said to the team.

I watched the Venom armor lumbering along, seeing how it could be an absolute nightmare if it was holding the entrance to a cave or tunnel. *They'll be the armor divisions' problems,* I reminded myself.

Thirty seconds later, the Mortar drones fired with a boom.

On the side of the tank, the ground exploded, sending Venom flying. The tank erupted in fire a moment later, debris flying from it.

"OPEN FIRE!" I ordered.

I sighted a Venom that was starting to move and shot a burst at it. It thrashed and lay down. I shot at another. It rolled, obviously hit, but not dead. It limped behind a fallen comrade and fired back in my direction. Some of the building near me broke into bits with the impacts. The walls in the room peppered me with little bits as they were shot. BI7 next to me shot, and then a moment later, it was hit. I held my fire and watched another BI shoot, and then after its second shot, the return fire was extremely close.

"Enemy can zero after two shots. Keep your position moving," I said to my team.

"Roger that. I have my POD firing in sequence. It seems to slow them down," Meyers said to the squad.

I told my POD to start rotating fire, and I only took shots when I had a kill shot. I reminded myself that my primary job was to stay alive so I could direct my drones.

The Venom were starting to take up positions in the building across from us, some in the alcoves and others running up the sides, stopping on the exterior with dust flying from where they were. They were starting to dig in.

"I have my team keeping their heads down. I've had two people get tagged," Royle said to me.

"Roger," I said to Royle.

"Advise Fireteam Bravo has had two people hit by the enemy. Keep your heads down and focus on directing drones," I said to my team.

I hid behind the wall, pulling up feeds from all of my drones. The Heavies were taking heavy fire from ground units. In their line of sight, I saw the large Venom working around the tank, presumably to start moving it out of the way.

"Keep the Venom off that armor. I want that area bottlenecked as much as possible," I said to Sweeting.

I could see what the Venom were doing on the sides of the buildings. They had burrowed into the walls, creating cover for themselves, and they had done it in just a few minutes. There were others on the ground doing likewise.

"Don't let them dig in," Monroe said to Royle and me.

I relayed the order to my team and popped up, targeting only those Venom who were digging in. The first wave that had begun the process was starting to get settled. I felt uneasy. In an alarmingly short period, the Venom had managed to dig themselves into concrete, giving themselves foxholes our units couldn't dream of penetrating.

The ones on the side of the buildings were still slightly exposed. I had to zoom in on them, which meant being still and taking more time —time that the enemy could use. I took out one and then moved. The spot where I was just a moment ago was peppered. My CCPU was connected with all my drones and the Arbiter, factoring trajectories of every shot the system could. Similar to how the Venom were finding me.

We knew that the Venom weren't as good at long ranges as we were. They preferred close to medium ranges, which made sense for a subterranean species. I had an idea. I ordered a BI to pop up and shoot and then duck down right away. As it did, there was fire in its general direction. It did it again, and the return fire was much closer this time.

"They are waiting to see if we use the same position. Fire, duck, then rotate, and we should be good," I said to the squad.

As we did this, we were able to move more quickly, using Whiskers to find targets and then popping up to shoot them before ducking down again. Unfortunately, we were not moving fast enough. The sheer number of Venom digging in was too much. Several on the ground were now inside holes with only their weapons poking out. BI3 went down.

From a whisker, I quickly inspected the dug-in Venom. Their nano-material was out making caps in their holes, so only their weapons stuck out; each of the bastards was like a mini pillbox. Our rounds ricocheted off the roads and buildings in the area, with the occasional round finding a Venom weapon.

SYSTEM WARNING: TEAMMATE ALLEN BETTS IS WIA. LEFT ARM FLESH WOUND. FULL FUNCTIONALITY AVAILABLE IN TEN MINUTES.

"What's your situation?" I asked Betts.

"I popped up, and they got me. I'm down four BIs," Betts said to me.

"Keep down. The enemy is watching the alcoves. Pull back drones and keep out of the line of sight from ground enemies," I said to my team.

I pulled up a drone count, seeing we were down by thirty percent, and Royle's team was down by twenty-five percent. There was a boom, and I pulled a feed, seeing the tank in pieces. It appeared the Venom had decided to just blow up what was left of their tank to get it out of the way. A new Venom tank came into sight and quickly shot at the Heavies, taking them out.

Shit.

I targeted the tank with Mortar drones, having them switch to armor-piercing shells.

"Advise enemy has wrapped around the building on the right side, flanking us," Royle said to the squad.

I sent a whisker to the building we were nearest. The Venom were doing likewise to us. I was now down to fifty percent of my drones. Some of the team, including myself, had tried having our BBALLs go above the Venom ground units and shoot them. It had worked great until Venom behind the building started targeting them. We were losing the BBALLs quickly. The building shuttered, and dust filled the air. The tank was firing on us. Again… shit.

"Pull back, pull back," I said to my team.

We were getting pinned down. The Venom surged without the Heavies, and now us to stop them. They were coming around and over the buildings in front of us. All the while, the dug-in units gave them more effective covering fire than I would have ever thought possible. If we left the cover of the building, we would get torn to pieces. I could see how this would play out. The Venom would surge and dig in, then the next group would move forward.

"We are taking heavy fire and are pinned down, requesting air support," I said to Monroe.

"Request granted. Be ready to retreat in two," Monroe said to me.

"We are bugging out in two. Get to the back of the building. Air is on the way. Keep your BIs up front until air support gets here," I said to my team.

I didn't want to lose any more BIs, and I wasn't going to leave them behind as there was a very real chance we'd get attacked on the way back to the landing parties. But my choices were quickly becoming limited. I made my way to the back of the building, my CCPU giving me a countdown as air support closed in.

SYSTEM WARNING: BOMBARDMENT COMMENCING.

The ground shook slightly as bombs dropped.

"Move out! Bring your drones," I said to my team.

The Mortar drones were moving to a waypoint in the canyon we'd come in through. Our BIs were capable of moving much faster than we were. Normally they didn't, so that we humans were harder to spot. I disabled that mode, allowing the BIs to catch up with us. I also disabled it on my fireteam's BIs as well. We came out from the back of the building, taking little in the way of fire as the Venom scrambled for cover. I rounded the corner into the canyon with my fireteam and Royle's. We continued to run, allowing our Whiskers to fan out, looking for an ambush. Our other BIs caught up with us, and I re-enabled their guards to act like humans.

I checked on Betts, seeing that he was fine now. He was still healing, but his biotech had created a temporary synthetic muscle to handle the damage.

"We'd be dead if that air support had been taken out," Kwasny said to the squad.

"Negative, there were two other birds headed our way. We aren't the only thing slowing the Venom," Royle told the squad.

It was good that she nipped the griping in the bud. What she said was true, but what Kwasny had said was also true. Had our initial air support been taken out, we might not have lasted long enough for their backup to arrive.

It didn't take long to start catching up to the Pike we had seen in the area. They were being picked up by their own air support, a hulking vehicle. One seemed to be motioning to us in some way. My CCPU said it was a gesture telling us to come to them.

"The Pike want to give us a ride," I said to Monroe.

"Their local command said they'd drop you by the LZ on their way to their rally point. Jump on unless you fancy a run," Monroe told me.

I didn't fancy a run.

"Load up on the Pike's transport; they're giving us a lift!" I said to my squad.

We ran up to the transport, which was more of a floating platform, and jumped on. As soon as our last drone was on board, the vehicle lifted off and headed away from the battle zone. We'd lost sixty percent of our drones in under forty minutes. This was going to be a long, hard war, I realized.

The ground dropped away, and Whiskers made a bubble around the transport, looking for Venom pursuit. There was none; their pace had moved back to what it had been before they'd encountered us.

The Pike transport vibrated softly as it flew. It wasn't the fastest thing out there, but it was better than running. I did an inventory of myself, POD, and the team. The losses weren't great, but other than a minor wound, we'd fared pretty well considering the circumstances. I turned and looked at one of the Pike. It didn't seem to have fared as well. Its woolly hide was caked with blood in various stages of drying. Its form was massive, and it was hard to believe that we were here to save them.

The turrets on its back swiveled around, looking for danger. Each turret had multiple barrel sizes. Sweeting had been right when he'd seen the Pike. Taking one down would be an absolute pain in the ass. Its thick hide and body would require high-caliber and high-velocity rounds that I suspected a Pike could take a lot of. Never mind dealing with the turrets that would continue to function after the Pike itself was dead.

"Thank you for the lift," I said to the Pike nearest me, my helmet's external speakers translating what I said into Pike.

The Pike next to me shifted, turning slightly towards me.

"It should be us that are thanking you for saving us from these demons," it said, or my CCPU said it said. "How did you last so long against that many?"

"We had cover and were ready for them. Still, we lost sixty percent of our drones. This isn't going to be easy," I said and instantly regretted it. "Don't worry though, we'll get better at killing them, and we'll win. We always win," I assured them.

"I am sorry you lost so many today. I hope you are right and that you kill these demons." The Pike paused. "Does it hurt you to lose your drones?" it asked in what my CCPU told me was an apprehensive tone.

Another Pike spoke. "You should not ask them that," it said.

By this point, the rest of the squad was paying attention to our conversation. It occurred to me that for the first time in my life, I was talking to something that wasn't human. Somehow, I didn't feel uneasy about it. Maybe it was the fact that we'd just saved them from some seriously nasty fuckers, and they'd given us a ride that made me feel a bit of a bond with them.

"It's fine. No, it doesn't bother us to lose our drones. Sure, I would have liked to not have lost that many, but that's what they are here to do. They are just machines to us. Do you feel the same way about your technology? I apologize if that's rude to ask," I said.

The other Pikes were looking at us now, and though I couldn't fully read their body language, they appeared to be interested.

The Pike I had been talking to before spoke, sounding relieved. "I'm not sure you can take offense when talking to another race for the first time. Or I should say it's not wise to. For us, we are extremely connected to our technology and environment. Our homes, communities, and what we build are an extension of who we are. Not the same as our families, but dear to us all the same."

That must have made the war even worse for them. I had to remind myself that they weren't just losing tactical ground. They were losing their homes and loved ones. I could see why they'd call the Venom demons. It was a fitting name. They certainly looked the part.

"I am truly sorry for your loss," I said and then added, "I know it won't bring back your loved ones, but we will get you back your planet and keep the demons from taking more worlds... for what it's worth."

"I hope you are right," the Pike said, and after a moment, "such a waste," it said, my CCPU telling me the last word had a tone of sorrow and resignation.

My CCPU pinged me that we were almost at our destination. The transport started to slow, and I stood with the rest of my squad and drones. Before we began to unload, I looked over the Pikes, trying to etch into my mind what our mission meant to them.

"Thank you again for the ride," I said.

"You are most welcome, and thank you," the Pike said.

I jumped off the transport.

NINETEEN

I am sure that Pike Prime was a wonderful planet. From what I had read, it had been wonderful... when it wasn't covered in Venom. Maybe someday, decades from now, I'd come back if I survived my time here. At the moment, I wasn't hopeful about either possibility.

Royle and I walked out of the temporary hospital at FOB 026. We had just finished a meeting with some of the medical staff about the injuries our team had sustained. We weren't in trouble by any stretch of the imagination, but we, like all fireteam leaders, had to hold these meetings after several injuries. In the case of Pike Prime, they were moving over to meeting with us every two weeks. The people overseeing our health didn't have the time to spend every waking moment in meetings. As it stood, everyone had been hurt except for Krista. How she had not been shot or blown up was a bit of a mystery. She joked and said it was her lucky necklace— the necklace Monroe had allowed her to wear inside her suit and said it would have been bad luck not to have it on. It was made from the bullet an Erie had been so kind to put in her shoulder on our first day in combat. Thus far, it had been difficult to argue with Monroe's logic.

The hospital was located inside one of the Pike's large, hill-shaped buildings that had been loaned out to the HFDF. They were great for the hospital and barracks. We could and would build structures better suited to humans, but for the time being, logistics teams were busy trying to keep the front supplied with drones and ammo. Nutrient packs were coming in regularly, but it would be a long time before normal meals would start to show up. If they ever did at all.

As we walked through the cavernous halls of the building, I heard the rumble of a barge drone landing or lifting off outside. It was something you could set a clock by. In this, Jon was being worked harder than I was. He was part of the crew of a military cargo ship. The ships would load up at a deep space anchorage, then make the jump to Pike Prime, where barge drones would be waiting to offload them. The cargo vessel would unload and then move at top speed to jump distance to start over again. They had a three-day turnaround time. Liz was also busy up on the Healer's Touch. We weren't taking heavy casualties yet, but we were losing people regularly, unlike Erie Prime.

Along with casualties, something far more common was major injuries— the kind that the hospital on Pike Prime wasn't equipped to handle. The Healer's Touch was filled to capacity. It wasn't the only hospital ship in the same spot. There were dozens of hospital ships, their hulls nearly bursting with the number of injured troopers on board. This was far more terrifying given the speed at which troops could be patched up and sent back planetside.

The Venom's advance had finally been halted. It had required a lot of resources and God knew how many drones. We were now holding the line while logistics finished building what we would need for the long road ahead. It was a difficult situation. We needed logistics to get a temporary infrastructure so we could start moving forward, but logistics needed the front stable so they could build what we needed to accomplish that goal. I'm sure it was a pain in the ass, and Royle and I both agreed that we never wanted to have to deal with something like that.

For us, the war was one patrol and scouting mission after another. Nothing deep into enemy territory or even that far behind the line. We spent most of our time in the areas between major battle zones. Our job was to find Venom scouting parties and take them out. It seemed that many Venom had the same mission. This meant both sides spent a lot of time trying to ambush the other in ways they couldn't escape.

Royle and I walked into a briefing room where Monroe appeared on a vid wall. The rest of our squad was waiting. Annoyingly, even though we were inside a building, we had to keep our helmets on since the structure wasn't airtight. Even if we weren't worried about chemical attacks, Pike Prime's atmosphere was toxic to humans... maybe I wouldn't visit someday.

"How was your meeting?" Monroe asked as we walked in.

"Long story short, try not to get shot as much, people," Royle said.

Everyone chuckled.

Royle and I stood at the head of the gathered group next to the vid wall. The wall displayed the area we would be hunting in, consisting of dense forest and rugged terrain. There were plenty of places to hide. The Venom had been looking for ways to flank us as soon as their advance had stopped. In other cases, they would find ideal spots to hide and wait for our army. The concern was that the Venom could be searching for gaps in the line where they could move breeders further into the continent. This posed the greatest threat. Our first objective was to contain the enemy. If the Venom managed to get a breeder set out of the area they were currently in, that could prove problematic.

That being said, it was likely that some had escaped and were waiting to start their own colonies. By treaty, we would be on Pike Prime for thirty years after hostilities ended to ensure that the Venom couldn't take root again. It also meant that we would be doing our utmost to find them. Already back away from the line, drones were placing detection devices that could scan all the way down to the planet's mantle.

As we'd walked in, Royle and I had grabbed nutrient packs sitting on a small table. I held the pack to my helmet, pressing it to the chin. Little feeders began the process of pulling the pack into my helmet. As they did, they removed its packaging, ensuring nothing was exposed to the atmosphere. From there, my helmet extruded it into my mouth in bite-size pieces. As Monroe began giving us our briefing, I tried not to think about the salty-sweet taste of the pack, which had been all I'd tasted for some time.

Our mission that day followed the template of most of the assignments we'd had lately: find Venom parties and kill them. Request backup when needed and provide it when necessary.

Since landing on Pike Prime, our standard drone arrangements had changed. The Venom were very aggressive and liked to dig into the ground, which lessened the effectiveness of our BIs. The best way to deal with them was to move fast and fire down on their burrows—something our BBALLs could do but didn't have the firepower to do effectively. As such, we each lost two BIs that were replaced by the BBALL's larger counterparts we called Spheres. Original, right? The Spheres were a little bigger than a man's chest. They boasted two guns capable of the same firing power as the SIRs, each with its own targeting systems. Also, in a pinch, they could carry a human a short distance. We had used them a lot in training. I hadn't liked that they didn't have hands and couldn't use tools, but they were handy to have against an enemy that hid in holes in the ground, shooting at you. Everyone also had more Whiskers and two extra BBALLs.

On a fireteam level, we also had changes, namely in the form of the Heavies. As amazing as they were, they struggled in rugged terrain, so no more Heavies. To replace them, we had another mortar drone, six Spheres, and a mule drone for carrying ungodly amounts of ammo and parts, along with eight large Whiskers. The large Whiskers were ten times the size of the normal ones, with significantly more power and abilities, including the ability to see a few meters underground. That last part was extremely useful. The big change, though, was that with all the extra drones to manage, Royle and I could not stay on the firing line. We had to manage our fireteams and all the drones while looking for new threats. As for our team members, they only engaged if they had a kill shot and one of their drones wasn't able to take it. It mostly fell to the BIs and occasionally human operators to keep the Venom pinned down while the Spheres did their thing.

We all left the briefing room and headed to the armory. The room was once a meeting space for the Pike, which meant it was like a warehouse for us. There were rows of shelves mostly lined with ammo and a few weapons in case someone damaged or lost their SIR or sidearm. Various drones worked in the armory, a few of which were stacking ammo blocks and explosives on a table that we were heading towards. As I got to the table, my CCPU pinged me from a group of drones that would be my POD for today, along with the drones replacing the Heavies.

I grouped the BIs into two groups of three. I then grouped one Sphere with two BBALLs for support. I didn't group the Mortars for the fireteam drones, but put the Spheres into two groups of three. With supplies at a premium, drones were working multiple missions with different humans daily. As I connected in, I started diagnostic programs on them. The diagnostic had never pulled any errors. The drones were kept in good repair, but I didn't want to get killed because I didn't dot my i's and cross my t's. I started loading up on ammo, explosives, and parts for drones. When I was done with that, I ran an inventory of the drones and the mule.

We walked out of the armory into the organized chaos of the FOB. People and drones moved around like angry insects. Materials were being transported from here to there, with a constant stream of air and spacecraft moving overhead. We walked with our PODs down the road, moving to the edge of the base. Construction drones were working on semi-permanent buildings, while others worked on base fortifications, including walls, trenches, and turrets. The ground was already wired, ensuring the Venom couldn't tunnel in without us knowing about it. In the far distance, I could see puffs of smoke. I zoomed in to see a squad of fighter drones engaging a squad of Venom. I turned back to the road ahead of me.

There was a rumble behind us, and I used the feed from the back of my head to see a barge taking off. The barges were tall cylinders with tapered noses. The craft was rising slowly into the sky, its engines thundering. As it climbed higher, it gained speed and turned away from the front line. Following its path, I could see another barge coming in to land.

We made it to an open area where transports were loading and unloading troops and drones. One of the upsides to the Spheres was that they didn't need to fly in the transport, giving us more room. We loaded up, and the transport lifted off, moving to our patrol. The transport moved away from the FOB, staying low to the ground, trying to keep out of view of the enemy. I looked through the transport's feeds as we flew, watching as Pike Prime passed below. The forest canopy was broken by large patches of thick shrubs that covered the rocky ground. The planet was surprisingly monotone, everything covered in various shades of green and brown. Not unpleasant, just simple. Occasionally, I would see spots of color, mostly in the form of animals. We skirted a Pike village where I could see Pikes wandering around, doing whatever it was they did. Nothing on the planet felt urgent. Everything was slow and mellow. Well, except for the war and all. We banked south towards the front, and my CCPU informed me that we were ten minutes out from our destination.

I checked my CCPU to see if there was any updated intel on the area. I saw a notification saying that another squad had encountered the enemy yesterday and the day before. That wasn't surprising. The Venom were looking for a way deeper into the continent. What it did tell me was that we would probably find something today. The Venom were nothing if not persistent. And why not? It had worked wonderfully for them so far. Unfortunately, we were just as persistent. And while the Venom were keeping up with us right now, sooner or later, that would change. Their defense grid would come down, and with it, a lot of HFDF ordnance. Also, while they bred fast, the Venom could not replenish their ranks as quickly as we could. The twenty-year-old in me wanted to go buck wild, but I knew the wisdom of the brass's strategy. Slow and steady would win the war and reduce our losses. This was not like the wars of old, where people debated the benefits between a fast, brutal war or a slow one. All of those conflicts had been between each other and not with drone warfare.

There was still both brutality and speed, but they were applied differently. On Erie Prime, we had moved fast, taking objectives fairly quickly. While we didn't target civilians or even Erie that dropped their weapons and ran, we were brutal in how we went after objectives and targets. Here on Pike Prime, we would plod along, not worrying about speed or objectives but rather thoroughness.

As we approached our LZ, we deployed our Spheres to scout the area along with my large Whiskers. The area we were landing in was covered with dense bushes and small trees. The transports came in low to the ground, and we jumped the few meters to the surface. It lifted into the air, going back the way it had come, keeping low. We raised our weapons, ordering our drones to fan out in a bubble formation. Our Whiskers pushed out in front of the large Whiskers, expanding our sphere of awareness. The brush was up to my chest, and I crouched down and started moving forward.

We were heading for a thick part of the forest with steep hills and uneven terrain. Despite all of the bioengineering in my body, I was going to be thankful for my suit's assistance. There was still foliage all around on the forest floor that provided some cover, and I kept slightly stooped as we entered the woods. The trees had long trunks with nubs where branches must have once been. At the top, branches unfurled into a dense canopy that cast the ground in muted dappled light. When we first came to Pike Prime, I was unsure how the Pike moved about the forests until seeing these trees. There was plenty of space for a Pike or several between each one.

We moved slowly through the brush, trying not to make any

sound. In the coming weeks, there would be a constant stream of Whiskers patrolling the gaps between the line to help out with missions like this, but for now, we moved forward twenty or thirty meters and then stopped, allowing all of the Whiskers to scan the area. It was slow work but also intense. We had spread out so the whole squad could cover as much ground as possible. If one of us walked into a Venom ambush, that person likely wasn't coming home, or at least not without injuries. So we went slow, taking our time. Move forward, scan and hold your breath, then repeat.

I moved forward slowly, allowing my Whiskers to do their job. I felt my heart beat a bit faster with each sound I heard. I squatted at the base of one of the towering trees as my Whiskers inched forward, scanning for anything amiss. If my suit didn't absorb sweat, it would have been running down my brow and back. I focused on keeping calm, taking even breaths and looking at the data. The OODA loop ran through my mind each time I stopped.

My HUD filled my entire field of view as I looked at my immediate area and the location of my team members. We had detailed maps of the location and had already marked where Venom were likely to set up an ambush. I checked those locations against where I and my team were. Then I looked at how I would get out or assist someone.

"Possible contact," Betts said to the squad.

I tapped into his feeds, seeing what he was looking at. One of his Whiskers had spotted what it thought was an abnormality in the forest floor. I couldn't see it, but that didn't mean much. It's not like I'm a Whisker that can tell if the pattern of soil on the forest floor looked messed with or not. I tasked a Large Whisker to the area. It moved in slowly and turned up a trail heading southeast of us.

Oddly, finding something calmed me down. I looked at the map again. Betts's Whisker was in an area that looked ideal for a Venom ambush. The enemy hadn't managed to change tactics as we'd expected. Or I should say, as my team had. We'd seen them be the definition of swarm and imposed our own way of thinking on them. The

HFDF had changed tactics many times already and would continue to do so as we learned. The Venom had not, or at least not in a significant way, and it was starting to cost them.

"Confirm enemy movement to the southwest," I said to the squad.

"Roger Alpha, how would you like to proceed?" Royle asked.

"Alpha, converge on Betts's position at waypoint one. Bravo, please proceed to waypoint two for support," I said.

I set out two waypoints: one for my team and the other for Royle's. The general deal was that whichever fireteam found the enemy dealt with them if it was a one-team job, or at least if we thought it would only take one team. The other team would set up a perimeter, watching the backs of the other team. I won't lie; I'd rather deal with the enemy whose location I knew instead of a possible counterattack from other enemies we didn't know were there. That happened sometimes. You would be spread pretty thin if you were playing the support role. When the other team would engage, different Venom that you hadn't found yet would attack, usually with small artillery outside of our effective range. As you were getting shelled and taking cover, more Venom would swarm your position, hoping to overwhelm you before backup could arrive.

As I moved toward Betts, I had my Whiskers follow the path they'd found. Not far away, they spotted the enemy. A group of thirty was in a bowl in the ground. Hidden in that bowl was what looked like small artillery. The Whiskers kindly informed me that the dirt in the area appeared to have been disturbed recently. I could see why the Venom had set up a position like this. They had lost two patrols in as many days in this area. Setting up like this was smart. It also meant that there were other Venom in the area that were within range of the artillery for it to support, and that if the enemy had invested the time to create this happy little place, there were probably several Venom patrols in the area. Peachy. We were potentially in the middle of a much larger group. If we were lucky, we'd beat the other Venom and get out of the area after we took out the artillery.

I sent everything we had found, along with my concerns, to Monroe.

"Treat this as any other mission. I have requested air support should you need it. Five Mini Gunships are deploying to your area. They will, by all appearances, be on a normal patrol," Monroe said to Royle and me.

I relayed the information to my team, trying not to come across too happy. Monroe would have been hard-pressed to get those Gunships a week ago, but with the front halted and logistics starting to get their feet under them, we finally had some support. I set waypoints for my team to surround the Venom while Royle moved into support positions, allowing me control of her mortar drones. I had them target the artillery and possible escape routes. Once that was done, I gave the order for sniping positions to be taken up.

This was one of the hardest parts of this type of operation. Like us, the Venom had very sophisticated surveillance tools. Also, like us, they had countermeasures for those tools. We were on par with one another in this regard, and there was a decent chance that one of our drones or people would be discovered. If we were found, the next question would be if the Venom would wait to see if they could find more of us or just attack. Historically, the latter proved more likely. The pro to this was that sometimes the Venom would give away their location before we found them. Sure, it would cost you a drone or two and make the situation a little crazy, but at least you found the enemy and could deal with them before they had a chance to mount a solid attack.

I was lying down behind a tree, clear of any enemy line of fire. I watched a map of the area as BIs moved into position. Four of them had solid shots, with a fifth moving into place. Once it was in position, I would give the order for the BIs to fire simultaneously, followed moments later by the mortars and Spheres. I waited as the last BI moved into position.

The enemy the BI was targeting moved, swinging both of its guns on the BI and fired. *Dammit.* The BI lost signal. Two other BIs went down. So it appeared the Venom had found us and had opted for option one: be patient and smart. Awesome. At least we outnumbered them. I gave the order to the other BIs to fire. Both did, hitting their targets.

"ENGAGE ENGAGE ENGAGE!" I called to my team.

The mortars fired, and the BBALLs and Spheres rocketed into the air, avoiding branches. There were explosions as the mortars hit. I ordered another volley on primary targets before the mortars moved onto secondary and tertiary targets. The BBALLs and Spheres popped into the air, arcing over the Venom and strafing the area. There were more booms of mortars. The bowl the Venom were in filled with flying bits of rock, trees, and metal from their own artillery as it exploded. The Venom covered their burrows with their nano-material caps. With the caps and the ground as cover, the Venom were nearly immune to small arms fire and shrapnel. What the caps couldn't stop, however, were armor-piercing explosive rounds fired from above. And that was the primary round the Spheres used on them. Sadly, if you were a Venom, the Spheres tried to shoot a three-round burst at you, so you were toast. Sure, the rounds didn't have a one-hundred percent chance of piercing vital organs. But the little holes the Venom hid in sure made a great place to keep all of a small explosion's energy contained.

Taking your strength and turning it into a potential weakness—that's how the HFDF turns smiles upside down. We're just dicks like that. It was also an example of how the Venom's reluctance to change tactics was costing them.

I coordinated the mortars, keeping heavy pressure on the Venom, each impact shaking the ground and providing acoustic data allowing the Large Whiskers to create an ever more detailed map of the enemy and their hiding holes. Meanwhile, the BBALLs zipped overhead, providing suppressive fire, trying to pin them in their holes. As their guns came out from under the caps, BIs shot them. Easy, right? But with every round a BI fired and every mortar shot, the Venom could zero in on them. Experience told us the mortars had four shots at most before they were targeted. BIs had two shots; the BBALLs and Spheres, fast though they might have been, were sitting ducks if the Venom had a moment to target them. This created a tempo for the engagement.

The mortars paused as they changed their positions. At the same time, the BBALLs and Spheres took cover, along with any BIs. Thus far, the whole fight had been fairly one-sided and only about thirty seconds. Now that changed. The moment we paused, a series of thumps came from the Venom position. They didn't have their large artillery anymore, but grenades, mortars and anything that could be carried by a Venom were still in their possession, safely hidden at the bottom of burrows. There were booms all around. Several of the tall trees around us exploded, their trunks rent to pieces. They fell to the ground all around the bowl. I ducked down, hoping that the tree I was under wasn't one that had already been targeted.

My CCPU pinged; there was a flurry of movement.

"Engage! They are trying to retreat!" I said to my team.

The BBALLs and Spheres popped back into the air, zipping to tree trunks for cover, firing on the enemy as they went. Three didn't make it. The Venom were spilling out of their holes. I could see all of the warrior casts together. Taking the data from all of the Whiskers, my first mortar drone targeted one of the large Venom and fired. It flew to pieces, a chunk hitting another Venom, knocking it off its feet. It rolled, corrected, and then dropped as it was shot by a BI.

"Be advised, Gunships have spotted enemy movement. Royle, they are heading from the southeast," Monroe reported to the squad.

"Roger that," Royle replied.

My map showed her sending her team to meet the oncoming enemy. The Gunships continued on their fake patrol route, not interesting the Venom. My map updated, indicating that they would assist Royle's team.

I rolled away from my position, taking cover behind one of the fallen trees. All the Venom were out in the open now, and I ordered my BIs to move forward, telling the rest of my team to do likewise. It could mean losing more drones by going toe to toe, but it would be faster, allowing us time to assist Royle or handle any other Venom that could be on their way.

Meyers charged forward with his POD, ever aggressive. They came over the top of the bowl in full auto, spraying the Venom, stopping their movement forward and focusing their attention on him. Betts and Sweeting went from the sides, taking out several Venom. My POD and Krista came from their rear. I crested the bowl, seeing the Venom below trying to fend off the onslaught. We were taking damage, to be sure, but for the most part, the BIs were moving from cover to cover. Four of Meyers' BIs jumped down next to the Venom, the material in their vambraces coming out in thin blades. All the Venom surged toward the four BIs. Something in their biology seemed to react to attacks like this. Once thought out, good formations would crumble as they rushed an enemy. It was also something that consistently lost them a fight. As the Venom moved, the rest of us dropped cover and went to work on what had become a turkey shoot.

The Gunships screamed overhead, and I saw a notification from Royle's team indicating they had made contact. The last of the Venom in the bowl died, and I ordered the team out. We retreated out of the bowl, quickly moving away from the area using the tree trunks as cover. There were booms as explosions shook the area we had just occupied.

"I guess that answers whether there is more than one artillery team out here," Sweeting said to the team.

"No shit, man," Meyers replied.

"Hopefully, the Whiskers gave us a location," I said.

"How can we help?" I asked Royle.

Royle sent me a set of waypoints behind her position at the top of a hill. I gave the order, and we moved quickly to the hill.

"Prep for cover," I said to the team.

Royle had her team leapfrogging back to us. Once the Venom were in our sights, we opened fire. Above, the Gunships shot through the canopy, slowing the enemy. As they stopped, I sighted in with the mortar drones, and they fired, taking out several Venom. They turned and began to retreat.

"The enemy is in retreat. Do we pursue?" Royle asked Monroe.

"Negative, head to waypoint Bravo for resupply," Monroe replied.

We headed to the waypoint, where a group of replacement drones, along with replacement ammo, awaited us. We loaded up our packs with ammo and replenished the supplies on the mules. While we did this, I watched a map of the area begin to light up. Squads from all over were starting to report action. All of the reports were spreading out from where we had just been.

"That's a lot of artillery our squads are finding," Betts said to me.

"That it is. My guess is they were planning a counteroffensive in the area. I guess our attack started the push," I said.

"So the question is, did we interrupt the preparation for this or just start it a little early?" he asked. "With all that action, I'd guess we just started it a tad early."

I studied the map. "I think you're right. At least this way, they lost getting the jump on us."

My CCPU pinged me. Our new mission was in. We were to help with fire control. If teams were in a tight spot, we were to assist them, or if they found something their CO didn't think was wise for them to handle, we would take care of it. It was going to be a long few days.

TWENTY

Our first few months on Pike Prime had seen us surrounded by life. Not animal life, mind you, as that had high-tailed it out of the area. We had been surrounded by all manner of foliage, but that wasn't going to remain the case. The Venom, like us, possessed rapid manufacturing, mining, and reclamation technology. As they advanced up the continent, they'd been harvesting resources. They'd erased entire cities off the map, and along with those cities went biomass.

Our main fighting units were machines, so we didn't really care about plant and animal life. For the Venom, their main fighting units were their warrior caste, and they were constantly replenishing their ranks, along with feeding those units. I didn't really understand biotech, but from what we'd been told, the Venom were able to process biomass from around them into food. I suspected it was similar to how humans were able to eat and consume plants and animals from other worlds. Once planetside, they consumed anything that was alive or had been alive. Orbital images showed that the deeper you went into Venom territory, the less life you found. The longest-held areas were void of plant and animal life. It unnerved me and the others. On Erie

Prime, we'd known that there would be some ecological damage to our presence in the short term, but within a few years, the damage caused by us would diminish, and for the planet itself, it would be as if we'd never been there. The Venom were literally killing Pike Prime. Even Meyers had come around to the side of "we need to kill the Venom as quickly as possible."

We'd been held up in our current position for about a week, or whatever passed for a week here. We were on the side of a steep hill. In front of us were much smaller rolling hills. The main army was in a stalemate with the Venom just beyond the hills west of us. To our east, the hills turned into mountains with steep terrain that made for slow movement and dick all for cover. There was almost no vegetation in the area thanks to the Venom.

We were dug into the side of the hill in alcoves, providing us easy cover and positions to attack the enemy from. It was kind of nice to turn that around on the Venom. Each alcove only held three troops, making it less likely that enemy artillery could take out a large group. Each one was dug so the entrance was big enough to crawl in and out. The floor sloped down, forming a chamber large enough to stand in if you stooped a bit. The upper edge of each alcove extended further than the lower edge, making it difficult or even impossible to attack from above without a lot of firepower. Which, of course, the Venom had but didn't tend to waste on small clumps of troops. Each alcove also had a reinforced ceiling.

We spent the vast majority of our time lying down on the slope to the entrance. There had been steady rain for most of the last three days, and water was managing to seep into the alcoves despite the over-hanging edge of the entrances. There was a small drainage hole bored into the floor of each one, but it wasn't quite able to keep up with the current rain. Currently, my alcove had a few inches of water in it.

The water didn't really make things uncomfortable for us with our suits, but it turned everything into slippery mud that was a pain in the ass to move through if you were in a hurry. The mud also coated our suits, making it difficult for them to camouflage us if we needed to move out of the alcoves.

We had large and normal Whiskers keeping a lookout for us, so none of the BIs or Spheres needed to risk getting shot if the enemy was in the area. It was pretty boring. There would be a lot of lying in a hole, then a brief firefight, and then some more lying in a hole. It must have been what life was like for the Venom. Mercifully, we had CCPUs and could talk to one another, send and receive messages from home, or take advantage of any entertainment our CCPU offered when we weren't on watch. It wasn't that I'd turned into a couch potato so much as a weird hole-in-hill potato that occasionally shot hostile aliens, or at least tried to have drones shoot them.

Cortez had told us repeatedly that every deployment would be different. I was starting to appreciate that now. On Erie Prime, after our initial setup, our forces had moved quickly across the planet, taking dozens of kilometers a day. At the time, I'd thought it was kind of slow, given how advanced the HFDF was compared to the Erie. And while I thought we could have moved a lot faster there, I was sure that command was moving at a speed they believed to be the smartest and best. Still, in the end, it was a smash-and-leave sort of job. We'd over-whelmed the Erie with sheer numbers and technological advantages. But we didn't clear the Erie out of every area we took. From towns and cities, we did, but from the countryside, we didn't.

We were there to destroy their technology and infrastructure, not them per se. Here was different. We were cleaning Pike Prime of the Venom. Plus, the Venom weren't the same pushovers the Erie were. The front was moving slowly. Centimeter by centimeter, meter by meter, day by day. Two kilometers behind us was the first of several containment lines. While the front moved forward from objective to objective, it wasn't a solid line of drones and people running from sea to sea. The containment lines, on the other hand, were.

On Erie Prime, we used the natural resources and the Erie's own property to build a massive army. Here on Pike Prime, we used none of the natural resources, and reclaiming the Pike's old cities and towns was difficult thanks to the Venom already having done it. So that meant bringing in countless millions of drones from off-world. Or the materials to make them.

Where the Erie wanted to go toe-to-toe in fights with little or no armor, the Venom dug into burrows with small caps on top of them that they shot out of. The two deployments were apples and oranges. For the first time in my life, I was starting to realize what the HFDF was really up against in the galaxy.

"So, Krista, what was home like for you? I know you're from a dead world, but I haven't heard you talk about it much," Sweeting asked over a comm line that he, Betts, Krista, and I had open.

"D324?" She said with a chuckle, "it was fine, not really much to talk about. Though there's something odd knowing that in a few thousand years, your home is going to burn up in a blue giant."

"Seriously? It's gonna burn up?" Sweeting asked.

"Seriously," she said. "But before that happens, the HF will pull a ton off-world. My parents are in mining, obviously. I grew up on the far side of the planet."

"How does a planet without a star have a far side?" Betts asked.

"The side opposite the space elevator," she said. "D324 is newer for a dead world. Most of them have four elevators, but we don't yet."

The thought of four elevators was amazing. I knew that unlike the elevators on Arrow or Orion with their sixteen lanes split between eight up and eight down, on a dead world, only one line was dedicated to traffic going back down to the planet.

"How many people were in your town?" Sweeting asked.

"Not many. And they aren't towns so much as hubs for drones. There were all of twenty people in my school. It wasn't bad; the hubs are nice. But there's no sun, so it's always night outside, and because there's no atmosphere on planets that cold, you can see more stars than anywhere else. I never really knew how nice that was until I joined the HFDF."

I knew all of this, of course. Krista and I had talked about her home a lot. She didn't understand why, but I was just as interested in her home planet as she had been with mine. She promised that sometime we'd visit her parents and go camping—something that required suits and mobile habitats. She said there were caves they liked to go to that were pretty neat. I told her I'd take her camping on Orion sometime.

"So, what made you want to join the HFDF?" Betts asked.

"I went to school with twenty people, remember?" she said with a laugh. "My life at home was nice, don't get me wrong, but I didn't want to go into mining, and sometimes you get a bit of a complex knowing that the 'D' in your planet's name stands for 'dead.' On that note, there's something slightly depressing knowing your home world didn't even get a name but a number. I wanted to get out and see the galaxy and make a difference. How about you, Betts?"

"Satcity," Betts said, "Hunter 56. I liked where I grew up for sure. Most of my family lives on 56. I've had a lot of family in the HFDF, so I thought I would follow in their footsteps, you know? Do any of you think you'll move back to your home when your service is done or you're on a cooldown?"

"Just to visit my family. Otherwise, I think Orion sounds nice. Or a planet like it," Krista said.

"I don't know; I kind of liked Arrow. I didn't think I would, but there's something about it. How about you, Taylor?" Betts asked.

"I don't know," I said. "Maybe it would be cool to live on Earth for a while, ya know? I still have family there and all."

"Have you ever been to Earth?" Sweeting asked.

"Oh yeah, loads of times. My parents were from North America; they grew up in Denver."

"I'd like to go to Earth someday," Sweeting said.

It always surprised me how many people hadn't been to Earth or the Alpha system at all.

"Contact, contact, contact," Meyers said over a fireteam-wide channel, interrupting our conversation.

I brought up a map of the area, seeing what Meyers was looking at. There was a column of Venom moving in our direction. They were on the other side of the hill in front of us, keeping out of the line of fire. They had to know where we were. I could send the Spheres out but held off. Instead, I told a large Whisker to go high and see if anything else was coming our way. There was. I could see several mobile artillery units. Three were of the standard projectile variety, but they also had a rocket launcher.

"Be advised, there is enemy artillery setting up. Prepare for bombardment. Again, I say prepare for bombardment," I said to the squad, trying to keep my tone even.

As if on cue, my CCPU pinged me that the Venom artillery had just opened fire. Moments later, the hill shook, and there was a deafening boom, followed by another and then another. I tucked myself as far back in my alcove as I could. This was one of the scarier things we had to deal with.

The lip on the top made it almost impossible to fire anything from above into the alcove itself. But hitting the edge of that lip, or right below the opening, sending God knew how much debris inside? That was not only doable but pretty simple for any sufficiently advanced species. We were still very protected inside the alcoves even during these events, but if the ground around us weakened or a shell hit just right, we were in a world of trouble. Rockets were another fear. They could zip around straight into the alcoves.

Some of the alcoves were smaller and only held missile defense systems. So long as the system held out in an attack, rockets weren't too much of a threat. But if the system went down, things could get bad.

The ground shook again as the Venom started another salvo. The alcove opening grew dark with dirt from the explosions. There was another thud and a flash right outside the entrance, and the alcove filled with dirt and rock as I was peppered with bits of debris. My BIs came in close, shielding me. As they did, there was another impact, forcing more debris inside the alcove. This time, one of the rocks was the size of an apple.

I reached around to my pack, pulling out the nano-material block and forming it into a kind of shield that I held in front of me. My BIs did the same. I couldn't see around them or the material. The alcove shook again, even harder than before. I felt the weight of one of my BIs slam into me and heard the crunch of rock. My helmet toggled view modes, trying to restore my vision. I tried not to panic and focused on my breathing and tried to calm myself.

As I started to calm down, I pulled up information on the BIs and ran damage reports. Thankfully, only one had taken minor damage to its left arm. The report said that the arm would be repaired in under five minutes. I shifted along with the drones. The floor of the alcove was covered in rock and dirt, the latter mixed with a small pool of water, forming thick mud.

There was another thud in the distance, and my CCPU notified me that a missile defense system had just been taken out. I instantly pulled up a map of the hill and looked at what the system was protecting. I could see that three alcoves were now missing coverage. All the alcoves were drones only, but I didn't want to lose them.

A volley of rockets zipped towards our location. Missile defense systems activated, taking out the vast majority, but one rocket found its mark in an unguarded alcove. *Shit.* I ordered the other two alcoves to EVAC, hoping that they'd make it to others that were still protected.

This was the part of a fight that I liked the least. I wasn't special right now. The rest of my team and squad were also cowering inside their holes in the ground, hoping they didn't bite it. They, like me, were also monitoring drones that couldn't do anything right now. The six drones from the other alcoves made it to others that were guarded by defense systems.

I could see a message from Royle requesting air support for the artillery. We might or might not get it. Lately, the Venom had taken to pounding the hell out of a position, waiting for us to send in aircraft that they would shoot at with ground troops. That meant no air cover. Eventually, our own artillery would move into position and take out the Venom, or at least push them back. In the meantime, it was a waiting game. Would the Venom get bored and send in ground troops? Or would they simply shell us until they were stopped? It was fifty-fifty on what they'd do.

I tried to relax as the ground around me shook, and my CCPU pinged me with notifications of impacts as if I couldn't feel them. During this time, you couldn't really do anything other than wait. There was no talking with others unless it was to share information. Instead, you just had to sit there and wonder what was coming.

I hadn't often felt scared on Erie Prime. Worried? Yes, but not scared. That was different here. On Pike Prime, I had to do something that humans didn't do anymore. I had to face mortality. Growing up, I'd never feared injury. I didn't seek it out, but fear it? Once you were old enough to understand just how little chance you had at dying, you lost that fear. If you got hurt, it was just an inconvenience.

All of us except Krista had spent plenty of time in MHUs. There was always a small fear that you would lose fingers or a limb in combat. That, while easy to survive, was something that people still seemed to worry about. But in the alcoves and with the Venom in general, you feared not only this but death. Even the little injuries could concern you in the field. You had a greater chance of losing if you weren't at one hundred percent. And losing meant dying.

It also meant that with each thud of the artillery, I feared for my team and Krista. She was just meters away from me, and there was nothing I could do to help her. I knew she felt the same way. We all felt that way about the whole team.

The only real upside had been that Meyers wasn't immune to this same fear. He was still an ass, but somehow there was a "I give a shit" attitude behind it. I suppose there's something that brings you together when you're in this kind of situation.

There was another thud, this time near a defense system that kept

Sweeting safe. *God, please don't let them zero it*, I said to myself. There was another thud.

After a bit, it stopped. The Venom had opted for option one: attack us with ground troops. Using the cover of the bombardment, they were able to get uncomfortably close.

I deployed the Spheres. Along with my BIs, I moved up to the lip of the alcove. There, scurrying across the ground, was the Venom. A lot of them. The Venom were smart to push as far as they could while we were getting shelled. In the open was the time the Venom were the most vulnerable. Their bodies were best suited for being in tight spaces like, you know, alcoves in the sides of hills.

In the front was a line of their larger soldier caste. They'd take the brunt of the damage. On their heels, so to speak, was the smaller castes. These would be able to get inside our alcoves if we didn't stop them. But it wasn't like we could ignore the big ones. While they couldn't make it in the alcoves, they could shoot inside them with large-caliber rounds or rip them open, making it simple for the other Venom to overwhelm us.

"Incoming. Focus on stopping the big bastards," I said to the team.

Above, drones were firing and weaving around, trying not to get shot out of the sky. Our BIs opened fire with heavy rounds on the advancing Venom. I aimed out of the opening with my SIR and launched a few grenades. Several of the Venom dropped while others behind them fired into the air. I lost several Spheres. They lifted higher above the Venom, making them harder targets but also limiting their accuracy. The Venom were coming up the hill now fast. Soon they'd reach the first alcoves.

I looked at the advancing column on the map, seeing which of my team would be reached first. It was Meyers. I zeroed the mortars right in front of his alcove.

"Meyers, take cover. Mortars on the way," I said to him.

"Roger that, we're tucked in," Meyers replied.

The mortars fired, hitting the oncoming Venom, sending limbs and carapace in every direction. As soon as the mortars stopped, BIs from other alcoves above Meyers popped out, shooting the dazed Venom. I looked back at the map, seeing that Betts and Sweeting would soon have company. Again, I told them to hide while the mortars fired. Again, this sent Venom flying.

Now it was my turn. The mortars fired, killing the largest of the Venom, but the others behind them surged forward, clamoring over their dead and wounded. I backed down to the bottom of the alcove, trying to keep calm. Moments later, my BIs backed down as the opening was filled with the form of a large Venom. I opened fire with my SIR, belching out a continuous stream of rounds. The two drones did likewise. Thankfully, one had a HIR as well as its SIR. The Venom's carapace burst as it was hit with the rounds from the HIR, sending its blood everywhere. It fell away from the opening, this time replaced by two of the medium-sized Venom and several small ones. My BIs targeted the two medium-sized ones. I dropped my SIR, letting it stick to my chest, and grabbed my sidearm, plinking one of the little bastards as the other Venom entered the alcove. The BI to my left went down. The Venom turned to the other BI, which was trying to deal with its companion.

I had the vambrace on my left arm extend into a blade and dropped my sidearm, a nano-material strip helping it swing around and snap to the bottom of my right forearm. The Venom on the left wasn't paying attention to me yet. I leaped forward, landing on the Venom's back. I could not afford to lose another drone if I wanted to live. I grabbed one of Venoms legs with my right hand and stabbed it with my vambrace. It thrashed, slamming me into the ceiling of the alcove. One of its gun arms swung around. I retracted the nano-material and grabbed the arm with my left hand, twisting it and putting pressure on the arm joint. It broke, and I used the vambrace on my right arm to stab the Venom again. This time, I killed it.

I rolled off the Venom, noticing that the BI had finished with the first enemy it had been fighting and moved onto another. As I got up, my sidearm snapped back into my hand, and I took aim at several small Venom approaching. I fired once, twice, three times, killing them. I grabbed my SIR, shouldering it, and buzzed several other Venom as they advanced. I was knocked back when one of the little ones managed to get off a shot. Two others fired as well but stopped when their rounds ricocheted, nearly hitting them. That was a plus. We could shoot, but they couldn't. My CCPU informed me that I had a broken rib. Thankfully, it had started turning off pain as soon as the fight broke out. Yay for technology.

Several more Venom made it to the opening, but we were able to shoot them before they got in. Luckily, the Venom didn't seem to use grenades very much. I suspected explosives could have negative results in cities that were, from what we had gathered, mostly underground. The Venom did not come back in through the opening.

"They are retreating," Krista informed the team.

"Report," I said to the team.

Reports from everyone started flooding in. Betts and Meyers had both been forced to hold their alcove openings. Both had lost several drones. Sweeting was down four drones, and Krista had apparently lost almost sixty percent of hers trying to keep me from being overrun. I was the only one who'd needed to fight inside the alcove.

"Thanks, I owe you one," I said to Krista.

"No, you don't," she replied, then paused. "But don't do that again, okay?"

I chuckled darkly. "No promises."

"How'd you fare?" I asked Royle.

"We lost a lot of drones. You okay?" she inquired.

"Yeah, I've got some broken ribs, nothing else. We sustained heavy losses," I said.

"Good work. I will let you know when replacement drones are inbound," Monroe informed Royle and me.

"Is there any more Venom in the area that we know of?" Royle asked.

"Negative," Monroe replied, "it looks like more rain is coming your way."

I breathed a sigh of relief. One of the issues with stripping an area of all plant life was that flash floods became fairly prevalent. When we got heavy rain, the little valleys between the hills turned into streams that churned up rock and dirt. Meanwhile, the sides of the hills turned to slick sludge that made it a pain in the ass for mechanized units and infantry alike. That meant the Venom would hunker down, giving my team plenty of time to refit.

I got to work hauling the dead Venom out of my alcove, and I wasn't disappointed when Monroe returned to us saying that we were rotating out of the area.

TWENTY-ONE

I pressed myself into a divot in the wall as rounds flew past me. To my right, one of my BIs was shredded. I raised my hands to my chest to reach a pack that was connected to me. It was new, and while it was a pain to have hanging on your front, I was eternally thankful for it at the moment. I removed it and slammed it into the wall to my right. It stuck and flung open to create a barrier about a foot wide that went from the floor to where my head was. Instantly, it registered several impacts. Nothing went through, though.

My POD and I were in a tight passage in one of the Pike's old buildings. Though a Pike couldn't fit into the passage, pipes and other service lines once had. Now it was empty save for the occasional chunk of debris on the floor. I checked on one of my other BIs further up the passage. It had managed to find some cover and deploy its shield before taking any damage. It was currently curled up on the ground behind its shield and had no real way of fighting back. That meant one of the two BIs at the intersection I came in with would need to take out the threat—something they were currently scanning for.

After a few moments, they thought they had something. I checked and agreed with them. Twenty-three meters ahead of the lead drone were four bumps in the passage. One on the floor, another on the ceiling, and the other two on the walls opposing each other. This passage was built into the building's concrete skeleton, so our density vision was pretty much worthless. I suspected the little shits were hiding in holes dug into the walls. I sent a ping to my team, letting them know I was pinned down for the moment.

I told the other two BIs to sit tight and keep cover. I didn't really want to lose any more drones. I looked at a map of the building and where my team was in relation to me. Betts was in an adjacent passageway. He'd stopped his advance. He was probably checking to see if he had any unexpected company as well. Krista was stationed right outside of the passage openings, ready to give us support. The room she was in was vast and cavernous. It had two entrances, one guarded by Meyers and the other by Sweeting. They weren't taking any fire.

I tried to assess my situation. In space, we had a clear advantage when fighting the Venom. Good for the fleet. But in regular conventional ground warfare, we would win just on the grounds that we had been doing this longer and had superior numbers. The same went for subterranean or close-quarters fighting in the long run. In the short term, however, the Venom were far better at tight-space fighting than we were, generally speaking. Humans left their caves and started killing each other in the open millennia ago. The Venom never did that. The four Venom down the passage from me would be of the small variety. That was a plus in that their weapons seemed to have difficulty penetrating the shields unless it was close range. Something they must have known, as they weren't pelting me or my BI anymore.

As it seemed I would be here for a little while, I used my CCPU to access my pack and extract the nano-material block inside it. The shields we were now equipped with had about four times the material of our normal blocks, and all of it for armor-related tasks. Our standard-issue block could be used for armor but was mostly for utility purposes. Still, some protection was better than none. I had it attach to the shield's edge and extend in front of me, essentially sealing me in my little wall divot. It would be able to stop low-caliber rounds, but more importantly, it could slow down anything from small explosions to the point where my suit could protect me.

The smaller Venom didn't have large explosives, but they would toss small frag grenades that could be effective in tight places. They, like me, also had extra cover. We could use larger explosives to kill each other, but that also meant killing yourself and possibly blowing up part of the building. That didn't work for anyone, so now we waited and, in my case, thought.

I had eight functioning BBALLs under my command, positioned with the drones at the end of the passage. I could have sent them ahead of the other two BIs and myself, but then I wouldn't have any BBALLs left to use, as they'd have been taken out. So there was a plus. After a few minutes, I made a decision. At the end of the passage, I had two of the BIs ready with small grenades. They were mostly like flash-bangs; I wasn't sure what the building could withstand, so I didn't want to use anything too powerful. I just needed the Venom to take cover. The flashbangs would work for that. I also prepped four of the BBALLs and the BI that was with me in the tunnel.

The first BI fired on my command, sending the flashbang down the passage. It exploded near the Venom on the floor. The second BI fired, and simultaneously, the BBALLs started to zip down the passage. The flashbang went off, and a second later, the BBALLs whizzed by and began to fire, moving down the passage past the Venom and shooting at them. The BI ahead of me advanced. The passage filled with a quick exchange. I collapsed my shield and nano-material block, putting them away.

"How'd it go?" Betts asked me.

"Lost a BBALL, but that was it," I said.

"Roger that."

I knelt by the downed BI. I grabbed its ammo blocks and block of nano-material. I then activated pockets of nanobots and robots that would break the BI and its weapons down into smaller and smaller pieces until it was dust. Normally, this protocol was unnecessary because reclamation units would come by and recycle the drone, but being close to a Venom colony meant no reclamation drones. I took the BI's shield and activated it. The shield covered the BI, and then I used its block of nano-material to cover the shield, having it take on the color and texture of the passage. In a few hours, this material would also be turned into dust, and there would be nothing left for the Venom.

When I was done, I moved up to where the Venom had been hiding in the wall. Whiskers had been down this passage before us and hadn't noticed them. I saw why when I got close. The Venom had cut out the lids for their holes from the concrete the passage was made of. The pieces were thick with a hinge they'd placed, allowing them to move the block up, use it for cover, and fire around it. The seams around it were extremely fine. I recorded all of the data that I could and sent it to my Fireteam, Monroe and Royle. I commented on the Fireteam's line.

"They had to put some time into this. The Whiskers didn't even notice it," I said to the team.

"Clever little shits, aren't they?" Meyers commented.

"Do you think this is something new?" Sweeting asked.

"I doubt it. The Pike hadn't had control of this area for months prior to our arrival. I bet they have a bunch of these things scattered around the buildings," Betts said.

"No way they have troops in them all, though," Meyers said.

"I agree. This will slow us down. If they'd waited just a bit longer, I'd be dead," I said.

"So slow down the Whiskers and keep the shields out?" Krista asked.

"Are you serious? That will take forever; we can't take all day in here," Meyers said.

"We get caught in too many firefights like Taylor had, and we'll be in trouble," Betts said.

I thought about it.

"I agree with Krista and Betts on this; we can't take the losses I did. But Meyers has a point too. I sent it to Monroe; maybe he has something for us," I said.

Before I could start moving down the passage again, Monroe contacted Royle and me.

"Taylor, we are starting to see reports like what you have found. As this is the first colony we have approached, we haven't seen this yet. I am sending some whisker settings that might speed things up a bit, but you will need to move with caution. So far, hiding holes like these have only been spotted in tight passages," Monroe said.

"So, ditch the passages?" Royle said.

"For now, yes," Monroe said.

"Roger that," I said.

I related the conversation to my team. This whole part of the campaign had been a pain in the ass. The army had been moving ahead slowly, but moving nonetheless. We'd reached one of the Pikes' old cities, a large one. In the center of the city lay one of the Venom's subterranean complexes that acted as a colony. We didn't know their makeup yet beyond the surface. On the surface, they appeared to have several forts. Each one was highly fortified with all manner of weapons. The Pike had taken a good deal of losses trying to take these in the early days of the war. They'd discovered two things.

One, if they did take one, the complexes went deep into the ground and were self-sustaining. They also found that, in some cases, the colonies were connected to one another, allowing the movement of materials and troops without relying on the surface. We'd noticed that. Material flowed out of the colony to combatants in the area, but all other supply lines were non-existent to our orbital assets, meaning they were underground. The Pike had also learned the hard way that you couldn't just leave a colony alone and try a siege to get rid of it. All that happened was that eventually, Venom would surge out of the colony along with units from the front line. The colony would cut off retreat, and the front-line Venom would press forward. This could lead to, as it had in the case of the Pike, the largest loss in their species' history.

We didn't feel like doing that. So, we were going to surround the colony, take out its surface fortifications, find its supply routes underground, and destroy them, and then begin the process of taking out the colony itself. Once the supply lines were gone, the rest of the army would be able to move forward, leaving a dedicated force to root out the Venom. I was sure it would be good times for the people dealing with it.

We started to move forward again. This time the Whiskers moved slowly, catching everything as we inched ahead. At the mouth of the shaft, the lead BI made a shield for itself, pressing the front of its SIR into the shield, which made a hole for it. Handy for sure, but it meant that the BI had limited mobility. The BI behind it did likewise, and my BBALLs prepped behind them.

The drones spilled into the room beyond the shaft, their shields getting hit by enemy fire. One of the lead BIs took a headshot and dropped. The BBALLs entered the room, taking out a Venom clinging to the ceiling that had taken out the BI. The BIs were able to take out the other two Venom in the room.

I came in after several more drones, followed by my Fireteam. The room, like every room, was large, though this one was not as much as some of the ones we'd been in. Its walls were scraped clean, with a hole in the side looking outside. I'd stopped trying to figure out what rooms used to hold or what purpose they served—partially because I couldn't wrap my head around a species like the Pike and also because it was depressing. For all I knew, this was some Pike kid's room, and that Pike could be dead or have lost everything it ever cared about. I didn't need those thoughts.

My team took up positions along the opening with their drones taking sniping positions. I waited for the mule to come into the room and then summoned all of the damaged drones to me. Meyers had a drone that had been shot in the arm, rendering the arm useless. I had one with a hole in its head. The other drones that had been hit were like the one I'd lost, rotting away in the building.

I walked up to the BI that lost its head and used my CCPU to access the drone's upper body. Most of its computing was done from this area, with only a small portion being done in the head. I ran a diagnostic on it and integrated it with one of the spare heads on the mule. I had the BI's body come up to a kneeling position. The diagnostic returned, telling me that the neck clamping and connections were undamaged. I held the sides of the ruined head and told the body to disengage. The head came off nicely, and I tossed it onto the mule and grabbed the new head.

Somewhere along the line, the Venom had figured out that head-shots killed the people commanding the drones. As a result, we took more losses. It also meant that I'd gotten pretty good at swapping drone heads. I should have been thankful for it, really. The Erie had just shot for the largest mass they could find. You did that, and the drone really wasn't worth repairing in the field, but a head was easy.

I took the new head and placed it on the BI's shoulders. My CCPU showed the head and body syncing, and the BI stood up as good as new. I repeated the process with Meyers's BI, which had the damaged arm. As soon as there was a pause in the battle, we could replace the heads, and then the unit was back in action. And the heads took up the least amount of room on the mule.

On the other hand, they'd figured out that humans weren't so easy to replace. I wasn't sure if they knew just how hard modern humans were to kill or not. You could riddle our bodies with holes, and we could live to fight again, but a headshot... well, maybe someday we could live through that.

At any rate, drone maintenance was something that was pretty new for us. We all knew how to do it, but the beauty of being bounced from mission to mission like we were meant that we didn't have a lot of downtime in the field, and when we got back to base, there were maintenance drones that took care of repairs.

I scanned all the other drones in my POD and my teams to make sure nothing was amiss. Then I started dividing up the ammo that we had left. In many ways, it was smart to figure out how to unload a mule. Once you did that, it could make its way back to a place where it could be resupplied and returned to you. For some reason, I got edgy whenever the mule was low on supplies but not low enough to justify sending it to get more.

The Whiskers were surveying the area, as were the BIs. In the building across from us, I was sure there was Venom. Whether they knew we were here or not yet was unknown. While the average Venom soldiers weren't tacticians, there were commanding Venom that were. The breeding caste had much higher intellect than the other two castes. And being as close as we were to a colony, I was sure that breeders were being extra diligent in managing front-line troops.

"Contact, there is a small group of them in the building across from us," Krista said to the team.

My CCPU pinged me with the data from Krista. Whiskers had managed to catch some movement in a window. On further investigation, it found three Venom setting an ambush in the room like we'd experienced.

"Shit, they're setting up an ambush like we had. I'm not seeing any friendlies in that building," Meyers said.

"Contact. They are doing it in another room," Sweeting said.

"Looks like they are setting up in every room they can," Betts said.

That hung out there for a moment.

"Be advised we see hostiles setting up ambushes in the building across from us similar to what we experienced here. Royle, are you guys in position yet?" I said to Royle and Monroe.

"Negative. We are about to take a room with a vantage point," Royle said.

"Give us an update after you enter the room. Alpha, hold your position and fire," Monroe said.

"Roger that," I said.

I ordered my team and drones to keep their heads down. I was starting to feel uncomfortable. We waited as Bravo approached their positions and then took the room. They took out three Venom. I felt a little sick.

"Be advised we encountered the same setup as Fireteam Alpha," Royle said.

"Roger Bravo. Alpha, have you deployed Whiskers outside the window to have a look in another window in your current building?" Monroe asked.

"Negative," I said.

"Do it but keep them as hidden as possible. Royle, do likewise," Monroe said.

We did. In the room above my team were three more Venom. There were three more in the room next to Royle's team, and they were moving out of their position.

"First squad, get out!" Monroe ordered.

"Up and at 'em; this place is infested," I told my team.

We'd left a few Whiskers along our trail up here. One of them pinged me with enemy contact. Royle then reported she had the same. The Venom had waited for us to take up positions. They'd probably hoped that we would start shooting across the street and get distracted before coming up behind us, but that wasn't going to happen.

One of Betts's BIs by the shaft entrance opened fire.

"Take cover," I said.

I ran to one of the walls, crouching down and deploying my shield, as did the rest of my team. A small canister popped out of the shaft a moment later and detonated. Nothing crazy, mind you. The Venom weren't about to commit suicide. My shield was peppered with shrapnel. It was followed by gunfire from across the street coming into our window. The room filled with ricocheting rounds. The Venom from the shaft started to poke their weapons into the room. One of my BIs launched a small grenade into the shaft. It didn't kill the lead Venom but flung it into the room where its companion's rounds shredded it.

The fire stopped.

"Advise. First squad prepare for EVAC. Armor is inbound, along with four gunships for cover. When they are on-site, they will cover the far building with fire. You will need to jump out of your current building and head to the armor. Be ready in five," Monroe said.

Great, I thought. The gunships would protect us from the Venom across the street, but not from anything shooting out of this building. At least as soon as we hit the ground, the armor would give us all the cover we needed. It would just be a long drop getting shot at.

One of my Whiskers kindly pinged me a warning, and I brought up the data. *Shit!*

"INCOMING!" I yelled.

Across from us, deep inside the building, the Venom were finishing setting up a cannon of some sort. The bright side? There wouldn't be any Venom in the shaft shooting at us in our building. They'd be in the building for sure, but away from our current position. The dark side? We were going to get the hell shelled out of us while inside a building.

On cue, the wall in the back of the room took a round, exploding and sending chunks of building flying around the room. A moment later, the outside wall shook, a hole opening in it above my head, sending more debris into the room.

"We don't have five," I said to Royle and Monroe.

"Roger, gunships on site in thirty seconds. Be ready to leave," Monroe said.

"Be ready in thirty seconds; we are running to the Rhinos!" I said to the team.

The room shook a few more times with Venom artillery. My CCPU became aware of four gunships above us. I had no control over them, but it was nice to see them there.

GUNSHIP ONE: COMMENCING COVER BARRAGE.

The gunships unloaded on the building across from us, forcing the Venom to take cover.

"MOVE MOVE MOVE!" I ordered.

I got up, my shield retracted, and ran to the window. We were up high and would need to clear as much of the dome-shaped building as we could. I jumped, pushing off the ledge as hard as possible using a burst of power from my anchor. Next to me, my team and POD did the same.

I could see Bravo team doing likewise. I twisted in the air, curling into a ball and deploying the shield to my right, giving me a little cover from the Venom in the building. In the near distance, I could see two Heavies along with a Rhino. The Rhino was our primary form of drone armor, and I had no idea where it got the name, as it didn't even remotely look like one. Dumb name or not, I was happy to see it.

I fell, watching the ground rush up to meet me. I was wrenched in the air as my shield took a hit. My anchor fired, stopping me. I kept my shield up as I sprinted toward the Rhino. The ground around me exploded with gunfire. Despite my CCPU trying to keep me calm, this was the most afraid I had ever been in my life, but we were close to relative safety.

The Heavies opened fire on the building we had been in. The Rhino, which looked pretty dang intimidating on the ground, turned, bringing its three cannons to bear on the building to our left and opened fire. My suit wouldn't let me hear the full power of the guns lest my ears explode, but I could feel it shoot. My chest thumped with each shot, and the dust around it curled in the wake of its shells.

We were home free.

To my right and just ahead of me, Meyers tumbled as he was hit in the leg. He recovered right away and started running again. My CCPU pinged me.

GUNSHIP THREE: ADVISE ENEMY HAS SMALL ARTILLERY OUT OF OUR LINE OF FIRE.

There was a flash next to me, my display went white, then black, and for a moment, I felt a flash of pain like nothing I'd ever felt before. My vision fuzzed, and I tried to focus on my display, which was just red.

I saw a timer that said consciousness elapse time was 34s. *Shit, I got knocked out?* I tried to clear my head, but I couldn't move my body. Nothing surprising there. My suit would keep me immobile until I was clear-headed enough to not move into enemy fire. In front of my eyes was a display of a body with the title damage report. I felt numb all over, so I must have been hurt badly. I looked at the report, thankful for my CCPU, all but shutting down my emotions. On the left side of the diagram, my ribs were yellow, and so was my arm. They were broken, which sucked, but what had me oddly not concerned, *thanks CCPU,* was my right leg and arm were red, along with the bottom of my left leg. Red meant not that they were really messed up but that they were gone. I was missing an arm, a leg, and half of another leg. My head showed that my helmet took some damage but wasn't penetrated.

CCPU or not, I started to panic. I couldn't even sense the world outside of me. I pulled up a list of my Fireteam. They'd have been hit with the artillery as well. The list came up slow to update as my CCPU was busy at the moment keeping me alive.

I was at the top of the list and labeled as OOA. Betts and Krista were IA or In Action, so no injuries there. Sweeting popped up as WIA. I couldn't tell how bad just now, but he wasn't out of action yet. Meyers was still just showing as updating. No surprise; he was close to me and probably got flung around. My CCPU told me that I had been retrieved by medic drones. Meyers's name updated from updating to KIA. I looked again, then again and told my CCPU to update. It did, and again, Meyers showed as Killed in Action.

I tried to bring up a comms line but couldn't. My CCPU warned me that I was starting to panic past its ability to keep me calm. No shit I was panicking. One of my teammates just died! I tried to bring up my visual feed but couldn't, nor could I contact any drones. I felt my breathing speed up, and my helmet felt like it was closing in on me. Anger and fear flared, and I tried to override my CCPU. My CCPU showed an emergency shut-off warning. *No!* I tried to yell but couldn't; I couldn't move, and there was nothing I could do as my CCPU put me to sleep, and my vision faded to black.

TWENTY-TWO

I knew that I was in a safe and quiet place, but I didn't want to open my eyes. All I could see in my mind's eye was a diagram of my mangled body and a message echoing in my head that one of my teammates was dead. How did I know I wasn't in danger anymore? Simple: my CCPU was doing nothing to keep me calm. At least I didn't feel any pain.

Logically, I knew that I'd be okay. Emotionally, I was less sure. Humans had spent most of their history unable to heal from anything major, and that reptilian part of my brain was screaming for me to confirm if my CCPU was right and I was disfigured. I knew that Meyers was dead. My CCPU wouldn't have been wrong about that. But it didn't really seem real to me just yet.

I opened my eyes.

Above me was a smooth white ceiling with a soft light shining down on me. I caught a glimpse of color out of the corner of my eye and turned my head to look into soft blue eyes and bronze hair. Liz didn't seem to really be looking at me, which told me she was focused on her CCPU. Her focus shifted to me, and at once, her expression changed from relief to concern, back to relief, some pride, and then it settled into controlled irritation. But beyond the irritation, there was something else in her expression. I doubted anyone who hadn't known her as long as I had would have noticed it. Liz had changed.

"How are you feeling?" she asked professionally.

"I think I'm fine," I said, trying to sit up, but was unable to.

"You can't sit up; you're in a medical bed. Do you know where you are?"

I shook my head in response.

"You're on the Healers Touch; you were routed to this ship partially because we are friends. You are still very badly hurt," she said, sounding professional. I was not surprised that it was Liz next to me. Having her here would be more soothing than someone else, and that's how the HF works.

"How bad?" I asked.

"You've lost your right arm, right leg, and lower leg on your left side. You lost most of the skin on your right side, broke some ribs, and then also managed to break several ribs on your left side." Her tone was even, and I suspected she had delivered news like this many, many times in the last few months. "Your ribs are healed along with your skin. Your arm and legs, on the other hand, will take roughly a week to grow back."

"Thanks," I said. "You did good at that."

"Thank you," she said, still professional, then her face darkened, "I've kept your family and our friends up to date on how you've been doing. I told you not to get badly hurt. I should be screaming at you right now... I want to."

"I know," I said, "sorry for worrying you, and thank you for patching me up."

She looked over her shoulder and then back to me, "I'll be back in a moment. Don't try to get up. You'll have more range of motion tomorrow."

She left and was replaced by Staff Sergeant John Monroe. His face was a mask of controlled emotion. He looked down at me, and I did my best not to look away.

"How are you feeling, soldier?" he asked.

"Fine, sir. Sorry, sir," I responded.

His face darkened. "I hate this part," he muttered. "I am here to check on you, but also to inform you that one of your teammates, Private James Gabriel Myers, was killed in action the day you were hurt."

Now things were getting real. "I am sorry, sir. What happens now?"

Monroe placed his hand on my shoulder, looked, and then moved it to my chest. I couldn't feel his hand before, but now I could. I assumed the medical bed wasn't exactly your standard mattress.

"I know you're sorry, but you didn't do anything wrong. After you were lifted, the information from your and Meyers' CCPU feeds of the battle, along with the rest of your team and every drone, was reviewed. It's standard procedure when there's a fatality. There was nothing you or anyone could have done. The mortar shell that tore you up hit Meyers almost dead on. Nothing you or our tech could have done to save him. As for your situation, you did the best that could be hoped for. The Venoms' ambush was well-executed. Sadly, this is war, and moreover, this is war with an equal enemy." He sighed. "Now you heal. Your squad is on the Arbiter, with some of them being patched up. When you are back aboard, Meyers' slot will be filled, and you and your team will prep to go back into action. I'm sorry; I wish we could go back to Orion or Arrow, but that's not on the table."

"I understand," I said, almost emotionless.

I was at a loss for what to say. The concept of someone I knew dying was utterly foreign to me. My only experience with human death came from the reports I'd received in the military. I'd never personally known anyone who had died. Yes, death was inevitable, even for the most advanced society, but it was not expected. I knew my parents hadn't been to a funeral in almost two hundred years. I didn't know how to think or feel.

"Sir, how am I supposed to feel?" I finally asked.

He looked away for a moment, his expression darkening further. "This is the one thing we don't really train for, you know? Dealing with someone under your command passing away or how to talk to your team about it. I have protocols and procedures to follow, but honestly, our society has largely forgotten how to mourn. Alex, I'm not sure how you should feel. I know right now I'm angry. I'm angry because one of my people is dead because of the Venom, and however else I feel, I want to get back at them."

I thought about it for a moment. I knew at some point I'd be sad. I didn't like Meyers, but he was still a brother in arms and someone I knew. The more I thought about it, the more I agreed with Monroe.

I just looked at him and nodded my head. He nodded back and told me to get better. Then he walked away, and Liz came back.

"I'm sorry about your teammate," she said.

"Thanks," I replied, suddenly not wanting to talk about Meyers. "What's new with you? I don't get chances to message you as much as I'd like."

She didn't seem to mind the change in topic. "I'm busy mostly," she sighed. "This war is nothing like Erie Prime. We got injuries there for sure, but most of them could be taken care of by MHUs planetside. I had several rotations on Erie Prime, sure, but we mostly spent our time making sure the drones were in top shape and, every now and then, working with soldiers. Here, even when planetside, it's constant, and up here..." She waved her hand around, "well, even more so."

"Lots of torn-up troops, huh?"

She nodded. "So many! I can't imagine what it must have been like before ageless tech came around in war."

"Do you lose a lot of people?" I asked.

She looked down at me, almost like she didn't want to answer. "Yes. Mostly in the field, though. Your CCPU put you to sleep before you were even out of the hot zone and onto a transport. If a medic drone with a stasis chamber can get someone in stasis before they go brain dead, we can generally save them."

"I take it that doesn't happen a lot," I said.

She shrugged. "No, it does. If someone gets decapitated, their chances are low, but most people make it to a chamber. Most of our losses are instant. People dying within moments of injury."

I thought for a moment about being in the field. "I've seen a lot of drones take headshots."

She nodded again, her emotions seeming less pronounced and more professional. "That is the largest group that we see. Those cases don't come to us. Any in-field fatality doesn't."

"What does happen?" I asked, part of me curious and the other wanting to know what happened to Meyers.

I could tell by the look on her face she knew why I was asking. "Is this about Private Meyers?"

"Yes," I said, not bothering to lie.

"Do you really want to know?"

I nodded after a moment.

Her expression went out of focus for a moment, and I assumed she was pulling data that I wouldn't have access to.

"There wasn't much of him left. It looks like the mortar hit at his feet." She looked at me, and I told her to continue. "A piece of shrapnel passed through his head, destroying his brain and CCPU. Drones recovered everything they could, and his remains are now on a morgue ship. Right now, his family has requested planetside services on his home world and has consented to standard military cremation."

"What's that?" I asked.

I knew what cremation was; it's what most people opted for. Your remains were burned and generally turned into gemstones for family and friends. I knew my parents planned on setting aside part of whoever died first's ashes until the other went so they could be mixed and turned into stones. I didn't know how the military would do it differently.

"He will be cremated on the morgue ship and then turned into gems. Most of those go home to his family, but others will be mounted and given to each of his Fireteam and squad mates, along with everyone in his command, with one going to the military memorial in Orion City. Someone from your ship will talk to you about him, I'm sure," she explained with a pained tone.

"Oh, ok."

I wasn't sure what I thought about that.

Liz touched my chest. "You need to rest now, and I have to work."

I could try to argue with her, but she was a doctor and Liz. She could pretty much tell my CCPU to do whatever she wanted, and it would comply. So, I could fight her, and she'd just put me to sleep, or I could be a good boy and do it on my own. I chose the latter and told my CCPU to calm me down and put me to sleep. I could deal with having lost Meyers tomorrow.

I spent a good amount of time the following day talking with the Arbiter's psychologist, Dr. Philips. He told me it was not uncommon to not know how to feel in situations like this and that emotions would come up with time. He also told me that the guilt I felt about losing a team member was also normal. While I was sure he was right, telling me it's normal and that nothing was my fault didn't make me feel any less like shit because Meyers was dead. Having a line open to my parents helped a lot more. They'd actually lost people in their lifetimes and had more experience with it than I did.

My movement was sort of better. The bed, or machine, or whatever it was that covered my whole body except my head, was busy helping to regrow everything that I lost in combat, which was pretty handy. The left side of my upper body was fine, but I still couldn't move it for a few days until I went into a different machine that had a lot more mobility. The thing was integrated with my CCPU—not that I could tell it to do much, but I could make it sit me up and turn me slightly so I could talk to other patients.

The room I was in was full of other people in similar machines as me. I was in the corner of the room with only one other person next to me. He was awake but couldn't move yet. I figured I might have someone to talk to when he could move.

Liz came walking up to me with a small smile on her face.

"Hey, how's it going?" I asked.

"That's what I'm supposed to be asking you," she replied with a smile.

For the eightieth time today, I was reminded that I couldn't shrug right now.

"Bored, honestly. I spent the morning talking to the shrink from the Arbiter. Talking to Mom and Dad was nice, but I'm supposed to be resting, so my CCPU is blocking most entertainment," I sighed. "Sorry. I shouldn't complain. Both my parents reminded me that I live in a time of medical miracles and that when I was their age, I would have died."

"Your parents have that lecture down," she said with a bigger smile.

I chuckled. My parents never told us that they walked to school naked in the snow, but they may as well have. There was a time when neither one of them could walk up a set of stairs and worried about getting sick. I could see where me bitching when I was a kid about how hard life was didn't go over well.

"The joy of first-gen parents," I said.

"Well, I think your day is going to get less boring, at least. Your squad is here in one of the waiting areas. I'm going to take you there now," Liz said.

I should have been excited to see them, but I suddenly felt a little nervous.

"Is that a good idea?" I asked.

She rolled her eyes, and I felt my bed start to move. It slid out into the center of the room and then turned towards a door. Liz kept pace behind me as I glided down the white hallways. I had to remind myself that while the Healer's Touch wasn't anywhere near the size of the Arbiter, she was still very large and expanded once in orbit to accommodate patients. A few moments later, we entered a small, empty room. My bed slid up to the far wall, and Liz let me know that everyone would be in shortly, which was medical speak for at least thirty minutes.

The door finally opened, and Monroe led the squad in. At the head of them was Krista. She moved around him, walking quickly up to my bed. She looked down at it, running her hands over its surface, her face red. She looked at me and bent over, pressing her forehead to mine. I felt hot tears drip onto my face.

"I am so sorry," I said, emotion getting the best of me as I felt my own eyes well up.

She didn't lift her head from mine. "It's okay, it's okay, it's not your fault. I thought I'd lost you."

"I know," I said, "I'm sorry."

She lifted her head off mine to look into my eyes. "It's going to be okay," she tried to smile.

The rest of the squad had been standing off to the side, giving us a little privacy. All of them wore somber expressions. They started to move in closer to me.

Sweeting looked down at me. "Man, you had me worried there, ya know?"

"Sorry," I said.

He shook his head. "It's cool. But man, I was worried. I've never been in command before, you know. And seeing how I was the obvious choice... well, let's just say I was anxious about taking on that mantle of responsibility."

Monroe snorted a laugh, along with a few others who chuckled, breaking the mood.

"Sweeting, I'd put a BI in charge first," Monroe said.

Sweeting shook his head and mouthed, "He lies; it was already in the works."

I couldn't help but laugh.

"Thanks, man," I said.

The others started talking now; everyone was feeling better. It was nice to talk to them. Everyone kept things fairly light, with lots of 'get wells' and 'feel betters'. Monroe didn't let them stay long, shepherding everyone out after only a few minutes. Krista kissed my forehead as she left, and I felt lonely for the first time since waking up. It hurt to watch her go.

Monroe came up next to me, looking at me. "How do you feel?"

"I'm doing better, thanks. Thank you for bringing them today," I said.

He nodded. "Of course. Get better soon. We have payback to work on."

That we did.

As he walked out the door, he let me know that I'd been cleared for comms for my team, and though they wouldn't have the chance to visit again, I could keep in contact with them.

Liz walked up to the bed, shooting Monroe a disapproving glare. "You aren't even healed, and you lot want to go back out there?"

I thought for a moment. How to explain to her how we felt?

"It's what we are," I said.

She glared at me this time. "You aren't some weapon, Alex."

"No, not a weapon. A shield. Did I send you the recording from my graduation?" I asked.

"Thank god no. I didn't want to sit through mine, let alone yours."

"That's fair. My training officer, Major Cortez, spoke at it. I didn't get it at the time. He said we were shields. He said we were what stood between Humanity and death. Our job was to go into harm's way and stop it. I know it's cheesy, but he was right. I don't want to go out and fight just for revenge. I want to go stop the harm before it hits others. Before it hits you, or Jon, or anyone else I love. I feel like I let Meyers down because I didn't stop what happened to him.

"You've seen what the Venom have done here, not just to Humans and me, but to the Pike. Don't you want us to make them stop?"

She looked into my eyes for a moment, not as a healer or even as a friend, but as another human. A human who had seen things, one who knew what it was that we fought against. Her controlled expression cracked. "I hate them," her face flushed red, "I hate what they have done. I haven't lost many humans in my care, but the Pike? I've heard them wail in agony and loss the few times I've helped them out. I've seen suffering that humans have forgotten. I've seen good men and women mutilated physically and emotionally. I hate them!" She sighed, regaining control of herself. "So when you put it that way, I do want you to go stop them."

"That's what Monroe and I are talking about. That's why I want to go back down there. We will stop them," I said, my voice hard.

Anger probably wasn't the best emotion to foster at the moment, but it did have its benefits. Liz seemed to calm down somewhat, and I wondered how long she'd wanted to let out her own emotions. I doubted the healing staff had any time whatsoever. I could only imagine what she'd seen and been through. She never saw the victories, only our losses.

"How are you holding up?" I asked her.

She looked down and thought for a moment. "I don't know, Alex," she said honestly. She gestured around the empty room we were in. "This is the calmest my day will be. It's also going to be the highlight. After this, I'm sure I will be called in to help with someone who is coming from Pike Prime in critical condition." She sighed. "Even if that's not the case, I will go tend to people who are overcoming an injury."

I thought for a moment. "How are they?" I asked, "the people you help?"

"Most are like you," she said, "hurt obviously, but for most people, their CCPU puts them to sleep pretty quickly. One moment they are in combat, and then they wake up here. But there are others," she continued, "people who were trapped for a while or were in intense action." She looked sad. "And those people... if they are asleep when they get here, they wake up terrified or shell-shocked. Others break down after they realize how hurt they are or after seeing their friends torn up." She said, emotion pulling at her expression. "I didn't appreciate how hard that would be to see."

"Yeah, I guess I didn't think about that," I admitted.

What must that have been like?

"And on Pike Prime, helping the Pike..." she said, looking off into space. I saw her eyes fill with tears. "Damn, they are watching their species die. The Pike are tough. They've never needed to invest in biotech like humans have. They aren't prepared for a traumatic injury like we are. Hell, their CCPUs don't even shut off their pain, so it's not like they can at least be comforted with the knowledge that their loved ones were numbed as they died."

"They don't?" I asked, surprised.

She looked at me and shook her head. "No. And when you've seen their history, it makes sense, but now? I've treated some of them that had a Venom burrow into them. Can you imagine what that would be like? Or to see someone you love have that happen to them?" she said. "These things are monsters. So, I guess to answer your original question, I'm not good or okay. I'm afraid, and sad, and depressed."

I reached my good hand out and took hers. She squeezed it. "I'm sorry. Can you get any help?"

She looked at me, a few tears rolling down her cheek. "Yeah, we have people we talk to. I'm not in any danger of losing it. I'm just..." She shrugged. "I don't know what I am. But I'm not special. We all feel this way. The only silver lining, if there is one, is that we don't have time to feel this most of the time. We're just too busy." She sighed softly. "Alright, let's get you back."

Liz brought me back to the room I was in before. The whole trip, I thought over what she'd said. As we got back in the room, I saw the guy in the bed next to me was awake. He introduced himself as Takeo Strode.

"Where are you from, Takeo?" I asked.

"I'm from Earth. You?" he asked.

"Orion. Where on Earth?"

"I doubt you've heard of it, but it's a city in North America called Fort Collins."

"No shit!" I said excitedly. "My parents were raised in Denver."

Takeo perked up a bit. "Really? That's cool. Have you been?"

"Oh yeah, we still have family there. My parents are first-gen."

He smiled openly now. "Very nice. Mine are too; heck, they probably ran into yours at some point. I'm going to be honest, I'm looking forward to talking to someone from a normal planet and someone with Earth roots."

"Why is that? And someone from a normal planet?" I asked, taken aback.

"I'm the only one in my platoon. Everyone else is from Mercury and satcities around Pluto, the two craziest planets in the Alpha System," he said with a sigh.

I thought for a moment. "I don't think I've met anyone from those planets before."

"Good for you," he said. "Don't get me wrong; I like the people in my squad and all, but the people who settled Mercury and Pluto either wanted to be as far out in space as they could without being around a dead world or as close to Alpha as they could. Not one of them had ever been outside of a satcity or megastructure before basic on Earth," he chuckled a bit. "I thought they were gonna explode being outside on leave."

I laughed. "I can feel you there. My girlfriend is from a dead world."

"So, what got you in here?" he asked.

I felt a pit in my gut at the question. "Venom artillery..." I paused awkwardly. "Sorry, I lost one of my teammates in it. How about you?"

Takeo grimaced. "Sorry about that... it's so rare nowadays... sorry man, I know how you feel."

"Have you lost a team member before?" I asked, and then added, "Sorry, not my business."

"Don't worry about it. It happened a year ago, and honestly, I think it's good to talk to people who have lost people. We were on Earth fighting some nuts, and she got tagged with a round to the head."

"Sorry," I said, and then curiosity got the best of me, and I asked, "You were fighting on Earth? Why not use drones?"

He smiled darkly. "Drone-on-human killing is still frowned on down there. Earth doesn't have the benefits that the other planets have. Though they are becoming more rare, there's still non-ageless humans down there."

"I've heard about that before. Several factions, right?"

"Yeah. Some don't believe in CCPUs, others think that there's a dome over the world and the HF is lying to everyone, and others think being ageless isn't natural. For the most part, they keep to themselves. Shit, they have to. What doesn't require a CCPU nowadays? Anyway, every now and then, one of the groups will get it in their heads to get violent. When that happens, normally, the cops can take care of it, but like I said, some people on Earth don't like the killer robot thing. So, we have to do it if the cops need help."

"I never understood that, but my parents seem to," I said.

"Yeah, I kind of see their side. Mostly now, it's the groups that don't like the HF that would lose it if BIs started offing people. Anyhow, this nut blew some stuff up, and then when we went to catch him, we couldn't use drones. It wasn't my first op. I'd never killed another human before, but in the first op I was in, I managed to wound the bad guy, and the cops arrested him. It was easy, as non-ageless humans are pretty weak compared to us. So, this guy was waiting for us and shot one of my team members in the head before hiding in a basement.

"See, they know at that point they're gonna die, they have to..." he was silent for a moment, "so they strap themselves with explosives. If we use drones to get them, then their group gets to claim that machines are killing people, and if we try to get them, then they might take out a few of us. For them, they see it as a win either way."

"So, what do you do?" I asked.

"We waited. The dude had about a week's worth of food and water, but it ran out. When he eventually died, he blew up, but no one else got hurt. He got a lucky shot. Most of them don't even get that. Eventually, my team was able to move on. There was nothing we could have done."

I thought about what Takeo said long into the evening. I replayed the data from a few days before over and over in my head. There was nothing that we could have done. No way to have prevented Meyers from dying, barring not being there to begin with. It didn't make me feel any better right now, but I hoped that someday it would.

———

MY RIGHT LEG TOOK THE LONGEST TO GROW BACK, AND WHEN IT DID, LIZ put me through a battery of tests and ran scans on my body until I was cleared for combat. The Arbiter's shrink also cleared me in that time, noting that generally, when someone lost a team member in this day and age, they either freaked out about being confronted with mortality —not the words he used, but that was the gist—or, like in my case, didn't seem to be overly impacted by it. To a certain extent, while I worked closely with Meyers, I never saw his face and generally communicated over messaging or comms. He said that at some point, I'd probably have a bit of a breakdown about it, and when that did happen, if I was in combat, my CCPU would flatline my emotions, and if I wasn't in combat, I would talk to him. My psychological profile suggested that I would most likely break down while on leave. Sometimes the things the HFDF could predict about us were just creepy.

Takeo had left the Healers Touch the day before I had, but I'd come to think of him as a friend, and we'd stay in touch via messaging. Monroe said that he'd spent some time on a hospital ship in his first term and still kept in contact with many of the people he'd met.

Liz gave me one last disapproving look as I boarded the shuttle that took me back to the Arbiter. The whole time I'd been aboard, she'd acted professionally and unaffected, save for her one outburst, but I knew her too well. She would have a hard time for the rest of this deployment, and while I was thankful she had been my primary doctor, part of me wished for her sake that the Healers Touch hadn't been deployed to Pike Prime.

Monroe, my platoon leader, along with my squad and the ship's captain, met me back at the Arbiter. It seemed that the captain made sure that each man or woman assigned to the Arbiter was personally greeted when they returned from a hospital ship. I'd been in contact with the rest of my team on the Healers Touch, but it was good to see them.

Monroe led Royle and me to his office. When we got there, he asked Royle to wait in the hall for a moment. We walked in, and standing in the center of the room was a tall girl with long red hair and pale skin. She was standing at attention, but her eyes flicked to me for the briefest of moments.

"This is Private Melanie Clay," Monroe said. "She is going to be permanently joining your Fireteam."

I walked up to Clay and extended my hand. "It's nice to meet you."

She took it, "You too, sir."

"You can stand at ease, Private."

She still looked tense, which I suppose I understood. Our team had been together since basic, and she was there to replace someone who'd been killed. That couldn't have been comfortable. My CCPU pinged, letting me know I had a new personnel file. Monroe had Royle come in, and I did a quick once-over of the file during that time. Clay was part of a replacement squad. She'd been in the HFDF as long as our team and had spent the time being bounced around to no less than eight different Fireteams.

"I see you've been on several teams," I said.

She nodded her head. "Yes, sir. Mostly injury replacement when someone was healing. I was also in a few training teams as well."

"Training teams?" Royle asked.

"They're teams that are used in exercises. Replacement squads don't see the same action as our normal units. The HFDF doesn't like to bounce them around from one combat zone to another, so they do a lot more training exercises," Monroe said.

"Okay," I said, "I see here you've been on Pike Prime."

Clay nodded. "Yes, sir, I have fought the Venom on several occasions. I won't let you down."

"I'm sure you won't," I said to her and then to Monroe. "May I take her to meet the rest of the squad?"

"Yes, please."

I wasn't worried about Clay; I could see her scores and assessments, and she'd scored extremely high, putting her in Special Teams, but then she continued to excel in different teams. I supposed you'd have to learn how to adapt if you were in a replacement squad. I led Clay down the Arbiter's halls, her rolling her suitcase behind her. It was going to be different having a new team member, but for the moment, I was optimistic.

TWENTY-THREE

I was hunched down behind a broken wall, watching my team work. I should say I was hunched down behind a simulated wall and wasn't really hunched but lying in a VR pod. As far as my mind was concerned, I was back on Pike Prime and not on the Arbiter. Strictly speaking, I didn't need to be hunched down in the sim, but it just felt right. While I had comms with my team, for the purposes of this simulation, I was a ghost. Later, I'd be able to examine every moment of the sim from every perspective. It was overwhelming, and something that was normally what Monroe and the people back on Arrow did, but I needed to learn how my newest team member worked and how she worked with the team.

I had been a little worried about Clay when she transferred in. Yes, she looked good on paper and was friendly, but she hadn't been with us for months. My worries, it turned out, were pretty unfounded. Clay had been extremely versatile, doing well with everything she was thrown into, whether it was working with others or on her own. Everyone on my team was competent at every type of job, but I, like most Fireteam leaders, tended to have people in the same roles. Betts was my point man, Krista had our backs, Sweeting tended to be more of a defensive support, and Meyers had been a bit of a lone wolf, not working well with others. That had made him ideal for roles where he was on his own. Scouting and recon were great for him, as was setting up ambushes. Clay did well in all these roles, like all of my team, but her willingness to work with others made her more useful than Meyers. I felt bad thinking that, but it was the truth.

She'd told us that she was always filling a hole in someone's team and therefore had gotten used to changing things up. I got up and walked over to where she was hiding, crouched down with her SIR to her shoulder. We were taking a Venom Colony, or at least a small part of one. The field before us was rubble with crumbling buildings in the center. The enemy didn't surge on the outside like they had in the cities but stayed inside, lobbing artillery and taking sniper shots. Above us, the sky twisted with color. Shielding against photonic weapons drained a ton of power, but the Venom only had to cover the top of their Colony. I knew that this simulation wasn't just some well-thought-out scenario. This was data from an actual battle that had taken place on the surface.

Like all my team, Clay kept her head down, moving slowly to positions where we could snipe the Venom as they shot at our main army. West of our location, armor and artillery were pounding the hell out of the Venom while infantry slowly pushed forward. Barring mortars, the Venom didn't seem to have any large weapons left on the surface. I walked around the field as rounds from both sides whizzed through me while I observed my team. The sim was about to end. We weren't going to take the Colony or heavy fire. This was just so I could see how the team worked together. It was also one of the last simulations we'd be taking part in before returning to combat.

We all exited our VR pods and headed to a debriefing room when the sim was over. I was happy to see Krista and Clay talking and smiling. I told everyone that they were doing a good job. Our debrief was fairly standard. Monroe and I both went over what we saw, with me taking more time to discuss my initial observations. After every sim, the system gave the team and each team member a score, which I also went over with everyone. Sadly, our scores as a team were on par, if not slightly higher than they were with Meyers. Most teams experienced a dip in performance for a few months after losing a team member. We did the week after Clay came on board, but those scores had gone back up.

I dismissed the team for the evening, telling them that they needed to sleep in and take it easy tomorrow before we went back planetside. I joined Monroe and Royle in Monroe's office. Behind him, his wall displayed Pike Prime. I could see little flickers of light and streaks from ship-bound ordnance. In the planet's northern reaches, it was a deep green that faded to brown in the Venom-held territory. Some of the display showed notes and ship labels. Above the North Pole, I saw labels for several cargo ships along with the fleet of surface-to-orbit barges that were constantly bringing materials to the planet. We sat for a few moments before Monroe finally spoke.

"What's on your mind?" he asked me.

I thought for a moment and sighed. "I'm bothered by our scores."

"They're up, aren't they?" Royle asked.

"Yes, but they shouldn't be," I countered.

Monroe nodded, "You're not sure if you should be happy that your team is doing as well as it is. Your team is performing at the same level with someone new, and you're worried that it's wrong to be happy now that Meyers is gone, and your team will only get better."

"I don't think I'm happy, but at the same time, I think I am," I said, sounding conflicted. "I know that it's good to have my team in a position where it will likely do better than it did before, but I'm bothered that it's because of a death."

"There isn't an easy way to deal with that. Meyers was good at his job but wasn't easy to work with and never fully engaged in the team. Clay, on the other hand, is good and engaged. In time, I think it will be easier to accept that."

I just nodded. What else could he say?

Monroe's expression changed back to business. "I got word today that our fleet in the Venom system has pushed the Venom back to their home worlds. Engineering teams have already been working on how to get the selected objects headed towards Venom Major and Minor."

"How long do you think it will take?" Royle asked.

He shrugged, "I'm not sure. I can't imagine it's easy turning a giant asteroid or comet into a missile. That said, I'm also not in the engineering corps. I also don't know what the HFDF's plan is on it or how they want the impacts to happen. They may send in some smaller rocks first to take out most of the surface, or they may not. I don't think we will see anything happen for a few months, if not closer to a year.

"What I do know is that the fleet has started to build up mining and manufacturing in the system, which tells me they aren't planning on going home any time soon. My understanding is that in these situations, we will build a counter-planetary grid to keep pressure on the surface and keep the Venom from leaving. The other thing that I know is that we don't need all the firepower in that system that has been there up to this point. Part of the fleet is being diverted to Pike Prime."

I was pinged with an informational packet. To Monroe's left, his wall showed a map of Pike Prime. There were markers for when we started fighting the Venom, to where we were now, and all the known ground defenses they had. Above it, there were icons for what was left of the Venom's orbital defense, which was small, to say the least.

The area south of the current line turned red. "This area is some of the oldest and most infested parts of the planet. There is almost no indigenous life left in that area, other than bugs and bacteria, and even that's sparse.

"The fleet is going to be tripling the number of ships in orbit. Almost all of them are flare class, with a handful of photon class ships." He let that sink in for a moment. The flares were our main damage dealers, and I could guess what their mission would be.

"Tomorrow, those ships will arrive. Upon arrival, they, along with every other ship in orbit, will finish off what little is left of the Venom's defense grid. They will then begin to unleash hell on the surface. Not enough to cause widespread ecological damage to the whole planet, mind you. No nukes or anything that will fill the atmosphere with too much garbage. That said, there's nothing left down there to burn that would fill the atmosphere. It's a wasteland."

"But we can't take out the colonies from space, can we?" I asked.

Monroe shook his head. "Sadly, no. And even if we could, we can't leave any stone unturned. What we can do is make the fighting on the surface much faster. When the Venom killed everything, they not only got rid of cover, but we would have to worry about ordnance causing widespread fires that could have a major negative impact on the rest of the planet, not to mention the damage it would do to wildlife. This would have been the case had we started our campaign this way, but when was the last time you found anything substantial that would burn that wasn't ours or the Venom's?"

"It's been a while," Royle admitted.

Behind the main line, several orange dots appeared on the map. Some had labels showing them to be factories, and others showed that they were reclamation and mining operations. Ten showed as being fully active, while the others indicated that they would be within a week.

We'd been hesitant to mine on Pike Prime. We'd reclaimed what we could, but we were not only not planning on staying on this planet but didn't want to deplete resources that belonged to the indigenous species or deal with the Venom trying to take out factories. Now that we were in wastelands, it appeared that hesitance was gone. Within a week, we'd no longer be completely dependent on what ships could bring in.

"The line will move forward quickly and shouldn't have to deal with heavy amounts of resistance, thanks to the fleet. When we reach a colony, we stop. Let the fleet finish blowing the hell out of it. Find and destroy its supply lines underground and then take the surface. From there, the main force will move on with teams left to deal with the Colony below," Monroe said.

"Didn't the Pike try this?" Royle asked.

"Yes, but they tried to starve the Venom out, and that didn't work. We aren't going the wait-the-enemy-out route. The line has moved on from the Colony you were last at, and teams in the area have already pushed fifty meters down into the Venom's complex there. We also have the benefit of having a much larger and more advanced military than the Pike do.

"The numbers are turning against the Venom now. We can make drones faster than they can grow soldiers. And while effective, their underground transportation system has a weakness. Tunnels large enough to move enough supplies to support a colony are easy for us to find. We can get to them and destroy them where the Pike had a hard time doing that. Swarm may be how the Venom naturally work, but we've perfected it. It's just a matter of time now," he said with a smile.

Monroe was right. The Venom were the embodiment of swarm warfare, but they were held back by biology. In all honesty, had they spent their time building drones and having either their soldiers or workers manage the drones, we wouldn't have had a chance against them. While placing value on the Colony and ignoring the importance of the individual had worked well for them in the past, in the end, it wouldn't save them.

After Monroe dismissed us and Krista was asleep next to me, I lay in bed wondering if the Venom knew what was coming. And if they did, what they thought about it. I didn't know any of their emotional traits, if they even had emotions like we did. I suspected they didn't, but I was sure that whatever they thought or felt was probably something to the effect of "oh fuck." Or maybe they thought they would make it out alive like they had every other time in their history.

The next morning, I slipped out of my bunk, and Krista and I made our way to the mess. There were a few of the ship's crew members eating, but for the most part, we had the run of the ship. I sat down to eat, trying to ignore any news coming from the fleet bombarding Pike Prime. Clay sat across from me and seemed to be the only one who wasn't watching every report that came in.

She looked down at the table at everyone. "I bet we could dance around naked, and none of them would notice."

"Oh, I would, but don't let that stop you," Sweeting said, looking at her and then back away.

We both chuckled.

"Have you ever heard that your name is the loudest word you hear?" I asked her.

"Yeah, why?" she asked, confused.

"That's not the case for Sweeting. For him, it's naked," I said.

She laughed.

"And boobs," Sweeting said. "Don't forget that." He barked a laugh, then his eyes went out of focus again.

"Why aren't you watching what the fleet is doing?" I asked her.

"I figure it's about to be our entire life again. I'm not complaining about being in the military, but it's just kind of nice not to have the Venom ruling my life for a day. How about you?"

"Same," I said. "The whole thing seems like a waste to me, you know? I get why we are here, and I believe in our mission to my core, but it is just such a waste to have to wipe out a species. It seems like an even bigger waste that they've killed countless billions and destroyed worlds. It's kind of depressing."

She nodded. "That's occurred to me a few times."

Royle broke her reverie. "It's messed up, but can you imagine being the Pike? It's not even like they have anything to come back to in the south. They're going to have to almost terraform that whole area. And all the lives lost..." She took a bite of food. "Have you seen any of the Pike?" she asked Clay.

She nodded. "My squad was on a reinforcement drop ship that jumped in with everyone else. In the first few weeks, if someone had two or more team members get taken out of action, we'd drop in. That really only happened if command wanted to hold the area long enough for the Pike to get out."

"Pretty bad, I take it?" I asked.

Clay looked down, shaking her head. "Yeah. The fighting could get really intense. There'd be us and the Venom and the Pike. It got pretty crazy. Then the Venom would focus on us for the most part, but you guys were there for that surge at the beginning, so you know what it was like. Plus, the Venom don't just burrow in non-living things. They burrowed in the Pike while they were still alive. I think they saw it as killing two birds with one stone. The Pike wouldn't fire on them if they were in another living Pike, and it's not like the Pike was likely to survive that."

I could see from her expression that what she'd witnessed bothered her. I could relate a bit to her. I still remembered when we first jumped onto the planet, seeing refugees fleeing the area. It was odd that I could kill other species without feeling overwhelming guilt, but I was bothered by the suffering of the Pike. Maybe it was because they weren't the enemy, and I knew that. Or maybe it was because they were more human than the Erie or Venom when it came to their emotions.

"Do you like being part of a permanent team?" I asked her.

She smiled. "Yes, a lot. I was part of a squad before, but we weren't together that often. It's nice to know that I will always be working with the same people and not have to worry about getting used to one group dynamic after another."

"Even though your Fireteam leader is a prick?" Royle asked.

"Yeah, there is that," Clay said, serious and dejected.

I chose the high road and didn't say anything. Instead, I took a bite of food and gave them both the bird.

Krista and I did a fairly good job of keeping our day low-key. There wasn't a lot that we could do. Finally, I gave in to curiosity and started looking over feeds of the fleet's progress. We'd come here with mostly comet and juggernaut class ships, with only a few flares and photons.

CHAPTER TWENTY-THREE

It was slightly awe-inspiring watching the damage dealers do their jobs.

The photon class ships were each firing several particle cannons and lasers at the surface, scorching or vaporizing wherever they aimed. I brought up feeds from one of the ships. It had several cameras watching where one of the beams was going. I zoomed in and watched as it fried a company of Venom that were burrowing into the ground.

"I wonder why we don't use the photon class ships more," I said to Krista.

"I hear they are a bit of a pain," she said. "They take a lot of power, and if the area is cloud-covered or if there is a ton of stuff in the air, they can't focus as effectively. And they're kind of newish for the fleet. I'm not sure they've really found their place yet."

I'd heard that too. I also knew they had to stay steady in the sky to focus the beams the way they did. The class had only really been in mainstream use for a few decades, and I wondered if, as we got better at using them, they would see more action.

On the other hand, the flares were well-rounded in killing everything. Streams of ordnance flowed from them like rivers. Most were like the pods I'd seen entering Erie Prime's atmosphere. I didn't look at any of the loads on the pods, but I could only imagine how much damage they were doing.

The next morning, we boarded a shuttle early. It felt odd. We only had two BIs for each person. As we left the Arbiter, I pulled all the feeds into my display, making the ship around me disappear. The Arbiter shrank behind us as we moved. The trip would take a lot more time than normal drops, as anything that wasn't urgent had to avoid cluttering up the space above the combat zone. Today we'd be taking a route that would take us over Pike Prime's North Pole. I was kind of excited about it. We'd be flying over parts of the planet that hadn't been torn apart by the Venom or us.

Our entry was supposed to be a "smooth" one, but smooth is a pretty relative term when it comes to entering a planet's atmosphere.

We didn't pull the Gs we did on jumps or combat landings, but I was still thankful I could turn off my body's ability to feel like it needed to throw up. After that, though, it was all smooth flying over the green of Pike Prime. The cities almost seemed to blend into the surrounding foliage and were only recognizable by the domed shapes of the buildings and the wide roadways they required.

There was more color than we'd seen on arrival, but not by much. Pike Prime was a very muted planet, but it looked peaceful. As we flew on, that peace and green shifted to HFDF temporary bases and fading vegetation until there was grayish-brown rock and dirt from horizon to horizon.

As we came in to land, I thought I could make out smoke in the far distance. We started our descent into a sprawling mass of drones and temporary buildings. We were meeting up with the rest of the troops from the Arbiter and other ships. The war had seemed so slow a month ago, but now I could see that while we only moved forward a kilometer or two a day, that added up over time. I suspected that going forward, our speed would increase.

Upon arrival, we were sent orders to go to a supply area to pick up our new PODs. Our PODs had changed significantly from before. We now only had the two mandatory BIs. Replacing the old BIs were Spheres and BBALLs. Each person was also assigned a utility digging drone called a Small Digger, or SD.

"I'm not sure I like where this is going," Betts said in a comm line to me.

"The utility drone?" I asked.

"Yeah, I bet that means we're going underground to root the enemy out," he said.

I didn't like the idea of that either. I checked with Monroe, and he said that we didn't have orders yet, but from what the rest of the Special Team squads had been up to, he suspected that we would be busting small underground bunkers that the Fleet couldn't take out or justify using ordnance on.

After getting our PODs squared away, it was time for chow. Which, this close to the front, meant that there wasn't a mess hall. Instead, we sat next to lines of bunks, placing sealed nutrient packs to the front of our helmets so they could bring them in, unwrap them, and stick them in our mouths. We chose the area that we did because other teams from the Arbiter were there.

From what we could gather, the front was starting to move faster. The Venom weren't extending as far from colonies as they had been in the past. It was making for a relatively quick trip up to a colony and then bitter fighting. For the Spaceborne, they seemed to spend a lot of time sweeping for the enemy, and like Monroe said, the Special Teams squads spent a lot of time clearing out enemy bunkers. I wasn't excited about it, but at the same time, it was good to be moving again.

TWENTY-FOUR

I stood in the transport ship, waiting for the inevitable to happen. One of the squads in our platoon would call in that they had found an enemy bunker, and it would be time to go to work. Since returning to service, we'd spent weeks on the same mission.

The main army was moving forward at a faster pace, while the rear line maintained its previous speed. The rear's job was to check every inch of the path ahead for the enemy, ensuring that the Venom could not reappear on the Pike. The Venom's policy of destroying everything around them was now working against them, as they had dick all for cover. Fleet and air assets were blasting the Venom off the surface whenever they found them. This was pretty easy since, again, there was nothing around on the surface. But underground bunkers weren't as simple. Enter the spaceborne.

The spaceborne's job was primarily securing landing columns, cleaning up messes, and generally being there to do whatever was needed. This was kind of the case for Special Teams as well. With the current movement of the front, the spaceborne found themselves scouring the planet for the enemy. Unfortunately, the Venom were ruthless and quite adept at killing shit underground. That meant letting the drones go in and do their thing while directing them, then going in to help clear out the bunker once you were relatively certain everything was dead. Part one was actually somewhat challenging and required that you were skilled at using your drones, understood the enemy, and could work well with your team, all while not being part of the action. But the latter part was what was dangerous. One in ten bunkers had at least a few Venom that a sweep didn't catch, and that meant you ran the risk of hand-to-hand or close-quarters combat in a space that was just slightly taller than your average human.

Normal spaceborne troops couldn't handle that action, at least not the hand-to-hand. That's where we came in. Firstly, we were much better at using our drones, significantly lowering the chance of any Venom remaining in a bunker. Secondly, we were trained for hand-to-hand and close-quarters combat.

A squad would find the enemy, surround them, and call us. While we were on our way, they used Ground Penetrating Whiskers, or GPWs, to map what they could of the bunker. The GPWs could see about three hundred meters into the ground in all directions. Super handy. The squad's primary objective was to see if there were tunnels leading into the bunker. If there were, then we'd need to call out engineering and get their take on the situation. Thankfully, most of the bunkers we found weren't connected to a larger network, and when they were, it was generally to only a handful of other bunkers.

Occasionally, a small network would connect to a single bunker that didn't have surface access and acted as a supply depot. We didn't deal with those; instead, regular infantry would set up shop and treat the network almost like a mini colony, digging their own access tunnels and taking their time clearing every inch. It was slow, monotonous work that could take days to complete. I didn't envy them.

One nice thing was that the Venom only went so deep into the ground. The furthest we, or any of our allies, had seen them go was about two thousand meters. That's still a lot of space, don't get me wrong, but it was a limit. The bunkers rarely went more than one hundred meters into the ground, which allowed the GPWs to map them entirely before we even fired a round.

After Special Teams took out the bunker, we hopped on a transport to refit and rest while the other squad went looking for more trouble. It wasn't a system that anyone really liked. For us, we spent our time waiting to deal with some seriously nasty stuff while envying the regular spaceborne for just having to scout. For them, they bitched to no end about how boring it was and how much it sucked to find the enemy, then babysit them until we came to kill everything and take the "glory," as they said. I was sure that they'd change their tune in a hurry if they had to clear one of those shitty bunkers. Nothing like getting into a knife fight with something from a horror movie that made you long for boredom.

My CCPU pinged with a message from Third Squad letting me know that they'd found a bunker. Our pilot was also in the loop and sent back an ETA of ten minutes.

"Up and at 'em, we are ten out from drop," I said to the team.

Monroe sent the official orders as the transport started to move towards Third Squad. Royle and her team were in their own transport but would not be helping us unless the bunker was big. Instead, they'd be waiting for one of the other squads to call in.

We didn't want the Venom to know we were coming if we could help it, so we dropped a few klicks away from Third Squad's position.

As we got on-site, my CCPU downloaded all of the intel that Third Squad had gathered. I had to admit that each squad did its best to give us what we needed. Despite their griping, not one had dragged ass at all in the last few weeks.

I pulled up a map of the bunker, seeing what we were up against. At first glance, any of the Venom's underground structures looked random, but after you'd seen enough, you could see that they were anything but random. They worked their way through rock and soil, finding the best spots and optimal routes inside the complex that was almost an art form. For humans, building on the surface allowed us to play with form and function. For the Venom, the sheer work of tunneling had given their buildings a functional simplicity and elegance that I wasn't sure humans were capable of. This one had four tunnels connecting to the surface. They each connected back to each other with a main shaft that mostly went down. Forty meters below the surface, the main tunnel split into others that also split. It broke the bunker up into sections with only one or two tunnels connecting them. Without a map, you'd get hopelessly lost in them. But they all flowed well together, each section easy to defend but still accessible.

I had my CCPU mark the tunnels by size. The Venom came in three different sizes, as did their tunnels. This one didn't have the ability to hold any of the larger caste, which was nice. But there were tunnels for the medium ones, which were the most common sized ones, along with a vast number of tunnels being small. The little shits could be the issue in these fights.

In most cases, their tunnels connected everywhere, making clearing a slow process. Also, there were pockets where the Venom could hide in a wall and pop out and kill you. Mind you, we could see these on the maps, but that didn't make them easy to deal with.

I sighed, looking at the map. Maybe thirty percent of the tunnels were big enough for a human. I opened a channel with Betts.

"What do you think?" I asked.

"I think I hate these things," he said. Betts was usually the calmest and most collected member of my team, but not when it came to the bunkers. There was something about them that seemed to seriously bother him. "I don't think we have enough BBALLs to cover the smaller tunnels. The little bastards will just flank the Spheres."

"That's my thoughts on it, too. We will have to clear slowly and have the BBALLs take a small tunnel, clear it, and then have the SDs close it off."

"Do you think they'll target the SDs?" Betts asked.

"I do. Hmm."

I checked our mule to see how much accelerant we had. We had a lot. Our suits protected us from fire, but the Venom's exoskeletons did not. I decided how I was going to go about this.

"I am sending you each entry points. Have the Spheres clear a small path if you can, and then use your BBALLs for the little tunnels. When a BBALL clears part of the tunnel, have them spray it and light it, then seal it with the SDs," I said.

The team all came back saying they understood. It sounded like a great plan, and in all fairness, this wasn't our first time clearing a bunker or using this approach. The problem was that the Venom were very good at what they did. If we came in aggressively, they'd flank us like they had in the past. If we went slow and steady, they would, in turn, keep pressure on our Spheres and keep our SDs from being able to do their job, also as they'd done in the past.

We could use explosives, but that caused cave-ins, and then you had to dig to clear the areas you missed with the explosives, which could take hours or days. Unfortunately, there weren't many good ways of doing what we were going to do.

By the time I had my team set, Third Squad had set up sniping positions in case any of the Venom popped their heads out.

I told my team to engage.

Dozens of BBALLs rocketed into the air and fired into the tunnel entrances. There was only one Venom in one of the entrances. This seemed to be a trend. They wanted to fight us in their tunnels, where they had the advantage. Spheres shot small frag grenades into each entrance and then rushed in after they blew.

I connected to my lead drones and watched them work. The frags managed to kill two Venom. As the Sphere entered the chamber, it started to take fire. It wove where it could and managed to take out another Venom before being destroyed. The next Sphere moved into position and was instantly shredded. I halted my progress. We had to be careful not to clog the tunnel with wreckage. I tried using BBALLs next. They didn't get destroyed but were pinned down by enemy fire.

From what I was seeing, there were two Venom in the walls with their guns pointed out. I had the BBALLs try fire. One sent a jet of flames down the tunnel. The Venom shielded themselves in their hiding places, which gave the Spheres time to move down the tunnel and take them out.

There was a bend in the tunnel, and I managed to hold it as the rest of my team took their entrances. Now we had the central shaft to deal with. They had a trapdoor over the opening with just enough room for them to fire from. The chances of getting a grenade in the opening were slim. We could use fire again. This time, it was the Spheres that belched flames into the small passage. We had to be careful with this, however. The tunnels could have ammunition in them that could go off, and our drones did have limits. In this case, we only needed a small amount of time for a BBALL to zip to the door before the Venom could fire. It attached itself to the lid and turned into a bomb, shattering the lid.

It was a waste of a drone, but in our experience, if you sent in a BBALL to place a charge, it might not get there and back. Three out of four drones didn't make it back from the trapdoor. By having the BBALL blow with all its charges, you were guaranteed to take out the hatch. The Venom had been taking a lot of losses, and it was showing in their ranks. This place would have a quarter of what it once did, with no hope of reinforcements. I had to think that they knew they were going to lose eventually. All they could do was slow us down, giving their colonies time to build up, or, like when they were fighting the Pike, come back out swinging. They knew all they had to do was take out enough drones, and we would have to pull out and wait for replacements. First platoon's Special Teams squad had a bunker that took them two days to clear because of how good the Venom inside were at shooting our drones. The Venom really didn't get the concept of giving up, and in a way, I had to give them respect for that.

The drones were sending a steady stream of low-charge frags down the shaft. Each thud of a frag was slightly more delayed. You could hear the progress the grenades were making. Two of them exploded in the same section of the shaft.

I sent a whisker to investigate. We'd reached the bottom, where the tunnels started to split. Tattered corpses piled at the bottom of the shaft. Our smaller Whiskers zipped down, searching for the Venom. They found more bodies and several Venom trying to clear the tunnel.

"Move move move; they're trying to clear the tunnel!" I yelled.

Drones rushed down the shaft and fired armor-piercing rounds into the Venom corpses, penetrating them and hitting the living Venom behind. The shaft split into three others. One led to a chamber. I had Sweeting and Betts press the other two shafts. Krista was to hold the junction we were at, and Clay and I were going to deal with the chamber.

"Wait for my mark before moving SDs into position," I said to Clay.

"Roger that," she replied.

I directed my SD down the main shaft into the junction. The entrance to the chamber was closed off. I had Clay cover the opening while my SD determined the best way to dig our own indentations into the wall.

"I'm at a junction," Betts informed the team.

"Me too," Sweeting added.

"Roger, Betts and Sweeting. Sit tight," I said.

The SD began its work. This would have been faster with Clay's units as well, but I didn't want to risk losing them if the Venom emerged. I checked on Krista's units while I waited and saw that she had her own SD digging indents for drones. We could use the Venoms if they were available, but unfortunately, there weren't any in this section.

The SD finished and retreated to cover. Drones took position in the indents while a BBALL placed a charge on the entrance.

"Breaching in thirty, clear units out of the line of fire," I said.

Thirty seconds later, there was a small thud as the charge blasted the door, followed by fire from both sides. A Sphere launched a frag into the chamber, and then units rushed in. They found eight Venom inside, none killed by the frag, but they had to take cover, giving our drones time. I lost a Sphere, and Clay lost one of hers and a BBALL. Once cleared, we moved forward to another junction and repeated the process again and again.

Four hours later, I got up from the rock I'd been taking cover behind and made my way to one of the entrances. I dropped down into it and then descended the forty-meter main shaft, my anchor keeping me from landing too hard.

I rose from a crouch and started to move forward. Thankfully, junctions tended to be a bit taller, so I didn't have to stoop. In my mind, I could almost see Venom scuttling around on the walls, floors, and ceilings. While I didn't have to worry about hitting my head in the junction, I did have to weave around dead Venom. Not for the first time, I was thankful that I could not smell with my helmet on. Given I didn't have any firsthand proof, but I suspected a group of dead Venom stunk to high heaven.

I was joined by the rest of my Fireteam, each of us with our sidearms in one hand and a vambrace blade extended in the other. These places were eerie to me. I could see fine, but I knew that was just because of my helmet. In reality, I was in a dark hole surrounded by dead aliens on an alien world. I felt my chest tighten a bit, and I focused on my breathing, calming myself. I pushed back on that ancient part of my brain that said *don't go in the monster's den, moron!*

"You know the drill. Move slow and careful," I said.

We split up, each with two BIs and some other drones. We checked every inch of the place. In some of the chambers, we found materials for ammo and weapons. Others were empty. Intelligence told us these were likely where the Venom rested. The oddest ones were full of thick orange-purple fungus, or at least something that resembled fungus. Some insects on Earth did something similar. The orange-purple stuff was the Venom's food. It seemed to break down and consume whatever it was given.

We knew that the Venom could eat just about anything on the planet, but they preferred the fungus. The Venom were good at modifying their genetic structure in some ways. On each planet they had been on, they had altered themselves to be able to live in the atmosphere and consume local flora and fauna. They had done the same with their fungus.

The Venom never seemed to venture into large bodies of water. We weren't sure why this was. They also didn't inhabit planets where there was no atmosphere or that had extreme conditions. They found homes as close to Venom Major and Minor as they could. This was something that was apparently a common trait in invasive races like the Venom. Some thought that because they only had the technology or inclination to inhabit areas where they could thrive without the constant aid of technology, they found the universe to be a very small place with not a lot of real estate. We were the opposite. We could and did live everywhere, though most of the time, we were completely dependent on our technology. For us, there was almost no end to places to live and no need to compete for them with other species.

The fungus squished when you stepped on it, with orange goo running over your suit. I was thankful again that I couldn't smell it. My BIs reached around to their packs and pulled out canisters that contained a poison that killed the fungus. Well, if we were being fair, it killed everything unless you had some serious biotech. The fungus didn't. The BIs sprayed some of the poison on it, and we moved on.

It took us another two hours to clear the bunker by hand. Thankfully, there were no Venom still alive. I started up the main shaft to the junction and then made my way to the surface. It was dark now, with dense cloud cover. To the southwest, I could see bright flashing lights. The main army was working its way to a colony. We had only lost forty percent of our drones, making this a pretty good day.

"Bunker is clear," I said to Monroe.

"Birds are on their way for pickup," he said.

We took cover positions and waited with Third Squad for the transports to show up. We were done for the day, and I was looking forward to getting back to base and to some sleep. On the transport back, I stood next to Clay.

"You're doing a great job," I said.

"Thanks, I really like the squad and team," she paused, "may I ask a personal question?"

"Go for it," I said, wondering what she'd want to know.

"Do you enjoy this?"

"Enjoy what? The HFDF?"

"No, this war. I mean, how do you feel about it?"

I thought for a moment, "I don't really care for it. I mean, I knew that this was the job and that we could be in a spot like this. But honestly, I thought we'd spend most of our time in drills and occasionally doing what we did on Erie Prime. How about you?"

She shrugged, "I know why we are doing what we are. The Venom have to be eliminated, but we are still taking part in genocide, and I don't like the way that feels."

"I know you were on Erie Prime. Did you feel that way there?" I asked.

"No, not really. I know that a lot of Erie died and still will, but they will bounce back. They have an opportunity for a future. Whether they take it or not is up to them. But the Venom don't."

"Nor did the species they wiped out," I said.

"Oh, I know," she sighed, "like I said, I know why we are here. Moreover, I believe in our mission, but it seems too wasteful to me. How many billions of lives are going to be, or have been, wasted because of them?" she said. "And should I feel complacent thinking that we have the right to do this? I know sooner or later, if we didn't do this, the Venom would attack us, they'd beat us, and, in the time leading up to it, they'd kill countless billions. I'm sure there are galaxies where one species has killed off everything else, but it just feels... wrong and bad... but...."

"Somehow comforting?" I asked.

CHAPTER TWENTY-FOUR

"Yes! Does that make me a bad person?"

"No," I said, "I think it makes you normal." I thought for a moment. "I had some of the same thoughts when I was on the Healer's Touch. If it makes you feel any better, I don't think the HF wants to be doing this. I feel a little guilty that I care more about what happened to the Pike than I do the Venom."

"I feel the same way. Seeing dead Pike bothers me now, but rarely does it bother me to see Venom piled around... well, I guess it does a little. God, it's creepy in those holes."

That made me laugh. "That's the truth. I suppose it's healthy to wonder about what you're doing, and I guess when we stop wondering, that's when we know that something is wrong with us."

"That works for me," she said. I decided to change the subject. "I see you and McLeod are becoming good friends; you seem to get along well with Kwasny in Bravo Team too."

"Yeah, I like them both a lot. I like the rest of our team too. Sweeting is funny," she said with a chuckle.

"Yes, he is."

"What's it like dating someone in the squad? If you don't mind me asking."

"I thought I wouldn't like it or that it would hinder the team, but it hasn't. Honestly, part of me thinks the HFDF set it up that way. Was it new to you?" I asked.

She shook her head. "No. It wasn't common in the platoon I was in, but that was just because of how often we were being shuffled around. In a lot of the teams, people have been together or at least fooling around a bit. And I think you're right about the HFDF thing. I've seen a lot of Special Teams together. Well, I guess not a ton, but more than I would have thought."

"Honestly, I think they do it so we stay in the service together. If Krista and I stay on the path we're on, we'll get married and won't have a spouse who might pull us from the HFDF. Monroe's soon-to-be wife is also HFDF," I said.

"He told me that. My brother is in exploration, and he said that happens a lot there too. You tend to be stationed with someone who either turns into your best friend or your significant other. It's like they make your service occupation a lifestyle."

"Kind of creepy," I pointed out.

"No argument here," she said, "but somehow not at the same time."

We were coming in for landing now, and I diverted my attention to getting the team squared away for some shut-eye and making sure we got drones for tomorrow. I saw a notification that my CCPU had finished compiling an action report for the day. I could skim it in a few to see if there were any areas I'd like to add more detail or insight to, but I doubted it.

We made our way to the chow station, which, being this close to the front, gave us a nutrient pack. Yum. I started digging into the pack and skimmed over the action report for the day, Clay's and my conversation weighing heavily on me. I checked on Royle's team, seeing that they were wrapping up a bunker found late in the day. They wouldn't be back for about an hour.

I found an open bunk in the sleeping area and slid in. I thought more about what Clay and I talked about and considered asking the shrink on the Arbiter if what we were thinking was normal. Instead, I wrote a message to my parents. I sent the message feeling better and told my CCPU to put me to sleep. As I drifted off, I wondered whether I would look back at this time in my life with pride or regret.

TWENTY-FIVE

The Venom hadn't landed on the southernmost part of Pike Prime's main continent. They'd landed one hundred kilometers north of it. The HFDF had named this colony Incursion Point Alpha; sexy, right? IPA was the one that had kicked the Pikes' asses. By and large, IPA was the Venom's largest colony, and from what we had been able to figure out, it was once several colonies that had now merged into one. Like its brewed counterpart, IPA was nasty. Don't fight it. You know deep down inside that IPAs are gross.

IPA also helped supply every nearby colony. It was the oldest and the most fortified, spanning fifty kilometers and going two thousand meters down. At least, that's what we suspected. We hadn't been able to fully image the entire colony yet, but it was a safe bet that clearing it would take months. The battle plan had been to isolate IPA from what was left of the Venom-occupied territory so it couldn't support other colonies or evacuate. Cutting off underground supply routes had taken several weeks, but we'd managed it. Or I should say teams of engineers managed it while my team and I killed Venom close to the surface.

Now every colony north and south of IPA was under direct attack by its own dedicated HFDF force, made up of career troops. Each force was more than up to the task of spending however long it took rooting out each colony. IPA was going to be no different. In fact, IPA was going to be our last area on Pike Prime. By "our," I meant the crew from the Arbiter. Once we were done with our mission here, we and most of the other Service Term ships would leave the system.

The war was far from over, but our part was almost done. From here, the Venom would be a problem for the career troops. The light at the end of the tunnel felt wonderful. We'd been on Pike Prime for a little over six months with constant fighting. Monroe told us that when we got back to Orion, we had one month of leave. After that time, we would be out of the main battle rotation for any conflict for at least four months, leaving us with just training exercises.

We weren't the only ones leaving. Jon had already been rotated out, and The Healer's Touch was also making its way out of the system. When we got back home, I was looking forward to having lunch with all my friends. We'd promised that we would do it after a year. We were a few months past that, but everyone was supposed to be around about the time the Arbiter docked at Orion station. But we had to get there first. I was brought back to this reality by the pilot of the Transport telling me we were inbound on our LZ.

I brought up a feed of one of the last surface fortifications. It had towers jutting from the ground that rose over a hundred meters in the air. They were made of thick material that shrugged off most of our attacks. It was a sight watching the main army go after it. Missiles and explosions were everywhere, but the Venom were far from being complacent. For each missile we fired, it was matched by one of theirs. It was like watching a movie as the two sides duked it out. The biggest difference was that our career and service troops were keeping far back from the line, controlling the countless drones that were being lost. For the Venom, they were taking very real losses.

We were flying on the outskirts of IPA when I got a notification that one of the battleships fired a salvo of KEPs, or Kinetic Energy Penetrators. Firing stuff from space had its drawbacks. The biggest was that you had a lot of air to go through. The KEPs had a lot of heat shielding on them and were pretty dang accurate. They were also large and hit with insane amounts of energy. You wanted a heads-up when one was about to hit.

I didn't see the first round as it came in, but I saw the results. The round hit the base of one of the towers, plumes of dirt and debris filling the air. I could see the air in the area ripple with a shock wave. Then the next one hit, and then the one after that. I couldn't see the damage they were doing with all the debris in the air, but I had a pretty good idea of what was going on.

Unfortunately, I wasn't going to get to watch the aftermath as we were landing. I made a note in my CCPU for it to record the feed for later.

Our mission for the day was an odd one. We'd figured the Venom would hold every inch of their colony they could. But they hadn't. They'd abandoned large sections of it on the outskirts, leaving only small forces behind. Command had known something was up when our drones trying to take the area stopped facing heavy resistance and then, in some cases, faced no resistance at all.

Where we were going today was part of a section that was mostly abandoned. Or at least what we'd found of it was. The section was huge, and we'd only explored about a thousand meters down. The Venom weren't completely absent. They were regularly found in areas that had been cleared before, showing a level of guerrilla warfare we'd yet to encounter. This forced a level of POD control that the career PODs weren't suited for. That meant Service Term troops had to deal with it.

We grouped up on the surface near one of the entrances we'd made into the complex. We were working in shifts with other platoons from the Arbiter. Landing with us was the rest of second platoon. We were working twelve-hour shifts with one hour for a break in the middle of the shift. A new shift started every six hours. We were relieving fourth platoon. We joined up with third platoon's fourth squad's Fireteam Alpha, which was babysitting the entrance.

Large-scale tunneling drones had been hard at work, boring from the surface to key parts of the Venom complex. It was these drones we thought drove the Venom out of the area, but it was more of a hunch among troopers than anything else. We greeted the troops topside, who told us we were good to enter. The hole was three meters across and dropped straight down, ending in a chamber.

I stepped off the ledge and fell into the black. After a moment, my anchor activated, and I landed in the chamber. I walked forward quickly as Krista landed a moment later. The bunkers we'd cleared had given us a false view of how the Venom lived. In the chamber we stood in now, there was no dirt or stone but a room of metal. The walls and ceiling were a series of textured flat planes, making it easier for the Venom to walk on them. Columns connected floor to ceiling and walls to walls. The room was entirely alien to me, yet it was easy to see that it was made by an advanced race. The consoles that the Venom could use were jutting out from the columns and walls. All of them were blackened and fried. The Venom had destroyed their tech as they'd left.

Fourth squad's Bravo team was holding the chamber that was acting as a staging area for the rest of us. Our drone PODs were fairly standard with BIs, Spheres, and BBALLs. What made the job more interesting, by which I mean a pain in the ass, was the number of Whiskers we had to manage and the separation between our PODs and team. Each of us had an ungodly number of large and small Whiskers to check in on. Also, with them were a host of GPWs. The Venom colony was not only vast but extremely complex. There were tunnels and chambers of every size, but not all were for Venom to move around. There were support lines and utilities. Some moved material from factories. Others moved larvae to brood chambers. We were learning loads of things about a species whose days were numbered.

The chamber we were in now appeared to be some sort of resting area. My CCPU synced up with the last bits of information from fourth platoon's latest sweep. With it, Monroe sent us orders for the areas we'd be in for the day. Deeper in this section, regular forces were busy pushing down further and toward lines that connected this area with the rest of the colony. Our job was to keep the upper levels clear so the troops below didn't get overwhelmed.

I reviewed the orders for the day and relayed them to the team.

"Looks like we're going deep today. Fourth platoon didn't have too many encounters, so hopefully, neither do we. This is possibly our last planetside mission. Let's make it a boring one," I said to the team.

It felt good to say that.

As fourth platoon's first squad reached our chamber, control over their drones passed to us. Mostly it was Special Teams that were sweeping the tunnels. Other squads guarded the top or key chambers with intel drones learning all they could. If we ran into too much trouble, they could come to help out, or we could fall back to their positions.

My CCPU plotted a route to where we'd be starting our sweep for the day. The tunnels, while larger than those of the bunkers, still seemed cramped to me, and it was strange being in a place with no windows or light, for that matter. We were completely reliant on our helmets feeding us information. We could use a small light in the helmet if we wanted to see the world in the visible light spectrum, but I'd gotten used to the monochrome of my current display. Not to mention that when we had looked at the inside of the colony, it was almost as monochrome as our displays were anyway.

The nano-material on our boots was working overtime, matching its texture to that of the sometimes steep tunnels, keeping us from sliding or losing our footing. Sometimes we'd have to use our vambraces to help us stick to the side of a tunnel so we could descend down it. We tried not to use our anchors lest they run out of power when we needed them.

That was something that was new for us as well. Our suits had power cells in them that could last for months. The cells were trickle-charged by our body heat, but that only covered a small portion of the energy we needed. Our suits used up energy, keeping us warm or cooling us off. The cells were fast-charging when we were in base, taking only a few moments. I gave more thought to eating a nutrient pack than I did to my suit's power supply. That was different down here.

The drops in the tunnels could easily run us out of power if we were wasteful. Power, we needed if we had to either drop down a tunnel for a fight or to give us a boost up when running from the Venom. But the real clincher was the heat.

As we went deeper into the planet, I could see the outside temperature rise. I didn't feel this, mind you, because of how good my suit was at keeping me cool. Humans had gotten very good with energy. We had to if we wanted to leave Earth. Our suits did a bang-up job converting heat into energy, but our suits were for combat and had limits. Right now, my suit was using more energy keeping me from overheating than it was producing energy with that heat.

This wouldn't have been the case if I had one of Jon's suits. His could handle this environment almost indefinitely. It was designed to thrive in what one could call crap conditions, but it couldn't stop enemy fire or do many of the things my suit could. Long story short, with the effort my power cells were putting into keeping me where I needed to be, their charge went from months to days. If I was careless with my anchor and depleted its power cell, and I needed it to keep me alive, my CCPU would tell it to pull power from the rest of my suit. I could run out of energy in hours. If that happened, I would need to hook up to a drone and drain its cells to keep me going. I'm sure you can see the problem here. If I had no power due to the situation, how much better off would my drones be? Also, how many would I have lost at that point, and could I afford to lose more? To be fair, the drones weren't wasting energy keeping cool. They could still last for at least a month down here, but I still found myself wary of using my anchor.

On the other hand, the Venom seemed to thrive in the heat. They also could naturally walk on the walls. They zipped around like it was nothing, and all around were in their element. Good for them.

We were deep now and splitting up to start our own sweeps. Mine started in a brood chamber. As the Whiskers did their thing, I looked around. The walls, floor and ceiling were covered in holes about the size of a man's chest and about a meter deep. At the ends were little ball-looking knobs that the Venom larvae attached to. There weren't any dead Venom larvae in the chamber as there had been when the HFDF first took this place, but I could see them in my mind's eye. Not dead, of course, but alive. The chamber was a cylinder about six meters in diameter. The construction was precise, and the chamber stretched for over a hundred meters. It made me shiver thinking about what it would have been like with however many thousands of little Venom must have been in here at any given time.

After the chamber was swept, I continued walking in the criss-crossing tunnels. The deeper I got, the closer I got to where actual fighting was going on, and I could hear it echoing up the tunnels as if from every side around me. I wondered what it had been like on the Venom's home world as they were developing into the race they were today.

My CCPU pinged me with a contact. I crouched down into a tunnel opening as my drones also took cover. Whiskers had found three hostiles before they were taken out.

"Be advised I have hostiles. Whiskers are down, and enemy heading is unknown," I said to the Arbiter team.

"Roger that. Please verify enemy heading," First Lieutenant Lisa Middleton said.

I deployed several more Whiskers to other tunnel junctions and waited. It didn't take long for a Whisker to find the Venom. They weren't headed in my direction, and my CCPU plotted likely targets, finding a chamber that had once held ammunition. That was currently being held by one of second squad's Fireteams. I opted for a private comm with Monroe and the platoon leader.

"Be advised the enemy is heading to second squad's position. They are twenty strong," I said.

"Thank you, please hold," Middleton said to Monroe and me.

Lieutenant Middleton was technically mine and Monroe's CO, but since we were Special Teams, we rarely worked with her. When I did, I liked her. Her job was usually limited to working with regular space-borne and their squad leaders. I was looking at the data I had, and second squad was not going to be able to handle this. There was a long pause before I received a reply.

"Second squad is confident in their ability to hold the chamber. Prep for backup," Middleton said.

I understood why second didn't want help. I really did, but the chamber still had Venom ammunition in it, and if the little pricks took root there, it would take us hours to get them out. And by us, I meant my team. But orders were orders. I glanced at my team members who were in the area, seeing that it was Betts and Clay. I couldn't justify pulling my entire team just to be potential backup, but if I had to pull people, I was happy with the two that I had. Fighting in the tunnels was a game of being really good at holding your position or being extremely aggressive in taking the enemy's position. If I had to hold a tunnel, I'd take Krista any day of the week, but Betts and Clay were my damage dealers.

"We are prepping to back up second squad. Move to waypoints alpha and bravo and await orders," I said to Betts and Clay.

They pinged their affirmations, and I moved quickly and silently to a position I thought would be useful. Clay was in place above the chamber. The Venom were coming from a tunnel lower than hers, but if they managed to breach the chamber, she could fire down at them. Betts and I were to the sides of the tunnel they were using. Betts would be behind them if things got ugly, and they would. The other squads weren't used to this type of fighting for one, and second, they didn't have the same skill and drive we did. We'd been trained not to hesitate; in our missions, hesitation could mean death. We also weren't afraid of getting hurt. Whether that was good or not, I wasn't sure, but it was how it was.

The Venom reached the chamber.

I pulled up a map of the chamber with all of the drones second had and the Venom. My feed showed a BI and four Spheres drop as two small explosives went off. I tried not to sigh, thinking about how they should have seen that coming and taken better cover. A firefight was starting now, and it was clear it was going to be one-sided. I checked my team, seeing they were in position.

"We are in position. Requesting permission to engage," I said to command.

"Hold your current position," Middleton said, sounding tense.

I watched as several more drones went down. The Venom were entering the chamber now, and I rolled my eyes. I was sure that the squad leader for second squad was insisting that his people could win, but I doubted it. I got a ping that someone in the room got hit in the arm.

"Second squad has an injury. Requesting permission to let my team engage," Monroe said to Middleton, his tone urgent.

"First squad, you are go to engage," Middleton said a little grudgingly.

"Taylor, you heard the Lieutenant. Neutralize the threat!" Monroe said.

"With pleasure," I replied.

"ENGAGE!" I ordered Betts and Clay.

I darted out of my hiding spot and raised my SIR to my shoulder, launching a grenade that bounced off the tunnel wall and through a junction. It exploded, taking out a Venom. My drones and I moved as quickly as we could, firing as we saw the enemy. The Spheres did fine in the tunnels, but the ones we were in had a lot of twists and turns, making it hard to maneuver and aim. I dropped my SIR, opting for close-quarters fighting so the Venom couldn't use their own explosives. As my BIs and I entered the main tunnel, I could see the chamber ahead. One of Clay's BIs dropped from the tunnel above the chamber, landing on a Venom and using the nano-material in its vambrace to stab the creature.

One of my BIs launched off the wall, taking out a Venom, and I jutted forward, stabbing it with my own vambrace. From behind me, Betts shot at another Venom. I got to work on a group that was close to me. The fight was over in less than a couple of minutes. The metal walls of the chamber were slick with orange blood.

"The enemy is neutralized," I said to command calmly.

"Thank you, first squad, and congrats on not losing any drones," Middleton said to Monroe and me.

"Thank you, ma'am," I said, doing everything in my power not to sound smug.

"You know this is why the rest of the platoon doesn't talk to us, right?" Sweeting said to the team, his voice sounding happy.

I didn't answer, but I was grinning.

At the end of our shift, second squad gave us a grudging thanks as we loaded up on the Transport. When we got back to the base, we got the news that all of the Arbiter crew was being recalled to the ship for departure. Spaceborne and infantry would load up first, and we'd stay in a ready position for the next two weeks as the rest of the crew were brought on board.

It felt amazing to be going back to the ship, even if it meant that for the next two weeks, we would be spending the bulk of our time hanging out in the launch tubes of the ship.

We stepped onto the shuttle with only our two mandatory BIs and launched from Pike Prime's surface. Maybe someday I would want to come back here, but I kind of doubted it.

The flight back to the ship was fairly uneventful. As we left the atmosphere, I could see there were fewer ships in orbit than there had been before. Above the planet's pole, there was still the constant traffic of cargo ships, and I doubted that would stop anytime soon. The war was only ending for me and mine. Not for the HFDF, nor the Pike. We held the south but had to deal with the colonies still. As for the Pike, they were working on making sure their territory was Venom-free and that none of the Venom had made it past us since we'd landed.

Once they were done, the Pike would have to start their sweep over again and repeat the process for years to come. We'd do the same, but I suspected that after what had happened to them, the Pike would make a habit of checking on their planet for hostiles on a regular basis for centuries. Someday thirty or forty years from now, their planet would be healed and their defense grid long rebuilt and strong, but I knew that the Pike would likely never be the same. You couldn't take the losses they had and come out of it without long-term scars.

The shuttle entered the Arbiter's gravity field, and I felt my body tug downward. The shuttle doors opened, and we walked out and through an airlock into the ship. My helmet slid off as we walked into the main ship where Monroe was, and so was Lieutenant Middleton. We stiffened and saluted them.

Middleton was of average height with long purple-red hair that she had back in a bun. She returned our salute and walked up to me, extending her hand. I took it in mine and shook.

"Well done today," she said.

"Thank you, ma'am," I replied.

She held my gaze for a moment, "Some of the other squads think we rely on Special Teams too heavily," she commented, "but I'm personally glad to have you and yours around."

"We'll always be here, ma'am," I said, trying not to smirk.

She gave a tight smile, "I suppose you will be. We appreciate your hard work as always," she said and then walked off.

Krista walked up to me, "Making impressions with command, huh?"

I looked over at her, leaned down, and kissed her before saying, "I guess so."

Monroe walked up to me, "I know some of the other squads complained about the lack of 'useful work' that they had to do."

"I don't understand why the other squads want to be shot at so badly," I said.

"It's because they haven't seen the action your team has. If they did, they wouldn't be complaining. At any rate, you certainly shut a lot of them up today. I talked to second squad's leader, and he was sweating bullets. Good work," Monroe said, not bothering to try and hide a grin.

He addressed the rest of the squad, "I recommend hitting the showers, getting some chow, and then sleeping in a real bed for a while. Tomorrow morning, we start our holding pattern as the ship pulls the rest of her crew on board."

He dismissed us, and Krista and I gladly beelined with the rest of the squad to the showers.

TWENTY-SIX

I t was hard not to have a bounce in my step as we left the mess and headed toward our prep room. I shouldn't have a bounce in my step. My day was going to consist of sitting in a tube just in case the shit hit the fan planetside, and the HFDF thought a squad of Special Teams could do anything about it. In short, I had another day of hanging out, bored in the launch tube, and I'd take it. In the last week, nothing had shot at me; I hadn't had to skulk in bug nests, I had a bed, real food, and I got to fool around with my girlfriend and see her face instead of a helmet. So overall, boredom sounded pretty great.

As we were getting geared up, Betts looked over at me and shook his head. "Try not to look so happy, man," he said with a chuckle.

I barked a laugh, "Whatever, I'm about halfway through a book, and if I'm lucky, I'll start another today. You can't tell me you're not as happy as I am right now?"

"Man, I can't wait to be rid of this planet. Erie Prime was fine, almost fun, but Pike Prime? No, thank you!" Sweeting said.

We finished loading up and entered the jump tube. I walked to the front. Excited though I was and convinced of my impending boredom, I didn't shirk any of my duties. I ran over my own checklists and that of my team. Once done with that, I reported back to Monroe and downloaded the day's global situation reports. I'd seen these a little in the field but had mostly glossed over them. There were reports for each area of the war and of the planet, giving the general situation we were in. I'd read the local reports exclusively planetside but hadn't paid any attention to the global ones. Now I looked through them every day. If we were needed, we didn't know where we would go, and I didn't care to go into a situation, no matter how unlikely, unprepared.

Royle and I opened a comm line, as we always did when looking these over. "Looks like things are running slower than expected at IPA," she noted. I looked at that section of the report, seeing that we were running slightly behind where we'd hoped to, but there was nothing alarming. We had teams doing in-depth screenings for the Venom moving north and south, creating a clean area. The Pike were doing the same in the north, but at some point, the HFDF would also clear the area. I finished looking through the report and forwarded anything I found noteworthy to my team. I then settled into my book.

A few hours later, I was lying on my back in the last chapter of my book when my CCPU pinged me with an incoming action message. I paused what I was doing and waited for the message to load, wondering what semi-useless update we were going to get. The last three had been about the Arbiter being in the area of another ship bombarding the planet.

I opened the message and sat up. During one of their sweeps, the Pike found something that piqued their interest near a small city. When they investigated, they'd found a Venom colony hiding under the surface. The message went on to say that the Venom were now pouring into the city. I forwarded it to my team.

"Couldn't have been big, or they'd have noticed it a while ago," Sweeting said to the team.

I watched the feed for a moment longer.

A ship-wide announcement came on. "Action stations, action

stations. All hands prepare for troop insertion," one of the ship's controllers said.

Shit, that meant us!

"Up and at 'em! Let's get ready to do our jobs!" I said to the team.

"First squad, prep for jump; this is not a drill. Orders will push to your CCPUs en route," Monroe said to the squad.

I was up now and doing a check of my drones and suit. When I was done, I checked on my team. All reported that they were ready to go. "Launch. First squad Alpha team is go for insertion," I said to the controller.

"Roger Alpha, Bravo has reported in. You are out in thirty. Good luck and godspeed."

The tube went dark, and the door to the outside opened to the cold vacuum of space. Below us, floating serenely, was Pike Prime. *Come on,* I thought, waiting for the order to jump. For all my looking forward to being bored, I was certainly ready to be back in the frying pan.

The lights on the floor turned green, and I ran, throwing myself from the safety of the Arbiter. There's a calm to space, a silence that can only come within a vacuum. But in the soundlessness, there's energy building inside you that violently pushes to get out. I felt that energy inside me, trying to claw its way to the surface.

Our orders arrived. As expected, the Pike Security forces were wholly unprepared for what was happening. We were going into a close fire situation. The Venom appeared on the outskirts of a city, and there were Pike civilians trying to flee. That meant no orbital support, at least not when we first got on site. Infantry and armor were being routed, and we were to contain the Venom until career forces could arrive. We were to help keep as many Pike alive as we could and slow the Venom before they spread too far. In my mind, that meant we needed to make sure the Venom cared a whole lot more about us than they did the Pike.

Monroe opened a line to Royle and me. "You need to take the Venom's attention from the Pike. Remember, this was not a planned attack. The Pike surprised them; the Venom are just reacting right now. You also don't need to hold the line for hours or days on end. Reinforcements are an hour behind you at the absolute most. Go in hot and stop the Venom advance before it happens."

"We're on it," Royle said.

We dropped comms as our space anchors kicked on and our heat shields unfolded. It had been so long since we'd dropped onto a planet that I had forgotten how exciting and terrifying it was. I tried to pull up intel on the area we were dropping into, but there weren't many updates since we'd jumped. We did have some discretion on our final landing site, though. I pulled up a map of the area and scanned it for spots where the Venom could dig in and slow us down. I found a promising section of buildings that also had a ton of Pike in it, making it a win. I set our destination spot, and everyone's anchors nudged them in the direction they needed to go.

The air roared by my helmet, and green ground and rolling mound buildings rushed up towards me.

"Hold your fire until we are on the ground. I don't want the Venom deciding they need to shoot the humans falling from the sky," I said to the team.

As I got close to the ground, I found a tight group of buildings that were forcing fleeing Pike to bottleneck. The Venom were taking full advantage of the situation. I didn't really want to land in the line of fire, so I angled myself to take cover behind a building. I was close enough to the ground to hear a low rumbling siren. The ground and I finally met. My anchor jerked, and I landed hard, coming down into a crouch. Reflexively, my SIR came to my shoulder.

I landed close to a group of Pike who clearly did not expect my arrival. They bleated loudly, moving surprisingly fast away from me until they seemed to realize I wasn't a Venom.

I set a waypoint on the building on the other side of the street where the Pike were bottlenecked and labeled it Alpha. I set Bravo back from the Venom, Charlie, and Delta in far-flanking positions.

"Betts, attack Alpha. Clay, you have Bravo. Krista's on Charlie and Sweeting, you have Delta. Keep the Venom from spreading and digging in," I said.

The building next to me was tall, but like most Pike structures, it was more of a dome. I started to run up the side of the building. All around us was chaos as Pike of all ages fled. The building was covered in a thick green moss-like plant that felt like I was running on carpet. When I crested the building, I took in the scene before me.

To my right was the building that Betts was on top of. In front of us was another one. If you were above them, they were arranged like a triangle. In the center of the triangle was a large intersection crammed with Pike. On the other building, Venom were crawling all over it, firing on the Pike.

I raised my SIR and sighted a Venom.

I opened fire, dropping a Venom and then rolled to a different location. I used my Whiskers and came back up and fired again, taking out another Venom. Above, the Spheres and BBALLs started to get to work, buzzing the enemy and taking advantage of them being in the open.

I got a notification from the Arbiter that all Spaceborne troops had jumped and were inbound.

"All squads have left the ship. We are to help keep the Venom hemmed in until reinforcements arrive. Drop ships will drop armor in ten. First squad is to press the enemy and keep their attention. All other squads, keep the Venom from flanking First. Be advised, the Pike government has authorized the HFDF to use whatever means we see fit to contain the enemy. Prep for close-quarters orbital bombardment," Middleton said to the platoon, her voice calm in a way that made me think of Monroe.

My CCPU pinged me with the landing locations of the other squads. Just ahead of them were the three other Special Teams squads from the Arbiter.

"Mark buildings for bombardment," Monroe said to Royle and me.

I marked the building across from us.

"Marked," I said.

"Expect an ETA soon," Monroe said.

"Help is on the way. Clay, advance forward. We are going to hit that building," I said to the team.

The Venom were starting to try to find cover and had completely overrun the building. They were also now ignoring the Pike. That was a good thing in that we'd done part of what we were supposed to. All but a few living Pike were clear of the area in the intersection.

"This is HFS Paris. Advise, ordnance inbound in ten, clear the area and take cover," a male voice said over the general comms.

"Be advised, there are Pike in the blast radius," Monroe said to the team.

I could see two of them in the intersection. A large Pike appeared to be shielding a smaller one. My CCPU informed me that one was an adult and the other an adolescent. The smaller of the two seemed unable to move on its own. *Dammit.*

"Paris, be advised there are Pike in the blast area," I said.

"Roger that, first squad. We can hold fire for five, but then we have to launch. You'll have ten minutes once we do," Paris replied.

"Thank you, Paris," I said.

I had to think of what I wanted to do. The building was crawling with Venom, and we didn't have much time before the Pike were either killed by the Venom or by us.

"Should we try to extract the Pike?" I asked Monroe.

"Your call. The rest of the platoon is on the ground and in position; the Venom are pinned down there," Monroe said to me.

"Are we going to help?" Betts asked.

I thought about when Meyers had gotten killed. It was because we had gone into heavy fire. This could be the same. I should sit tight. I looked at the Pike in the center of the intersection, and it made me think of talking to Clay and how it had bothered her seeing the Pike die. We had the ability to do something.

"We are extracting local civilians, requesting extra cover," I said to Middleton.

"Roger that, first squad, the rest of the platoon has your back," she said.

"We are pulling the Pike from the area. Clay, you secure the Pike. Use your BIs to help them move. Betts and I will press forward. McLeod and Sweeting, we need extra cover. Unleash hell," I said to the team.

Krista and Sweeting began peppering the Venom with fire.

"Move out!" I ordered.

I stood from where I was and ran down the side of the building, doing my best not to make an easy target. At the base of the building, I knelt down next to a dead Pike. I popped out from cover and launched a grenade into the building where the Venom were.

I moved forward, advancing towards the Pike, with Betts keeping up on the other side of the intersection. I lost two drones. And then another, but I'd made it to the Pike alive. Thankfully, the Venom were green from hiding out, and they weren't the battle-hardened ones we'd been fighting. Had they been, I was pretty sure I would have died.

The smaller Pike struggled to move. It looked like one of its legs was hurt. Blood oozed everywhere. I lost another drone. Clay was there now. She had lost several drones herself. This wasn't going to be good.

"Third squad is in your old position," Middleton said to me.

"Third has us covered. We don't have any time. Let's get moving," I said to Clay and Betts.

The larger Pike seemed a little uneasy with us being there but didn't stop us. I approached the injured side of the Pike, and my CCPU informed me that it was more than its leg that was hurt, but it should live if it made it out of here.

"Small" wasn't really the right term for the Pike, though. It still had to weigh a couple of tons. I pulled out my block of nano-material, as did all of the BIs with us. Our helmets could produce sound, but I'd rarely had the need to use that feature before. Of course, I couldn't speak Pike, but my CCPU could do a decent enough job of it. I instructed the Pike to try to raise itself so we could get cords of nano-material under it.

With some effort, it lifted itself enough for us to slide the cords of nano-material beneath it.

My CCPU kindly informed me that the HFS Paris' bunker buster was ten minutes away. *Great.* We got into position and heaved, lifting the injured side of the creature. It wailed as we did so, and blood squirted out of it, covering me. We started to move away from the Venom.

"Get a move on! You don't have a lot of time," Monroe said to the team, his tone holding an edge to it.

"We need to get moving. If you want to take cover, go for it," I said to Betts and Clay.

"I'm good," Betts said.

"Me too," Clay said.

I told the other Pike that it needed to go take cover and that we could handle this. It squawked something I couldn't understand, but my CCPU translated it as essentially "no." That was fair.

We moved as fast as we could, and I was pinged that we had five minutes until the round hit. We rounded the building I had been on top of at the two-minute mark. Four Pike were there with what looked like a stretcher. They rushed up to us, taking the injured Pike.

The round hit.

With it, the ground shook and was accompanied by a deep boom. Dust filled the air, and bits of debris scattered on the ground between the two buildings. The Pike cowered but soon started to move away with the stretcher. The large Pike hesitated for a moment and said something that my CCPU translated as a thank you. It turned and left.

Above and away from us, I could see orbs the size of houses rapidly slowing down as they approached the ground. As they landed, the orbs fell apart, revealing the hulking form of Rhinos. They started moving forward, passing Pike that stopped to look at them.

"Shit, even with how big the Pike are, they still think those things are intimidating," Sweeting said to the team.

"Second platoon, prepare to fall back. Armor and career troops are taking positions," Middleton said.

They didn't have to tell me twice. We moved out of the area as the heavy hitters came in to do their thing. As they did, we were shunted back to support positions, and after a few hours, we were told that shuttles were coming to take us back to the Arbiter. Before boarding the shuttle, Betts, Clay, and I found a broken pipe that was spilling out water and rinsed the blood from our suits.

As the shuttle took off, my feelings about my time on Pike Prime had changed. I now felt good about what I had done and been a part of. I felt like, at least today, I'd left the galaxy a better place than when I had found it.

———

WE ALL SAT IN OUR SQUAD ROOM SILENTLY AS THE SHIP'S PA ANNOUNCED that we were approaching jump distance from Pike Prime and would be entering Orion's orbit shortly. The trip to jump distance had been calm, and it was only now that I realized I was just slightly tense, as if we could be called to fight at any moment.

We hadn't had any training during the trip, and our days were only broken up by a meeting or two for Royle and me. There had also been a medal ceremony for everyone aboard. The ship and all her crew—including us—received one for being part of the Venom offensive. My team members and I received numerous decorations for our time during our part of the war. My Fireteam also received one from the HFDF for helping out the Pike. The Pike apparently didn't have military decorations, as they really hadn't even needed a military up until a few years ago. But their government sent a thank-you for what we'd done, which felt nice.

I was watching the external feeds as we jumped. In one moment, the sky was filled with stars, and then my field of view swam with blue and green as I looked down on Orion. As I took it in, I felt my body relax in a way it hadn't done in a long time, and I sighed deeply. I was home, and at least for now, not in the frying pan.

TWENTY-SEVEN

As the Arbiter slid into dock at Orion Station, one could almost feel the crew's excitement about their upcoming leave. Krista and I were looking forward to our month off. It would be nice to catch up with family and friends, but I was really looking forward to the downtime. Krista and I had one trip planned for just the two of us and another with my family. I was also looking forward to that evening. It had been just over a year since my friends and I had all been on the same planet at the same time.

Krista and I disembarked from the ship, merging with the throngs of people in the station. We headed to the Lift, and I enjoyed the smooth transition from space to planet without being jarred by a shuttle or having a heat shield stuck to my ass. It's the little things in life. I had to admit, though, that there was something about jumping to a planet's surface that the Lift couldn't replicate.

From the main terminal, we headed to a hotel that catered to people in the HFDF. It was in the heart of Orion City, and we'd only be there for one night. The building was tall, shining glass with a large entryway and welcoming staff. From its appearance, you'd think it was a normal hotel. Our room said otherwise. Everything about the room indicated that it was intended for HFDF personnel. For one, it was small by most people's standards. It was only the size of our squad's quarters, but the difference was that we had a real window here, and it was just the two of us, so as far as I was concerned, this place was like a stadium. The decorations were simple, with a desk and a bed. There were cubbies in the wall that were the size of our suits. We didn't need a closet because we would be in our combat suits on leave. The bathroom was likewise simple, with the exception of the shower, which had every kind of showerhead you could want and a tub. Whoever designed this place had spent a lot of time on ships or in the field.

The first thing we did upon entering our room was take off our suits and jump in the shower. You might think, hey, I bet they're going to get it on shower style, but you'd be wrong. The showers on the ship were nice, but Krista and I were so excited to have a real shower. We spent the first twenty minutes or so just enjoying being able to move around. Then we had fun shower style.

After the shower, we left the hotel. Krista was meeting up with Clay, and I was meeting my friends. I felt a twinge as we parted. After the last year, I'd grown dependent on having her around whenever I wasn't getting shot at. It was nice to know I'd miss her a bit.

I walked to the restaurant where we were having dinner. It was wonderful to feel the wind on my face and to see people around me whose faces weren't concealed by helmets. Orion City had so much more color than I had thought when I lived near it. Everyone wore different clothes, not the same matte black of the HFDF. I didn't dislike the service; if anything, I loved it and knew that my life would never be the same. I thought it was because we'd gone from one deployment right into another. We hadn't had the weekend leaves that so many had while training on one planet or another.

I walked into the same restaurant we had been in on the day we left. The hostess took me up to a seat on the second-floor patio. There, sitting at a table laughing, were Jon, Liz, Monica, and Charles. Only

Monica and Liz were in their service suits. When they saw me, they all got up and came over.

Charles was the first one there. I gave him a hug.

"Hey man, how are you?" I asked.

"Great! How about you?"

"I'm good."

We'd all been messaging over the past year, but there was something about actually seeing them that made me happy. I'd seen Liz not too long ago, but she bounded up next, not hugging me but looking me over.

"I'm fine. You'd have found out if I wasn't."

She looked like she disapproved. "We'd just jumped here from Hunter's deep space medical complex when I heard that you were deployed. How was it?" she asked.

I'd talked a lot to Jon, too; he'd been over Pike Prime. But he hadn't really seen the war. Liz had. She may not have seen a Venom, but she saw what happened. She'd also seen Pike and assisted them, and she'd been on Erie Prime. Out of all my friends, Liz was the only one who had an idea of what it was like.

I thought for a moment, thinking about that last fight. I felt good about what I'd done, but I had also been thinking about what I'd seen that day.

"It was bad. No one on my team got torn up, but the Pike did," I said, shaking my head. "The Pike found a Venom colony. A small one, but they weren't prepared for it. I'm a little shocked the Venom made it that far north. It was easy pickings for them."

I could see her face darken as our friends listened silently.

"Did you guys stop it? Did you make them pay for it?" she asked.

Before Pike Prime, I would have never expected those words from Liz. I still didn't completely, but I understood.

I nodded. "We slowed them down, got the Pike out of the area, then Fleet hit them with Kinetics, and armor came in to rip them up," I said.

"Good," she said with a satisfied nod.

We both noticed that our friends were all around us and didn't look as bright and happy as before. Liz touched my arm, and then she withdrew.

Monica recovered from the sudden somber mood, slugging me in the arm. "You ass! Why did you go out and get hurt?"

I smiled. "One of us needs to be tough."

She snorted.

I greeted Jon, and we all sat down at the table. I looked around at my friends, and I could see that they were different. We all were.

Monica talked about life as a cop. She was currently working on a satcity and had made sure to point out that she had to get permission to come back to Orion for the weekend. Jon had gone back to working on the Lift.

"Do you miss cargo runs?" Charles asked him.

"Yes and no. It kept us really busy, which made the time go by, but it got a little grueling. I think I'd like being on a ship when things aren't so crazy. How about you? Do you like what you've been doing?"

Charles smiled. "I still think I've got the best job out of all of us." He pointed at me. "It's all about learning about new places, unless these stiffs need something."

"What would we need?" I asked him.

He shrugged. "I only did a little for the HFDF. They had me scan some systems to see if the species there had a radio bubble."

"What's that mean?" Monica asked. "Don't be a nerd, Charles."

"I am a nerd, and you love it! Well, we use Alt-comms communications, but most newer species use radio first, like we did. Sometimes, like in the case of the Erie, when a new hostile race shows up, we park radio observatories a few light-years from the system and see what we can find. It isn't glamorous work, and it can be hard to decrypt signals when we get them, but it gives the HFDF a lot of info they need," he said.

"So, you had to do this for us?" I asked.

"Yep," he said, nodding his head.

CHAPTER TWENTY-SEVEN

"What did you find?"

"Not sure, honestly. I was part of a team. We were pointed at the Venom system. My stations picked stuff up for sure, but then the data went off to other people to be analyzed."

"Huh, that's kind of cool," I said, and it was, but I wondered why we'd be looking at the system when we had so much data about the Venom already.

"So, Liz, where does the Healer's Touch go next?" Monica asked.

"Hopefully, nowhere," she said. "I've only got a few months left on her, and then I'll get transferred. I'm not sure where to yet."

"And you, Alex?" Monica asked me.

I checked my CCPU to see if we had orders yet on where we were going after our leave. "Nothing yet," I said, "but my CO told me that we would see time on dead worlds and water worlds. It should be kind of fun. See, Charles, you and I are kind of the same. We go to new places."

He laughed. "Yeah, totally. I study the galaxy and find new places, and you go blow stuff up on them."

After dinner, I walked back to my hotel with Monica walking next to me. She kept eyeing my sidearm.

"What's up?" I finally asked her.

She shook her head. "It's nothing."

"Come on."

She sighed. "Fine. Every time I see your sidearm, it reminds me of that time before you went to Erie Prime. Do you remember?"

I chuckled. "When I kicked your ass? Yeah, I remember."

She hit my arm. "Yes, and when I found out you can do more with my gun than I can. I saw things on feeds about Pike Prime, and honestly, it bothered me."

"How so?"

"One, you were there. I've known you my whole life. I've always pictured myself as the tough one, and while I'll never say this again, I know you can beat me one-handed, but even you almost... well, you know...."

"Died," I said soberly.

She looked at me and then back to the ground in front of her, no bravado or confidence. "Yeah. Being a cop isn't what it was like before people were ageless, I know that. I have trainers who tell me that all the time. But I kind of thought that we were something, ya know? But now I wonder: could I hold my own against something really bad?"

I stopped walking, and so did she. "Why would you have to?" I asked. "You're more than capable of dealing with any Human, trust me."

She looked kind of scared—something I'd never really seen with her. "But what if it's not Humans?" She started walking again. "Some of the people in the satcity I'm at were convinced that the Venom were going to jump in and kill us all. Not a lot of people, mind you; everyone talked about the war, and I'm sure they still are, but I don't know, they kind of take the HFDF for granted."

I could see why people would be freaked out. The HFDF hadn't taken losses like we did on Pike Prime and in the Venom system like that in over a hundred years. On their feeds, they saw people dying and drones being blown to bits. They didn't appreciate how well our commanders had done and how low our losses had been. The Pike had almost been wiped out, and the Venom had killed many races, but we pushed them back and were going to kill them.

"Monica, you aren't going to have to deal with that. If a satcity were to be attacked, the fleet would jump in within seconds of the enemy arriving. And let me tell you, our fleet is amazing at what they do. Honestly, they are a little freaky. And our people on the ground are the same. I know Pike Prime looked bad, and it was, but trust me when I say that by and large, it was a one-sided fight."

"But what happens if someday it isn't a one-sided fight?" She sighed again. "Don't answer that. I know nobody can win everything.

I've just always felt like I was in total control of my life, and over the last year, I've learned that's not the case."

I laughed darkly at that. "I completely understand."

We arrived at my hotel, and I looked at her. "I know this won't make you or the people you're around stop worrying, but I promise the HFDF is here, and we aren't giving up. Losing isn't really our thing."

She smirked. "I know. No more getting all messed up, okay?"

I laughed again. "I really wish I could promise that."

She looked at me for a moment as if I were insane. She was right, of course. I'd have thought the same of myself a year ago, but now? Well, now I knew that when you're fighting aliens, you're just going to get torn up sometimes. And as long as the Lizs of the universe are around and you don't lose your head—quite literally—you'll probably be okay.

She left me, and I went up to the room. Krista wasn't there yet, so I lay down in bed, stretching out my arms and legs. Eventually, she came in, and we fell asleep. The next day we left Orion City for a vacation spot by a large lake.

After a week there, we met up with my parents and vacationed with them. Then we returned to the city, and at the end of the month, I was actually looking forward to getting back on the ship. As we boarded the Arbiter, I felt like I was home.

"God, I didn't think I'd be so happy to be back here," Krista said. "Who in their right mind gets bored sitting by a pool and misses being on a warship?"

I put my arm around her. "Someone who is my kind of crazy," I said with a cheesy smile.

But she was right. I was ready to get back to work. I didn't know it when I joined, but the HFDF was my home, and it was what I was.

EPILOGUE

EPILOGUE

"**G**ood afternoon, Mrs. Koffski. Can I get you anything to drink?" a greeting drone asked as I entered the general's office.

"No, thank you," I replied.

The drone led me down a hallway and stopped at a large wooden door. It opened, and I walked into a windowless conference room with a round table in the center. Five people sat around the table—two women and three men. They stood as I entered and greeted me.

I took my place at the table, and all of them looked at me. Each person in the room was a high-ranking member of the HFDF. The man across from me spoke.

"What do you have for us today, Mrs. Koffski?"

I had my CCPU send each of them a packet of information.

"I am sending each of you the full report from the Venom system and our findings."

Their gazes drifted off into the distance. I gave them a moment.

"The report seems comprehensive and rather large. May I ask why this meeting was requested with such urgency?" one of the women asked.

"We were tasked with finding the Venom's origins and as much of their history as we could. We collaborated with the other races in the coalition, primarily the Quiver," I explained.

"And what were your findings?"

I paused for a moment. This type of information gathering was fairly standard. When the HFDF went into action, we liked to know what we were up against. But after the conflict started, we wanted to understand why the enemy had reached their current state and how we could potentially spot enemies like them in the future—or how to curb them before deploying troops.

"Initially, we and our allies assumed that the Venom originated on Venom Minor. We believed that another race developed on Venom Major, which was more technologically advanced than Venom Minor and, at some point, traveled to Venom Minor. From there, our hypothesis was that the Venom reverse-engineered the technology from Venom Major's population and then started a campaign against the species on Venom Major. They used that technology to jumpstart their space industry to what it is today."

"But we no longer believe that, do we?" one of the other men asked.

"No."

"Then what do we believe now?"

"Up to the point where the Venom overtook the population of Venom Major. While the Venom have shown the ability to take and use the technology from others, they don't aggressively pursue their own R&D. Furthermore, their temperament suggests that had they not received technology from Venom Major, they would have never left Venom Minor. Even with that being said, we do not think that Venom Major had sufficient technology to leave their solar system," I explained.

There was an uncomfortable silence for a moment.

"In short, someone helped them. Or I should say, nudged them several times," I added.

"Please explain," another general urged.

"The Venom are extremely hostile. The only reason they banded together was either that they found a larger threat in the rest of the universe or, more likely, one of their bloodlines was able to wipe out the others. We think the latter is the case. All of the Venom we have been able to take samples from share the same lineage. It is our view now, and the view of several of our allies, that another race allowed some of their technology to be discovered by the Venom."

"You said 'nudged' several times?"

"Yes. We don't think Venom Major was able to do more than what we could shortly after humans first went to Earth's moon. The Venom didn't develop their own technology and couldn't make the leap from basic chemical propulsion to ships capable of faster-than-light jumps. The same goes for their CCPUs, genetics, and nanotech. Someone provided them with little pieces, let them figure it out, and then allowed them to find more. And by 'find,' we mean basically give it to them. The Venom do not explore the galaxy other than to find planets similar enough to their own that they can colonize. Though they destroy those worlds, showing no concern for their future on that planet."

"Do we know who helped them or why?" another general asked.

"No, we don't. There have always been races that try to alter others, but in the case of the Venom, whoever it was did a very good job. We have found three other races in the last few years that show similar 'help' to what the Venom received. All of them target similar planet types as the Venom."

This was what concerned us most. A race playing god was common enough, but a race that was playing god and choosing targets that would destroy certain types of worlds was not. It was hard to alter other species. It was harder still to make them do what you wanted.

One of the generals sighed, "It could be a nomadic race."

I had thought of that too. They didn't stick to one system, and a race that left its home system mostly did so because they had to. Those that did generally tried to colonize elsewhere or chose to leave. Those that left because they wanted to typically did not return to living on planets. These races were small, relatively speaking, and did not often interfere with others. Planets not only provided room for a large population that could then go on to attack others, but they were also massive reservoirs of resources—something essential for any military unless you planned on turning another race into your army.

"They could be," I acknowledged. "We considered a race that was forced off of their home world and is looking for a new one. But there are easier ways to acquire a planet. The Venom also destroyed the worlds they attacked, making them almost uninhabitable for other races. We don't find it likely that whoever this is wants to take up residence. We haven't been able to find out enough yet to determine motive or who might be doing this. All we know is there's someone out there playing with fire."

ABOUT THE AUTHOR

Nicholas Taylor is a fantasy and science fiction author. He was born in 1981 in Denver, Colorado, where he lives with his wife and family. Nicholas was an imaginative child who enjoyed writing stories and daydreaming about new worlds and places from a young age.

In his twenties, Nicholas rekindled a love for reading and consuming fantasy and science fiction. The culmination was his decision to write a novel in the winter of 2007. That first novel was Legon Awakening, which ran as a weekly podcast and was later released in print, digital, and audio editions that thousands have enjoyed.

Nicholas enjoys writing fiction that pulls readers into immersive worlds with likable and relatable characters. He strives to draw the reader into the scene with the characters, allowing them to explore magical realms or distant planets.

For more about Nicholas Taylor

Visit:

www.NicholasTaylor.co

www.ingramcontent.com/pod-product-compliance
Lightning Source LLC
Chambersburg PA
CBHW030807260626
47169CB00001B/229